Also by Sean Moynihan

Here - A Robert Falconer Mystery

THE Fall

A ROBERT FALCONER MYSTERY

Sean Moynihan

The Fall: A Robert Falconer Mystery
Sean Moynihan

ISBN (Print Edition): 978-1-09838-360-2
ISBN (eBook Edition): 978-1-09838-361-9

This is a work of historical fiction. Apart from the well-known historical figures and events, all persons, events, and names are products of the author's imagination and are used fictitiously. Any resemblance to actual persons, living or dead, is purely coincidental.

To Shaun Moynihan

1936 – 2020

Son, Brother, Husband, Father, Grandfather, Teacher, Cousin

Is cuimhın liom thú

I couldn't have thrown that bomb. I was at home making bombs.

—Louis Lingg, Haymarket Bombing Defendant, 1886

For the anarchist himself, whether he preaches or practices
his doctrines, we need not have one particle more concern
than for any ordinary murderer. He is not the victim of social
or political injustice. There are no wrongs to remedy in his
case. The cause of his criminality is to be found in his own
evil passions and in the evil conduct of those who urge him
on, not in any failure by others or by the State to do justice
to him or his. He is a malefactor and nothing else.

—Theodore Roosevelt, 1901

The most absurd apology for authority and law is that they serve to
diminish crime. Aside from the fact that the State is itself the greatest
criminal, breaking every written and natural law, stealing in the
form of taxes, killing in the form of war and capital punishment,
it has come to an absolute standstill in coping with crime. It has
failed utterly to destroy or even minimize the horrible scourge
of its own creation. Crime is naught but misdirected energy.

—Emma Goldman, 1910

PART I

1

The young man entered the waiting room outside the inner office of the notorious steel magnate and looked around. He saw several other men sitting there—obviously, hopeful suitors bent on securing a job with the wealthy industrialist, or perhaps simply angling to procure an investment from him—as well as a few clerks sitting behind a wooden barrier with a gate attached. As he looked around the room, he reached into his pocket and fingered his revolver delicately, as if to reassure himself that he did, in fact, bring it with him. He could feel sweat dribbling down his forehead, so he quickly dabbed at it with a handkerchief that was stuffed into his breast pocket.

Over at a small desk behind the barrier that blocked access to the office's inner sanctum, he saw the wealthy man's attendant sitting by dutifully.

Hm, he thought. *A negro. Typical of such a capitalist master. Ordering this young fellow around just like the American slave drivers of yesteryear.*

He took a deep breath and walked up to the attendant, and then coughed deliberately a couple of times to get his attention. The man looked up at him. "Yes, sir?" he asked.

"I am from New York," the man replied in his rather broken English as he handed the attendant a faked business card. "I run an employment agency and I believe that Mister Frick could find use for my services, given the workers' strike."

"I see," the attendant said. "Well, sir, let me go see if Mister Frick is available."

"Thank you," the visitor said as the attendant stood up and moved over to the door to the private office.

As the attendant went inside and started to close the door behind him, the visitor caught a glimpse of a distinguished-looking gentleman with a dark beard sitting in the back of the room. Then the door closed, and he stood there nervously amongst the other men and the clerks for what seemed to be an eternity.

The door then finally opened, and the attendant walked out. "Mister Frick is engaged," he said. "He can't see you now, sir," and he handed the business card back to the visitor.

"Um, yes, I see," the visitor said, as he placed the business card into a briefcase he was holding. "Thank you."

He then turned and slowly walked out of the waiting room. Stepping out into the hallway, he took a deep breath, reached into his pocket for the revolver, and walked briskly back into the waiting area and through the gate in the long, wooden partition. The attendant looked up from his seat with a confused look on his face and started to stand up, but the visitor simply brushed past him and opened the door to the private office. Stepping purposefully inside, he beheld the man with the beard sitting in an ornate chair at the end of a long, beautifully crafted table. Near to the man in another chair on the side of the table was another man, very trim and small of frame.

"What is this?" the small man demanded before starting to get up.

The intruder stood for a moment, unsure of what to do or say, after all those weeks of planning and preparing, all those sleepless nights spent thinking about this exact moment that would change the course of history for the working man in America. And then he yelled out the rich man's name, but the look of dread on his intended victim's face stopped him from completing the utterance: "Fri—."

He then raised the revolver and saw the bearded man gripping the arms of his chair with both hands as if in a desperate attempt to stand up. The visitor then aimed the gun at the man's head, but in the last second, the man turned his face away, and as the sound of the shot reverberated through the cavernous office, the now wounded man fell from his chair.

The shooter could no longer see his target, who had disappeared beneath the table, and so he walked a few steps closer to get a better look. His movements, however, were immediately halted when the smaller man leaped upon him and struggled with him over the gun.

"Murder! Help!" someone shouted. In his struggle with the smaller man, the visitor could tell that the anguished cries were coming from his victim, and so with all his might, he flung the small man off him and pointed the gun again at the wounded man now crawling across the floor.

"BLAM!"

The shot missed, however, for just before he pulled the trigger, the small man had managed to strike him in his hand, misdirecting the bullet. The two men then struggled feverishly across the room, yanking arms and pulling at hair. The visitor finally grabbed his opponent by the throat and spied the victim cowering behind a chair in the corner. He managed to get his shooting hand free and aimed just beneath the arm of the small man who still clung to him.

Nothing.

The gun misfired and failed to emit a bullet.

He attempted to fire off another round, but just before he could, he felt his head explode from something crashing into the back of his head. He dropped the gun and sank to the floor, semi-conscious.

"Where is the hammer?! Hit him, carpenter!" he heard a voice shouting through the chaos and pain swirling in his head. He also heard the voice of the victim over in the corner, moaning, and so he determined to finish the job by stabbing him with the dagger in his pocket. Reaching down, he extracted it and struggled mightily against the weight of the several men who know lay upon him, trying to impede his movements. Ignoring their commands to stop, he crawled closer to the wounded man and managed to stab wildly at the man's legs, piercing them several times. But then he was lifted bodily up off the floor and his arms were pinioned behind him, and he could no longer move.

"Mister Frick, do you identify this man as your assailant?" a voice asked as the would-be assassin was held sturdily up in front of the bleeding businessman. The shooter then looked straight at the man whom he had intended to kill, and he saw the man slowly nod his head.

He then felt himself carried out roughly through the waiting room and down to the city street to a waiting police wagon.

I have failed, he thought to himself, as a crowd gathered in the street. *My attentat failed to kill the capitalist monster.*

A policeman then interrupted his despondent ruminations. "Are you hurt?" the officer asked him. "You're bleeding."

"I've lost my glasses," he replied.

"You'll be damn lucky if you don't lose your head," the officer replied.

ㅅ

2

The grimy-faced thug peered around the corner of the brick building through the settling fog and whispered to his partner standing slightly behind him in the alley. "Ah...here comes one, Johnny Boy—a real baldy. Should have plenty of greenbacks on him. Get ready."

The man pressed himself against the brick wall as his younger confederate did the same, and he could hear footsteps slowly approaching the opening of the alley where they lay in wait.

"Almost here, Johnny...almost here...get ready now, boy...."

He glanced to his left as the old man came up the sidewalk through the fog and into view where the alley opened onto the street, and as the old man walked by, the thief reached out quickly, grabbed him by his lapels, and swung him hard back into the alley against the brick wall.

The old man grunted loudly, and the veteran hoodlum slapped him against his head and shoved him violently into the alley. As the old man stumbled and fell to the asphalt, the thug motioned to his younger companion to help drag the stricken old man deeper into the alley away from any passersby who might hear their activity at this late hour of the evening.

"Come on, Johnny!" he growled at the younger accomplice. "Grab the sheeny bastard and bring him back here!"

The two men then dragged the older man another forty feet towards the back of the alley and threw him down in a heap near the back wall.

The lead assailant then straddled the whimpering man, slapped him violently a few times in the face again, and then leaned over him, placing his own face within inches of the old man's. "Well, well," he said as he rifled through the man's coat. "What do we have here? Another old Shylock carrying some dough around late at night. You really shouldn't do that, old man—you could lose it!"

The two robbers chuckled as they took the old man's cash and started counting it. "Not bad, Johnny Boy," the leader said as he finished counting the bills. "Looks like this old bastard had forty bucks on him tonight—a decent haul."

"Yeah," Johnny Boy replied with a smile. "Pretty good for one job, ain't it, Nick?"

"Sure is, Johnny," the older thief replied as he stuffed the old man's bills into his pockets. "And these old Hebrew pin-heads just make it so easy."

A sound of footsteps suddenly came from back closer to the street, and the men froze. They both looked back to where they had initially grabbed the old man, and the footsteps appeared to be getting closer.

"Step back, Johnny," Nick said as he moved back away from the wounded man lying on the ground and peered forward into the thick fog enveloping the alley. "Be ready for anything."

The two men kept looking until a figure slowly appeared: a man, on the tall side and dressed in dark clothing with a dark bowler atop his head. He was beardless and was walking very slowly until he came into full view approximately fifteen feet away from the two criminals. Then he spoke: "Evening. What seems to be the problem here?"

Nick stepped forward with a menacing look. "Nothing's doin' here, friend. We were just looking over this boozed-up old coot...making sure he's okay."

"I see," the stranger said. "So, you two aren't the men I saw grabbing him from the street a moment ago? I couldn't quite tell—I was watching from down the street a piece."

Nick looked over to his young friend, and then turned back to the stranger. "Nah," he said, pulling out a switchblade and opening it with a flick of his wrist. "That ain't us. So, you'd best be moving on, guy, or you might have trouble, see?"

The stranger looked at the blade in Nick's hand and frowned slightly. Then he spoke again: "You know, a man pulls a blade on me like that—I usually pull out my revolver." The stranger reached into his jacket and pulled out a large pistol, and the two thieves moved back quickly. "But tonight, I thought I'd bring something else along," the tall man continued. His left hand, which had been hidden behind his back throughout the entire encounter, now came out brandishing a policeman's two-foot-long, wooden billy club.

"Do you know what one of these things can do to a man's head if used correctly?" the stranger asked, holding the club up in front of him and gazing at it. "It's not pretty, I can tell you that."

"Hey, listen, mister," Nick said. "Are you a cop or somethin'? If so, we can give you some of our loot here. There's plenty to go around if you know what I mean."

The stranger looked at the two men and then walked slowly towards Nick. "You know," he said, "there are basically two kinds of people in this city. There are the hardworking, law-abiding kind who do what they have to do to feed their families, whether it's working fourteen hours a day in some darkened shop with no windows like this old fella' lying here, or handing out papers on the street corner, or maybe even making important decisions in a boardroom of one of those big companies uptown. Those people get up in the morning, go to work, and generally mind their own business. They want to contribute to the world and not bother the next guy in line.

"And then," he continued, "there are...the troublemakers. Those guys are out just to cause mischief and bother other people. They don't hold jobs, they expect a free hand-out, they take what they want, and they don't mind hurting people at all. In fact, they go out of their way to do it. And you know what, 'friend?'"

The stranger slowly jabbed the end of the nightstick directly into Nick's nose, pushing the thief's head back hard against the brick wall.

"You are a troublemaker, pal," the man said. "I could spot it a mile away. Just like your friend over here is a troublemaker, too." The stranger gazed over at Johnny standing nervously to the side.

"Detective Sergeant Falconer?!" a voice suddenly yelled from back towards the street. "You there?!"

"Yes!" the stranger answered back loudly. "Back here in the alley. I got 'em here with our victim!"

Moments later, two young men came running up breathlessly. Nick looked at them and noticed that they had badges affixed to their coats and were brandishing revolvers.

"Arrest these men, Detective Waidler," the stranger instructed one of them. "And Jimmy, help me out with the gentleman here."

"Right, Detective Sergeant," the other young man replied, moving over to help the injured victim up off the ground.

The two of them gently grabbed the old man underneath his arms and slowly lifted him up to his feet. "Ugh," he groaned as they held him in a standing position. The old man then squinted and looked directly at the stranger who had come to his rescue in this dank, barren, little corner of the city. "Thank you," the old man managed to say through bloody and swollen lips. "Who are you?"

"I'm Falconer, sir," the stranger replied. "From the police department's Central Detective Bureau."

New York City Police Headquarters
Mulberry Street
July 25, 1892

3

Falconer stood outside the office of Police Superintendent Thomas Byrnes. It had been approximately 36 hours since Falconer and his colleagues had interceded in the robbery and assault of the elderly Jewish shopkeeper, Mordecai Rosen, in the back alley off Hester Street. Now, after arriving for work, he had discovered that he was wanted in the superintendent's office for some unexplained reason, and so he stood patiently in the hallway as police personnel drifted by him in the typical day's fashion—clerks, detectives, and secretaries, all busy with the duties of keeping the citizenry safe in a rapidly growing and modernizing city.

The door to the boss's office suddenly opened and Inspector Alexander "Clubber" Williams poked his head out. "Ah, Falconer, you're here," he said. "Come on in."

Falconer followed Williams into the ornate, spacious office and saw Byrnes—recently elevated to the very top position of Police Superintendent—standing behind his desk. Two other of Byrnes' top advisors—his replacement as Chief Inspector of the Detective Bureau, Henry Steers, and Detective Sergeant Charles McNaught—stood close by, along with the always pugnacious-looking Williams. "Afternoon, Falconer," Byrnes said. "Thanks for dropping by."

"Sure thing, superintendent," Falconer replied.

"Have a seat," Byrnes said, motioning for Falconer to sit in one of the chairs fronting his large desk.

Falconer sat down, as did Byrnes and the other three men. "Well," Byrnes said, "I heard you took down a couple of those miscreants who have been fleecing the shopkeepers over in the Jewish sector on Saturday night. Well done, Falconer."

"Thank you, sir," Falconer replied. "It's only two, but it's a start."

"Yes, indeed," Byrnes said, lighting a cigar. "We'll break up that crew soon enough, and I'm proud of the work you and your men are doing over there."

"Thank you, sir," Falconer said.

"I wanted you in here, Falconer, because of something that's come up," Byrnes said. "Do you know who Henry Frick is?"

"Yes," Falconer replied. "The steel company man who just got shot over the weekend."

"Yes, he's the chairman of the Carnegie Steel Company up in Pittsburgh," Byrnes explained. "A real important man, and unfortunately, one of those anarchist agitators just tried to assassinate him—shot him twice in his own office on Saturday."

"I heard Frick survived, though," Falconer said.

"Yes, he did, Falconer," Byrnes said, tapping the ashes of his cigar into a glass tray on his desk. "In fact, he's apparently doing remarkably well considering he got shot twice, including a wound to the neck, and was stabbed in the legs, too."

"What happened to the suspect?" Falconer asked.

"Oh, they roughed him up a bit and now he's sitting in jail up there and not saying much, I'm afraid," Byrnes replied. "His name is Berkman—Alexander Berkman. Young foreigner type from Russia, another of these crazed, Red anarchists bent on destroying everything for whatever idiotic reason they have. It's an open and shut case, though. He'll get decades in prison for this, and he's just lucky Frick didn't die. Otherwise, the chair would be waiting for him."

"So, may I ask why you wanted to see me about this, sir?" Falconer asked.

"Well," Byrnes said, "we've communicated with the Pittsburgh police, and it's agreed that Berkman probably didn't do this alone and had some help in effecting his plans. We need to round up his gang of anarchist bomb throwers before someone else follows up and tries something new, and the main suspect is none other than Miss Emma Goldman. You've heard of her?"

"I have," Falconer replied. "She gives lots of speeches around the country, supposedly on behalf of the working man. A real firebrand, they say, but that's about all I know of her."

"Yes, you've painted an accurate picture of her," Byrnes said, looking over at McNaught, Steers, and Williams and smiling slightly. "Except that she's also likely trying to perpetrate acts of violence to make her point, I'm afraid. These Red agitators are all basically the same: no sense of decency, no sense of basic moral principles, all just complaining about how the state has ruined their lives. And now it's time to stop them."

"And you want to focus on Goldman first?" Falconer asked.

"Yes, indeed," Byrnes answered. "She was known to cavort with this Berkman character, lived with him for a time, and they share the same fanatical attachment to the anarchist creed—tear down the world as we know it so that chaos will reign and there will be no authority to ensure order and public safety. We simply can't have these people out there, sowing discord, and clearly now they've raised the ante by trying to kill Frick, a symbol of all that they despise. Goldman is probably planning more incidents—it's well known that she idolizes those bomb throwers who were hanged for the Haymarket affair in Chicago back in eighty-six, and we believe that she'll try to pick up where Berkman left off. So, we need to shadow her and gather evidence against her. Do you understand?"

"Yes, sir," Falconer said. "Any idea where she might be hiding?"

Byrnes looked over at the other men again, and then Steers spoke up for the first time. "She's not exactly hiding out," he began. "In fact, she's been pretty brazen about her whereabouts. She gave another anarchist speech on Saturday night here in the city. She has lots of contacts and friends who are sympathetic to her cause, and they will obviously try to protect her. We believe that she probably knows we're on her trail, but she's been telling everyone that she's not involved with the Frick shooting. We think otherwise, of course. We have good information that she's currently staying with a woman over on Fifth Street—a lady by the name of Mollick. That lady's ex-husband, Frank Mollick, is likely involved with Berkman, too. Pittsburgh PD believes that he sent Berkman some money just before the assassination attempt. We'll need to keep any eye on Goldman and see where this leads us. She's a very clever bird, and dangerous, too."

"Got it," Falconer said. "I'll need some men to help out, of course."

"Certainly," Byrnes said, standing up from his chair. "You'll be off your current cases for now—we'll see to that—and you can pick a team of your own from the Detective Bureau. This is a priority. We need to nip this in the bud and take care of these people."

"Yes, sir," Falconer. "We'll get on it. Anything else?"

"Not at this time, Falconer," Byrnes answered. "Good luck to you, and please keep us posted."

"Will do," Falconer said, and then he turned to move to the door.

"Oh, and Falconer?" Byrnes stated.

"Yes?" Falconer said, stopping and looking back at the chief.

"Don't take chances with these people," Byrnes said. "As Chief Inspector Steers just pointed out, they are dangerous and there's no telling what they might try to pull. Do what you have to do to stop them. Understand?"

"I do," Falconer said. "Thank you." He then stepped out into the hallway and moved quickly to the stairs leading down to the offices of the Detective Bureau.

4

"So...who is this Goldman lady?" Jimmy Halloran asked Falconer as they walked briskly out of the Mulberry Street Headquarters with Detective James Waidler shortly after Falconer's meeting with Byrnes and his men. The day was growing hot, with the temperature rising towards 90 degrees, and the men had removed their jackets and loosened their collars.

"She's an anarchist," Falconer answered, dodging various people walking along the busy sidewalk in front of the large building. "It's a group of people who essentially believe that government is oppressive of the people and should be abolished."

"I don't get it," Jimmy said. "If you don't have government, you have nothing. It's just chaos and every man for himself."

"Well, that's where I stand on things, too," Falconer said, "but there's no question that these anarchist types do exist, and they can be trouble."

"How so?" Jimmy asked.

"Well, they blow things up occasionally, for one thing," Falconer said. "Like the Haymarket riot."

"What's that?" Jimmy inquired.

"You don't know of Haymarket?" Waidler asked, incredulous.

"No," Jimmy replied, looking at him. "What's that?"

"A bunch of these anarchists blew up a bomb in Chicago back in eighty-six," Waidler answered. "The bomb and some shooting right after killed some cops and a few workers, too. You never heard of this?"

"Well, I was only sixteen and was in school," Jimmy said, "so I guess I missed it."

"Well, they hanged some of the anarchist leaders," Waidler continued, "and now all these new anarchists consider them heroes and want to continue with their crazy work."

"And this Emma Goldman is one of these types?" Jimmy asked.

"Yes," Falconer replied. "A very prominent one, too."

"So where are we headed, detective sergeant?" Jimmy asked.

"Over to Fifth Street," Falconer replied. "She's apparently staying in a tenement over there with some woman and her kids. And she also hangs out at a German club down the street that's popular with the anarchist crowd."

"So, what do we do if we see her?" Jimmy followed up.

"Nothing," Falconer said. "We'll just split up, keep our badges concealed, and keep an eye on her—see who she converses with, that sort of thing. Got it?"

"Sure, detective sergeant," Jimmy answered.

"Right," Waidler said.

"All right," Falconer said, "let's head over to Bowery and walk up to Fifth. It's not far."

The three men then headed toward the German sector of the Lower East Side, where noted provocateur and anarchist rabble-rouser, Emma Goldman, was allegedly scheming to wreak havoc on the city.

5

Falconer approached the bustling corner of Fifth and Bowery with Waidler and Halloran. They had just entered the German district, full of hard-working immigrants from Berlin, Hamburg, Frankfort, and other Teutonic strongholds, or from the hinterlands of Bavaria and Alsace-Lorraine, all seeking a better life within the embrace of Lady Liberty, who welcomed them all with her commanding presence as they streamed into New York Harbor.

Although just as crowded as the tenements near Mulberry Bend and Little Italy, those in the German district were not as filthy or disease-ridden. Indeed, somehow the stout and disciplined German residents had managed to make the teeming enclave reasonably livable and pleasant, despite the lack of room and privacy.

Falconer stopped the men just before rounding the corner. "All right," he said, "we're just giving it a look and not trying to raise any alarms here. You've seen photos of Goldman, so you should be able to recognize her if she shows herself. She's staying in Number 340 on the first floor, down near the corner of First Ave. next to the police station there. Jimmy, you walk down and find some little spot across the street and see if she shows herself. James and I are going to go into this beer joint right up here across from Beethoven Hall. It's called Zum Groben Michel and it's supposedly a big anarchist gathering spot where Goldman hangs her hat a lot. Like I said, keep your badges hidden and if any of us see her, just quietly alert the others and we'll keep an eye on her. Understand?"

"Yes, detective sergeant," Halloran answered.

"Right, boss," said Waidler.

"Okay," Falconer said, "let's move."

As they turned the corner, Falconer saw the normally boisterous ale house called Zum Groben Michel standing amidst the brick walk-ups and noisy tenement houses of Fifth Street. Stepping up to the place, he turned to Halloran. "All right, this is our stop, Jimmy," he said. "You head down another two blocks and keep an eye on the place she's been leasing. Remember—it's first floor of Number 340."

"Got it, detective sergeant." Halloran replied.

"All right, James," Falconer said. "Shall we head in?"

Waidler nodded, and then the two men stepped inside the strangely quiet tavern.

6

Falconer looked around the barroom with Waidler standing by his side. It was drab, dark, and only half-full of patrons at this early hour in the mid-afternoon. To the left was a long bar fronted by perhaps fifteen beaten-up, old, wooden stools, and on the right were approximately six round, wooden tables with chairs. The walls were nondescript, with only an occasional framed painting, some with German phrases on them.

Falconer estimated that there were roughly twenty customers loitering at the bar and tables, some visibly drunk, while others simply played cards together or smoked silently by themselves. What got his attention immediately, however, was the enormous man standing behind the bar cleaning glasses with a dish rag while a couple of minions tended to the customers. The bartender must have been close to seven feet tall, Falconer figured, and weighed surely over 250 pounds.

Falconer motioned for Waidler to go find a seat in the barroom while he went over to see the giant, who appeared to be in charge of the place. He walked over slowly and leaned next to the bar near to the big man. "Afternoon," he said to him.

The man only nodded and kept to his task of cleaning the glasses.

"Nice place," Falconer said, scanning the room. "How long have you been here?"

The man looked at Falconer for a moment with a look of annoyance on his face, and then spoke with a clear German accent. "Nine years. You vant drink?"

"Sure, sure," Falconer said. "How about just a lemonade? I don't typically have a drink until evening if you know what I mean."

"Sure," the imposing man said, and then he walked down the bar to pour the drink. Moments later, he returned with a glass of the lemonade and handed it to Falconer.

"Thanks," Falconer said, handing the man a nickel. "Appreciate that."

The man said nothing and only went back to his task of cleaning the glasses and looking around the room in silence. Falconer walked slowly across the room to where Waidler had taken a seat at an empty table. "I don't see Goldman," he said to the young detective. "You?"

"No," Waidler replied. "Just a few women, but none match her."

"The big guy behind the bar doesn't seem too thrilled about our presence," Falconer said, taking a sip of his lemonade. "Probably doesn't like strange intruders."

"You know what the name of the place means?" Wailer asked. "Sorry, but I'm not up on my German."

"No, I don't know," Falconer answered. "Maybe one of these guys can tell us," he said, looking at the a few men playing cards at the next table. "Hey, friend," he said to the man sitting in a chair closest to them, "can you tell me what the name of this place means, 'Zum Groben Michel?'"

"Ja, sure," the man replied with a German accent. "It mean, 'Tough Mike's,' you understand?" He pointed over at the tall bartender. "For Mike over der," he said. "He is de owner."

"Got it," Falconer said. "Thanks." He turned back to Waidler. "Well, there's no sign of Goldman," he said. "I figured she wouldn't be here this early in the day."

"Should we go check out her place with Halloran?" Waidler asked.

"Yes, let's do that," Falconer answered. "But first let's go ask the big guy if he's seen her lately."

The two men got up out of their seats and walked over the bar to where the large, sullen proprietor was silently arranging glasses.

"Hey, mister," Falconer said to him. "You ever had a woman in your place by the name of Emma Goldman?"

The bartender looked up with an angry look, and then went back to his glasses without saying a word.

Falconer and Waidler looked at each other, and then Falconer spoke up again. "You hear me, pal? We're looking for an Emma Goldman. She's known to frequent your establishment. Have you seen her lately? Mid-twenties, brown hair, very petite, wears spectacles..."

The big man looked up again and peered directly at Falconer. He then moved closer, reached out and grabbed Falconer's lapel roughly in his large hand, pulling Falconer closer to him over the bar. "Look, friend," he said threateningly. "I don't like stranger coming by and ask qvestions, you see? You get out of here or I take you and your girlfriend and throw you both into ze barrels out back after I break faces in, you understand?"

Falconer glanced back at Waidler and shook his head almost imperceptibly as if to tell him to hold off on pulling out his revolver. Then he looked back at the large man who was grabbing his lapel and instantaneously grabbed the man's wrist, turning it severely such that the bartender's face went straight down onto the bar and Falconer was essentially looking down over him and holding him in place.

"Ah! Ah!" the giant yelped as Falconer slowly twisted his wrist, torquing the man's arm and causing more pain. The customers in the place immediately stopped what they were doing and looked over at the bar.

"You must be 'Tough Mike,'" Falconer said slowly as the big man winced in pain. "Well, let me just say, we're the police, see? And we're interested in this Emma Goldman lady. We hear she likes to have a drink in your place with the rest of her fellow anarchist types."

The big man struggled to look up at Falconer as he spoke up in a series of grunts and groans. "I don't know no Emma Goldman," he said. "I get lots of women in here, and I don't know what you mean by this anarchist word."

"You just remember us, Tough Mike," Falconer said, tightening his hold on the man's wrist. "We'll be back, and I don't want any funny business out of you or your workers. You see us again, you act like nothing's wrong—you got it?"

"Ja, ja, I got it, sir," the man said, grimacing.

"Good," Falconer said, letting go of the man's arm. "And thanks for the lemonade. Let's go, James."

The two men then slowly walked out of the deathly silent bar and headed down the street to check on Jimmy Halloran at 340 East Fifth Street.

7

Falconer stood inside Byrnes' office with Waidler, Halloran, McNaught, Clubber Williams, and another unfamiliar police official after a couple of fruitless days of trying to shadow Emma Goldman.

"Falconer," Byrnes said, pointing to the man, "this is Chief O'Hara of the Pittsburgh police. He's traveled here to look into some things with us concerning the anarchist attack on Mister Frick."

"Afternoon, sir," Falconer said to O'Hara.

"Afternoon, Detective Sergeant Falconer," O'Hara replied.

"The chief here went out to East Branch over in Jersey yesterday with one of our men," Byrnes said. "There are indications that a certain Frank Mollick, another anarchist sympathizer who lives and works as a baker out there, was in on the Frick assassination attempt, and sure enough, the chief here uncovered evidence that Mollick wired Berkman six dollars just a couple of days before the shooting. So, he's likely in on the deal."

"Understood," Falconer said.

"Well, it doesn't end there, Falconer," Byrnes said, slowly walking around his desk and coming forward. "The chief also found in his search of Mollick's place a telegram that Miss Goldman had sent to him earlier this month. It was found amongst his papers and is most interesting. Here—take a look."

Byrnes picked up a small piece of paper on his desk and handed it to Falconer, who slowly scanned the writing on it. It was a typical telegram, short and to the point, and Falconer read it out loud so that his men would know its contents, too: "'Come as soon as possible, Nothing dangerous. Goldman.'"

He looked up at the superintendent. "Nothing dangerous," he repeated. "I wonder what that means."

"Why, in all likelihood, it means that she's asking him to meet up as part of the conspiracy," Byrnes said. "She's sure to be on it, too."

"I suppose so, sir," Falconer said, handing the telegram back. "But there could be other meanings to it."

"Other meanings?" Byrnes said. "What sort of meanings are you referring to?"

"Well, sir, I imagine that you're aware she's been talking to the reporters already," Falconer said. "And she's denying knowing about the assassination plan—it's all over the front pages today."

"Yes, we are aware, Falconer," Byrnes said, walking back to the chair behind his desk. "So, she's denying everything—what of it?"

"Well, she was asked by the reporters what the telegram meant," Falconer said, "and she told them that it simply referred to her attempt to get Mollick back to his apartment because his wife was sick, but not dangerously sick. It seems a reasonable explanation to me, that's all."

"It's clearly a lie," Byrnes said, "and we need to get some solid evidence tying her to the conspiracy. She's one of the main Red agitators out there, Falconer, and she was Berkman's girl. There's no way that she's not involved, understand?"

"Yes, sir," Falconer replied. "We're trying to get something on her, but she's shifty. She moves around town quietly and doesn't slip up. I think she's a smart one."

"Well, not smart enough," Byrnes said. "We're getting a warrant to search the place on Fifth, and we'll do that tonight. Can you handle this?"

"Yes, sir," Falconer answered. "We'll take care of it."

"Good," Byrnes said, sitting down in his chair. "Miss Goldman might be a clever one, but she won't be so clever when we're clearing out her drawers of all her anarchist papers tonight. There will be something tying her directly to Berkman and his act—I'm sure of it. See to it that you coordinate the search of the place with Chief O'Hara here, and report back to me."

"Understood," Falconer said. He then motioned for Waidler and Halloran to follow him out of the office, and the three men departed.

"Think we'll find anything in her place, detective sergeant?" Halloran asked as they stood outside the office.

"We'll see," Falconer replied, placing his bowler on top of his head. "Let's meet back here at 8:00 PM and we'll head over together. I'll have the warrant ready."

"Yes, detective sergeant," Jimmy said.

"Got it," Waidler answered.

Falconer then turned and headed for the stairs down to the first floor of the large police headquarters building.

8

Falconer stood before the anarchist group's apartment building at 340 East Fifth Street with Waidler, Halloran, and several other men from the Detective Bureau. In his hand he held a search warrant signed earlier in the day by a judge of the court of general sessions. Looking up and down the block briefly, he saw no one except a lone, wandering drunk, tapping haphazardly on some wrought iron window bars on the ground floor of an apartment house about fifty feet away with a gnarled wooden stick. It was eight-thirty in the evening, and now that the sun had finally set beyond the Hudson River to the west, the oppressive 92-degree heat of the afternoon had finally yielded to a bearable seventy-five degrees.

Falconer motioned for the men to walk around the back of the building with him to where the fire escape rose to the top of the building. "We'll go in through the back," he said. "Doesn't seem like anyone's home, so we'll just have to make entry through a window. Let's go."

The men walked to the back and a few of them immediately entered an open window on the first floor. Falconer, Halloran, and Waidler followed, edging over the windowsill into a bare kitchen. The place was silent and devoid of people, which pleased Falconer, as it would allow them to avoid a ruckus with Goldman and the Mollick family.

"All right," he said to the gathered men. "Start looking for anything that might tie these people to Berkman or Mollick. Anything—papers, letters, money—you know the deal."

The detectives then started to upturn the apartment in a search of evidence of a conspiracy—rifling through drawers, uplifting mattresses, peering into vases—as Falconer walked around the place and took in the surroundings. It was a drab, messy, three-room apartment, and things were strewn about everywhere—newspapers, pamphlets, letters, clothing, discarded vegetables, and dirty plates in the kitchen area—and it looked as if the residents had had many visitors in recent days, as the newspapers had reported.

He looked up on the walls and saw several framed mottoes, all clearly announcing central tenets of the anarchist faith: "Down with Government;" "Law is a Farce;" "Marriage is a Failure."

Strange folk, these anarchists, he thought.

The men searched the place for the next hour, and then, with bags full of documents, photographs, and literature, they carefully exited the back window again and traipsed back to headquarters as onlookers gaped at them in wonder. Falconer made sure to leave a copy of the signed warrant on the kitchen table before leaving, and on the walk back to Mulberry Street, he pondered the efficacy of the search, for it didn't appear to him, at least, that they had uncovered anything of note relating to the attack on Frick.

"Well, we sure got a lot of stuff in there," Halloran pointed out on the walk back to headquarters.

"Yes," Falconer replied absently. "We'll have to sift through it all. Maybe there's something there."

"I wonder where they were tonight," Halloran said.

"Who knows?" Falconer answered. "These people seem to move around a lot—they're really a strange crowd."

"I'll say," Halloran chuckled, and the men continued walking through the breezy nighttime air of the summer evening.

9

"Nothing, you say?" Byrnes inquired from behind his desk at headquarters the day after the police raid of Emma Goldman's flat on Fifth Street. "No note or letter referencing the attack?"

"That's correct, sir," Falconer answered as he stood in front of the desk with his men. "We turned the place upside down, but Miss Goldman didn't leave anything incriminating in there, unfortunately."

"Well, that is unfortunate," Byrnes said, slowly walking away from his desk as he rubbed his chin with his hand. "She must have expected this and burned anything that ties her to the crime. As you've said, Falconer, she's very clever."

"Indeed," Falconer said.

"Any idea of her whereabouts today?" Byrnes asked, looking back at Falconer.

"We've got some info on another speech she's giving tonight," Falconer said, nodding at Waidler.

"Yes, superintendent," Waidler said, stepping forward. "There's a meeting of radicals scheduled for tonight at Military Hall on the Bowery. There have been a lot of pamphlets flying around town advertising it as a rally for the working man, and she's listed on the bill. It should be pretty crowded."

"I see," Byrnes said, slowly walking back to his desk. "Well, make sure you men are in attendance, too, and see who she fraternizes with. I want to catch her when she slips up. There's no telling what this little foreign agitator is cooking up next, but she's surely up to something. She's in deep with Berkman and the rest and is probably the leader."

"Right, sir," Falconer said. "We'll check it out."

"Good, thanks," Byrnes said. "That will be all, gentlemen."

The men then shuffled out of the office and headed downstairs to the Detective Bureau.

"I read in the paper today that Goldman's mad as hell at our search of her place," Waidler said as the men walked down the stairs. "She's furious."

"Oh, well," Falconer said, "if you don't want your place searched, don't go around telling people to burn down the damned government."

Waidler and Halloran both chuckled and the men continued walking down the stairs past the steady stream of humanity moving up past them in the great headquarters building in the heart of Lower Manhattan.

10

The driver pulled on the horses' reins and the police wagon bearing Falconer, Waidler, and Halloran stopped in front of Military Hall at 193 Bowery. The three men jumped off as a second wagon pulled up near to them carrying another three plainclothes detectives from the nearby Eldridge Street station.

As the second group of men clambered down from their wagon, Falconer scanned his surroundings. It was evening and a large crowd was slowly moving through the front door of the three-story brick building that stood before them. The temperature had dropped significantly as the sun had gone down, and due to a cool front that had slipped into the city in the past 48 hours, the air was almost pleasant, giving the city's residents a satisfying break from the suffocating heat of the summer months.

Falconer motioned for the men to gather around him. "All right," he said amidst the din of the conversing throng stepping into the hall, "we're obviously not hiding who we are tonight, so wear your badges on your jackets. They know we're here and why. Just keep to the back of the room and don't interfere unless you have to. They won't be happy with us, so just expect that."

He looked at one of the detectives from the Eldridge Street station, Michael Arndt. "Arndt, are you okay with translating if they start speaking German?"

"Sure thing, detective sergeant," the detective replied. "I'll just stand by you so you can hear me."

"Thanks," Falconer replied. "They probably won't speak English because this is largely a German crowd. All right, let's move in."

He led the men from the sidewalk up to the front door through the multitude of spectators waiting to get inside the assembly hall. As they pushed through the crowd, some of the people grunted in frustration, but the policemen just ignored their protestations and moved quickly into the place. Stepping inside, they moved to either side of the entrance and stood against the wall as the crowd followed them in.

Falconer looked around the room. It was a long, narrow lecture hall, and at the end, below the dais, was a table where an assemblage of reporters had already taken their seats and pulled out their pencils and notepads. The regular spectators had no chairs, however, and thus, they were forced to simply stand where they could and try to see what was happening up on the dais.

People continued streaming into the hall, and soon the air grew heavy and oppressive in the absence of the cool, evening breezes outside. After another fifteen minutes had elapsed to allow the last of the spectators to enter, a man finally walked up onto the dais and the crowd cheered. He then motioned for them be quiet and spoke.

Waidler turned to Falconer and whispered into his ear. "That's a fella' named Dyer Lum," he said. "Important Red agitator and general troublemaker."

Falconer nodded and then looked toward the dais to hear what Lum was saying. He was already shouting in English and gesticulating wildly, telling the people how heroic Berkman's deed in Pittsburgh had been, and how the working men now had to face down their capitalist oppressors like the wounded Henry Frick. Building his exhortation to a crescendo, he raised one hand high in the air and shouted to the wild-eyed and smiling spectators: "When an anarchist like Berkman decided to leave the world, he considered it his duty to take a good Christian like Frick along with him!"

The crowd roared with approval and Lum stepped down from the dais with a host of hands being held out to shake his own. Then, after he had made it to a seat in the front, another man stepped up and took his place at center stage. The crowd cheered heartily for the man who was noticeably tall and sported a very dark beard.

"Who's this?" Falconer asked Waidler.

"Joseph Peukert," Waidler answered. "Leader of a certain group of anarchists called the 'Autonomists.' Not sure what that means."

Falconer nodded and turned back to listen to Peukert, but quickly learned that the tall firebrand would be speaking in his native German tongue. As Peukert looked down disapprovingly at the reporters sitting in front, Arndt slipped closer to Falconer and began translating the speech: "This meeting," he said, "is an expression of approval on the part of the working class of the deed of Berkman. When the working men of Homestead were ground down by the capitalists, one man elected himself the champion of the oppressed classes and tried to liberate them from their slavery, not by shooting Frick, but by showing them where the source of their misery lay. We approve of the act most heartily. You paid vassals of the press cannot stop the wheels of history. The people are awakening, and they will crush you, with those who pay you, these murderers, these robbers, the capitalists. So long as there are people who are starving, there will be a Berkman, and these Berkmans will shoot without any conspiracy."

The crowd cheered, and then, after Peukert had quieted them, he continued. Falconer listened closely as Arndt continued to translate the words into English. "We are proud of Berkman's act," Peukert asserted. "We were associated with him and we don't deny it. The working men must fight and that soon. Hundreds of Berkmans will arise to do their duty. These reporters before me are the people who declare us unwashed and unkempt.

We do not wash ourselves because we have to work. When we are through work, we are tired, and we cannot afford to change our shirts twice a day. Now the question is whether we are dirty or you. You have been trained like parrots and are the parasites of capital."

The spectators erupted into applause once more, and then, after taking a long bow, Peukert walked down the steps to his chair near the other speakers. Falconer and the men next heard from an Italian anarchist doctor by the name of Merlino, who struggled through broken English to decry in a wild and frenzied speech the crimes of the capitalists and the promise of approaching revolution.

After the doctor at length composed himself and sat down to the cheers of the assembled workers, Emma Goldman then finally ascended the stairs. Falconer peered intently at her as she walked slowly to the center of the dais and looked down at the clapping spectators with a stern and almost reproachful look on her face. Her brown hair was pulled back into a bun, and her large, bright, blue eyes glared behind her silver pince-nez spectacles, giving her the appearance of an unpleasant schoolmarm displeased with her pupils. He was surprised at her tiny frame and wondered how such a petite creature could have instilled such fear and worry in the authorities. But here she was—the woman who was considered a prime danger to the country and possibly even a terror mastermind—in league perhaps with countless unnamed bomb throwers and secret assassins bent on tearing down the government and the existing capitalist structure of society.

Falconer reached into his jacket and pulled out a cigarillo as the applause continued. Lighting it, he noticed that Goldman's intense gaze now appeared to be settling directly on him and his men standing against the back wall near the entrance to the hall. For a moment, despite the distance that separated them, he almost felt that their eyes met, and he felt strangely uncomfortable. Then, still seemingly staring at him, Goldman finally spoke to the people: "Comrades, I would warn you to be quiet in this hall tonight, for it happens to be filled with detectives who want to raise a row and kill the speakers."

A loud chorus of boos immediately filled the room as the spectators started looking around, searching for the police interlopers who would so deviously try to sabotage the meeting. Falconer and the men just looked at each other, and Falconer chuckled briefly, amused with Goldman's tart opening. He then leaned back against the wall to hear more from her, but she then started to speak in German, and he quickly motioned to Arndt to come translate again.

"Got it, boss," Arndt said, leaning over towards Falconer's ear. "The condition in America," he began as Goldman started to speak, "is worse than in Russia because here it is cloaked by a sham republic. The report of Berkman's shot will be heard throughout the world, and these shots will continue until capital is dead."

The crowd gave a sustained cheer, which forced Goldman to pause momentarily, and then she continued. "We must make the most of this deed of Berkman's and follow it with other similar deeds until there are no more despots in America." The crowd then interrupted her again with a huge roar, and she was forced to pause again for almost a minute. Quieting the attendees, she went on speaking in German for another twenty minutes or so, expounding on the blessings of anarchy and lauding the heroic actions of her close friend, Berkman, and when she was done, the people cheered her mightily for several minutes.

As the people clapped and shouted, Falconer looked out at them all. He thought nothing of them, really—just a band of strange, manipulated, poor, working people who were being led down a path by a bunch of foreign crazies who liked to hear themselves speak. But then he suddenly noticed something off to the side of the darkened hall: a lone man, walking slowly down towards the front of the room where the stairs led up to the dais. He could have been just another acolyte—a young, aimless ruffian taken in by the fancy speeches of the anarchist leaders who wanted to get closer to his heroes. But there was something odd about the man, about the way he pulled his cap down low over his brow and held his hands firmly in his trouser pockets.

"See that guy over there?" Falconer asked Waidler.

"Yeah," Waidler replied. "What of him?"

"I don't know," Falconer said. "Just something odd about him. He just appeared out of nowhere and he's trying to get close to the stage. I'm going to go check it out."

"Right, boss," Waidler said, and then Falconer started walking briskly down the side of the hall, with the loud cheering of the crowd still reverberating off the walls. The people were still whooping and yelling their approval of Goldman's inspiring speech, and she remained standing at the center of the dais, not smiling but occasionally nodding her head in appreciation.

Falconer had to fight his way through more and more packed bands of people as he got closer to the dais, and he could see the strange man drifting ever closer to the small set of stairs that allowed the speakers to ascend and descend from the stage. He shouted at the spectators standing in his way as he got closer to the man—"Police! Move aside! Move! Get out the way!"—and as he finally got to within ten feet of his target, he saw the man finally stop and look up at Goldman standing not twenty feet from him. Falconer could see that the man was fiddling with something in his pocket, and so he himself reached into his own jacket to unholster his Colt revolver. He then realized that the man was now looking directly at him, and amidst the loud cheers and frenzied cries from the people for more remarks by Goldman, he locked eyes with the man.

They both stood still there, looking at each other while the wild din of the crowd continued all around them, and Falconer gripped his gun tightly in his jacket but did not pull it out. Then, with an icy look and not even the faintest expression of fear or worry or apprehension, the mysterious man slowly backpedaled and disappeared into the mass of humanity that was slowly enveloping the dais. Falconer watched him disappear out a side door that had been left open to allow more fresh air into the meeting, and then he was left alone with a thousand thoughts racing through his mind.

Letting go of his gun, he then looked up on the dais and saw Goldman staring first directly down at him, and then staring out at the door through which the strange man had just departed. She did this a couple of times before the next speaker interrupted her and held her hand aloft to the resounding cheers of the people. Falconer then slowly drifted back to his men near the entrance of the hall, pondering what had just happened.

11

"What's that, you say?" Byrnes asked Falconer. "You noticed what?"

Falconer and his men stood before Superintendent Byrnes in Byrnes' office the next morning with Chief Inspector Steers, Detective Sergeant McNaught, and Inspector Clubber Williams standing off to the side. Falconer had just given a brief, oral report of the raucous meeting that had taken place at Military Hall, and the superintendent appeared confused.

"I said that I noticed a lone figure slowly approaching the stage from the side," Falconer said, "and I grew concerned."

"Concerned?" Byrnes asked. "Why?"

"There was something about him," Falconer answered. "I'm not sure what, but he just didn't seem like he belonged there—like he was out of place."

"Hm," Byrnes snorted. "Tell me more."

"Well," Falconer said, "I approached this male party through the crowd, and as I got closer, I could see him fingering something in his pockets, and he was slowly walking towards the stage where Goldman was standing. Then I got to about ten feet from him, and he saw me. He just stood there, looking at me, and we had an odd moment for a second or two."

"Odd, how, Falconer?" Byrnes asked.

"I don't know, sir," Falconer replied. "It was as if I knew exactly what he was doing, and he knew that I knew, and he just stood there looking at me, then he slowly retreated from the room and disappeared outside."

"Well, what of it?" Byrnes asked. "So, another of Goldman's Red followers got nervous around you, a police detective, as he tried to get closer to his heroine agitator, and then he departed. What's so odd about that? There were probably hundreds of followers like him in the hall last night."

"There was something different about this one, sir," Falconer said. "From his behavior and the way that he tried to get closer to Goldman from the side of the stage, I believe that he was actually trying to harm her, sir."

"Trying to harm Goldman?" Byrnes said. "Isn't that a bit of a leap?"

"I'm sorry, sir," Falconer answered. "I know I don't have solid evidence for you, but it's what I believe. I'm convinced someone was trying to hurt Goldman last night during her speech, but I don't know who or why."

Byrnes walked slowly back towards the open window overlooking Mulberry Street behind his desk, and then he turned back to face Falconer and the other men in the room. "Well, what of it?" he said. "Goldman is a controversial figure, a firebrand who has incurred the anger of half the country due to her inciteful and traitorous speeches. She's bound to have enemies. We can't just eliminate the danger that she has created for herself."

"I understand, sir," Falconer said, "but I'm concerned that if we don't act in some way, we may have a murder on our hands."

"Falconer," Byrnes said as he walked back to his desk, wiping his neck with a handkerchief, "Goldman is a known anarchist who has espoused violence against the government and the people of this country. We are convinced, in fact, that she helped to engineer the assassination attempt on Mister Frick and is likely plotting additional attacks this very minute. So that must take precedence over any perceived threat to her own safety that she has incurred herself through her own reckless speeches and writings. Do you understand?"

"Yes, sir," Falconer answered tersely, "but we shouldn't be surprised if Miss Goldman ends up dead in the near future. That's all I'm saying."

"Well, your concerns are well-meaning and duly noted," Byrnes said. "And, of course, if you somehow come across more evidence of a possible threat to the woman, let us know. But as I said, we need to get a case against her soon, or it could blow up in all our faces. Do you understand?"

"Yes, sir," Falconer replied.

"Very good then. Keep me apprised of the situation. That is all."

"Will do, sir," Falconer said, and then he motioned for his companions to follow him out into the hallway. When they got outside and Byrnes' door was shut behind them, Waidler turned to Falconer. "So, what now?" he asked. "We aren't getting much on Goldman."

"Right," Falconer said, adjusting his bowler on top of his head. "Well, we'll just keep shadowing her, and maybe it's a waste of time, but Byrnes obviously is intent on incriminating her somehow."

"Yes," Waidler said. "And now you think she herself is a target, too?"

"I do, James," Falconer answered, "and I actually think I need to warn Miss Goldman about it." He then started to walk off down the hallway.

"Warn her?" Waidler said, grabbing Halloran and walking quickly to catch up to Falconer. "What's that?"

"Come on," Falconer said as he continued walking down the hallway. "I'll explain." And then the men disappeared down the stairway to the first floor.

12

Falconer, Waidler, and Halloran stood outside the entrance to the Zum Groben Michel tavern on Fifth Street. It was late in the evening and the word on the street was that Emma Goldman was holding court with her fellow anarchists at a back table in the place, as she typically did on late nights after she had finished giving a lecture somewhere.

"Are you sure you want to do this, boss?" Waidler asked Falconer.

"Yes, James," Falconer answered. "I think we owe it to her to tell her about the possibility that someone's targeting her."

"We don't have much hard evidence of that," Waidler pointed out, "and we're supposed to be keeping our distance from her to catch her doing something incriminating."

"You're right," Falconer conceded, "but there's just something telling me that someone out there wants to hurt her, or worse. She's got a lot of enemies in this town, with all her crazy speeches, so I feel we have to at least warn her. I'll take the blame if the brass has a problem with it. Plus, it's not as if we've uncovered any evidence linking her to the Frick assassination attempt. The search of her place didn't give us anything, and she's been very good at not slipping up. Hell, maybe she isn't even involved, as she keeps saying to the papers."

"Got it," Waidler said tersely.

"All right then, boys," Falconer said, "let's go in. I'll deal with Goldman and you just keep an eye out for trouble. But I don't think there'll be any problems."

"Okay," Waidler said.

"Got it, detective sergeant," Halloran replied.

The three men went through the door into the busy tavern. Falconer saw Tough Mike looming over the bar to the left, and their eyes met briefly. The huge bartender simply went back to his work behind the bar, and Falconer continued walking farther into the place as Halloran and Waidler spread out to opposite sides of the room.

The bar was busy, with lots of patrons—mostly speaking German—sitting at tables and drinking large mugs of beer and conversing loudly. A few looked up at him but then quickly turned away, as if they expected the policemen to be trolling around the neighborhood bars like this.

Falconer looked farther back in the room and saw, through the hazy smoke of lit cigarettes and cigars, the petite figure of Emma Goldman sitting with eight or nine other people at a single table against the far wall.

Just as I thought—lording it over her subjects late into the night.

Falconer walked past the various tables and approached the sullen group of apparent anarchists sitting with Goldman, who stopped speaking to them suddenly and looked up at him with a glare. "Well, look who's here," she said. "If it isn't that police detective who was present at my lecture the other night. Are you here to perhaps arrest me for some trumped-up charge, sir?"

"Can't say that I am, Miss Goldman," Falconer replied calmly.

"Well, then why are we so lucky to have you gracing us with your presence, detective?" she asked. "Are you perchance interested in taking part in some anarchist discussions?"

The men and women sitting at the table chuckled.

"Not really," Falconer said, smiling slightly. "But thanks for the offer."

"Well, then, out with it," she said with a scolding tone to her voice. "Tell us what you want and then please leave us alone."

"Certainly, Miss Goldman," he said. "I'm here to actually warn you about possible threats to your safety."

"Threats to my safety?" she asked. "What do you mean?"

"It's true, I was there at Military Hall last night," he continued. "And I know you saw me after your speech dealing with an individual who was approaching the stage."

"Yes, I saw you," she answered curtly.

"I believe that that man was sent to harm you, Miss Goldman," he said.

"Sent to harm me?" she asked. "What makes you think that, sir?"

"Just the way that he was acting, and how he departed when I got close to him," Falconer said. "I just had a feeling that he was not there to hear your speech, miss, and I've been in this business a long time."

"Your suspicions sound like just a lot of melodramatic speculation without any real evidence," she said. "But I do appreciate your concerns."

"You do know that your speeches and writings inflame many people, don't you?" he asked. "You have many enemies out there, Miss Goldman, and some of them are not above doing violence."

"Of course, I'm aware of that," she replied blithely. "But we cannot let the apes intimidate us into silence, now can we? The enemies of progress will always try to stifle the voices of the people as they fight for their rights and freedoms. Good people cannot shrink in fear and be muzzled. I think you know that."

"Yes, I understand," Falconer said, "but you need to be aware that these people out there who disagree with you—they can be very dangerous and will try to harm you...even kill you, I'm sorry to say."

Goldman paused and sat still for a moment as if deep in thought, and then she looked up at him again and spoke. "I thank you for your concern, and I will be on my guard, but we will not let anyone dissuade us from our mission, and that is to empower the workers to overcome the yoke of oppression thrown onto them by the forces of capitalism. No one and nothing will scare us into submission."

"Yes, I see," he said to her. "I just wanted to alert you. If you'll excuse me."

He turned away and started walking back to the entrance to the bar, but Goldman stopped him with her voice. "Detective? May I have your name?"

"Certainly," he replied, looking back at her. "It's Detective Sergeant Falconer, from the Central Detective Bureau on Mulberry Street."

"Thank you, detective sergeant," she said. "I do appreciate your warning tonight."

"Certainly," he said, and then he turned and walked away.

13

The World

Evening Edition
August 4, 1892

ANARCHISTS BREAKING CAMP

The Mollick – Goldman –
Timmerman Crew Are Moving

Queen Emma Angrily Refuses to
Tell Where They Are Going

The red flag was at half-mast at the Mollick-Goldman-Timmerman Anarchist nest at 340 Fifth Street this morning. To-morrow the most rabid of radical Anarchists must obey the mandates of a law they hate more than the fate of sinful man.

Michaels & Sons, agents of the tenement, 340 Fifth Street, have issued an edict that Emma Goldman and her subjects must pull up stakes and get out.

This morning the entire colony was engaged in pulling up the stakes.

The Anarchistic camp was on the rear of the ground floor. It was dirty. So were the inmates. But never since Rip Van Winkle rubbed the moss of his eyes and brushed aside a foot or so of mother earth that had accumulated on his face and hands during his long sleep has there been so much terra firma on any one person as seemed to surround Mrs. Mollick as she opened the door of the apartment this morning and said, "Git out."

A cloud of dust like a Sahara sandstorm rushed through the door with the words. When at length the dust and Mrs. Mollick's wrath subsided the cause of the disturbance could be seen.

It was this—the Anarchists were breaking up house-keeping. A rag carpet, a bedstead, a table, a stove, a cradle, a baby carriage and a baby were piled up together, and from out the mass came mingled infant's screams, the odor of unwashed furniture and the accumulated dust of months. Back of it all was the voice of Emma Goldman reviling law, order and work.

"I have nothing to say," she screamed, as she threw a pile of Anarchistic literature in the baby carriage.

"Moving are you?" the reporter asked.

"Well, d'ye think we're doin' this for exercise?" was the answer, as Emma wiped the perspiration from her dimpled chin and rosy cheeks with her dust-covered hand.

"Where are you going?"

"Fifth Avenue; where did you suppose? We've got a corner lot among the 'ristocrats, and I guess we've a right to use it, hain't we, even if we don't stand in with the police and capitalistic press?"

"Donner, blitzen, bomben und grenaden," interrupted a voice mingled with the crash of a thousand falling pieces of stove pipe. At the same moment the door banged in the reporter's face and the interview with Emma ended.

Mrs. Walsh, the housekeeper of the tenement, said she did not know where the Anarchists were going. She added that the neighbors were very glad to get rid of the unwashed crowd and sympathy would be extended to the people in whatever community they move into.

14

F alconer walked into the Detective Bureau at the Mulberry Street headquarters and sat down at his desk a little before noon. He glanced at a tray that held recently arrived telegrams and messages and noticed that there was one from "E. Levine."

Well. The professor.

He sat up a little straighter and eagerly opened the envelope to read the contents:

> *Can you possibly meet me at 1:30 today at the new Hotel Savoy on Fifth Ave. and 58th? I have something interesting to report to you. I will be on the 2d floor landing as you go up the main staircase.*
>
> *Regards,*
>
> *Levine*

He placed the telegram on his desk again and pondered what the professor had written. Something interesting? Why so vague? Regardless, he decided that he would, indeed, go see his old friend from the prior year's East River Hotel murder investigation. Levine was always refreshing company—he would be a good break from anarchists, assassins, and smoke-filled German beer joints.

15

The imposing Hotel Savoy, newly opened just two months earlier, stood before Falconer on busy 5th Avenue. The building rose 12 stories and dominated the block. Falconer craned his neck to see the very top floor looming high over the street.

Fancy joint. Now why is the professor wanting to meet here?

He walked up to the front entrance and moved inside. The interior was fancy indeed, with shiny, marbled walls leading upward to gold-colored, coffered ceilings displaying intricate, painted designs within each coffer. The carpets were smooth, colorful, and equally ornate, and hanging from various points in the lobby were huge, crystal chandeliers that seemed to be hand-crafted from the world's finest jewels.

As various well-dressed customers walked by him in the lobby, Falconer looked over to the main staircase with its delicately lacquered, wooden bannisters.

The professor said he'd be up on the second floor.

He moved over to the staircase and walked up to the first landing. He immediately felt as if he were standing in a lush rainforest in South America: about seven or eight small, circular tables were surrounded by chairs and a forest of sweeping palm fronds growing out of large vases strewn throughout the area. Falconer looked for Levine, but it was difficult to see through all the tropical vegetation decorating the landing, so he decided to slowly walk through the area and scout out for his old friend.

After a few moments of this, he finally caught sight of the professor apparently doing the same scouting. "Professor," he said as he held up his hand.

"Ah, Detective Sergeant," Levine replied with a slight smile as he walked toward Falconer. "This is all very impressive, isn't it? Quite a beautiful place. I wonder why you wanted me to meet you here."

"What?" Falconer asked quizzically. "Why did I want to meet you here? What do you mean? You were the one who invited me."

"I beg your pardon?" Levine said, apparently just as confused as Falconer. "I received your message this morning asking me to come and meet you here at 1:30. I'm not sure what you mean by saying that I invited you."

Then Falconer suddenly heard a voice from behind him, and he immediately recognized its eminently British owner: "Well, well, now that we're all met, shall we have a drink together?"

Falconer looked at Levine, who appeared slightly in shock, and then they both turned and looked to where the voice had come from. Falconer saw two trousered legs sitting near a vase with its large palm fronds draping downwards, and above the legs, a newspaper held open by two sturdy hands, thus, shielding the reader. Then the newspaper in an instant came down to reveal the mysterious speaker. "Penwill!" Falconer and Levine exclaimed in unison as they both looked admiringly at their old friend from Scotland Yard.

Inspector Charlie Penwill smiled back at them with the faintest n'er-do-well sense of triumph and spoke: "So good to see you both, old chums. And now that my little ruse has apparently worked, I'd say it's about time I apologized and introduced you to another friend of mine. Come along—he's waiting in the dining room downstairs."

16

Penwill led Falconer and Levine into the fancy, grand dining room on the first floor of the hotel. Walking past various tables populated by groups of obviously well-heeled patrons, Falconer thought for a moment that he had been suddenly transported in time to the regal interior of the Palace of Versailles under Louis the Fourteenth. The ceiling of the room was spectacularly high, and was supported by a series of grand, square Corinthian columns topped by gilded capitals that appeared to be wrought from pure gold. Within the coffered ceiling were enormous, detailed paintings of, among other things, angels, planets, and animals that loomed over the diners like giants hovering over a village of miniature Lilliputians. The carpets were like those in the lobby—elaborately decorated and spotless—and the dishware on the tables seemed to have been taken from the cupboards of the finest mansions on the Upper East Side of Manhattan.

As the men reached the opposite end of the cavernous room, Falconer saw a lone man sitting at a table, and Penwill hailed the man as they got close. "Ah, here we are," he said. "Gentlemen, allow me to introduce Inspector Prosper-Isidore Houllier of the French Sureté. Inspector, this is Detective Sergeant Robert Falconer of the New York Police Department's Central Detective Bureau, and Professor Eli Levine of the Columbia College of Law."

Falconer saw the man stand up and straighten out his jacket and tie. He appeared to be in his thirties and was on the short side, but stocky and powerfully built. He had dark, slicked-back hair and sported a thick but trimmed, black mustache. He extended his meaty hand to Falconer, and as they shook hands, he spoke in English but with a thick French accent. "Detective Sergeant Falconer, I am most pleased to meet you finally."

He then turned to Levine and extended his hand again. "Professor," he said, shaking Levine's hand, "pleased to meet you, too, sir. Gentlemen, I have heard much of your investigation last year into the murder of Miss Brown and the other unfortunate ladies in New York, and eventually, I would love to speak to you more about it, if you would not mind."

"Yes, indeed," Penwill said, "but first, let us sit down and get better acquainted," and the men joined him in taking a seat at the table. "Well," he continued, "you're probably wondering why I asked you meet the inspector and myself here. No particular reason for the setting—I suppose I just fancied a new hotel and wanted to get a look at things. Lovely place, isn't it? In any event, I do want to catch up on the past seven months or so, but Inspector Houllier and I are actually here on urgent business, and we wanted to fill you in, as they say."

"Understood, inspector," Falconer said. "Go on."

"Do you gentlemen know who Ravachol is?" Penwill asked.

"Ravachol?" Falconer replied. "Can't say that I do."

"I do know of Ravachol, actually," Levine said. "He was just executed as few weeks ago in France for committing certain murders."

"Yes, he was, professor," Penwill said. "His real name was Francois Claudius Koenigstein, but he eventually took on his mother's surname, Ravachol, and that became his nom de guerre. He became politically active in the past couple of years, and eventually became an anarchist devoted to destroying a government that he felt was keeping the workers under the boot, as they say. He was convicted of setting off several bombs and killing a few men in the process, and he eventually met his day with the executioner just last month."

"Well," Falconer said, "too bad for him."

"Yes, well, the problem didn't end there, I'm afraid," Penwill said. "The bombings have continued."

"Continued?" Falconer asked. "So, this Ravachol character was part of a group?"

"Yes, indeed," Houllier said. "He was working with several other of these anarchists, and unfortunately, some of them are still on the run."

"On the run?" Falconer said. "You mean on the run here to the states?"

"Yes, that's correct, Falconer, unfortunately," Penwill said, "but only one appears to have escaped to your country."

"One?" Falconer said. "And who might that be?"

"His name is Theodule Meunier," Penwill replied, pulling out a photograph of a swarthy, mustachioed, and dark-haired man in his thirties. "Here is a photograph of him."

Falconer took the photograph and looked at it briefly, then handed it to Levine. "So, he's tied up with this Ravachol character?"

"Yes," Houllier replied. "Meunier was associated with Ravachol, and he set off a bomb in an army barracks this past March, but fortunately it did not cause any casualties. But to truly understand his motivations, one must first know what happened to Ravachol. The Surete finally caught him when a waiter at a café overheard him boasting about his bombing exploits. The waiter told the authorities, and the next time Ravachol showed up at the café, he was apprehended after a fierce struggle. Then, this past April, on the day before Ravachol was to be sentenced, Meunier set off a bomb in the same café, and it killed the owner and another patron, but the waiter survived. Clearly, this was an act of revenge for Ravachol's prosecution."

"So, what makes you think he's come here to the states?" Falconer asked.

"When the French government started to tamp down on the anarchists in the past few years," Penwill explained, "my government allowed some of them to seek refuge in Great Britain, believe it or not. Sort of a free speech thing, I suppose, but I can't say that I agree with the decision. Anyway, some of Ravachol's associates have been hiding out in England, and now my unit, the Special Branch under Inspector William Melville, has been rounding them up. But this fellow, Meunier, managed to escape to Canada. We lost his scent in Montreal, but all indications are that he got across the border and headed south, and we think he was headed here, gentlemen."

"Why here?" Falconer asked.

"Because it is the biggest city in your country," Penwill answered. "And Meunier wants to make a big statement. He doesn't want to leave a bomb in a small town. No, he would like to leave a lasting impression on the world by causing the maximum amount of damage on as big stage as he can find—New York City."

"I see," Falconer said. "And you gentlemen are asking for our help in tracking down Meunier."

"I suppose we are, Falconer," Penwill said. "My Special Branch has been in close contact with your federal government, and now your police department has been briefed, as well. I understand that you are currently assigned to shadowing several anarchists of your own here in the city."

"That's true," Falconer said. "Byrnes and the Pittsburgh police department are trying to find evidence tying our most notorious anarchist agitator, Emma Goldman, to the recent assassination attempt on Frick, the Carnegie Steel man up in Pittsburgh. You've heard of that business up there?"

"Yes, indeed, we have," Penwill replied. "Berkman and perhaps some of his associates have already been arrested."

"Right," Falconer said. "Unfortunately, we haven't found much of anything tying Goldman and her crowd here in the city to Berkman's act. You know of her, I assume?"

"Yes, that is correct, detective sergeant," Houllier said. "We are very well acquainted with Miss Goldman and her band of Autonomists."

"Autonomists," Falconer repeated. "I keep hearing that word, but I'm not really sure what it refers to."

"If I may, detective sergeant?" Levine interrupted. "I've actually studied the varied forms of anarchism in recent years, and I have grown familiar with the Autonomists. They are members of a particular faction within the anarchist camp that emphasizes the independence of the self from all forms of organized authority. In their view, all collective forms of civil order—the bureaucracy, government, capitalism itself—form the roots of tyranny, and the worker can only find true freedom by being free from the shackles of this organized society. And the ultimate expression of this autonomist creed is propaganda of the deed—attentat. Freeing oneself from the tyranny of the existing system by acts of violence that will serve as a catalyst to revolution."

"Hm," Falconer snorted. "That sounds like a lot of bughouse to me, professor."

"I suppose many people would agree with you, detective," Levine said. "They are obviously not very popular anywhere around the globe."

"Yes, well, it looks like you have another one on your hands, I'm afraid," Penwill said. "And we are here to catch him."

"I understand, inspector," Falconer said, "but I have to say, looking at this Meunier person's photograph, he looks like any one of thousands of dark-haired foreigners walking around the streets of New York. I'm not sure how you can pick him out of the crowd."

"Well, there is one thing, gentlemen," Penwill said. "He happens to have a back problem—he's a hunchback."

"A hunchback?" Falconer asked. "You mean like the guy in Notre Dame? All malformed and such?"

"Well, not exactly," Penwill said, chuckling. "He doesn't look like Quasimodo from the novel, as you can see from the photo, but he clearly has a hunchback and people have said it's obvious when you see him."

"Hm," Falconer muttered. "That would definitely help, I have to agree with you there. So where do we all start with tracking him down, I wonder?"

"Well, he is a Red agitator," Penwill said, "just like the ones you already have here. And if there's anything we've learned in dealing with these anarchist types on our end, gentlemen, it's that they like to mingle together and keep in contact. So "

"So, you're thinking that he'll make contact with Goldman and her band of anarchists here in New York," Falconer said. "To help facilitate his plan."

"*Exactement*, gentlemen," Houllier said. "That is what we believe."

Falconer set back in his chair and pondered what had been said. What a strange position they found themselves in: shadowing a leader of the anarchist movement here in the states to pin a recent assassination attempt on her and perhaps on some of her followers, and now faced with the very real possibility that a dangerous French anarchist bomb thrower was also in New York and planning—perhaps with Goldman's help—a big show of it here on American shores. It was a mess, indeed, and also a very dangerous situation: one well-placed bomb could kill dozens or more in the blink of an eye, and he and his men might not be able to do anything about it.

"Well," he said to the men sitting with him, "the only option now is to get on with it and try to track down Meunier and take him down. Agreed?"

"Agreed," Penwill said.

"Yes, agreed," Houllier answered.

"I think you have a chance," Levine said. "And you, of course, must try."

"Well, the first thing to do is to confront Goldman," Falconer said, "and question her about Meunier."

"Confront her?" Penwill asked. "Isn't she famous for despising police and not cooperating with them at all?"

"Well, yes," Falconer replied, "but I've had a few words with her recently, actually, and I think she'll at least listen to me."

"Really?" Penwill said. "What makes you think that?"

"I believe that she is being targeted for assassination herself—by whom, I don't know—and I've told her that recently, and she seemed open to hearing me out."

"I see," Penwill said. "So, where shall we find her in the near future, I wonder?"

"She had to leave her flat after we turned it upside down with a search warrant and the landlord kicked her out," Falconer answered, "and word has it she's living with her grandmother now over on East Tenth Street. But during the evenings she's been hanging her hat at a couple of popular anarchist watering holes, and we can probably find her at one of them tonight."

"Jolly good," Penwill said. "I'd actually like to meet the woman. She's known to be quite fearless about speaking her mind—quite the bricky girl."

"Yes, I'd say that's fairly accurate," Falconer said. "There's a lot of stubbornness in that little body, if you know what I mean."

"Well, then, where and when shall we meet, gentlemen?" Houllier asked.

"I'll get my men and we can meet at one of the places this evening," Falconer replied. "It's called 'Zum Groben Michel'—'Tough Mike's'—and it's on 5th Street just east of Bowery. We'll meet you outside at 9:00 PM. Professor, care to come along?"

"Me?" Levine asked. "Well, if I'm not getting in the way, of course, I'd be happy to join you."

"Well done, then," Penwill said, smiling. "Just like last year when we were chasing that demon from the East River Hotel."

"Yes, that's true," Falconer said. "It's good to be back together again."

"And I am most grateful to be included in your company, gentlemen," Houllier interjected. "We shall track down Meunier in your great city, and he will face the guillotine in my country, too."

"Or he'll face a bullet from one of our revolvers in this country, inspector," Falconer said. "Either way, we need to stop him before he lights his dynamite."

"Indeed, *mon ami*," Houllier said. "Indeed."

17

Falconer checked his watch as he stood with Waidler, Halloran, and Levine beneath the gaslit streetlamps outside of Tough Mike's Saloon.

Nine o'clock.

He looked to his right towards the Bowery and saw a couple of dark-clad men walking towards them on the sidewalk. One was larger—like a heavyweight prizefighter—and the other, short but thickly-set with a very purposeful stride.

Penwill and Houllier.

As they approached him outside the bar's entrance, Penwill spoke. "Evening, gentlemen—I do hope we aren't late. Quite a time getting over here on the train."

"No, you're fine," Falconer said. "Good timing, actually. You remember James Waidler and Jimmy Halloran from last year."

"Ah, yes," Penwill said, smiling and extending his hand to the two young men. "Jolly good to see you chaps again. And this is Inspector Prosper-Isidore Houllier from the French Surete."

"Pleasure to meet you, gentlemen," Houllier said, shaking Waidler and Halloran's hands.

"Inspector," Waidler said.

"Nice to meet you, sir," Halloran said.

"So, this is the place?" Penwill asked. "Tough Mike's?"

"That's correct," Falconer said. "A German joint, popular with the anarchist crowd."

"Is our girl inside?" Penwill asked.

"She is," Falconer answered. "She's been in there for some time now. We've been hanging off in the distance, though—didn't interact with her or her friends."

"Excellent," Penwill said. "So, what's the plan, detective sergeant?"

"You, me, the professor, and Inspector Houllier will go inside and try to speak to her," Falconer said, "and James and Jimmy will wait out here and keep a watch over things."

"All right," Penwill said. "Sounds easy enough. Shall we, gentlemen?"

Falconer turned to Waidler and Halloran. "Just keep an eye on people going in and out," he instructed. "We shouldn't be long."

"Right, boss," Waidler said.

"All right," Falconer said to Houllier, Levine, and Penwill. "Let's head in."

The four men walked up to the bar's entrance and walked inside. It was crowded and noisy, with scores of revelers swilling mugs of beer and jabbering busily in their native German tongue. As waves of smoke wafted up towards the ceiling, no one seemed to notice the four men amidst all the celebrating going on in the room until the policemen started pushing their way through the throng. Then, Falconer could sense that eyes were settling on them and voices were being muffled.

He looked ahead to the back of the barroom and saw Goldman sitting at what he now discerned was her favorite table. She was talking in an animated way to several companions and gesticulating sharply with her hands as if to emphasize the point she was trying to make. Falconer turned to Levine, who appeared slightly unnerved by the chaotic atmosphere in the room. "See her over there?" he said to him. "That's her speaking to her followers."

"Yes, I recognize her from her picture in the papers," Levine said. "Strange seeing her in person now."

"Well, let's get this over with," Falconer said to the other men. "Just be prepared for some angry responses from her. She's like that."

The men nodded and they pushed forward until they came before Goldman and about six others sitting at the table. As Falconer took off his bowler, Goldman stopped talking and looked up at him. Then she glanced at the other three men and frowned. "So, you're back, detective," she said, sitting back jauntily in her chair. "And with more friends, I see. Are you here to arrest me or to save me?"

"I'll get right to the point, Miss Goldman, so as not to intrude on your evening too much," Falconer answered. "These men here have been investigating an anarchist bombing in Paris. They've come to our city because they believe that the French suspect has perhaps come here to try out some more dynamite on our shores. And they're just wondering if perhaps you've heard from this man."

"Really, detective?" Goldman said. "Are you insinuating that I am somehow involved with the machinations of a Paris bomber? Are you joking, sir?"

"No, not joking at all, miss," Falconer replied. "This bomber happens to be an enthusiastic anarchist by the name of Theodule Meunier and he's wanted for blowing up a café over there—killed a couple of people in the process. The good inspectors here believe that he did it to avenge the execution of his leader, a guy named Ravachol. Maybe you've heard of him?"

Goldman sat silently for a moment and then spoke again. "I have, in fact, detective," she replied. "Another martyr condemned by a ruthless and corrupt state."

"Well, I don't know about that," Falconer said, "but I do know that he committed some murders with bombs of his own, and he had his followers like this Meunier character."

"And?" Goldman asked. "What is your point, sir?"

"My point is, Meunier is a rabid anarchist by all accounts," Falconer said, "and if he has, in fact, come to New York, chances are he'll want to get in touch with some notable anarchists who live here. So, my question for you is this: has Meunier been in touch with you?"

"That's quite an accusation, detective," she said. "I'm not sure I want to even dignify your question by giving you an answer."

"Well, let me put it this way," he said. "Lives may depend on your answer, and I'd hate to see the authorities find out after a bombing that Emma Goldman knew of Meunier's whereabouts and didn't say anything about it. That wouldn't be good for you."

"Well, if you must have an answer, detective," she said, "it is no—I have not heard from this Meunier person. I don't even know why he would be in touch with me. I'm not that schooled in the art of dynamiting buildings, frankly."

"I see," Falconer said. "Well, if he does happen to be in touch, I would hope that you would alert the authorities immediately."

"I shall keep that in mind, detective," she answered tartly. "The authorities are never that far off, as you know, as they are constantly surveilling me."

Falconer put his bowler back on his head and doffed it slightly in Goldman's direction. "Good evening, Miss Goldman."

"Good evening, detective," she answered. "I'll be seeing you outside my grandmother's place on Tenth, as it's obvious your men know I've been staying over there lately."

Falconer smiled and then motioned for the other men to follow him outside. When they had pushed their way through the barroom crowd and exited into the summertime air, Penwill grabbed a handkerchief and patted his sweaty brow. "Well, you weren't joking when you said that she could get a bit angry," he said. "Quite a church-bell, that one."

"Yes, I'm getting used to it by now," Falconer said.

"So, what now, gentlemen?" Houllier asked.

"Well," Falconer said, "I suppose Jimmy, James, and myself stick around and see where Goldman goes, and we'll keep you posted."

"Very well, Falconer," Penwill said. "Thanks for including us, and we'll stay in touch. But sorry you have to stick around. She might be in there all night."

"Um, actually, I don't think we'll have to," Waidler said, motioning to the tavern's front door. "Look."

Falconer turned around and, like the other men, saw Goldman and a few companions exiting Tough Mike's Saloon.

18

"Ah, Detective Falconer," Goldman said as she moved closer to the men standing on the sidewalk. "Still lurking around, I see. Well, we'll be headed to my grandmother's place now, if you want to follow."

Penwill chuckled.

"Thanks, Miss Goldman," Falconer said. "We'll follow your lead from a distance."

"I'm sure you will," she replied, and then she motioned for her friends to follow and started walking down the street. Falconer shook his head in amusement and then lit a cigarillo as the other men followed suit and lit cigarettes.

"This woman is most amusing," Houllier remarked. "It is rather hard for me to view her as a dangerous assassin or bomb thrower."

"Yes, I suppose you're right there, inspector," Falconer said. "But as they say, looks can be deceiving."

"Most assuredly," Houllier said.

The men stood for a moment chatting and waiting for Goldman and her retinue to walk some distance down the street. Falconer listened impassively for a moment until something suddenly caught his eye: a hansom cab rustling past them and headed in the same direction as Goldman. It looked like every other of the thousands of hansom cabs in the city—a dark, two-wheeled, covered carriage with a gas lamp attached to its side and led by a single horse and a driver sporting a top hat sitting high up on top behind the cab—and it normally wouldn't have garnered his attention but for the way in which it appeared to slow down slightly as it got closer to Goldman ambling down the sidewalk. Falconer took a couple of steps closer and peered intently at the cab in the distance. He then saw a gloved hand holding a small dark object suddenly protruding out of the carriage's window, and he immediately threw down his cigarillo.

"What is it, Falconer?" Penwill asked.

"Gun!" Falconer replied as he took off at a sprint down the sidewalk. As he ran, he kept glancing at the cab in the street as it got closer to Goldman and her friends. It was very close to them now—perhaps twenty feet or so—and he worried that he would be too late. But still he ran as fast as he could on the hard, concrete sidewalk lit by gaslit lamps. And, as he approached the group in the hazy light, he thought it would be prudent to alert them to the impending danger, so he yelled at the top of his lungs as best he could, given his exertions. "Goldman! Look out! The cab! Get down! Get down!"

Then, just as the cab was about to pull up next to Goldman and the others, he saw that she did hear him, for she stopped and turned back to look in his direction. He saw the confused look on her face just as he dove for her, tumbling down onto the sidewalk with her as he heard a series of gunshots going off.

BLAM! BLAM! BLAM! BLAM!

As they fell to the ground, Falconer wrapped his arms around her body and took the force of the fall on his back, so as not to expose her to injury. They skidded briefly on the sidewalk and then came to stop just as the driver of the cab slashed at the horse with his whip and the horse took off at a full gallop. As Falconer rose to his feet, unholstering his revolver, he heard Goldman exclaim, "What on earth?!" and he saw her friends stand up from their crouching positions and go to her aid. He turned his attention back to the fleeing carriage and fired off a couple of rounds, but the carriage flew off down the street and rounded the corner just as fast as the horse could pull it.

Falconer placed his gun back in his shoulder holster and turned to see Penwill, Houllier, Levine, Waidler, and Halloran all arriving at the scene themselves, having also sprinted down the sidewalk. "Good god, man!" Penwill exclaimed. "What the devil was that?"

"Someone just tried to assassinate Miss Goldman," Falconer responded. "That's what that was."

He turned to Waidler and Halloran, whose guns were also drawn. "James...Jimmy...run down to the corner and see if you can spot that carriage."

"Right, boss," Waidler answered, and both men took off running down the street.

Falconer then turned his attention to Goldman, who was still sitting on the sidewalk being attended to by her companions. "Are you all right, Miss Goldman?" he asked her as he crouched down next to her.

"I...I think I am," she replied vacantly. "Did someone just try to shoot me?"

"Yes, I'm afraid so," Falconer answered. "But it looks like they've gotten away, unfortunately."

"My god," she said, looking at her friends. "My god...I almost died just now."

"Yes, yes, Emma," one of them, a young bespectacled man, said to her soothingly. "But it's over now, and the danger is passed."

"I...I think I owe you my life, detective," she said, looking at Falconer.

"No need for that, Miss Goldman," he replied. "But we need to get you out of this city, and quickly."

"Out of the city?" she asked. "What do you mean?"

"It's clear that you are being targeted," he said. "By whom, I don't know, but if you stay much longer here in the city, I fear that you will be killed."

Penwill, Levine, and Houllier walked over and stood next to the crouching figure of Falconer as Goldman appeared to be lost in thought.

"But where?" she finally said, looking at the various people crowding around her on the sidewalk. "Where shall I go?"

"My bureau has a safe house up north," Falconer replied. "I'll take you there while my colleagues look into whoever did this. You'll be safe there for a while."

"But I have my lectures," she protested. "My meetings."

"You need to let those things go for a while," Falconer said, "until we figure this out."

"Please, Emma," the young man said to her pleadingly. "He's right. This has moved to a new level of dangerousness and you must disappear for a while. I'm begging you."

"All right, all right, Claus," she said. "I will heed your warnings and do as the detective says. But where to right now, detective?"

"We'll go to our headquarters on Mulberry Street where I can get some supplies," Falconer answered. "What do you need from your lodgings? I can send my men to do that."

"I...well, I'll need a change of clothes," Goldman replied, "my toiletries, and I'll need some of my books. I can't go sitting in the woods somewhere without something to read."

Falconer looked up and saw Waidler and Halloran running back to the group, signaling that they could not find the cab.

"We'll attend to that, Miss Goldman," Falconer said. "Give your house key to Detective Waidler here, and your list of belongings. He and Officer Halloran will meet us at the headquarters."

"Very well, detective," she said, standing up with the help of her friend and Halloran. "Mister Timmermann here can accompany them over there. My grandmother knows him and will let him gather up my things. And thank you again, detective, for saving my life, it appears. That was quite close."

"It was," Falconer said. "And unfortunately, it won't be the last time, I'm afraid."

"Well, then," she said, dusting off her skirt, "I suppose we must be getting on. Please lead the way."

Goldman then conferred briefly with her friend, the man named Claus Timmermann, and with Waidler, and then she turned and walked off into the night with Falconer, Levine, Penwill, and Houllier as her escort.

19

After walking a few blocks, Penwill hailed a cab and the four men and Goldman packed themselves into it and rode over to the stately headquarters building on Mulberry Street. It was late in the evening, and thus, when they arrived, the building was largely quiet and not the busy control center humming with activity that it typically was during the day. A couple of overnight desk clerks sat behind a grand, wooden counter inside the front entrance, and three patrol officers were trundling a dusty inebriate into the building for drying out in a cell downstairs.

Falconer led Goldman and the others down a hallway to the Detective Bureau and offered Goldman a seat in a conference room with some coffee. "Thank you," she said. He then went to a locked cabinet in a back room of the bureau and retrieved a Winchester Model 1890 .22 caliber repeating rifle with several boxes of rounds, as well as more rounds for his .45 caliber Colt revolver. Grabbing a canvas duffel bag, he placed the rifle inside it with the boxes of rounds and collected some extra clothing items from some of his colleagues on the nightshift.

After retrieving some extra cash from the bureau lockbox, he gathered the men. "Well, this should be enough to get us through several days up there," he said. "I'll keep in touch via the local telegraph office up there, and I know there are places close by to keep us stocked with food."

"I say, Falconer," Penwill said, "where exactly is this safe house, if you don't mind my asking? We might have to come find you."

"It's in a town called Cohoes, just along the New York Central and Hudson River Railroad line," Falconer answered. "There's an old house overlooking the Mohawk River just a half mile west of the big falls that are right there. You can't miss them—big waterfalls. Take the road along the south side of the Mohawk as you leave town and right past the last set of houses is a dirt path leading through the forest. The house is back there all alone on the river."

"Understood," Penwill said. "Any idea how long you'll be up there?"

"Just long enough to convince whoever is trying to kill Miss Goldman that she's skipped town," Falconer replied. "Then, I'll try to get her back under cover."

"Right," Penwill said. "Meanwhile, we'll work with your men here to try to figure out who's up to this."

"That would be great," Falconer said. "And James, we don't have time to request permission from Byrnes or Steers, so you'll just have to alert them that I had to get Goldman out of town in an emergency. I'll take the blame later."

"Got it, boss," Waidler said. "We'll take care of that."

"All right, I'm going to go get her," Falconer said. "We'll take a hansom cab up to Grand Central—more inconspicuous than a police wagon."

He walked down the hallway and entered the room where Goldman was quietly sipping her coffee. "Miss Goldman," he said, "it's time. I see that James managed to get you some of your books and personal items. Are you ready?"

"Indeed, I am, detective," she replied. "Lead the way."

"We'll go downstairs and exit through a back door to avoid anyone noticing us," he said. "We'll take a cab up to Grand Central and take a train upstate."

"How far upstate?" she asked. "You obviously know that I have family in Rochester and lived there for a time."

"Yes, I'm aware of that," he said. "We're not going near that far. We're headed to a town on the Mohawk River called Cohoes. It's a little bit past Albany."

"I see," she said. "Well, much as I hate to leave the city, I also recognize that those were real bullets tonight, and that they were aimed for me. So, I am yours for concealing."

"All right, then," he said. "Let's go."

20

Falconer led Goldman into the expansive, roofed Grand Central train shed at 42nd Street and 4th Avenue with two tickets for Cohoes in his hand. He looked at her at his side to make sure that she was still covering up most of her face with a thin shawl, then he motioned for her to head down a concrete walkway with him to the train that was slated to depart shortly for points upstate.

Normally, the enormous glass panels held in place high overhead in the roof by a system of wrought iron lattice work would allow plentiful sunlight in to drape travelers as they waited for the trains. At this late hour, however, the place was only partially lit by a series of gas lamps, and Falconer hoped that the lack of sunlight would allow them to better avoid detection as they entered the train.

Walking up to one of the several cars that were attached to the powerful steam engine at the front, the two of them stopped in front of a purser and Falconer handed him their tickets. The man uttered a casual "Thank you" and pointed the way for them to enter the car. Moving inside, Falconer motioned for Goldman to head to the back of the car and take a seat against a window. "It's best to stay back here," he said to her quietly.

They sat in silence for several minutes as other passengers boarded and took their seats. Then, Goldman turned to him. "You know," she said, "it's really very fascinating, detective. For two weeks you and your men have been following me, a target in your little investigation following Berkman's atten-tat in Pittsburgh. I was the bad guy—the prey to your predator. And now it appears that I've become the prey to someone else, and you have switched hats to being my protector. I don't quite know how that all happened so quickly, but it's happened. Odd...."

"I suppose so," Falconer said. "Maybe now you won't treat me quite so harshly."

"Perhaps, detective," she said. "Perhaps. But rest assured, when this little adventure is over and you are once again sent to sneak around behind my back and those of my comrades, you will become the enemy once again. Don't think that we're getting friendly or anything."

"I wouldn't think of it," he replied quietly, and then he felt the train finally shudder and start to move slowly out of the enormous train shed towards the thundering Great Falls of the Mohawk 160 miles away.

21

The Sun

New York
Sunday, August 7, 1892

RAVACHOL'S AVENGERS

The Man Who Blew Up the Very Restaurant
Believed to be On His Way Here

Paris, Aug. 6—The police have seized a placard, evidently issued by Anarchists, and urging the extermination of the Judge and jury that sent Ravachol to the guillotine. Several dangerous Anarchists, who had come to Paris with the intention of avenging Ravachol by blowing up simultaneously several public buildings, have been arrested within the last few days. The police have been earnestly searching for Joseph Meunier, the Anarchist known as Ravachol's avenger, and who is believed to have caused the fatal explosion at the Very restaurant.

A man named Bricon was arrested at Havre while trying to throw himself under the wheels of a heavy cart. He gave information which led to an energetic search being made for Meunier and

Francois. These men were in London, and officers were dispatched to arrest and extradite them. In spite of the fullest assistance given by the London police, the Anarchists slipped through the fingers of the Frenchmen.

It is believed that they have gone to America, as they were traced as far as Liverpool.

Penwill looked up from his newspaper and turned to Houllier, sipping some tea next to him in the dining room of the Grand Central Hotel on Broadway, just blocks away from Police Headquarters on Mulberry Street. "Look here, chum," he said. "The paper mentions Meunier coming to America."

Houllier took the paper and scanned the page for a moment, his dark brow furrowing. "Ah," he finally said. "So now it is out in the open and he will be on guard, as it were, my friend."

"I agree," Penwill said, taking back the newspaper. "He will certainly hear of the newspapers talking about his travels and will be even more vigilant—which makes our job that much harder."

"*C'est vrai, mon ami,*" Houllier said. "But not an impossible task. This man is unique with a noticeable limp due to the extraordinary curvature of his back—the hunchback. He will stick out in a crowd, inspector, and then we just need to get word of this and fly upon him. I am confident that we will bring him to justice. You and me together."

"Agreed, Prosper," Penwill said. "Meanwhile, when the professor gets here, we will mine him for ideas. He's really a very knowledgeable chap and has a good intuition for the next right step in an investigation."

"Yes, I can see that," Houllier said. "The man obviously has an exceptional mind and a knack for thinking what the criminal is thinking. His expertise is most welcome."

"Ah, speak of the devil," Penwill said, looking beyond Houllier's shoulder to the approaching figure of Professor Eli Levine. "Glad you could make it, professor."

"I was glad to be invited for lunch," Levine said cheerily as he took a seat at the table.

"*Bonjour, professeur*," Houllier said. "Very nice to see you again."

"And same to you, Inspector Houllier," Levine said.

"We've actually just seen a little story about Meunier in today's newspaper, professor," Penwill said. "Here, take a look. It says he's likely on his way here having last been seen in the port city of Liverpool with his accomplice, Jean-Pierre Francois."

"Ah," Levine said, scanning the news story. "So, your theory finds even greater credence in the newspapers."

"Indeed," Penwill said. "But, of course, even anarchists read the papers, I'm afraid. So Meunier will likely be aware that he's being tracked here now."

"So it appears," Levine said.

"What we've got to do now, professor," Penwill said, "is figure out what he's trying to destroy here—his intended target."

"Yes, absolutely," Levine said.

Penwill opened his mouth to speak, but then a waiter suddenly approached and asked if the three men wished to give their lunch orders. After they had done so, he returned to the subject at hand. "As I was saying, we feel that Meunier will hit a target here, but we have no idea what that target is. A government office? A hotel like this one? A particular person?"

"Do you have thoughts on this puzzle, professor?" Houllier asked.

"Well," Levine began, "Meunier is an acolyte of the executed Ravachol. He is utterly devoted to the man, and to his memory. He even tried to gain revenge on behalf of Ravachol by blowing up the café that was the cause of his leader's capture. Thus, he is animated by feelings of retribution and pure revenge, as the newspaper has referred to him: 'Ravachol's Avenger.' So, what does this tell us, gentlemen? Well, it at least points us in the right direction. Meunier is seeking to harm someone or something that is tied directly to Ravachol's downfall."

"But what could that be, professor?" Houllier asked. "We are, after all, in America, not France. What did the U.S. have to do with Ravachol's capture and execution? *Rien*, gentlemen. Nothing."

"That may be so, inspector," Levine said, "but I can't help feeling that Meunier feels unsated—like he has failed in his quest to truly avenge his prophet's government-sanctioned killing and he wants another try at it."

"I agree, professor," Penwill said, "and something tells me that it will be bigger than just one little café. We need to search for an event or a gathering that will take place here in the city and that would be an enticing target for Meunier. Professor, is there anything unique about this time of the year in the city, or unique about the country in general this year?"

Levine rubbed his beard and took a few moments to think. Then he turned back to the two men. "Well, something that is unusual this year is, of course, the presidential election. We are only three months from Election Day, and it is a presidential election—Harrison, the incumbent, for the Republicans, and Cleveland, the former president, for the Democrats. It's a big news story, of course."

"Yes, that's true," Penwill said. "So, a presidential assassination attempt, perhaps? Do you think that's what Meunier's aim is?"

"It would certainly be in line with what radical anarchists would do," Levine answered.

"But still," Houllier interjected, "this is just one man who would be attacked. And how is one of these candidates associated with the French State and the execution of Ravachol? I don't believe either of these men is particularly tied to my country."

"I believe you are right, inspector," Penwill said. "They might be running for the highest office in this land, but what had they to do with Ravachol's prosecution and execution? Professor?"

"I must admit that I, too, am not aware of any particular tie to the French government that either of these men have," Levine said. "But then..."

"Professor?" Penwill said.

"Well, maybe it's not any tie that a presidential candidate has to your country, Inspector Houllier," Levine said. "Instead, it's a tie that a vice-presidential candidate has."

"Vice-presidential candidate, you say?" Penwill said. "What do you mean, professor?"

"As I recall, gentlemen," Levine explained, "Whitelaw Reid, the current running mate of President Harrison, was Ambassador to France until just this past March. Were you aware of that, Inspector Houllier?"

"That name actually sounds quite familiar, professor," Houllier replied. "He is the newspaperman who became your ambassador to our country a few years ago, I believe. Correct?"

"Correct, inspector," Levine said, "and he is now running with Harrison on the Republican ticket. If he perchance had any dealings with your country concerning Ravachol, he would make a logical target of your Meunier."

"You're bloody well correct there, professor," Penwill said. "Good god, you might have struck something."

"What we now must do," Levine said, "is figure out if Reid did, in fact, figure in the prosecution of Ravachol in anyway."

"*En effet*, gentlemen," Houllier said, as the waiter approached with some drinks and set them on the table. "We shall look into this Mister Reid and his time in Paris. But first, my cognac."

He raised his glass to his two companions. "To the capture of Meunier!"

22

Falconer stood next to a window inside the remote, rustic cabin and raised its dark curtain slightly to peer outside into the darkness. He and Goldman had reached the town of Cohoes just before noon and had trudged to the cabin on the far side of town where it lay deep inside some woods along the wide Mohawk River. On the way, they had stopped at a mercantile store to get some supplies and then had settled into the small, three-room cabin for a stay that was open-ended. After unpacking, they had shared a spartan dinner of beef with potatoes, and now, in the darkness of evening, Falconer stood watch at the window while Goldman read by candlelight near the hot stove.

"Why are you still standing there, detective?" she suddenly asked him, putting her book down on a small table by her chair. "You have been looking out that window for over an hour now, and perhaps it's time you took a break."

"I have to keep a lookout for any movement out there," he said taciturnly. "There's no telling if someone followed us on the train."

"Really?" she asked incredulously. "Do you honestly think that these people, whoever they are, somehow got wind of our movements and secretly followed us up here? That sounds rather preposterous."

"Maybe," he answered, "but I can't take any chances. These people seem very determined, Miss Goldman."

"Well, have it your way, then," she said, "but eventually, you'll have to sleep."

"That's where you come in," he said. "I'll stand watch until 4:00 am while you sleep, and then I'll wake you to take over. Agreed?"

"Certainly," she replied. "But I still cannot believe that I'm actually hiding out in the woods with a police detective—a man who represents all that is corrupt and insidious about society. Imagine that—me."

"I'm sorry I make you feel that way," he said with a hint of sarcasm.

"But really, it's rather odd," she continued. "You appear to me to be a man of character, and yet you align yourself with forces of persecution and tyranny."

"Persecution and tyranny?" he said. "I'm not sure where you get those terms when you speak of the police."

"Ha!" she exclaimed. "Are you saying that the police are not tyrannical or despotic in their friendly relations with the powerful and rich who step on the throats of the weak? You must be joking."

"I'm not really sure what you're talking about," he responded calmly. "I'm just a police detective sergeant doing my job, that's all."

"You are a part of the problem," she said, "despite your obvious strengths. In doing your 'job,' you are, in fact, being complicit with the forces of domination over the working class."

"Oh, really?" he said. "Please tell me how I'm complicit."

"You are the muscle of the government and of the powerful, moneyed interests that really control society," she said. "You are their billy club, as it were. Without you, they would not be able to control the masses so much."

"So, solving crimes and running bad guys into the jug are actually helping out the rich barons and hurting the little people?" he asked, turning to her. "Is that what you're saying?"

"Yes, indeed," she replied, "when you clearly aim your crime fighting skills disproportionately at the poor and the weak, as you and your fellow bullies do."

"Disproportionally at the poor and the weak?" he said. "What's this you're saying?"

"Well, it's no secret that there are vastly greater numbers of prisoners in the Tombs and Sing Sing who are poor, uneducated, and struggling to survive. Not so many of the robber barons appear to be in there, though, it seems."

Falconer chuckled momentarily in exasperation, then spoke again. "Lady, I don't know where you get your ideas, but they're crazy as a loon. All I do is find the suspects and arrest them if I have the evidence, whether they're a bum on the Bowery or the richest toad in the puddle. It doesn't matter to me, and if most of the bad eggs in jail are poor guys, well, they put themselves there and it's probably because it's the no-account losers on the streets who are committing the most crimes."

"'No-account losers?'" she said, getting angry. "Spoken like a true capitalist pig. You have shown your true colors, detective."

"At least I don't give these irresponsible criminals a pass, like you do," he retorted.

"What?" she asked. "A pass? What do mean by that?"

"Well, like your pal, Berkman," he said. "You don't think he did anything wrong, do you? He just walked into an office and shot a guy a couple of times—almost killed him—and now you give fancy speeches in his defense, saying that he was put upon and it was the old rich guy who was wrong and deserved it. Some responsible citizen you are."

"He did deserve it!" she said, her voice rising. "Shooting Frick was an act of attentat, a brave gesture on behalf of untold thousands who suffer at the hands of a wicked tyrant who exploits the suffering workers to line his own pockets and those of his shareholders with cash. But you're too blind to see that."

"As far as I can tell," Falconer said, "your pal shot a guy who was defenseless in his office, and that's against the law. And we enforce the laws in this country, miss. I'm not sure if they do where you come from, but here, we do."

"What's that supposed to mean?" she asked sharply.

"What?" he muttered, looking out the window.

"Where I come from?" she said. "What are you saying? That I don't belong here in the United States, like you do?"

"I didn't say that," he answered.

"Not in so many words," she said, "but that's what you meant. I know what you're really saying, I represent the 'other' who has come to your shores and has infested the cities with disease, grime, and unpleasant ideas."

"Well, now you've really gone bughouse," he said.

"Not really, detective," she said. "I know what you and your native-born citizens feel about us who have come from other countries and other societies. It's not hard to discern your true feelings towards us."

"I don't give a damn where you come from," he said. "Just please abide by the laws and don't make mischief, if that's not too much to ask."

"I'm done with you," she said, returning to her book. "Just get me back to New York as quickly as you can, and I'll part ways with you—with my thanks for your assistance, of course."

"That's fine," he said. "I'll get you up at four."

"Sounds just splendid," she said. "Thank you."

23

Falconer awoke with a start to the sound of Goldman's voice in the room. He blinked his eyes several times and then looked up towards the front door of the cabin. It was light outside, and as he squinted in the morning sunlight, he could see the silhouetted form of Goldman standing in the middle of the doorway looking in. "Time to get up, detective," she said. "It's seven o'clock and it's a glorious day. You really should go outside for some fresh air."

He realized then in his sleep-soaked mind that he was lying on the floor, in the cabin up in Cohoes, and Goldman was standing in the doorway speaking to him. He paused momentarily as that thought became clearer in his mind.

Goldman is standing in the doorway.

He shouted at her quickly as he got up and reached for his revolver lying next to him on the floor: "Get out of the doorway! Move!"

Grabbing the revolver, he then leapt over to her in a burst of motion and grabbed her around the waist with one arm and swung her inside the cabin against the wall next to the doorway. Just as suddenly, the room erupted with tiny explosions against the far wall, with vases and glasses set up over the sink shattering into many pieces. Falconer covered Goldman with his body and pushed her along the floor towards a bedroom off the main living area and kitchen. She screamed above the din: "What is happening?!"

"Gunshots!" he yelled as he pushed her closer to the door leading into the bedroom. "They've found us!"

"My god!" she yelled desperately. "When will it end?"

"Here!" he shouted as more bullets flew into the cabin, cracking beams and ricocheting like lightning strikes off the steel wood stove. "Get in the bedroom! We're going to go out the back!"

"Go out?" she yelled at him. "Why go out into that?"

"If we stay inside, we die," he said loudly into her ear. "Let me just grab my rifle and we'll go out a window here."

He pushed her against the side of an old bureau standing in the bedroom, and then, waiting for a moment in between fusillades, he crawled back quickly into the kitchen area and grabbed the Winchester .22 rifle that was leaning up in a corner of the room along with a box of rounds nearby and raced back into the bedroom.

"Here," he said as more gunshots rang out, striking all over the cabin's exterior. "We'll go out this window and head for the river down the embankment."

He opened the window, crawled out, and turned to Goldman waiting inside. "Here," he said to her. "Give me the rifle and box of rounds."

She did as he instructed and then he beckoned for her to grab his hands. "Reach outside," he said. "I'll take you and help you down."

Slowly she managed to grab onto him and extricate herself from the bedroom. Then, standing on the soft ground alongside him, she asked him what they were to do.

"Come on," he said as more bullets struck the front of the cabin. "We'll head down to the river and make our way down along the town."

"But where will we go?" she asked plaintively.

"Back to New York," he said as he led her through the thick woods that descended sharply down to the river in the distance. "We have no choice.

We'll have to confront these people with the full weight of my police department now."

"If we survive this," she said despondently.

"Come on," he said. "Let's head down to the river quickly."

24

Falconer led Goldman quickly through the tangled brush and hanging tree limbs that barred their way to the shores of the Mohawk far
below them. He held the rifle with one hand and Goldman's hand
in the other, and behind them, he could still hear gunshots at the cabin, but
they were lessening in number now. He listened intently as he fought his
way through the woods, and he heard men's voices as the gunshots finally
stopped. The attackers would soon realize that he and Goldman had escaped,
and thus, the men would be quickly on their heels. He would try to get to
the river and somehow elude the mysterious assailants, but it would not
be easy.

They kept moving as quickly as they could through the woods—
around large trees, under overturned logs, through the sharp branches
covered with green leaves and spider webs—and eventually, Falconer could
hear a roar in the distance.

The falls.

They would have to figure out how to avoid the 75-foot cascade of
water thundering down towards town, he knew, but he wasn't quite sure
how. He would just have to adapt and make it up as they went.

The men's voices were getting closer now and so he stopped and bent
down briefly with Goldman and looked back from whence they had come.
He thought he could see forms fighting through the brush and he realized

that it was true: several men dressed in dark clothing and carrying rifles were just seventy-five yards or so up the embankment and were closing fast. He turned to Goldman and spoke quickly: "I need to stay and delay these men, and you need to get hidden. Do you see that big boulder down there near the bottom of the falls?"

Goldman turned and peered through the undergrowth and branches, and then turned back to him. "Yes, I see it," she said, breathlessly.

"Go down there and find somewhere to hide," he said. "I'll come for you shortly. Here, this is my Colt revolver. Take it with you. All you have to do is pull this metal lever back here, and then squeeze the trigger, but be ready for a big kick when it fires. You have to hold it firmly."

"But, detective," she said pleadingly, "I can't fire a gun, especially an enormous one like this. Plus, there are several of them and you're just one man. You'll never make it on your own."

"Take the revolver, just in case, and don't worry," he said to her. "I'm only going to delay them. I'll be there soon—I promise."

"All right," she said, "but be careful."

"I will," he replied, and he stood up and turned, but before he could leave, she spoke up again, stopping him: "Remember, Falconer: just delay them for a minute. I don't know what I'd do without you up here."

"I will," he said, and then he turned away again and ran off up the embankment.

25

F alconer ran up the hill and then crouched down behind a large, grizzled oak tree that provided good cover. He peered around the tree's gnarled trunk and saw two men slowly walking down the embankment less than forty yards ahead.

Time to get serious, he thought to himself as he quietly loaded five rounds into the barrel of the pump-action rifle. Moving it up into firing position, he leveled the barrel in the direction of the two men, peering down at the front sight sticking up at its end.

First the one slightly in front, then quickly move to the bigger one behind him.

As the two men crept down towards him with their rifles held in front, Falconer took a deep breath and pulled the trigger.

CRACK!

The first man dropped his rifle and fell backwards, groaning in pain with a belly wound. As the second, larger man looked down at his friend in shock, Falconer quickly aimed the rifle at him and squeezed off another shot. The larger man winced and grabbed at his thigh, falling next to his stricken companion.

Falconer wasted no time in running off for a different position as he heard one of the men yelling out in pain: "We're hit! We're hit! Help! Help!" He ran in a crouching position laterally across the hill and managed to find another tree, slightly smaller but effective nonetheless for cover, and looked up the hill again to spot other targets. Seeing none, he quickly reloaded the rifle and looked out into the dense woods.

The two wounded men continued to yell out for their companions, and Falconer wondered if perhaps the remaining men had abandoned them and fled the scene. But these ruminations were quickly interrupted when he saw another figure in black creeping across the hill towards his stricken comrades.

Falconer shouldered his rifle again and tried to get a good view of the man, but the many branches and trees in the way kept obscuring the target just when he thought he had a good shot. He nonetheless continued to try to track the man's path across the hill, and finally, as the man got to within twenty yards or so of his companions, Falconer saw him for a moment in between hanging branches and fired off a shot. The man yelped and dropped his rifle but did not fall. Instead, he clutched his upper arm and ran back up the hill.

Falconer sat for a moment and heard additional voices back where the cabin stood.

More coming.

He glanced down to where the great falls rumbled incessantly in the river like a great locomotive rushing by one's window at night and decided to make an escape and get to Goldman down near the big boulder lying at the foot of the falls. Seeing none of the men nearby, he quickly jumped down the hill, sometimes sliding on his buttocks and back, sometimes managing to get to his feet and trot haphazardly through the brush. But as he finally came to where he thought there would be a clear path down to the shore, he realized that the ground suddenly ended and there was actually a sheer drop of thirty-five feet or so to where the huge falls settled into the river in a violent and discordant cauldron of mist, foam, and bubbles.

He wondered where Goldman had gone given this unfortunate situation and scanned the nearby woods for some sign of her. Then, looking farther down the shoreline, he saw that there was, in fact, a way to get down to the shore and to the boulder lying sturdily in the water: a steep embankment about fifty yards distant that jutted out from the cliff briefly, allowing a person to carefully tread down to the water right at the foot of the enormous falls.

He started walking quickly along the cliff to make it over to the steep embankment, but after only a few steps, a bullet suddenly whizzed by his ear, smacking solidly into a tree three feet away. He threw himself to the ground and looked about, readying his rifle in case the unknown marksman tried to rush him, but he saw no sign of any of his mysterious trackers.

Crawling over to a tree, he sat up and carefully looked around for any sign of the gunman. After a few seconds, he spotted him: a young man with a dark newsboy cap and a menacing scowl holding a rifle and peering around a tree of his own. Falconer knew he was trapped now—if he tried to make it over to the embankment leading down to the river, he would be shot off the cliff by the young hoodlum; if he tried to retrace his steps and go back, there clearly would be others who would intercept and encircle him, making for a quick and violent end.

He leaned back for cover behind the tree and pondered his next move, and, after a brief respite, decided on a third option: he would find someplace to hide nearby and would see if the scowling gunman would somehow decide to come down and get closer. Then he would ambush him up close and without the use of a rifle.

He looked around and saw a large rock, perhaps three feet high and five feet long, jutting out of the mossy ground much like the sharp, pointed top of an iceberg rises above the waves in the cold, northern reaches of the ocean. He scampered over to it and hid on his side, shielding himself.

Crawling to one end of the rock, he very carefully peered around it with one eye in the direction of his would-be assassin. Then, he waited.

After lying still for several minutes with the enveloping sound of the roar of the falls thundering down into the river behind him, he saw the young man slowly approaching through the trees, rifle at the ready. Falconer reached down and unsheathed a five-inch hunting knife lashed to his ankle and held it close to his shoulder. The young man was getting closer and was swaying the end of his rifle from side to side, ready to shoot in an instant. He walked slowly, and after about thirty seconds, he had bypassed Falconer's position at the rock and had come close to the edge of the cliff.

Falconer quietly edged around the rock and got into a crouch, holding the knife in front of him and waiting for an opportune moment to strike. The young man had turned away and was scanning the river, as if Falconer had mistakenly fallen the 80 feet or so into the swirling waters below. The gunman then turned and faced downriver and slowly started walking in that direction. As he did, Falconer hid closely behind the rock and waited for the right moment. After the man had walked about ten paces, he made his decision and leapt out, running directly at him and holding his knife out at arm's length. The young man must have heard him, however, as he suddenly turned and tried to raise his rifle. Falconer grabbed it with his right hand and swung the knife at the man's throat but missed and felt the knife drop to the dirt as he himself fell to the ground, too.

Quickly turning to face the shooter, who had dropped his rifle and now appeared to be trying to draw his own knife out of his belt, Falconer raced at him and hit him with a shoulder directly in his midsection, sending him flying backwards to the ground. He then leapt upon his adversary and rained blows down on his back and head, trying to daze him, but the man twisted out of the barrage and kicked out at Falconer, hitting him hard in his cheek.

Falconer got up and saw the man doing the same, dusting off his jacket and pants. They circled each other briefly, each trying to find an opening for an attack, and then the man reached at his belt again and pulled out a large Bowie knife and pointed it at Falconer with a smile. "Looks like this is the end of the road for you and the lady," he said loudly over the roar of the water.

Falconer stood and thought about running to retrieve his rifle behind the rock, but the man was too close now and he wouldn't have time to get off a good shot. He glanced around and saw his own knife lying on the ground fifteen feet away.

"Try for it!" the man shouted. "See if you can get it in time!"

The man then started walking towards him slowly, waving the large Bowie knife in front of his face. Falconer walked backwards slowly towards the edge of the cliff with the rushing falls just behind him, bellowing throughout the area and drowning out all other sounds of the forest. Then he felt himself step on something hard and he instinctively looked down: a rock about the size of a baseball. He reached down quickly and grabbed it, and then looked at the young man, who hesitated and started biting his lip.

Might as well try. It's all I've got now.

He reached back and hurled the rock directly at the man's chest, and the man turned quickly, shielding his head as he did. The rock slammed into the man's side and he groaned loudly as Falconer rushed him again. The man turned back and tried to slash at Falconer's shoulder just as they collided, but Falconer managed to grab his forearm and wrench the big knife to the ground. The two men then struggled together on their feet, but Falconer finally grabbed his opponent firmly by his jacket and swung him hard towards the cliff's edge. The young man went flying and started to roll over the edge, but he managed to reach out and grab a small branch growing out of the side of the cliff face.

Falconer rushed up and looked down at the struggling man, who now dangled 80 feet above the turbulent waters.

"Give me your other hand!" Falconer yelled over the sound of the onrushing falls. "Reach up!"

The man, however, refused to extend his hand, and only looked up at Falconer as he strained to hold onto the small branch. Falconer again yelled out to him: "Give me your hand, damn it! It's your only choice!"

The man, though, still refused to reach up, and then, looking at Falconer, he smiled slightly as he swung from the bending branch in the morning breeze.

"Who do you work for?" Falconer demanded. "Who sent you here?"

The man smiled again and then finally spoke loudly above the overwhelming noise of the crushing waterfall: "You don't even know who you're dealing with, do you? You don't know how powerful we are!"

Then the man started to laugh, and Falconer desperately reached out for him. But the man then let go his grip and fell quickly down into the foaming waters below.

26

Falconer stood up and looked down through the enveloping mist at the angry, swirling waters below, into which the mysterious young man had just disappeared seconds before.

Why? he thought to himself. *Why give up and release yourself into that fury and a likely death? What was the calculation? What—or who—were you protecting?*

His labored ruminations on the subject, however, were interrupted by the sounds of more voices higher up the embankment, and he knew that he must be going, that he must find Goldman and travel down the river quickly to New York. After retrieving his rifle and knife, he quickly trotted over to the steep incline of grass and dirt that jutted awkwardly away from the cliff and down towards the shore. Carefully descending, he came upon the large boulder that sat at the bottom like an enormous elephant silently bathing in a cool pond amidst the scorching savannah in Africa.

Because the sounds of the nearby falls were so overwhelming and deafening at this spot, he knew that his shouts for Goldman would likely be for naught and would go unheard. Thus, he quickly jumped from rock to rock and started to explore the various individual depressions and small, naturally formed embrasures dotting the circumference of the huge, stone edifice. As he did so, he shouted out her name, hoping that she might hear his familiar voice. He did this for several minutes, but not seeing any sign of her, he was about to give up, thinking that she had departed down the shoreline on her own, when he suddenly heard a female voice faintly rising above the clamor of the great descending wall of water.

"Detective! Detective! Are you there?!"

He quickly made his way towards the voice, and, after climbing a few feet up into the opening of a small, hidden cave in the side of the giant rock, he saw Goldman, pressing herself against the darkened walls of its interior and shivering.

"Hold on!" he yelled to her. "Here I come!"

He clambered over some overturned logs and sizable rocks littering the entrance to the cave, and, finally coming upon her, clutched her about her shoulders. "Are you all right?" he said loudly into her ear.

"Yes!" she replied, also equally loud. "But what about you? What happened?"

"We'll talk later!" he said. "We need to get moving down the shoreline because there are more of them up there! Are you okay to walk?"

"Yes, fine!" she said. "Here, take your gun back!"

He took the large revolver out of her hand and carefully placed it into his shoulder holster, then grabbed her hand and gently led her out of the little cave and back towards the shoreline.

"Where are we going now?" she asked as they stumbled across the rocks and broken driftwood lining the shore. "Should we go up to the town and hop on another train back?"

"No," he said quickly into her ear. "They'll be monitoring the trains, so we'll have to get back another way."

"Well, how do we do that?" she asked as the sounds of the great falls slowly grew more distant. "Surely we can't walk the whole way."

"No, we can't," he said, still clutching her by the hand as they navigated the jumbled path down the river's edge. "So, we'll have to go down the river by boat."

"By boat?" she asked. "What sort of boat are you meaning?"

"I don't know the answer to that yet, I'm afraid," she said, "but there'll be some boats down at the town's marina. We'll try to hire one and get down the river as far as we can. Then we'll figure out something else. Does that sound all right to you?"

"Anything to avoid those murderous ruffians back there," she answered drily. "So, I'm all yours. Please lead the way."

27

Falconer led Goldman along the Mohawk's rock-strewn shore for about a mile. As they got closer to the town's center, he could see large, industrial, brick buildings pushing up into the sky among smaller, wooden dwellings high up on their right. Every now and then, he could see people moving about near the buildings and wagons rumbling down the street closest to the shore. He looked ahead and saw a few short docks jutting out into the river with a host of boats tied up alongside them.

"Here," he said to her. "We'll try to hire a boat up at these docks."

They walked another quarter of a mile and traipsed over to one of the docks. Various men were busy preparing fishing lines and nets on smaller fishing boats, while others were simply lounging about on sailboats that appeared to be meant for recreational purposes only. Falconer stopped mid-dock and surveyed their surroundings.

"Do you see one that looks like a possibility?" Goldman asked him.

"Yes," he said slowly, settling his gaze on one, small sailboat that was docked farther apart from the others. "That one over there."

"You mean the small one with the black man tending to it?" she asked.

"Yes, that's the one," he answered. "Let's go inquire."

They walked down the dock and came upon a man coiling up some rope inside of a small catboat approximately fifteen feet long. The man did not look up at them, and instead, remained fixed on his task at hand. Falconer glanced at Goldman and then turned again to the man. "Pardon me, mister," he said, "but we're looking to hire a boat to take us down the Hudson a ways, and we were wondering if you might be willing to do that."

"Maybe," the man said after a pause, still working with his rope. "Depend on how much you pay."

"Well," Falconer said, "I can give you two dollars to get the lady and me down as far as you can. Would that do it?"

"I suppose," the man answered, looking up at Falconer finally. "Two dollars is pretty good. But I gotta' say, you two lookin' like you're running from somethin', mister. You in trouble with her old man, or maybe with the law?"

Falconer and Goldman glanced at each other, then Falconer addressed the man again. "No trouble," he said. "Just trying to get down to New York, but we're a little tired of the view from the trains."

"Mister," the man said, "two dollars'll go a long way for anyone around here, and my apologies if I'm wrong, but I got the feeling you ain't bein' truthful with me. And I just don't need no trouble, you understand? I think you'd better go find yourself another boat."

"We aren't looking to cause you any trouble now," Falconer said. "We're just trying to keep from the crowds and see the river is all."

"All the same," the man said, "I think it best if you go hire one of them other boats. You'll have a fine time with them."

"Sir," Goldman interrupted, "if you could see your way to assisting us, I'm sure we could come up with additional funds for your fee. We have friends in New York who will see to that, I can promise you."

The man looked at Goldman for a moment and appeared confused. Then he got up out of the boat and walked a little closer to her on the dock, as if to examine her face. After a few seconds staring at her, his face then erupted into a large, bright smile. "Well, I'll be," he said. "You that anarchist woman from the papers. Yes, yes, I recognize you from your pictures. You're the lady they been talkin' about lately since that fella' got shot up in Pittsburgh."

Goldman paused and then turned to Falconer. "Well, it appears that our cover is blown," she said glumly. "What do we do now?"

"Listen, mister," Falconer said to the man, stepping closer towards him and showing him his badge. "The fact is, you're right about this lady, and I am the police, actually. The truth is, there are some men up near the falls who have been trying to hurt Miss Goldman here, and I need to get her safely down to New York. I'm not going to commandeer your boat here, but our offer still stands. If you could take us downriver a bit, it would be much appreciated."

The man stood silently on the dock, and after several seconds, Goldman turned to Falconer. "I'm afraid we're out of luck," she said. "Let us go find different means of escape."

She turned and started walking back towards the shore, but the man then spoke out to her. "Hold on there, Miss Emma Goldman," he said.

She turned to face him, appearing surprised to hear her name exclaimed in such a remote, bucolic setting.

"Yeah, I know your name, miss," he said. "I may be just a river man up here, but I do read the papers, too, like I said. And I know all you do to help them workin' men in Pennsylvania and New York City, and how you stand up to all them rich fellas'. You one of us, Miss Goldman, and I ain't about to let some group of hostile men come down from those hills there and put harm to you or to this here police detective. You got yourself a deal, miss. I'll get you downriver, no doubt. But I can't go too far. I got a family to deal with here. I can bring you down as far as Albany and then you can catch a day line steamboat from there. The 'Albany' or 'New York' will be running by there in a couple of hours, and we can make it if we leave soon. Is that all right?"

Goldman walked back towards the man, extending her hand. "Why, thank you very much, mister...."

"Lloyd," he replied, shaking her hand. "Tom Lloyd."

"Thank you ever so much, Mister Lloyd," she said to him. "You don't know what this means to us."

"Yes, thank you, Mister Lloyd," Falconer said, walking up to him and shaking his hand, as well. "We'll see to it that you are recognized for your assistance to us."

"It's okay, folks," Lloyd said. "Whoever those men are that been botherin' you up there, they can't be on the good side of the law, and I'm not about to make their life any easier, if I can help it."

"Are we able to shove off soon?" Falconer asked him. "The men you're speaking about aren't far behind and will be looking around here soon."

"Yes, indeed, detective," Lloyd replied. "And what's your name, sir?"

"Falconer—Robert Falconer with the New York City Police Detective Bureau."

"Well, Detective Falconer," Lloyd said, "I don't know what you've gotten yourself into, but it sure don't look good, so we'd best get movin' past the islands and out onto the Hudson. There's washrooms for men and ladies just over there on shore, and I got food stuffs and water stored on the boat. Let's be leavin' in about ten minutes."

"Right," Falconer answered. "Ten minutes. Oh, and one thing, Mister Lloyd. Do you know how I can get a telegram sent to my colleagues down in New York? It's important."

"Why, there's a telegraph office at the freight depot just up the hill here on Oneida where it hits the railroad tracks," Lloyd answered. "Ain't too far at all."

"The only problem, is, I should probably avoid town for obvious reasons," Falconer said. "I don't suppose you know anyone around here who might drop the telegram for me for a fee?"

"Sure, I got someone," Lloyd said. "Little Willie Jones is around here somewheres, and he'll do it if I ask him. Give me a second here."

Falconer watched as Lloyd walked away and hopped off the end of the dock onto the shore. He continued walking another fifty yards to a barn-like structure that appeared to be a general maintenance shed for the boats and then disappeared. Moments later, he appeared again with a young black boy perhaps ten years old or so in tow. They both walked onto the dock and approached Falconer and Goldman.

"This here is Willie," Lloyd said, pointing to the boy. "He'll get that telegram to the office for you, detective."

"Thank you, Mister Lloyd," Falconer said, as he reached into his jacket pocket and pulled out the small notepad and pencil that he always carried with him. Placing the notepad onto a tall crate that stood empty nearby, he wrote down several lines and then folded it up and handed it to the boy. "Willie," he said, "I need you to get this to the telegraph man up on the hill there. It's very important. Can you do that for me?"

"Yes, sir," the boy said shyly.

"Good," Falconer said. "Here's a dollar. Give this to the telegraph operator and you keep whatever change he gives back to you. Understand?"

"Yes, sir, I do," Willie said.

"All right then," Falconer said. "Thank you."

"You get goin', boy," Lloyd said to Willie, "and make sure that telegram gets sent."

"Yes, sir," Willie said again, and then he ran off down the dock and sped up the hill.

"All right, folks, you get yourselves ready and we'll leave in ten minutes," Lloyd said.

"Ten minutes," Falconer replied. "Understood."

28

Tom Lloyd eased his small sailboat out into the narrow portion of the Mohawk that ran between the town of Cohoes on one side, and Simmons Island on the other. The morning breeze caught the vessel's sail and propelled it southwards towards the much larger Van Schaik Island on the left, and then around a sharp curve in the river towards the wide expanse of the Hudson River in the distance.

"You've been sailing the river long?" Falconer asked Lloyd from his seat near the bow.

Lloyd nodded as he manned the tiller and chewed on some sunflower seeds. "Yup," he replied. "Ever since I was a kid, to be honest."

"Do you just give sight-seeing tours? That sort of thing?" Falconer inquired.

"No, I do some fishin', too," Lloyd said. "Anythin', really, s'long as it pays."

"Well, this part of the river certainly is very picturesque, Mister Lloyd," Goldman interjected. "It's a lovely part of the country."

"It is indeed, Miss Goldman," Lloyd said. "It is indeed."

"How far down to the Albany dock?" Falconer asked.

"Oh, 'bout ten miles," Lloyd answered. "I think we get maybe five knots or so with this wind and we'll be there in under two hours. I think you'll make your steamboat. It moves on at eleven o'clock."

"Well, thank you again," Falconer said. "This is a big help."

"Ain't no problem," Lloyd said. "Plus, I get to meet a world-renowned, famous anarchist. Ain't that right, Miss Goldman?"

"Well, I wouldn't say world-renowned, Mister Lloyd," Goldman replied. "But you are right—the newspapers are making me a little more notable lately. I'm not so sure that's a good thing, frankly."

"Yeah, you 'bout the most famous person I ever seen up close, I'd say," Lloyd said. "Well, exceptin' for President Grant."

"You saw the president?" Goldman asked.

"Yup," Lloyd said. "He done come through Cohoes on the train on his way to that mountain cabin of his back in '85. The man was dyin' for sure, but he still come to the window and waved to us all in the crowd that day. Yes, sir, a good man, that President Grant. A real good, decent man."

"Yes, he was," Falconer said, and then he turned to gaze down the river in the morning sunlight, down towards the city of Albany, where he and Goldman would start the next leg of their journey back to Mulberry Street headquarters, as the questions about Goldman's mysterious pursuers swirled within his troubled mind.

29

aidler sat at his desk in the Detective Bureau on Mulberry Street. It was 8:30 in the morning and his shift was just starting. He hadn't heard from Falconer since the detective sergeant had left under cover of darkness with Emma Goldman two days earlier, and he assumed that this meant things were quiet up at the safe house and that Falconer would just wait things out for a few days and then give an update when convenient.

He looked at the various papers strewn about his desk and pondered his other pending cases that were piling up—a thirty-nine-year-old woman who had fallen, or perhaps jumped or been pushed, out of a twenty-fifth-floor window on 39th Street; a 12-year-old boy found strangled to death behind a drug store on Fulton Street; another young woman—always, always it seemed to be young women—who had disappeared without a trace three weeks earlier.

He thought of these cases and of the many others, and of how difficult it was sometimes to solve them, and how this inability to crack the cases continually gnawed at him and made him perhaps a little difficult to deal with at times. But his broodings in this vein were suddenly interrupted when a young clerk from the telegraph office approached him with a paper in hand. "Detective Waidler," he said, "a telegram just came in for you. It's from Detective Sergeant Falconer."

Waidler took the telegram quickly from the clerk, thanked him, and then carefully unfolded the paper as the young man departed. He scanned the message quickly and felt perspiration suddenly appear on his forehead. He looked down at the telegram and read it again, just to be sure he had read it correctly:

> *Cabin attacked by multiple gunmen this morning. Escaped by sail. EG and I unhurt. Will seek to board day line steamer 11 AM from Albany. Rendezvous w us at Bear Mountain this evening. Falconer*

He was wondering what to do first in view of Falconer's alarming news when Jimmy Halloran ambled into the bureau, coffee in hand. "Morning, detective," he said. "How's the day looking?"

Waidler looked up at his young colleague. "Well," he said, "we're off to Bear Mountain up near West Point. It seems Detective Sergeant Falconer and Miss Goldman were attacked again up at the safe house and they need us to meet them on the docks up there."

He then got up and grabbed his jacket off his chair and started walking to the door to the hallway as he heard Halloran's short response coming from behind him: "Wait—what?"

30

Falconer looked at the docks of Albany jutting out into the river just ahead as Lloyd angled his sailboat over towards the shore. A large, white-colored paddle steamer was moored to a dock, and hundreds of people milled about the dock or upon its decks.

"Is that our boat, Mister Lloyd?" Falconer asked.

"Yup, that'll be her," Lloyd replied. "The New York—sister boat to the Albany. See? I knew we'd get you down here on time. You got about twenty minutes before she pulls out."

"It certainly is a grand vessel," Goldman said. "So new looking."

"Been in service since eighty-seven," Lloyd said. "She runs about 300 feet long and can hold 1500 people. And oh, how she looks on the inside—mmmmmmm. That'll be one of the fanciest boats on the river—like you're in some millionaire's mansion or somethin'."

"Well, thank you again for getting us down here," Falconer said. "We're grateful to you for this."

"It's no problem, detective," Lloyd said. "Like I said, it's an honor to have Miss Goldman here on my boat."

"Thank you, Mister Lloyd," Goldman said, turning to him. "And I shall not forget this little adventure of ours on the high seas."

"No, miss," Lloyd said. "Me neither."

He turned the boat slightly and headed directly towards a smaller dock that ran parallel to the longer dock holding the New York steady in the water. Soon, they were sidling up next to the wooden pilings, and Lloyd and Falconer fastened the vessel to some dock cleats screwed into the wood.

"That'll do," Lloyd said. "You just go up to that building there and get yourself some tickets. You got a little more time yet."

"I'll do that," Falconer replied, extending his hand. "And thank you again."

"My pleasure," Lloyd said, shaking Falconer's hand. "And Miss Goldman, I'll be readin' about you in the papers now—hopefully, good things."

"Yes, hopefully," she answered, shaking his hand, as well. "Thank you ever so much for your assistance this morning. I don't know what we would've done without you."

"Well, you just stick close this here detective," he said. "He'll get you home safe, I'm sure."

"Indeed," she said to him. "Good day to you, sir."

"So long now," Lloyd said with a wave of his hand. "You folks stay safe."

Falconer then helped Goldman up out of the boat and down the dock to the shore, intent on securing two tickets' passage to New York on the gleaming steamboat that bore the same city's name.

31

Falconer walked out onto the bow deck of the paddle wheeler, New York, with Goldman by his side as the boat slowly began to move away from its moorings. The boat's steam whistle erupted loudly behind them, seemingly filling the entire river valley with its anguished groan. Falconer looked around at the other people on the deck and turned to his companion. "Stay close to me," he said. "There's no guarantee that we managed to leave those men behind."

"I understand," she said as she glanced furtively around the deck. "How long until we make New York, do you think?"

"They say it typically takes eight hours or so, I'm afraid," he replied. "But hopefully, we'll be meeting some of my men at Bear Mountain later today. That will give us some reinforcements, just in case."

"And then, when we arrive back in New York?" she asked. "What then?"

"Then we find whoever's been responsible for this, and we send them to prison for the rest of their lives."

"I suppose if I were to agree with you," she said, "I'd be a hypocrite, given that I've railed against my friend Berkman's long prison sentence. But I can't argue that these men don't deserve some sort of long punishment. They are murderous brutes."

"Imagine that," he said, looking down at her. "We actually agree on something."

"Yes, fascinating, isn't it?"

"Come on," he said, gently touching her arm. "Let's go find some quiet corner of the boat where we can stay out of view."

"That sounds fine to me," she said. "Just as long as there's enough light to read by—I managed to retain two of my books, believe it or not. Eight hours on a boat without reading material sounds like torture to me."

"I think we can arrange that. Let's move towards the back."

32

The elegant steamboat, New York, let out a series of loud toots from its steam whistle as it neared the dock at Bear Mountain. Falconer got up out of his seat in a corner of a small lounge located aft of the great paddle wheels on the main deck and turned to Goldman, who was reading intently by the electric lights fixed to the bulkheads. "Here we are finally," he said. "Bear Mountain. Let's go out and see if we can spot my men on the dock."

"Very well," she said, closing her book. "It looks as though the sun is going down now."

"Yes, it is. Probably only another hour or two to New York."

They walked out of the lounge and onto the deck and found a spot on the railing where they could look down at all the people milling around on the dock. Soon, crewmates had extended a gangway for passengers to load and unload, and a steady train of people started to transfer to and from the shore. Falconer scanned the dock and finally saw the two policemen standing quietly in the back of the crowd. He motioned for them with a subtle waive of his hand, and Waidler responded by raising his hand to his cap. Falconer then motioned for them to join them on the boat and Waidler nodded again.

Shortly thereafter, the two men walked up the gangway and handed their tickets to the waiting crewman, and then headed up a flight of stairs to where Falconer and Goldman were standing. Falconer greeted them quietly and led the group back inside to a quiet alcove away from the bustling crowd. "Glad to see you two made it," he said.

"Well, sounds like you've had quite an adventure," Waidler said. "Any idea who these suspects are?"

"None, unfortunately," Falconer replied, "but we can't take any chances. They're armed and obviously very good at tailing us."

"You think they're on this boat?" Waidler asked.

"I'd doubt it," Falconer replied, "but you never know with this group. They could be standing around here right under our noses, so keep your guns ready at all times. Any sign of mischief, shoot them. They've shown that they're not messing around, so we won't, either. Got it?"

The two men nodded, and then Falconer pointed in the direction of the rear of the boat. "Come on," he said. "Let's go try to be incognito in the back of the boat until we reach the city. Miss Goldman, this is Detective Waidler and Officer Halloran from our Detective Bureau. They're going to help us get back to New York safely, so please listen to them at all times, all right?"

"Good evening to you both, gentlemen," Goldman said. "I guess you were investigating me with the detective here originally, but now due to unforeseen circumstances, you're a part of my personal bodyguard. Very strange how things work out, isn't it?"

"Well," Falconer said, "I guess strange is our business, so we can handle it. Shall we?"

They then moved off down the passageway towards the rear of the boat as more loud whistles signaled the vessel's impending departure from the darkening bend in the river called Bear Mountain.

33

The imposing steamboat chugged southwards down the Hudson River, which now lay draped in soft moonlight after the sun had finally set over the rolling mountains to the west. Falconer stood amongst a crowd of other passengers at a snack bar in the bow of the boat after having instructed Waidler and Halloran to stand watch over Goldman in the quiet, empty lounge near the stern. He ordered several coffees and pastries from the snack bar and then headed back to his companions.

Walking carefully through the many passengers milling about the deck, he marveled at the steamboat's impressive appearance and its ability to churn powerfully and quickly down the great river. The paddle wheelers were getting more and more ornate and were able to navigate the trip to and from Albany faster and faster, with speed records being broken every year, it seemed.

He walked down a passageway to the stern and noted that passengers at this part of the boat became fewer and fewer, as most appeared to prefer to observe the passing shore from the windows and railings situated in the front section of the vessel. Stepping up to the entrance to the small lounge, he turned and almost dropped his small tray containing the snacks and coffees: Halloran lay face down on the floor before him and Goldman and Waidler were nowhere to be seen.

34

F alconer leaned over the prostrate Halloran and turned him over to see his face. The young officer appeared to be only dazed and was trying to speak.

"What happened, Jimmy?" Falconer asked. "Where did Waidler and Goldman go?"

Halloran blinked a few times, and then, after Falconer helped him up into a sitting position, he finally spoke, slowly at first, as if searching for his words: "Detective Waidler went out to make sure things were clear down the passageway, and then a couple of ship's stewards came by and asked if we wanted anything to drink. I turned to Miss Goldman, and right then, I must have gotten hit from behind and things went black. Not sure what happened next."

"Stewards?" Falconer asked. "You sure about that?"

"Well, that's what they said they were, and they were dressed that way. I'm sorry, sir."

"It's all right, Jimmy," Falconer said, handing him a glass of water from the tray he had just been carrying. "You stay here, and I'll go find them."

"Yes, sir," Halloran said, taking a sip of the water.

"Are you able to handle your weapon?"

"I am, sir. Thanks."

"All right," Falconer said, standing up and unholstering his revolver. "I'll be back. And take no chances if they return when I'm gone. Shoot them, understand?"

"Yes, sir."

Falconer then ran out into the passageway and headed toward the boat's stern. As he got closer to the very rear of the deck, he saw no one save for several passengers glancing out over the fantail. He turned and saw a stairway leading up to the boiler deck and decided to head up. Quickly ascending the stairs, he moved forward slowly through the passageway, keeping an eye out for sudden movement and listening for any sounds of a struggle. The noise of the huge boilers and steam engine nearby made it much harder to hear at this level, however, and he had to strain to hear anything beyond the steady *whoosh-whoosh* of the engines hurling the great boat through the waters below.

Walking carefully past several surprised passengers, he glanced to his right and saw a large, red door with black, painted letters on it: NO ENTRY – ENGINE ROOM. Looking down, he saw that the door was slightly ajar. Moving closer to the door, he gently pushed it open, keeping his revolver cocked and at the ready in front of him.

Peering inside, he saw an enormous two-story engine room enveloped with the overwhelming noise of the great steam engine churning just fifteen feet below him. He looked around for any engineers or stokers but strangely saw none. Walking farther into the space, he saw the great black boilers down below and the attached giant levers that were, in turn, attached to the thick axle, which moved the two, enormous drums inside the paddle boxes fixed to either side of the boat. As the powerful engine steadily turned these great, steel components together, he could see the huge paddle wheels revolving violently down through the waters of the Hudson, propelling the long steamboat quickly down the river.

He decided to walk around the elevated walkway upon which he stood, as he felt something was amiss in this enormous cathedral of sound and machinery. Where were the engineers? Where was Waidler?

As he carefully made his way around the walkway, he looked down at all the hidden places and crannies in which an assailant could lay in wait and wondered if Goldman and Waidler were, in fact, already dead out in the waters now, floating down the Hudson River like logs discarded from a riverside sawmill. If this were, in fact, true, he would not stop until he found the mysterious "stewards" that had attacked Halloran and had exacted retribution on them. He would not take them into custody, as he would be expected to do—he would kill them with a swift and unmerciful violence. This would be his penance to the dead, to those he had failed to protect.

Something in his way suddenly interrupted his pained thoughts, and he squinted his eyes to get a closer look: a foot, appearing out from behind a large gear box down below. Quickly moving down a nearby stairway, he ran over to the gear box and saw an engineer lying unconscious on his back. Falconer knelt next to the man, who appeared to be in his fifties, and tried to rouse him. The man groaned slightly and then finally opened his eyes. "Are you all right?" Falconer asked him. "Can you speak?"

The man just peered at Falconer and appeared to be trying to form coherent thoughts and words, but none came immediately. Falconer grabbed some rags resting on top of the gear box and placed them underneath the man's head, and then spoke to him again: "Did you see anyone come into the engine room? What happened here?"

The man then took a deep breath and spoke finally, in a faint whisper. "A couple of men came in here holding onto a woman," he said. "She was struggling with them. I told them to let her go, and then they pointed their guns at me, so I put my hands up. They came down here and started mumbling to each other, something about how to get rid of her. Then some other guy came in pointing a gun at them and telling them to hand her over.

Shots were fired, and I went for the lady, but one of them smacked me on the head. Not sure where they went."

"All right," Falconer said. "You take it easy here, and I'll get help to you."

He stood up and looked around the cavernous room and was about to head up the stairs when he heard a female voice yelling out angrily.

Goldman.

He looked above and saw the two men coming back into the engine room with Goldman resisting them violently. They were both dragging her forcefully into the space from the passageway, and she, in turn, was trying to wrench herself free. Falconer tried to make out what they were saying but the din from the engines muffled their words, and he could only hear angry utterances and shouted commands of some sort. He quietly moved backwards towards another stairway leading up to the attached walkway, and walked gingerly up it, getting his gun ready for use, if need be.

At the top, he peered across the room and saw that the men were dragging Goldman closer to him, closer to the great, revolving paddle wheel that heaved around and around on the side of the boat. As they dragged her down the walkway, he then realized what they were about to do: they were going to throw her over the railing into the swirling chaos of the paddle wheel below, where her death would appear accidental, or perhaps the result of a suicide—tossed about violently in the powerful turns of the huge wheel and then left floating behind the great vessel like an old, torn, rag doll.

Goldman screamed and ranted as the men dragged her closer and closer to the top of the wheel, which turned steadily just a yard or so from the walkway. Falconer thought of what to do, and, seeing a small supporting bulkhead coming out perpendicularly from the side of the boat nearby, he moved quickly behind it away from the sight of the men. Holding his revolver up near his shoulder, he peered around the bulkhead and saw them struggling with Goldman at the apex of the great wheel's revolution through the waters below. Now he could make out words coming from the three of them.

"No! Let me go!"

"Get her damned arm, Sid! Hold her now!"

"Help me! Help me! Someone!"

"Push her up! Hurry! Throw her over!"

"No! Help me!"

Then, just as the two men managed to lift Goldman off her feet, Falconer sprang from his hiding place and ran directly at them.

35

Falconer could hear the clanking of his shoes on the walkway as he ran headlong towards the two men, who were now attempting to lift Goldman up and over the railing and down to where the great paddle wheel moved forcefully and violently into the churning waters below. He kept his revolver gripped tightly in his right hand but was concerned that a gunshot might hit Goldman instead, and thus, he intended to use it merely as a clubbing weapon.

Just as the men were about to tip Goldman over to her certain death, he reached back with the gun and unleashed a hard blow against the head of the smaller man, who grunted and fell limply to the walkway. At the same time, Falconer grabbed Goldman by her jacket and pulled at her mightily, dragging both her and the larger assailant down to the walkway, too. As they fell together, Falconer's gun was knocked out of his hand and it slid over the other side of the walkway to the floor of the engine room below. Looking back at the man, he saw a look of shock on his face, and then the man yelled out, "What the hell?!"

The man quickly pulled out his own gun and started to level it at Falconer's head, but Falconer deftly kicked it out of his hand, and it slid down the walkway. They both then got up to their feet as Goldman scurried away a few feet down the walkway. "Get out of here!" Falconer yelled at her. "Go back to the lounge!"

Falconer kept his eye on the man as Goldman got to her feet and ran swiftly along the walkway. As she disappeared out the door, he directed his gaze back at the man and stepped forward towards him. The man then reached into his jacket, and, with a smile, pulled out a knife and waved it threateningly at him.

Falconer raised his hands in front of him in a defensive posture and the two men hesitated. The man then swung out wildly with his knife several times, missing him by inches. Falconer waited for the next thrust, attempting to time it right, and when the man lunged again, Falconer ducked underneath his arm and grabbed it solidly with both of his hands, pushing the man backwards towards the railing.

The two men struggled to gain an upper edge over the other, grunting and straining against the railing, and when the man tried to strike Falconer in the face with his free left hand, Falconer leaned over and avoided the blow and simultaneously punched the man hard in the ribs, causing the man to yelp out in pain.

Falconer then stepped back slightly and saw the smaller man moving now where he lay on the walkway. The larger man, still brandishing the knife, shouted out to his companion, urging him to get up. "Lance! Get up, boy! We got company!"

Falconer saw the injured man look up and appear to realize finally what was happening, and then rise to a standing position, rubbing his head. He then slowly reached into his jacket with his other hand, and Falconer knew that he was moving for a weapon of some sort. Moving quickly upon him, Falconer grabbed his arm just as he was extracting a small revolver. The two struggled over the weapon, and, while it was pointing straight up in the air, it went off several times, with the sounds of the shots reverberating throughout the room despite the loudness of the steam engines rumbling below.

Falconer wrenched the young man's arm down to the railing and struck his hand hard, causing the man to yell out in pain and lose his grip on the weapon, which, like Falconer's gun moments earlier, fell to the engine room floor. Falconer then kicked the young thug solidly in his ribs, and the man doubled over in pain and retreated several steps.

The bigger man, still standing back with his knife, yelled at his young companion to converge on Falconer, but the stricken lad instead turned and fled down the walkway towards the door leading to the passageway. The bigger man yelled out in protest: "Lance, you get back here! You hear me?! Come back, you son of a bitch!"

Falconer turned back to his remaining assailant, and they both started moving slowly in a small circle, as if probing for weaknesses and the right opportunity to strike. The man feinted some strikes several times, attempting to get Falconer off-balance, but Falconer didn't take the bait, and then finally, when the man lunged directly at his torso, Falconer moved quickly backwards and kicked out at the knife. The man managed to keep hold of it, however, and he swung again wildly at Falconer's face, missing it by inches.

The man quickly recovered, and he again approached Falconer slowly, waving the large knife threateningly in front of him. Falconer stepped backwards and tried to find an opening through which to strike a hard blow, but the man was adept with the knife and allowed no opportunities.

"Who the hell are you people?!" Falconer shouted over the noise of the steam engines and the great paddle wheel revolving just feet away from them. "Who sent you here?"

"You'll never know, cop!" the man replied loudly with a grin. "You and the lady will be at the bottom of the river!"

"You're coming into Mulberry Street!" Falconer yelled. "You've got some explaining to do!"

"Oh, really?!" the man yelled. "Who's gonna' make me?!"

He then lunged at Falconer and swung the knife directly at his neck, but Falconer parried the thrust and struck the man hard in the face with the back of his hand, sending him backwards against the railing. Falconer quickly grabbed his arms and struggled with him closely against the railing while the huge paddle wheel rolled menacingly a few feet away.

The man tried to push Falconer off, but Falconer was stronger and managed to bend the man's upper torso backwards over the railing, ever closer to the paddle wheel. The man raised the knife one last time despite Falconer's hard grip on his arm, and the man grimaced with rage and desperation, growling like a caged beast.

"Give it up!" Falconer yelled. "Drop the knife!"

The man looked up at Falconer as he bent backwards over the railing towards the churning wheel. "Go to hell, Falconer!" he sneered, wrenching his hand free and ramming the knife directly at Falconer's neck.

The blow missed, however, as Falconer was able to duck, and the man's inertia caused him to twist around where he stood, such that he was now facing the paddle wheel. Falconer reached down quickly to the man's belt, grabbed it solidly, and lifted him up and over the railing as the man looked back with a pained look on his face.

"You first!" Falconer yelled.

Then, with a hard shove, he threw the man over the railing and down into the swirling waters where the paddle wheel churned, moving the great boat down the river. The man screamed in agony momentarily and then Falconer saw him disappear for a couple of seconds only to see him reappear all tangled up in the wheel's paddles as it moved around and around.

The man hung awkwardly in the metal and wood structure as it moved quickly past Falconer's gaze and down to the water again, and he saw the man like this, a rag doll caught unmercifully in the unyielding movements of the great machinery, until, after several revolutions, the body disappeared, lost somewhere in the boat's bubbling wake, and Falconer turned where he stood and decided on his next move.

36

Falconer stepped carefully out into the passageway with his recovered revolver at the ready. He peered to his right and saw several people standing over someone, so he ran down to find out what was wrong. Stepping through the small crowd, he saw Goldman kneeling before Waidler, who was bleeding from his shoulder.

"James," Falconer said. "What happened? Are you hurt bad?"

"Sorry, boss," Waidler said. "I took a knife wound after two suspects grabbed Miss Goldman here. It'll be all right."

"He's right," Goldman said, dabbing at the wound with a handkerchief. "I'm also a trained nurse, you know, and this is just a slight wound—not too deep and nothing to be alarmed about, thank goodness."

"Well, I'm sorry about this, James," Falconer said. "If it helps any, the older one is now floating behind us after he had an accident with the paddle wheel."

Goldman turned and looked up at Falconer. "You killed the man?" she asked him. "Really—was that necessary?"

"I'm sorry if it upsets you," he replied, "but at the time, I didn't really have many options when he was trying to gouge my neck with a buck knife."

"I see," she said, turning back to Waidler's wound. "I suppose men like those don't leave one any choice."

"There's still one left on the boat," Falconer said. "We've got to locate him."

"Too late," Waidler said. "Passengers reported that they saw a young guy run up to the railing and jump off. Sounds like he thought he'd try to make it to shore rather than stick around here."

"I see," Falconer said. "Well, even so, we need to get away from everyone for the rest of the trip—can't afford any more risks."

A crew member who looked like an officer suddenly made his way through the crowd and came upon them. "What the devil happened here?" he asked. "People said they heard shots."

"We're with New York police," Falconer said, showing the officer his badge. "We're escorting this young woman down to the city, and unfortunately, a band of thugs is after her. I won't go into why, but rest assured, they've jumped the boat and fled, so your boat is safe. We're going to need a safe place to stay for the rest of the trip, though. Can you help us?"

"Certainly, certainly," the officer said, glancing down at Waidler. "And we'll get your man's wound here looked at, too. Come along with me to the bow and we'll get you situated."

"Thanks," Falconer said. "And I've got another man who took a blow to the head over in the lounge, and there's a crew member hurt in the engine room. They'll need help, too."

"Understood," the officer said. "Shall we now?"

Falconer then reached down and helped Waidler to his feet, and with Goldman's assistance, they slowly made their way through the gawking passengers and followed the officer forward to the lounge as the steamboat continued its journey down the Hudson River towards New York City.

PART II

37

"Well, that's quite a tale," Byrnes said grimly as he stood before Falconer and Halloran in his office on the second floor of police headquarters. Nearby stood Clubber Williams and Chief Inspector Steers, both also apparently dumbfounded by Falconer's recitation just moments earlier of his dangerous journey with Goldman up to Cohoes and the Mohawk River and back in the past few days.

"I suppose I don't blame you for rustling her quickly out of the city," Byrnes continued, "given the events over the past several days. It's clear someone wants her eliminated, although who that could be beats me—Lord knows many people despise the woman. You did the right thing trying to protect her until you could figure it out, although we cannot forget that she is still a prime suspect in the Frick assassination attempt with Berkman."

"Understood, sir," Falconer said.

"And how is your man, Waidler?" the superintendent asked. "Not too serious, you say?"

"No, fortunately not, sir. Just a slight knife wound. I think he'll be back on duty very soon."

"Well, that is fortunate, indeed," Byrnes said, lighting a cigar at his desk. "He's a good man. Very dedicated—like his brother, Sergeant Waidler, over at the academy. Both top-notch men."

"Yes, sir."

"Well, what to do from here?" Byrnes asked. "Any suggestions?"

"I think I'll need to stay with Miss Goldman for now given the extreme threat posed to her," Falconer replied. "I know it presents some difficulties with the investigation of the Frick shooting, but we can't just leave her out there in the cold—I think she'd be dead within the week."

"I would agree with you there, but unfortunately, we can't order her to stay with you and your men."

"Actually, sir," Steers interjected, "we just received a note that she's left the building and has disappeared into the streets with some of her Red friends, it appears."

"What's that?" Falconer asked incredulously.

"Well," Byrnes said, "looks like she just up and left. Without any thanks, it appears—can you imagine that?"

Falconer stood still and wasn't sure what to say. Why had she just left knowing that she had a target on her back? Why risk her life so openly after all that had happened?

"I suppose you can track her down, though," Byrnes said. "You always seem to find your man—or woman, in this case. Do what you can do to shadow her, even if she apparently doesn't want the protection. You might just fall upon her attempted assassins and crack the case—and find evidence against her in the Frick matter while you're at it. Do what you can."

"Yes, sir," Falconer answered, and then he nodded to Halloran and they both turned to leave.

"Oh, Falconer?" Byrnes said suddenly.

"Yes, sir?"

"Your British inspector friend, Penwill, is back on a case here with a representative of the French police, Inspector Houllier. But I believe you're aware of that?"

"I am, sir."

"I know you're stretched thin already with this Goldman business, but I told him that you'd offer support, as you are able. All right?"

"Yes, sir. Will do."

"Thank you, and welcome back."

"Thank you, sir," Falconer replied, and then he strolled out of the office with Halloran right behind.

38

Penwill stood with Houllier and New York City police detective sergeant Frank Corsi in the waiting room outside vice-presidential candidate Whitelaw Reid's office high up in the New York Tribune Building on Park Row. Reid, the owner of the Tribune, had returned to his plush haven on the eighth floor after completing his three-year ambassadorship to France in March, but there was little time for relaxing now, as he was in the middle of a busy campaign season and was about to head out to more Republican Party gatherings in the Midwest.

The door to Reid's office opened and a man stepped out and approached the detectives. "Gentlemen," he said politely, "Ambassador Reid will see you now."

"Thank you," Corsi said, and the three detectives followed the aide through the doorway. Inside, Penwill saw Reid get up out of his large, leather chair and walk around an impressive, oak desk to greet them. He was tall and slender, perhaps in his mid-fifties, and had wisps of gray in his hair that was parted down the middle, and a full mustache.

As Reid moved closer to the men, Penwill noticed his dark blue eyes and found them rather arresting, as if they could freeze a man in place with a sudden glare. "Gentlemen," Reid said, "it's not often that I am requested to meet with police detectives. What can I do for you?"

"Yes, thank you for receiving us, Ambassador Reid," Corsi said. "I'm Detective Sergeant Corsi from the Central Detective Bureau, and this is Inspector Penwill from Scotland Yard's Special Branch, and Inspector Houllier from the French Surete. They are here in our country working with my department on a special assignment."

"Special assignment?" Reid said. "What sort of special assignment?"

"If I may?" Penwill interjected. "Ambassador Reid, you are familiar with the recently executed French anarchist bomber, Ravachol?"

"Yes, I am," Reid said. "He was on the loose during my last days in France, then was finally caught right after I had left."

"Yes, you are correct there, sir," Penwill said.

"So, what do I have to do with this man, Ravachol, Inspector Penwill?" Reid asked.

"Well, perhaps nothing, but we are here just in case, concerning your own personal safety."

"Personal safety? But as you mentioned, Ravachol is dead—executed last month. How can he affect my personal safety?"

"He can't, of course, but one of his acolytes might be able to, I'm afraid."

"Acolytes? You mean to say this Ravachol had followers who would like to take up his mantle, as it were?"

"Yes, and we have a belief that one of them—a Theodule Meunier— might be in this city now bent on committing further acts of destruction."

"And…I might be a target."

"Yes, perhaps, given that you were the United States' official representative in France for the past three years. But it's just a hunch at this point, which brings us to this visit. Do you mind if we ask you just a few questions?"

"No, not at all, gentlemen," Reid said, walking back to his chair behind the desk. "Please, have a seat."

"Thank you, ambassador," Penwill said, motioning for Houllier and Corsi to join him in taking a chair in front of the desk. "Do you recall having any role in the investigation and prosecution of Ravachol? Any influence at all?"

"No, no, I don't believe so," Reid said. "That was an internal affair for France's Ministry of Justice to handle. I was involved largely with our own foreign relations with the French government, of course—treaties, trade agreements, that sort of thing."

"I understand, but could there have been any sort of minor contact with the Ravachol case, even if seemingly brief and insignificant?"

Reid sat back in his chair and appeared lost in thought for a moment, then he turned back to the detectives. "I'm sorry, gentlemen," he said. "I just don't believe I had any role in that whole thing. And, as I mentioned, the prosecution only occurred after I had already left, so I don't see why this Meunier individual would have anything against me."

"Yes, yes, of course, ambassador," Penwill said. "Like I said, it was only a hunch, and we wanted to follow through on it—you understand."

"I do," Reid said, getting up out of his chair, "and I thank you all for looking into this. One can't be too careful these days, you know."

"Indeed," Penwill said, getting up, as well, as Houllier and Corsi followed suit. "Well, then, good afternoon, sir."

"Good afternoon, gentlemen. My aide will see you out."

"Oh, ambassador," Penwill said, turning back to Reid suddenly, "although it appears that Meunier would not have any reason to seek you out, I should nonetheless recommend that you stay vigilant and alert your men to his possible presence—just in case."

"I shall do that, inspector," Reid said, "but I can assure you that I've dealt with worse threats in my day. I was the only war correspondent present in the field for the full three days of Shiloh back in sixty-two. I think the Rebel charges against Grant's lines were a bit more dangerous than this Meunier character."

"Yes, I should think so," Penwill said. "Thank you, sir."

"Thank you, gentlemen," Reid replied.

Penwill, Corsi, and Houllier then followed the ambassador's aide out to the waiting room and headed for the elevators leading down to the first floor.

Friday, August 12, 1892

39

Halloran nudged Falconer as they watched Goldman hug a young man outside the Zum Groben Michel tavern on 5th Street before entering the place with him. It was late and the two men had been following her throughout the evening.

"So, who is that guy?" Halloran asked as they stood concealed behind the corner of an apartment house down the street from the tavern.

"His name is Aronstam," Falconer replied quietly. "Modest Aronstam—a Russian. He's a so-called artist and longtime companion of Goldman and Berkman. Some say he and Goldman even got married at one point, but who knows? What we do know is that there are rumors that he's actually in Pittsburgh right now trying to finish what Berkman failed to do—kill Frick—so we're going to keep him company for a bit."

"In Pittsburgh?" Halloran asked confusedly. "But he's here. Why would people think he's in Pittsburgh trying to kill Frick?"

"Because he was. We had some detectives tailing him in the days following Berkman's assassination attempt, and he went to Pittsburgh, but he must have gotten cold feet because he came back quickly. But he's been good at covering his tracks—even today the papers were talking about how he might still be in Pittsburgh."

"Do you think he's in on it and really tried to get Frick?"

"I don't know, but it is concerning enough that he traveled to Pittsburgh right after the shooting. So now we have to keep an eye on him and Goldman—and watch out for her damned personal safety, too, of course."

"It's odd that it's been quiet for several days and there haven't been any attacks against her."

"Yeah, but that won't last. I'm more concerned about that mysterious group than about Aronstam or Goldman doing something up in Pittsburgh. Those bastards will be back, and Goldman's just walking around like there's nothing to it and she can give her anarchist lectures whenever she wants. Crazy lady."

"So, what do we do?"

"Let's pay Miss Goldman and Aronstam a visit, shall we? Let's go inside."

Falconer then strode off towards the tavern and Halloran quickly followed at his heels.

40

F alconer led Halloran into the tavern and then stopped just inside the entrance. As usual, it was filled with many men and women speaking loudly in German or Yiddish and drinking hefty glasses of beer. Smoke wafted through the main barroom and no one appeared to notice the two policemen at first. Falconer nodded at Halloran and then strode purposefully into the room, looking towards the back. Walking by several tables packed with patrons, he spotted Goldman speaking with eight or nine companions at her favorite table against the back wall. He kept walking and ignored the stares of the various customers who were finally looking up from their chairs. With Halloran close behind, he walked a few more steps and then finally stopped at Goldman's table, and she stopped talking mid-sentence and looked up at him with a frown. "Detective Sergeant Falconer," she said, sitting back in her chair. "You're visiting me again."

"Miss Goldman," he said, doffing his bowler.

"Is it to try to find more evidence against me in the Frick matter?" she asked. "Or to protect me against my own assassins perhaps?"

"Both, I'd say. Any sign of your tormentors lately?"

"No, actually. Perhaps they've given up and found more consequential persons to eliminate."

"I'd doubt that. Something tells me they still place great importance on you, but they're lying back and waiting."

"For what?"

"For the right moment. I'm sorry to be so pessimistic, but you saw how hard they tried to get you upstate."

"Yes, I did."

"Are you taking precautions, I hope?"

"I have many friends who would like to protect me. Like Mister Aronstam here." She nodded towards the swarthy young man sitting quietly next to her with a scowl on his face.

"Yes, Mister Aronstam," Falconer said, looking at him. "I heard that he's actually supposed to be up in Pittsburgh right now—even the newspapers are saying that. Funny how he appears right here, in the flesh."

"Well, we're not responsible for the foolish drivel that the newspapers put out there," Goldman said. "If they can't do their jobs right, it's not our problem."

"So, how was it up in Pittsburgh a couple of weeks ago, Mister Aronstam?" Falconer asked. But Aronstam remained mute, and only glared more intently at Falconer.

"What's the matter?" Falconer continued. "Cat got your tongue?"

The young man then shoved his chair backwards and stood up angrily, with his fists clenched at his sides.

"Now, now, Modest," Goldman said, touching his arm and trying to calm him. "There's no need to get upset. Detective Sergeant Falconer didn't mean anything—he's just not very artful with his words."

"Right," Falconer said. "I'm no orator like Miss Goldman here. I only catch criminals and assassins—and their accomplices, too, of course."

"Please sit down, Modest," Goldman said to the young man who was still standing and peering straight at Falconer across the table. "The detective sergeant and his man were just leaving now, I'm sure."

"I heard you were a bit of a hothead, Aronstam," Falconer said teasingly. "Pushing guys around if they got in the way of your anarchist friends here…being quite the tough guy. I wonder…do you want to step outside with me right now? Is that it? I wouldn't be acting in the role of a police detective, of course. We'll just say it's two men dealing with each other in their own way. Is that what you'd like, friend?"

"Detective sergeant, please," Goldman said, raising her voice. "You are acting entirely inappropriately, and I would ask you to leave us now. Please."

For several seconds, no one at the table spoke, and then finally Falconer looked at Goldman.

"Certainly," he said. "I only hope that Mister Aronstam here is ready for them when they come for you. Good evening."

He then signaled for Halloran to move back towards the bar's entrance and they both turned and made their way out through the crowd. Stepping outside, Halloran turned to Falconer and spoke: "You think that guy Aronstam went up to Pittsburgh to finish the job, detective sergeant?"

"I do, Jimmy. I do. Let's stay on Goldman, though. I can't believe those killers we encountered up north have given up on her, as she says. They're going to strike soon."

"Yes, sir, understood," Halloran stated.

Falconer then turned and started walking up the street, and Halloran went with him at his side as the moon cast a glow on the dark, empty street.

Monday, August 22, 1892

41

The dark-haired visitor to the city quietly tailed his subject by about fifty yards as they slowly ambled their way down 14th Street with a crowd of other pedestrians. Approaching the intersection with 3d Street, he saw his young quarry stop suddenly and look to his right at the building adjoining the large 14th Street Theater that stood mid-block like a colossal Roman structure from ancient times. The theater—with its large, front portico supported by four, sturdy, Corinthian columns, and its triangular pediment higher up that sported a tympanum inlaid with detailed relief sculptures of Roman figures—dwarfed the other buildings on the block and currently advertised a play: "A Flag of Truce," by William Haworth.

The crafty spy stood back at a distance as the younger man stepped up to the front entrance of the five-story structure next to the theater and walked inside. By its signage, the building housed a publishing firm on the lower floors—"Taylor's Publishing Co."—but it appeared to rent out apartments on its higher floors.

The dark-haired man walked down the sidewalk to the building, limping slightly, and stepped inside to see where the object of his surveillance had gone. There was no sign of him amidst the various people milling around inside the publishing shop, but he could hear voices above and the sound of footsteps slowly ascending the staircase. He smiled and nodded to one of the firm's clerks and then moved over to the stairs. Walking up, he heard the voices getting louder as he approached the top floor. Reaching the last step, he moved over to a door that was closed and heard some of the discussion occurring behind it: "Am I able to take possession tomorrow?" a man said with a French accent. Then came the reply, presumably from the host and lessor: "Yes, of course, sir—the gas fixture has been installed and it's just about ready for you. How about eight o'clock this evening?" The lessee with the French accent agreed heartily. "*Tres bien,*" he said. "Thank you so much. I will be here at eight."

The interloper outside the door then quickly moved to the stairs and descended to the first floor, smiling again at the clerk as he exited to the street and walked away.

So…taking accommodations here. How perfect. But how to do the job? One cannot simply throw a stick of dynamite into a window on a floor so high up like one can at a street café in Paris. No. How to manage it up on the fifth floor? But wait—the man mentioned a gas fixture being installed. Yes…I have heard of such explosions. A proper gas leak lit by a candle at night would do the trick. And it would seem like just a terrible accident—a gas leak that no one could have foreseen…

He turned in his tracks and walked quickly back to the building, searching for an alleyway to its rear, where an access point to a back stairway would certainly be found.

42

Falconer sat down in a booth already occupied by Penwill, Levine, and Houllier at Brackley's Tavern near the Mulberry Street police headquarters. It was evening, and the men had agreed to meet to discuss the possibility that Meunier—if he had ever been in New York City—had now left and moved on to targets unknown.

"Ah, Falconer," Penwill said, "right on time, I see. How are things, my friend?"

"Not too bad, inspector," Falconer replied, nodding at the others. "Gentlemen."

"I was just looking at the evening paper," Penwill said, "and it appears that this Borden woman up in Massachusetts had her preliminary hearing today. Can you imagine that? A young woman kills her own father and stepmother with a hatchet? What the devil could be the motive, I wonder?"

"I have seen such terrible acts of violence committed by otherwise refined young women," Houllier said. "There is no telling what a desperate person may do if pushed too far. Even if that person is *une belle jeune femme*."

"Yes, I suppose you are right there," Penwill said, "but why did she do it? Money, I suppose. Wasn't the old codger fairly wealthy?"

"I believe that he was," Levine chimed in, "but he was known to be particularly frugal. In fact, I read recently that the home didn't even have indoor plumbing or electricity despite the man's obvious financial ability to pay for such things."

"Well, that's quite odd," Penwill said. "Why would the old man live like that?"

"Afraid to lose it—all that money," Falconer said. "Not all of these rich types live large. Some of them live with the constant fear that they'll fall on hard times and have to go back to living like they once did—like normal men do."

"Well, I dare say, it's a good thing I'll never have to worry about that," Penwill said with a smile.

The men chuckled at his remark, and then, as the laughter ebbed, Falconer spoke again. "So, I suppose the trail has run cold with Meunier."

"It has," Penwill replied. "I'm afraid we have no leads or sightings. Perhaps he's run along to another country—if he ever was here, in the first place."

"I agree, *mon ami*," Houllier said. "I am convinced that he did come here to your fine city, but alas, there is no sign now."

"And you have bulletins out with his description, I assume?" Falconer asked.

"Yes, everywhere," Penwill answered. "At least, we've tried."

"Well, then, I suppose you've done all that you can," Falconer said, "and we all just have to wait for him to make his next move. I know that isn't really what you want to hear, but it is the situation."

"Very true," Penwill said. "Very true."

"And what about your mysterious assassins, Detective Sergeant Falconer?" Houllier asked. "Any leads?"

"Unfortunately, not," Falconer replied. "It's been quiet all around, and Goldman is acting as if none of it ever happened. She's very brash, that one. Quite the 'bricky girl,' as you would say, Inspector Penwill."

"Yes, it appears so," Penwill said. "But who could have been behind it? A band of marauders intent on killing this young woman, and for what? For her political beliefs, perhaps?"

"I believe so," Levine interjected.

The men all turned to him.

"She is an anarchist," he continued, "and thus, who does she appeal to? To the workers, of course—the multitude of forgotten factory hands and sweatshop toilers who gather at all those loud and boisterous rallies. She is their protector and their voice, and through her rousing speeches she keeps them from forgetting how they are constantly exploited and used by—"

"By the corporate bigwigs," Falconer interrupted. "Like Frick."

"Yes," Levine said. "Like Frick."

"I say, Falconer," Penwill said, "do you think it's Frick who was up to those attacks on you up on the Mohawk River?"

"No," Falconer answered, pulling out a cigarillo and lighting it. "Why would he? Berkman is in jail and about to face trial, but he was captured in the act, after all, so there's no question as to his guilt. His goose is cooked and he's going to prison."

"A *fait accompli*," Houllier said.

"Yes, exactly," Falconer said.

"Well, then, who?" Penwill asked. "Any ideas?"

"Detective sergeant," Levine said, turning to Falconer, "you said that right before that one particular gunman let go of the cliff up in Cohoes and fell into the water, he said to you, 'You don't know how powerful we are.' Isn't that correct?"

"Yes," Falconer answered. "That's exactly what he said. Why?"

"Well," Levine said, "he said 'we,' and chances are, he was not merely referring to the gunmen who were with him that day; he was more likely referring to his employers—to those who tell him what to do."

"And?" Penwill asked.

"And," Levine continued, "if we stick with the notion of Miss Goldman frustrating the aims of the great financiers and the corporate titans, then perhaps the 'we' is, well…"

"Yes?" Falconer asked.

"Perhaps the 'we' is actually a band of these corporate heads who are issuing orders to eliminate any rabble-rouser who gets in their way."

The other men looked at Levine for a moment, and then at each other, and then Houllier finally spoke. "I see, *professeur*…a secret society, if you will, driven to promote the aims of their companies even to the point of committing murder."

"Well, isn't that just a bit fanciful, perhaps?" Penwill asked. "A group of wealthy owners meeting in secret to dispense their own brand of justice? You mean to say Carnegie, Rockefeller, Morgan, and all the others like them are members of a secret, organized crime gang?"

"I'm not saying exactly that, inspector," Levine said. "I'm only postulating that perhaps those assassins whom Detective Sergeant Falconer faced are getting their instructions from some people who are very powerful and very high up in the chain, as it were."

"It makes sense, actually, gentlemen," Falconer said. "Goldman advocates the upending of our capitalist society and the government that supports and enables it. She is a sharp thorn in the wealthy owners' sides and only makes things worse for them—just look at what happened in Homestead."

"What is that?" Houllier asked. "Homestead?"

"Yes," Falconer said, "Homestead, Pennsylvania, where striking steel workers engaged in a gunfight with Pinkerton agents at one of Frick and Carnegie's factories just last month. It's why Berkman went after Frick."

"Ah, I see," Houllier said.

"Perhaps the professor here can better explain," Falconer said, looking at Levine.

"Yes, certainly," Levine said. "The striking workers were from a union, the Amalgamated Association of Iron and Steel Workers, and they went on strike after Frick and Carnegie refused to increase wages and improve work conditions at the factory. Frick, determined to destroy the union, locked the men out of the factory and hired hundreds of Pinkerton agents to keep them out. Well, the workers fought back, and a gun battle ensued just last month along the banks of the Monongahela River, which fronts the plant. Several agents and workers were killed, and many more were wounded. Eventually, the Pinkertons—who were vastly outnumbered and outgunned—were forced to surrender, but then the governor called in the state militia, and the workers found out quickly which side the governor was on. They were strong-armed into capitulating and had to go back into the factory on Frick's draconian terms just a couple of weeks ago."

"I see," Houllier said. "Thank you, *professeur*."

"So," Penwill said, "perhaps these mysterious assailants who have dogged you and Miss Goldman, Falconer, have been sent by unnamed representatives of the companies' ownership—or perhaps even by the owners themselves."

"Maybe it's a stretch," Falconer said, "but the motive is certainly there. Goldman is a firebrand and she's continually sticking a hot poker right in the owners' eyes every time she gives a speech to hundreds of angry workers."

"The problem is, of course, *messieurs*," Houllier said, "how do you find out if this is true?"

"That's a hard question to answer," Falconer said. "But I think the only way is to catch one of these thugs and put the squeeze on him until he talks. Don't you agree?"

"Yes, indeed," Penwill said. "But where are these thugs now? Where are you to find them? As you've pointed out, they've melted away."

Falconer said nothing in response to his companion's pointed remark, and only took a long drag of his cigarillo as he thought of Emma Goldman.

43

The young Frenchman followed the apartment manager up the darkened staircase with a suitcase in hand as dusk slowly settled over Lower Manhattan. The manager also carried a bag, having offered to assist the new lessee with his belongings. As they reached the top floor, the manager lit a candle to better see in the darkening hallway.

"Here, we are, sir," he said to the young renter. "That's a little better."

They then both approached the room, and the manager, leading the way, opened the door to enter. The younger man instantly felt a rush of hot, pungent air—gas—hit his face, and then a bright flash lit up the hallway like the sun. He felt himself suddenly tumbling backward and heard a loud roar—like a freight train rushing by inches from his face.

He landed with a thud on his back in the hallway, and in his dazed state, he felt something burning: his mustache and hair. He reached up and tried to douse the embers that were singeing his face and heard the low rumbling sound around him that reminded him of the fireplace back home in France as a boy: the popping and hissing of the firewood as it slowly burned and the crackling of the blue and orange flame as it lapped the air and danced upward into the chimney.

He did not know what had happened, and was having trouble forming coherent thoughts, but somewhere in his tangled and pained mind he realized that an explosion had occurred—a gas explosion. He moved his head slightly to the side as he lay on his back and tried to see Mister Colon, the manager, but he could only see flames and smoke, and debris falling all around him.

Then he heard voices from below, and—somehow summoning the strength—he determined to get up and away from the encroaching flames. He rolled over to his side and lifted himself up to a sitting position, and then, struggling to his feet, he looked for the stairwell leading down to safety. Seeing it through the glare of the surrounding inferno, he limped over to the top step and slowly made his way down to the voices.

44

The World

Tuesday Evening
August 23, 1892

HURT IN A GAS EXPLOSION

Two Men Thrown Down,
One Burned and Furniture Wrecked

I t is reported that a severe gas explosion took place last evening in the dwelling-house at 103 West Fourteenth Street, adjoining the Fourteenth Street Theatre. The house is occupied by Mme. Taylor, a dressmaker, and the explosion occurred in a room upstairs which had just been rented. The tenant had requested that a private gas meter should be placed in the apartment, and this had been done by the Consolidated Gas Company.

About 8 o'clock last evening the tenant came to take possession and was shown up to his room by Harry Colon, the son-in-law of Mme. Taylor. They entered the room with a lighted taper, and as the door was opened a volume of gas rushed out, followed by an explosion, which shook the whole building.

Both men were thrown down violently, and the prospective tenant, who was a little in the rear, scrambled to his feet and ran downstairs. He was slightly burned about the face and his hair and face were singed. Mr. Colon, however, was seriously injured. He was taken out of the room in an unconscious condition, with burns on the face, arms, and breast.

The upper story of the house was partially wrecked and the furniture injured by the explosion.

45

Falconer glanced upwards at the smoking ruins of the top floor of the apartment building on 14th Street. He had heard of the explosion that had occurred the night before and had thought nothing of it—a gas leak that had been turned into a sudden inferno by a landlord lighting a candle—but Houllier had shown interest in the incident and had asked Falconer and Penwill if they might join him at the scene, if only to confirm the source of the explosion. Now, Falconer stood with the two inspectors and Levine, who had managed to break free from his students at law school for a while and had taken a train down to 14th Street.

"So, only the two men hurt, is it?" Penwill asked.

"Yes," Falconer replied. "It appears that only the landlord and the renter were injured, if you can believe that. Look at that damage—it looks like a bundle of dynamite went off up there."

"I should say so," Penwill said. "Can't believe the two men weren't killed outright."

"Well, the renter escaped with only minor burns, luckily," Falconer stated. "It was the landlord's son-in-law, actually—a guy named Harry Colon—who took the brunt of the explosion. He's at Bellevue now in serious condition."

"And what of the man who rented the apartment?" Levine asked.

"No information on that, I'm afraid," Falconer answered. "But maybe the landlord herself will know—Mrs. Taylor. She's apparently inside here with men from this precinct."

"Well, then, shall we go introduce ourselves?" Penwill suggested.

"Yes," Falconer said. "And just know that the fire inspector said that the gas is off now and the air has cleared, so there's no danger of another explosion happening in the building—in case anyone is wondering. After you, Inspector Penwill."

The four men then walked into the entrance of the building. Inside, there was much activity going on. Workmen were going up and down the stairs, some carrying charred remains of furniture or buckets of smoking ashes. Policemen stood about, as well, ensuring that no thieves would come by and try to take anything of value that remained up on the higher floors.

Falconer looked over to the corner of the room—which was clearly a shop of some sort—and saw a middle-aged woman speaking with a couple of detectives. As she wiped her brow with her handkerchief, Falconer and his companions approached her and the policemen. "Pardon us," Falconer said, showing his badge to the detectives. "We're with the Detective Bureau—I'm Detective Sergeant Falconer. Mind if we just take a minute to ask the lady a few questions?"

"No, not all, detective sergeant," one of the detectives replied. "Take your time."

"Thanks," Falconer said, and the two roundsmen walked off and went outside the building. Falconer then turned to the woman seated before him.

"I'm very sorry to have to speak with you under these circumstances, ma'am," he said, "but I'm wondering if we can just ask you a few questions. We just want to be clear on what happened here."

"No, that's fine, sir," Mrs. Taylor said to him. "I just can't believe it all—utterly destroyed…apparently a gas leak after workmen had placed a new meter up in the apartment."

"Yes, that's our understanding," Falconer said. "Again, we are very sorry. How is your son-in-law doing, if I may ask?"

"Well, he's terribly injured, unfortunately," she replied, "but the doctors say he will live. It appears, though, that he will be permanently crippled by his burns, I'm afraid. The poor boy."

"Yes, I see," Falconer said. "And do you happen to know the name of the man who was with him? The renter?"

"Well...I...yes," she said, as if searching her mind for the name. "I believe his name was...was...wait—yes, it was French. He was a young Frenchman newly arrived to town. The name was Antoine Boucher, I believe. A very pleasant young man."

"Boucher, you say?" Houllier asked intently. "Antoine Boucher?"

"Yes, I believe that is correct, sir," she answered him. "He spoke just like you—with that lovely French accent."

"Something up, inspector?" Falconer asked Houllier.

"Yes, perhaps, *mes amis*," Houllier replied. "We must talk of this, but first, madame, do you know where this Antoine Boucher was taken last night?"

"Well, I believe he went to the Bellevue Hospital with my son-in-law, sir," she stated.

"And do you know if he remains there?"

"I'm sorry," she said, "I do not know the answer to that. He was fortunately not hurt as badly."

"Yes, that is most fortunate," Houllier said.

"Well, I think we are done asking you questions, Mrs. Taylor," Falconer said. "We appreciate your time very much and hope your son-in-law has a swift recovery."

"Yes, thank you very much, gentlemen," she said. "I just don't know how we're going to recover from all of this...just devastating."

"Yes, we understand, ma'am," Falconer said.

"*Madame?*" Houllier said.

"Yes, sir?" she replied.

"If you don't mind, we would like to examine the remains of the room upstairs. Is that all right with you?"

"Why, yes, if you'd like, sir. You can take those stairs right over there. It will take you up, but it's a horrible scene."

"Yes, understood," Houllier said. "*Tres bien.* We are most appreciative for your assistance. *Merci beaucoup.*"

"Thank you, ma'am," Falconer said. "We'll do that now. You take care."

"Thank you, detective," she said.

Falconer then led Houllier, Penwill, and Levine across the shop, and they ascended the stairs as other men came down. At the top, Falconer beheld amidst the various workers and fire inspectors a scene of utter destruction: burned-out walls, incinerated furniture, and broken, charred wood everywhere. As the workmen sifted through the wreckage, he approached one of the fire inspectors. "Morning, inspector," he said. "I'm Falconer, detective sergeant from the Central Office on Mulberry. I'm here with a few men just to check around, if you don't mind."

"Not at all, detective sergeant," the man said. "But you won't find much, as you can see."

"Yes, I can tell. So, you're thinking it was just an accident?"

"That seems to be the conclusion. Someone must have mistakenly left the gas burner open on the new gas meter that was just installed. Then, when the two men opened the door with the lit candle, they were met with an enormous collection of gas, and...well, you know what happened then."

"So, the gas burner was in the open position, huh?"

"Yes, it appears that way, but unfortunately, we've seen that before. People get careless with these things. They fall asleep and never wake up because of the gas that keeps coming in. But in this instance, the men actually lit the gas up with their candle."

"I see. Tough break."

"Right."

"Well, anyway, thanks for letting us take a look around."

"Sure thing. Have a nice day."

Falconer walked back to where the other men were looking around the blackened room.

"Anything from the fire inspector?" Penwill asked, as Levine and Houllier joined them.

"Well, yes," Falconer answered. "They say the gas burner on the newly installed gas meter was left open accidentally, and when the men walked in with the lit candle, the gas blew."

"And so, it was an accident, as the newspapers reported," Penwill said.

"No accident, *messieurs*," Houllier announced, "but a deliberate act of retribution."

"Deliberate, you say?" Penwill said. "Retribution? How so?"

"Come with me," Houllier said. "It is time for a *café*. I will explain."

46

Falconer lifted his cup of coffee and took a short sip inside the local café that he, Houllier, Penwill, and Levine had found just a couple of blocks from the damaged building on 14th Street. He then placed the cup back down on the round, wooden table around which he and the men were sitting and looked over at Houllier. "So, inspector?" he said. "You felt for some reason that this explosion was a deliberate act against someone. Why do you think this?"

"Gentlemen," Houllier began, "I was stunned when I heard the name from the lady: Antoine Boucher. I could not believe my ears for a moment."

"Why?" Penwill asked. "Who is this Antoine Boucher person?"

"Well, of course, there are probably many Antoine Bouchers," Houllier continued, "but it simply could not be a coincidence. No—*c'est impossible.*"

"What is impossible?" Falconer asked. "Do you know this Boucher character?"

"I know *of* him," Houllier answered. "If, in fact, it is he. Antoine Boucher was an anarchist in Paris, or at least he was a lost, young man who wanted to be one."

"The man who was injured after renting the room back there was a French anarchist?" Penwill asked.

"Yes," Houllier replied. "But, as I say, he was just a neophyte—a young follower who idolized Ravachol and got swept up in the frenzy of the French anarchist movement. He never blew anything up, nor tried to kill anyone, but he did get close enough to Ravachol to provide helpful evidence to the authorities."

"So, Boucher was a turncoat, huh?" Falconer asked. "He testified against Ravachol?"

"Indeed," Houllier said. "The French prosecutors had enough evidence against Boucher to charge him as an accessory to several of Ravachol's murders, so he eventually agreed to testify against his former leader in return for a very lenient sentence. And thus, Boucher became a villain in the minds of Ravachol's avengers."

"May I ask, inspector," Levine said, "what happened to Boucher following the trial?"

"But of course, professor," Houllier said. "He only had to serve three months in the local jail, and then he essentially disappeared—a ghost of Ravachol's murderous spree. No one really knew where he went, but there were rumors that he left the continent—headed towards India, or perhaps to Germany, or perhaps even here to the States. And now, gentlemen, we know that he did come here to, in effect, disappear."

"But Meunier found him," Falconer said. "Or at least, that's your theory."

"*Oui*," Houllier said, taking a sip of his coffee. "I believe that this Boucher is our former compatriot of Ravachol's band of *criminels*, and because of his act of betrayal against Ravachol, Meunier is responsible for this explosion."

"Remarkable," Levine said, leaning back in his chair. "To slip up into the room and open the gas burner, knowing somehow that the target would be returning in the evening, when a candle would likely be lighting his way into the room. It is ingenious, in a way."

"I agree with you, professor," Houllier said. "No need for a stick of dynamite. No need for a dagger or pistol. Simply an open valve, and *voila*—the room goes up in flames."

"It is an interesting theory, I'll admit," Falconer said, "but we'd need more proof than simply a French name that happens to be in the record of Ravachol's trial."

"What do you suggest, Falconer?" Penwill asked.

"Well," Falconer said, "I think if we can confirm that this Boucher was the Boucher who testified against Ravachol, then it's clear this wasn't a coincidence or an accident."

"But the problem is," Levine said, "where is Boucher now? I would doubt that he's still at the hospital—his wounds were only superficial."

"You're right," Falconer said. "And this has probably scared him enough that he'll high-tail it out of New York pretty quickly. I suppose we'll just have to start at the hospital, though. Inspector Penwill, can you get over there with Inspector Houllier and Detective Waidler and find out anything you can about where he might have gone, any plans he might have mentioned?"

"Righto," Penwill answered.

"Professor," Falconer said, turning to Levine, "how about you? Do you have a little time to join me over at the 15th Precinct station on Mercer? We could get any info they got on Boucher last night."

"I'd be happy to join you," Levine answered, grabbing his hat.

"Good," Falconer said. "Well, gentlemen, we need to find Boucher, and find him quickly. If we find him, we'll probably find Meunier, too."

47

Falconer and Levine walked with a police officer towards the back of the Mercer Street station house. Near the end of the hallway, the officer stopped and pointed into a room that was full of desks, clerks, and detectives busily at work on their typewriters.

"That's Detective Delmonico over there," he said. "He was with the victims at Bellevue last night."

"Thanks," Falconer said, and then the officer turned and went back towards his post at the front desk of the station house.

Falconer nodded at Levine and the two then walked through the maze of desks to the back of the room where Delmonico sat working at his typewriter.

"Morning, Detective Delmonico," Falconer said.

Delmonico stopped typing and looked up. He appeared to be in his early fifties with dark hair speckled with gray and a face that had the deep, tanned complexion of a sheep herder who had spent his life tending to his flock in the sun-drenched hills of Sicily.

"I'm Falconer from the Central Detective Bureau, and this gentleman here is Professor Eli Levine, who's consulting with us on an investigation. We're wondering if we can ask you a few questions about your investigation of the Fourteenth Street apartment fire last night."

"Sure thing," Delmonico said. "Have a seat."

Falconer and Levine sat down in a couple of wooden chairs before Delmonico's desk and then Falconer spoke again: "So, we understand that the renter who escaped serious injury was a Frenchman named Antoine Boucher. Is that correct?"

"Yeah, that's the name given," Delmonico replied.

"Did you get a chance to speak with him?"

"I did, but he didn't have much."

"Did he say why he was here in New York?"

"Only that he was just here to sight-see. You know—a young guy trying to see the world before settling down. That sort of thing."

"Right. And I suppose he's no longer at Bellevue?"

"No, he was discharged pretty quick. He only had a few minor burns and bruises, so they let him go."

"Any idea where he was going?"

Delmonico paused for a moment, then reached across his desk for some papers. "Let me take a look here," he said. "I think I took it down."

He sifted through several pages of notes and then finally stopped on one page. "Right," he said. "Here it is: he said he knew a French couple down on 4th Ave. who would help him out while he figured things out, get his plans in order—know what I mean?"

"Sure, sure," Falconer said. "Any names or an address given for this French couple?"

"Well, I did ask him if he could provide that, in case I had to do any follow-up, and he gave the address of 58 4th Ave., right near Union Square. No names, though. He was saying he didn't want them getting involved in all of this."

"Got it. Well, we certainly appreciate your time on this, detective. Thanks for meeting with us."

"Yeah, no problem," Delmonico said as Falconer and Levine stood up to leave. "Hey—mind me asking what this is all about? It looks like it was just an accident last night—a gas burner left open by someone."

"Well, we can't go into it in too much detail right now," Falconer said, "but we're thinking it might not have been an accident."

"Not an accident?" Delmonico asked, appearing surprised. "How so?"

"I wish I could go into it, but it's just a theory right now, so probably not smart to start up a bunch of rumors. Suffice to say that we believe someone had it in for Boucher. I'll be sure to follow up with you just as soon as I have more."

"Yeah, understood. I'd appreciate that."

"Sure thing," Falconer said. "Have a good day, detective."

"And you gentlemen do the same," Delmonico said. Falconer and Levine then moved off and headed towards the hallway leading out to the front of the old station house.

48

F alconer stood before 58 4th Ave. with Levine and glanced down the sidewalk. He saw Penwill, Houllier, and Waidler approaching on foot, and when they got to within earshot, he spoke out to them. "Glad you got my telegraph. We might need Inspector Houllier to translate if anyone's home."

"Indeed," Penwill said, stopping in front of the address. "That's a right smart move on your part."

"And I am happy to be of service, gentlemen," Houllier said.

"Thanks," Falconer said. "Well? Shall we try them?"

The men nodded and followed him up the front stairs of the stone brownstone that stood on the corner of 4th Ave. and 18th Street.

"Nice place," Waidler remarked.

"Yes, it is very impressive," Houllier said.

Falconer knocked on the door, and, within 30 seconds, a woman dressed as a housemaid appeared. "Yes?" she asked with a French accent as she looked at the men.

"Allow me, messieurs," Houllier said, stepping forward. He then began to speak with the young woman in French, and after a brief discussion, she moved to let the men in.

"Well, this is a good start," Penwill said, and Falconer nodded.

The housemaid led the men down a central hallway until they reached a large, well-furnished drawing room on the left. She motioned for them to enter, and then she strode off to a nearby staircase and ascended. As the men stood silently in the drawing room, Falconer could hear voices speaking in French upstairs. Moments later, a rotund, well-dressed man in his fifties appeared. "*Bonjour*, gentlemen," he said with a smile. "My name is Henri Lavaud. Please—have a seat."

The men all sat down in chairs or on two fancy couches that sat squarely in the middle of the room. Lavaud motioned for the housemaid as he spoke to her in French again, and the woman departed. He then turned back to the men.

"I understand that you are looking for young Antoine Boucher after his terrible accident last night," he said. "Alas, he was here overnight after leaving the hospital, but he is gone now, I am afraid."

"Thank you for meeting with us, *Monsieur* Lavaud," Falconer said. "I'm Detective Sergeant Falconer from the New York City Police Central Detective Bureau, and we are investigating the fire from last night. We fear that Mister Boucher was actually targeted, and that it was not an accident."

"Not an accident?" Lavaud said, sitting back and appearing surprised. "*Mon Dieu*—this is not good. Why would you say this?"

"Well," Falconer said, "it's our understanding that Mister Boucher testified earlier this year in the trial against the anarchist, Ravachol. Is this correct?"

"Yes, detective sergeant," Lavaud said quietly. "I am afraid that is all true. Antoine was a fine young man, but regrettably, he got caught up in… unfortunate events."

"I see," Falconer said. "Well, we believe that a follower of Ravachol—a Theodule Meunier—is here in New York and that he deliberately sabotaged the gas burner in Mister Boucher's room to start an explosion as soon as a lit candle was brought into the room."

"Oh, my," Lavaud said. "Meunier...here in New York..."

"Do you know Meunier, *Monsieur* Lavaud?" Penwill asked.

"Well, I know of him. We all followed the events from this past spring, and it was well known that Meunier tried to exact revenge in Paris for Ravachol's execution, and that he then left the country for parts unknown."

"Yes, I see," Penwill said.

"*Monsieur* Lavaud," Houllier said from his seat at the end of a couch.

Lavaud looked at Houllier and then the two men began speaking to each other in French as the others looked on. After a moment of discourse in their native tongue, Houllier turned to Falconer and spoke: "I just asked the gentleman what Boucher had told him last night and where he had gone. He said Boucher was convinced, as we are, that this was no accident, and that Boucher felt compelled to flee the city. I asked Mister Lavaud where he went, and it appears that he just left a half hour ago for your Grand Central train terminal."

"Sir," Falconer said, looking at Lavaud, "do you know where Mister Boucher is going?"

"I am sorry, detective sergeant," Lavaud said, "but he felt it would endanger my wife and me if he revealed his planned destination. And so, he only said that he would be headed west, and would contact us when he could."

"West," Falconer said. "I see. And do you happen to have a photograph of the young man, just so we can familiarize ourselves with him?"

"But of course. Just over here on the mantle."

He walked over to the fireplace, reached up and grabbed a framed photograph on top of the mantle, and then brought it back to his seat.

"Here you are," he said, handing the framed portrait to Falconer. "That is him just about a year ago."

Falconer looked down at the photograph of a thin, young man with dark hair and a trimmed mustache sitting amiably in a chair and looking off to the side.

"Thank you, Monsieur Lavaud," Falconer said, handing the framed photograph to Waidler, who then shared it with the other men. "This helps us very much in our efforts."

"Yes, my pleasure," Lavaud said.

"Well, I think that's all we need to talk to you about today," Falconer said. "We certainly appreciate your assistance, and we will keep you informed of your friend, Mister Boucher."

"Yes, please do," Lavaud said dolefully. "He is the son of an old friend of mine back in France, and I have a special affection for him. I just fear that he has gotten himself into a most difficult situation from which he will not be able to escape."

"Well, we will do our best to find him and get him to safety," Falconer said, standing up as the other men followed suit. "And we will find Meunier. I promise you that."

"*Merci, merci*, detective sergeant," Lavaud said, also standing up. "I wish you men all the best, and good luck to you. *Bon courage*."

"Thank you, sir," Falconer said, shaking Lavaud's hand. "We can see ourselves out."

The men then skirted past Lavaud and walked to the front door of the home. As they stepped outside, Penwill turned to Falconer. "Well," he said, "looks like it's on to the train terminal immediately."

"Yes," Falconer said. "There's no time to lose. Let's go get a cab and head up there."

The five men then briskly descended the front staircase and headed off to 4th Avenue on their way north to the great train station in the heart of the city.

49

alconer leaped out of the covered carriage as it pulled to a stop on 42d Street and looked back briefly to see the other four men following him out. He turned again and glanced across the sidewalk at the busy entrance to Grand Central Railroad Station, which was swarming with people. "All, right, gents," he said, "we know generally what Boucher looks like, and thanks to Inspector Penwill here, we also just saw that photograph of our target, Mister Meunier, that he brought along. We don't know if Boucher is still here, or if Meunier is tracking him. Basically, we know nothing for certain, but we have to start somewhere, so let's go inside, spread out, and start looking for either of them. Agreed?"

The men nodded and he immediately turned and started walking to the entrance. Stepping inside and wading through the crowd of people in the large, front lobby, he led the men into the cavernous train shed beyond. Travelers were walking everywhere amidst the many trains that sat idling on the various tracks, and it was difficult to get a good look any faces in the chaos of hundreds of people milling about and moving quickly from point to point in the large space. Nevertheless, Falconer quickly formulated a plan.

"Inspectors, you two head over to the right," he said to Penwill and Houllier. "James, you head up those stairs and get a good look from above, while the professor and I will head over here to the left. All right?"

"Got it, boss," Waidler said, and Falconer watched as the young detective slipped through the crowd and quickly ascended the large staircase leading up to a balcony that overlooked one end of the enormous train depot. "Well, professor?" Falconer said turning to his companion. "Shall we have a look over near these tracks on the left?"

"Certainly," Levine answered, and the two men began to struggle through the mass of people entering and exiting the trains on the long platforms.

"This seems futile," Falconer said to Levine after a few minutes as they both peered around the bustling room. "But I'm not sure what else to do, frankly."

"I recall, "Levine said, "that Inspector Penwill mentioned in the cab that Meunier would have a noticeable limp due to his spinal affliction—correct?"

"Yes," Falconer answered. "That's the case, apparently."

"Well then, I would think that that is our surest way to find him in this mob, if in fact, he is here. That's not a very common condition."

"Yes, you're right, so we look for the limp."

"Exactly."

Falconer looked back towards the balcony overlooking the end of the tracks and saw Waidler scanning the crowd intently. "Waidler will be looking for that, too," he said, "so maybe he can spot something. Let's keep moving along the side here."

The two men then moved farther down the platform that lined the wall of the train shed and kept scanning the crowd and the interiors of the cars through their windows. After several minutes, they moved on to the next long platform that ran parallel to the first one that they had just traveled, and, after walking its length, moved on to the third one.

"Well, nothing yet, I'm afraid," Falconer said. "I hope the others are having better luck."

"Yes," Levine said.

"Imagine," Falconer said, stopping midway down the platform. "Coming all this way to exact revenge against a turncoat. That's dedication, professor. What strange people these bomb throwers are. They spend all this time and energy on—"

"There!" Levine interrupted.

"What?"

"Look back fifty yards. There—the man in the buttoned-up, gray coat and hat with the red hat band. Do you see him?"

"Yes, I do, and he's—"

"Got a noticeable limp," Levine said, interrupting again. "And look how his coat fits—it's got a bulge on his back."

"His hunchback," Falconer said, removing his revolver. "Let's go!"

He took off at a sprint through the many people walking down the platform, followed closely behind by Levine. As he got closer to the man they had spotted, he saw him move towards an open door to one of the train's cars. As the man stepped up to enter, however, he suddenly stopped and looked down the platform, as if to make sure he wasn't being watched. Falconer slowed down to a walk and held his revolver hidden behind his back, but he saw the man look directly at him and appear to recognize that Falconer was not just a regular passenger looking to find his train.

Falconer stopped and looked back at Levine, who also stopped in his tracks. Then Falconer looked back at the man, who still looked intently at him, not twenty paces away. The man appeared to hesitate, as if he were deciding on a course of action, and Falconer gripped his gun tighter behind his back. The man then slowly edged away from the door of the car, all the while looking straight at Falconer. Then he quickly turned and fled back towards the doors leading to the train station's lobby lining 42d Street.

"MEUNIER!" Falconer shouted above the din of the platform, and many people stopped and looked at him. He started sprinting again towards the lobby and looked up at the balcony to see if Waidler could see him, and he saw that Waidler was himself sprinting over to the staircase to come down to the train platform area. Meeting together right in front of the doors to the lobby, Falconer explained the situation rapidly to the young detective: "It's him—Meunier—he just ran out into the lobby. Let's go!"

Waidler followed him at a run without a word and they both burst into the lobby area with their guns drawn, eliciting shrieks and gasps from the people who were assembled there.

"Quick," Falconer said. "He's gone out to the street." But then before running outside, he saw Levine running up, panting for air.

"Professor," Falconer said, "he ran outside. Go find the inspectors and tell them to follow us!"

"Understood," Levine said, and then Falconer and Waidler ran out through the front doors of the station. Stepping out onto the busy sidewalk, they looked around for a moment, scanning the street and sidewalks for their suspect.

"There!" Waidler finally shouted, pointing down the street. "Getting into the carriage."

"Right, I see it," Falconer said. "Let's go."

The two men then ran swiftly along the sidewalk, dodging the many pedestrians who blocked their way, in an attempt to reach the carriage that was just pulling away from the curb.

"It's leaving," Falconer said breathlessly. "Hurry!"

But as they ran, the swift horses leading the carriage began to trot much faster down the street, and Falconer realized that they could not close the distance. He finally slowed down and motioned for Waidler to stop, too.

"It's no use, James," he said. "We lost him."

"I'm sorry, boss," Waidler said. "Too many people out here."

"You're right, but at least now he knows we're onto him."

As he stood and slowly caught his breath, he looked in vain far down the street and saw the carriage disappear around a corner. Then he looked over at Waidler and nodded for him to join him in walking back to the train station.

"Let's go meet the professor and the inspectors," he said. "This isn't over."

50

Halloran wiped the sweat off his brow as he waited outside Odd Fellows Hall on Forsyth Street down on the Lower East Side. Falconer had left a message for him earlier in the day instructing him to keep an eye on the place while Emma Goldman was inside speaking to a group of working-class German immigrants. Falconer and the others were pursuing some leads on Meunier, and Halloran preferred to be with them, but of course he heeded his detective sergeant's orders and arrived with several other plainclothes officers from the Detective Bureau and set up surveillance outside the place.

He looked down the block as the sun slowly disappeared behind a row of buildings to the west and saw Pat Long, the crafty and jocular sergeant who was filling in as a plainclothes detective in his last days with the department before retirement. Long looked up at him and nodded his head slightly before turning to face the street that was still alive and busy at this late hour in the day with pedestrians, horse-drawn wagons, hansom cabs, and dirty ragpickers lugging their wooden wheelbarrows full of refuse and junk.

Halloran slowly started walking towards Long, and, when he arrived to within a couple of feet of the beloved sergeant, he spoke quietly to him while scanning the street and adjoining sidewalks: "Well, Sarge, see anything?"

"I don't, Jimmy," Long answered. "Seems pretty normal, huh?"

"You think this Goldman lady is secretly up to something new? Maybe another assassination of some bigshot here in the city?"

"Possibly. You know, she hasn't been in the papers much for the past month. Maybe she's wised up and is just going to lay low for a while."

"Well, sounds like she's raising a ruckus in there by the sounds of the crowd."

"Yes, but I don't understand German. Just English, a little Gaelic, and a lot of annoyed wife."

Halloran chuckled and wiped his brow again. The street was now getting dark, and a lamplighter appeared nearby, raising his ladder to light the gas lamps for the evening.

"Sounds like it might be getting over," he said. "I'll go inside and see what's happening."

"All right, Jimmy my boy," Long said. "We'll be right here."

Halloran walked over to the entrance to the hall and flashed his badge to the doorman, who promptly moved aside and let him in. Walking through the small lobby, he entered the big meeting room and saw that the proceedings had ended, and many people were now grabbing their hats and coats and slowly winding their way to the exit. He looked at the back of the room and saw various people surrounding Goldman and shaking her hand. Standing aside for a few minutes to let the crowd leave, he stepped back into the lobby and exited the building. Outside, he encountered Long again, speaking with another plainclothes detective, Eric Jahn.

"Well, it's over, as you can see," Halloran said. "She'll be stepping outside in a minute—she's just being congratulated by a bunch of followers."

"So, what's next?" Long asked. "A few of us tail her, I suppose?"

"Looks like Detective Sergeant Falconer wanted that," Halloran replied. "You guys up for it?"

"I've got nothing else to do, Jimmy," Long said, looking over at Jahn. "You, Eric?"

"Sounds fine by me," Jahn, a sturdily built, German-born detective in his forties with a thick crop of brown but slightly graying hair, said with a smile.

"Well, then, sounds like we have a plan, gentlemen," Long said.

"You okay with this, Sarge?" Jimmy asked.

"Jimmy," Long said with a stern look, "I've handled the streets for thirty years. I can handle this young agitator for an evening. We'll keep you updated."

Halloran heard some noise coming from his right and saw Goldman and a small crowd exiting the building. As she walked by the men, she looked at Halloran and leered at him momentarily, then turned and started walking down the sidewalk with her retinue of followers. Halloran followed them a few steps and then turned back to Long and Jahn as a couple of other detectives approached from across the street.

"All right, fellas," he said to them, "she's all yours."

"Sounds good," Long said with a grin. "You have a good night and we'll be in touch."

Halloran nodded, and then stared beyond Long's shoulder for a moment, looking confused.

"You okay, Jimmy?" Long asked. "You look like you've seen a ghost, my boy."

"That carriage coming at us," Halloran said quietly. "It's going kind of fast."

He looked at the approaching carriage in the distance as Long and Jahn did the same, and he realized that something was wrong—the large, black carriage pulled by two horses was going significantly faster than normal as it careened towards them, and the driver wasn't doing anything to retard the horses' progress.

Halloran looked back towards Goldman down the street, and he knew then that this was no accident—these were no wild horses running astray as the driver attempted to pull back on the reins.

"He's going for Goldman!" he shouted at the detectives. "Quick—grab her!"

He then started running towards the carriage that was barreling down the street as Long and Jahn took off as fast as they could in the opposite direction to warn Goldman and her followers. Halloran ran hard up the sidewalk and waved at the driver, who ignored his orders to stop. As the powerful horses and carriage came close to where he stood, he suddenly darted out into the street and jumped up onto the side of the carriage, almost falling to the ground. Gripping a silver handle on the carriage's frame, he reached up to grab the driver's leg, but the driver swiftly brought a whip down and struck him on his forearm, causing him to yell out in pain and almost release his hold.

"Stop the carriage!" he shouted over the din of the thundering hooves and rolling wheels. "Police! Stop!"

But the driver ignored his commands again and pulled the reins to the right, forcing the horses to change their direction slightly. Halloran looked ahead as he held on desperately to the carriage, and he saw Pat Long coming up closer to Goldman, who seemed oblivious to the approaching catastrophe. Jahn was running right behind Long, waving his arms. The carriage kept moving powerfully at the mass of people walking on the sidewalk, and in one last desperate attempt to avert a collision, Halloran reached up and punched the driver forcefully in the ribs, and he could tell that the blow had some effect, as the driver winced audibly and bent over slightly.

But then it was too late, and Halloran looked ahead again to see the figure of Long leaping to push Goldman out of the way just as the horses ran straight into the small group, throwing people in every direction. The carriage rattled and bumped violently, and the driver then yanked on the reins to get the horses out into the street again, but Halloran reached up and grabbed the driver by his collar and pulled down hard, throwing his mysterious foe to the sidewalk.

Halloran then leapt down and ran over to the assailant, who was slowly getting to his feet. The young officer rammed into the man's torso with his shoulder, and the man crumpled to the ground. "You are under arrest!" Halloran yelled into the injured man's ear. "Put cuffs on him," he said to his fellow officers, who were fast approaching.

Standing up, he looked back at the moaning, injured forms of several people who had been walking with Goldman. Jahn was kneeling next to Long, who was on his back and bleeding from his mouth and nose. Halloran quickly ran over to them. "How bad?" he asked.

"Pretty bad," Jahn answered, holding Long's hand. "He got hit with the full force of the team."

Halloran looked down at Long, who was still alert.

"Sarge, I'm sorry," he said. "We'll get you to a hospital soon."

"Did she get clear?" Long asked haltingly. "Miss Goldman...did she avoid getting hit?"

"She did, pal," Jahn said reassuringly. "You got to her just in time."

"That's good, that's good," Long said.

"It's okay, Sarge," Halloran said. "You're going to be okay—an ambulance is on the way."

Long just smiled and closed his eyes as Halloran heard the moans and wails of the injured victims lying all around him.

"We need Detective Sergeant Falconer," he said, looking over at Jahn. "We need him now."

51

Falconer strode into the hospital ward at Bellevue with Waidler, Penwill, and Houllier at his heels. He stopped and looked around the large room with various nurses, attendants, and doctors tending to the many patients in their beds, and he recognized Halloran standing with Jahn and a few other men near one bed midway down the wall to his left.

"Over there," he said to his companions.

They walked quickly over to the bed, and Falconer saluted Halloran.

"Thanks for the message, Jimmy," he said. "How's he doing?"

"Well," Halloran replied quietly, "the doc says he got some broken ribs, a broken leg, a sprained shoulder, and a bunch of bumps and bruises, but he'll be okay."

"Good to hear. Could have been much worse, obviously."

"Right, sir," Halloran said, looking over at Long lying in his bed.

"Is he awake?"

"Oh, sure. Come on over—he'll be glad to see you all."

Falconer walked over to the bed with Halloran and sat down in a chair next to Long as the other men gathered around. The sergeant's left leg was encased in a large cast, and he had a wide bandage wrapped around the top of his head with scattered bruising about his face. Long looked at Falconer and smiled. "Robert," he said weakly. "Hello there…I guess I was a step too slow this time, huh?"

"Well, Pat," Falconer said, "I'm sorry it happened this way, but I heard that you saved some people's lives tonight."

"Yeah, that's what they're saying. Can you imagine that? Me?"

Falconer chuckled. "And we even caught the guy," he said. "How about that?"

Long smiled again. "Yeah, well, you know what they say down at headquarters: I always get my man."

The men standing around the bed laughed with Falconer.

"Hey, Robert," Long said, grabbing Falconer's hand, "I know this lady Goldman isn't liked too much around here being an agitator and such, but the fact is, she has as much right as you or me to speak her mind in this country—know what I mean?"

"Sure, Pat."

"So, you're doing the right thing, Robert. She's a victim here, and we have an obligation to protect her and get these guys, no matter what the people and the papers say about her. That's the oath we took."

"Yes, I understand."

"I want you to know your dad would have been so proud of you for what you're doing—so proud. You just keep going and you get these guys, you hear?"

"Yes, Pat. Thanks for that."

"Sure thing, kid. Sure thing."

"Well, well," a loud voice said from behind Falconer, "is this your gang from down by the docks, sarge?"

Falconer and the men turned to see a doctor in a long, white coat standing just a few feet away. He was in his forties, with his hair shaved almost down to his scalp, and Falconer could see that he was powerfully built, with his coat stretched tightly over thick shoulders and arms.

"Ah, look who it is," Long said. "Gentlemen, meet Doc Leland, who somehow patched me up."

The men all exchanged brief greetings with the doctor, who stepped forward to the foot of Long's bed. "So how are you feeling, sarge?" he asked Long.

"Oh, not bad, doc," Long said. "Not bad, considering."

"Well, gentlemen," Leland said, looking at the men surrounding the bed, "I can tell you that the sarge here had only one question as we treated him when he first came in, and that was whether he'd be okay enough to ice skate up in Central Park in December. And I said yes, he would."

Long chuckled.

"In fact," Leland said, "this guy wants me to join him, and let me tell you—I'm pretty good on my skates, too, if I do say so myself."

"Well, I'm going to hold you to it, doc," Long said.

"Yeah, well, just don't ignore me and spend all your time with all the ladies up there," Leland said. "I heard about your reputation, sarge."

The men laughed again.

"All right," Leland said, looking at Falconer. "I was just checking in. Just know that your sergeant here is going to be all right and we'll have him up and on his feet in a few weeks."

"Thanks, doctor," Falconer said. "Appreciate your help."

"My pleasure," Leland said. "Okay, sarge, we'll see you a little later."

Long raised his hand slightly and waived and Leland stepped away and moved off to other patients.

"Well, Pat," Falconer said, "I think we'd better get back to Mulberry. We'll check back with you tomorrow, okay?"

"Sounds good," Long said, grinning. "I'll be right here."

Falconer smiled. "All right, we'll see you then," he said, and then he signaled for Halloran and Jahn to join him a few feet away from Long's bed.

"So, the suspect is over at Mulberry?" he asked.

"Yes," Jahn answered. "But he ain't talking, so I doubt we'll get any information from him."

"Well, we'll see about that," Falconer said. "Let's go, Jimmy."

Falconer then signaled for the other men to join him, and they walked out of the ward, headed for police headquarters on Mulberry Street.

52

Falconer, Penwill, Houllier, Waidler, and Halloran all sat down inside Superintendent Byrnes' office after being let in by Clubber Williams.

"Well, gentlemen," Byrnes said, "this is an unfortunate turn of events."

"Yes, it is, sir," Falconer said.

"Pat Long is a good man and a good cop," Byrnes said. "I spent a lot of time with him on the streets back in the day, and I'm just glad he and the others are apparently going to pull through."

"It looks that way, sir," Falconer said.

"And it's clear from Officer Halloran's story here that this was a deliberate act. This suspect intentionally tried to drive over these people."

"Agreed."

"Although we don't actually know his identity yet. He's not giving anything up."

"Yes, we've heard."

"So where do we go from here?"

"Well, I think we can change this suspect's attitude and eventually get to the organization's leadership. But I'm going to need a couple more men."

"That's easy enough," Byrnes said, looking over at Chief Inspector Steers, who was standing off to the side.

"They'll have to be men of…a certain quality, sir," Falconer explained. "This band of thugs is obviously ruthless and plays to win. I need some men who, shall we say, aren't afraid to get their hands dirty…who will be willing to do what is necessary to bring these men to justice…who are willing to do what most other men aren't."

"I get your meaning," Byrnes said quietly. He then turned to Detective Sergeant McNaught standing over near Steers. "Are those two officers, Kramer and Winter, still on desk duty downstairs following their latest problems?"

"They are, sir," McNaught answered.

"Go fetch them for me, please, and grab their personnel files, too."

"Right," McNaught said, and then he quickly exited the office.

"Meanwhile, I suppose we should get the suspect in here," Byrnes stated. "I think I can change his mind about talking."

"If you don't mind, sir," Falconer said, "I would like the opportunity to interrogate this suspect."

"Oh? Well, by all means, please do. Meanwhile, Inspectors Penwill and Houllier, how are things going with your French bomb thrower?"

"Well, superintendent," Penwill said, "we got close to him at your Grand Central terminal yesterday, but alas, he managed to give us the slip."

"I see. But it's good that you are onto him, and he knows it now."

"Yes, Monsieur Superintendent," Houllier said. "This man cannot escape apprehension forever. We will chase him to the ends of the earth, if necessary."

"I trust you will, inspector," Byrnes said. "And our city is most grateful for your efforts and those of Inspector Penwill here."

Falconer heard the door to Byrnes' office open again, and he turned and looked to see McNaught enter, trailed by two uniformed officers. McNaught directed the two to stand before Byrnes' large desk, and they complied.

"Gentlemen, this is Officer Winter," McNaught said, pointing to the larger officer with snow white hair and a barrel chest. "And this here is Officer Kramer."

Falconer and the others stood up as Byrnes spoke to the two men: "Well, then, officers, we've summoned you here today to talk about something rather important."

"Uh, superintendent, sir, may I ask what it is we did?" Winter interrupted.

"What's that?" Byrnes asked.

"Well, sir, I'm just wondering what it is we're accused of, because I'm sure there's a good reason why we did it."

"Relax, Winter, you are not in trouble. We've actually asked you to come upstairs to take on a special duty, and I'll let Detective Sergeant Falconer here from the Detective Bureau explain things."

Falconer walked over to McNaught and asked for the officers' personnel files. After examining them for a moment, he walked back to where Winter and Kramer stood. He then looked up at Winter, who appeared to be in his fifties, with a sturdy frame, bright blue eyes, and large, meaty hands that appeared to have been in many physical altercations over the years.

"William Winter," Falconer said, reading from one of the files. "Formerly with the U.S. Navy, then joined the department in 1877, served on the street for over a decade and was advanced to the rank of corporal, but then, due to repeated citizen complaints of excessive force, was reduced back to patrol officer first grade."

Falconer looked up at Winter, who appeared to fidget slightly where he stood.

"So, Winter," Falconer said, "what's with all the problems? Seems like you've had a habit of putting suspects in the hospital over the years, as well as causing excessive damage to local businesses when apprehending said suspects. Can you explain yourself?"

"Well, sir," Winters said slowly, "maybe I've gotten a little too rough at times, but most of those mopes deserved it, as you know, being a former beat cop yourself. And I've tried to be a little nicer lately—that's a fact."

"Right," Falconer said, and then he turned to the dark-haired Kramer, who was younger, perhaps in his forties, slightly smaller, but still showed a sturdy frame with thick arms, wide shoulders, and had a hard face that seemingly could batter through a brick wall without suffering any appreciable damage. Falconer looked at one of Kramer's eyes, which appeared to be slightly blackened and swollen.

"What's up with the eye, Kramer?" he asked.

"Just a scrap, sir," Kramer replied nonchalantly. "Nothing major."

"I see," Falconer said, turning to the files in his hands. "So…Jason A. Kramer, aged forty-six, entered college here in New York City in 1866 to study the classics and philosophy, but was promptly expelled two months into his term for throwing a fellow student through a plate-glass window."

Falconer looked up at Kramer, who shrugged.

"You then went to work on the docks," Falconer continued, "and became known as an avid participant in underground prize-fighting, where the rules were, shall we say, relaxed and competitors could use any means necessary to win the match. You did well in this avocation, but then applied for the police department in 1878, and rose from patrol officer first grade to corporal, was passed over several times for sergeant, and then finally was reduced in rank three years ago after the police board found you guilty of a pattern of using excessive force. Does that about cover it, Kramer?"

The stone-faced officer looked at Falconer for a moment, and then shrugged again. "If that's what it says," he replied.

"Well, not the best records, gentlemen," Falconer said, walking away and glancing at the files again.

"Begging your pardon, sir," Winter said. "We were just told that we're here for some special duty, but it seems to me that we ain't really looked upon so favorably. So, I'm not sure why we're here. Sounds like you want a couple of fellers who aren't so much into the physical aspect of the job and we aren't the men you're looking for."

"You're exactly the men I'm looking for, Winter," Falconer said, turning back to face the two officers.

"Sorry, sir?" Winter said, appearing confused.

"We face a very determined and ruthless band of unidentified cut-throats, men," Falconer said. "They've already tried to kill our victim four times in the past month, and almost succeeded last night in taking her out and several persons who were with her when they deliberately rammed into her with a team of horses and a carriage. We almost lost one of our own sergeants in that incident. I need men who are willing to stand up to these killers. Men who are fighters, and who aren't afraid to kill, if necessary. Men who are used to…excessive force, if you get my meaning. Are you two willing to take on this job with my team?"

Winter looked over at Kramer, who looked back at him before turning to face Falconer again.

"Where do we sign, sir?" Winter said, with the slightest hint of a smile creasing his face.

"Good," Falconer said, handing the files back to McNaught. "Now, listen, you are officially off your desk duty and will be reporting directly to Detective Waidler here. You might also be working with these gentlemen—this is Officer Halloran, and this is Inspector Penwill from Scotland Yard, and Inspector Houllier from the French Surete. They are here in our country assisting on another matter, but we might be using them in our investigations, and they might be using us. We are a team—understood?"

"Yes, sir," Winter said.

"Got it," Kramer replied.

"Now," Falconer said, "the first thing you need to do is go home and change into plain clothes. You won't be wearing your uniform on this duty, all right?"

The two officers nodded.

"We'll see you back here in two hours," Falconer said. "You are dismissed."

Winter and Kramer then turned and exited the office, and Falconer looked over at Byrnes. "Sir, I think it's time to get our prisoner, if that's all right," he said.

"Certainly," Byrnes said. "Charlie," he said to McNaught, "could you please fetch our suspect?"

"Yes, sir," McNaught said, and then he left the office.

"There was no identifying information found on him?" Falconer asked.

"None," Steers answered from his position next to Byrnes. "Just one item: this napkin from a bar up in the Tenderloin with handwritten notes on it pertaining to the time and place of Goldman's lecture last night. It was found in his pocket. That's it." Steers handed the napkin to Falconer, who gazed down at it. In printed letters on the edge were the words, "The Black Swan," and then, handwritten nearer to the middle of the napkin, the words, "Odd Fellows Hall – Forsyth St – 7 pm."

"Black Swan?" Falconer said. "Up in the Tenderloin?"

"That's right, Falconer," Clubber Williams said, walking closer. "It's been there for years on 36th just off Broadway. I knew it well when I used to walk the beat up there. It's a quiet place generally—not swanky, but not a dive, either. Business is usually fairly slow—no big parties going on in there, if you know what I mean."

"Understood," Falconer said. "Well, then, I think it's time to have a little chat with our mysterious carriage driver."

53

Falconer stood in front of Byrnes' desk as McNaught and another officer brought the chained suspect into the room. Falconer studied the man as they forced him to sit down in a wooden chair in front of him. He was young—perhaps in his mid-twenties—and was very pale, clean shaven, and had a shock of tousled black hair. The man looked around at the several men surrounding him, and Falconer was surprised to see an almost nonchalant, peaceful mien about his face.

After McNaught stepped back and the other officer exited the room, Falconer stepped forward a couple of feet and spoke to the man. "So, you drove that carriage into a crowd of people last night. You didn't kill any of them, fortunately, but you did hurt some of them. Were you targeting Miss Emma Goldman? Was that it?"

The man just stared back at Falconer and said nothing.

"Who sent you to do this?" Falconer asked. "Who are you working for?"

The man again remained silent.

"Do you have a name, kid? You know, you're going to have to give up some information eventually."

The man smiled slightly. "I don't think so, detective," he said.

"Well, one of the people you hurt pretty badly was a sergeant on our police force," Falconer said quietly. "He's a friend of mine, actually. He was a close friend of my father and was very good to me when I was a kid."

He then walked slowly towards the man as if he were going to circle around behind him. "I don't take kindly to you driving a team of horses over him, understand? It makes me pretty angry, actually."

SMACK!

The man fell violently backwards in his chair after being struck by Falconer's fist just under the nose. He groaned in pain and writhed on the carpeted floor but could not tend to his injured face, as his hands were still chained behind his back.

"Get him up, please, boys," Falconer said to Halloran and Waidler.

They both moved over to the man and grabbed him under his arms and lifted him forcefully back into the chair, and he moaned audibly as he bled from his mouth. Falconer stepped back in front of him slowly. "Now then," he said, "let's try this again. Who sent you to do this last night?"

The man just gasped for air several times, and then looked up at Falconer, "I don't know what you're talking about."

"I see," Falconer said. He then walked back around the man and stopped directly behind him. "You're protecting someone. I get it—you don't want to betray your handlers and would prefer to just be the honorable guy who goes down for everyone else. That's very noble of you, but unfortunately, that's just not going to work." He then grabbed one of the man's fingers and bent it upward at an awkward angle.

"AHHHHHHHHH!" the man shouted out in pain, but Falconer refused to let go.

"Whose plan was it!" Falconer yelled out over the man's agonized screams. "Whose?"

The man just continued screaming in pain and shaking his torso as if to force Falconer to let go.

"Who do you work for, damn it!" Falconer shouted into the man's ear as he bent the finger farther.

"Never! Never!" the man yelled back in a rage. He then looked up at Falconer and smiled through gritted teeth. "We are coming," he hissed. "We will protect all real Americans, and you won't stop us."

Falconer grabbed the man by the front of his shirt, lifted him up out of the chair, and threw him into the wall a few feet away, and the man feel down onto his back, seemingly unconscious.

"Well, he's sure a tough nut to crack," Byrnes said, walking over and looking down on the man.

"Sorry," Falconer said, catching his breath. "Got a little excited there."

"It's no worry," Byrnes said, "This one had it coming, and we're not done with him yet."

He then looked at the other men gathered in the room. "This stays here, gentlemen."

"I'll go grab some men to get him out of here, sir," McNaught said.

"Yes, thanks, Charlie," Byrnes said. "In the meantime, maybe we should move him over here and put some water on him."

"Yes, superintendent," Waidler said, motioning for Halloran to help him.

The two men went to grab the stricken prisoner by his arms when suddenly Falconer pointed at them. "Hold on," he said. "What's that?"

"What's what, boss?" Waidler asked.

"Right there, just under where his shirt is buttoned at the top," Falconer replied. "Hidden by the shirt."

Waidler unbuttoned the top button and opened the shirt to reveal a tattoo on the man's chest.

"'PF,'" Falconer said, looking at the tattoo.

"What do you think it is?" Byrnes asked. "His own initials, perhaps?"

"Maybe," Falconer said, "but something's bothering me about it."

"Bothering you?" Penwill said. "How so?"

"I don't know," Falconer answered. "I feel like I've seen this before somewhere, but I just can't quite remember where."

"Hm," Penwill said. "That's most interesting."

"Maybe you have seen it on another suspect?" Houllier asked, stepping forward.

Falconer turned and looked at him. "Another one?" he said. "Yes... yes, I believe it could be...I..."

He looked down at the floor for a moment and then suddenly looked back up at the men. "That's it—the man I fought near the waterfall in Cohoes. As he hung onto the branch high up over the falls right before letting go, I remember now seeing something imprinted on his fingers. It was these same letters—'PF.' I can see it so clearly now, in dark ink: the tattoo that this man here has on his chest."

"Well, by Jove, that's something," Penwill cracked.

"Yes, gentlemen," Houllier said. "They both have the same signature, if you will. The markings of—"

"Of some secret society or group," Falconer interrupted.

"Yes," Houllier said. "Secret...and deadly serious, it appears."

"Well, then," Byrnes said, "how do we go about finding out who's behind this group?"

"I think a good start would be to go see the people who run this Black Swan Saloon," Falconer said, looking down at the napkin confiscated from the prisoner. "And I know just the men do it."

Byrnes smiled. "I get your meaning, Falconer," he said.

"But one thing first," Falconer said. "Is Goldman still in the building? I'd like to speak with her."

"Yes, she's still downstairs in protective custody, but I can't keep her against her will for much longer. She has those rights, you understand."

"Yes, sir. Understood."

"Very well, then. Good luck and keep me posted, gentlemen."

"Right, sir," Falconer said, motioning for the other men to follow him out of the office. "Shall we?"

He then led Waidler, Halloran, Houllier, and Penwill out into the hallway and towards the stairway leading down to the main floor of the police headquarters building.

54

Falconer showed his badge to the officer standing guard outside the room in which Goldman had been placed temporarily after the incident with the carriage. The officer moved aside and let him enter, while Penwill, Waidler, Halloran, and Houllier waited outside.

"Detective sergeant," Goldman exclaimed as he shut the door behind him. She was sitting in a chair by a long wooden table with a scowl on her face, and was joined by her friend, Claus Timmermann. "Why am I not surprised?"

"Miss Goldman," Falconer said, doffing his bowler. "Mister Timmermann."

"Good evening, detective sergeant," Timmermann said.

"Are you here to release me, I pray?" Goldman asked.

"Well, if that's what you want, I suppose I am," Falconer replied.

"Good, then. We've been cooped up long enough in your headquarters."

"I wouldn't advise leaving, of course."

"Well, thank you, but nonetheless, we'll go now."

"Miss Goldman, as you know, this is the fourth time that someone has tried to take your life in the past month, and you've been lucky enough to escape unharmed yet again. However, I think your luck is going to run out soon. We have safe houses here where you'd be protected by armed men around the clock. It's the best thing for you now."

"I am aware of the peril that I am in, but I will not—I cannot—let these forces of persecution and tyranny silence me in this way. I must continue the march, no matter what the cost."

"The march? What march?"

"The one that started on November 11 of 1887, detective sergeant," she answered flatly.

"Am I supposed to know why that date is important?" he asked.

"Well, you should," she said. "It was the date when the four martyrs to our cause were hanged by the bloodthirsty state after a pretend investigation and sham trial of the Haymarket incident in Chicago. Four men who were simply there for the revolutionary gathering and labor protest, and no real evidence to show that they were responsible for any of the deaths that occurred that day. Engel, Fischer, Parsons, and Spies—all murdered by the state, hanged at the gallows, with no cause. But we continue their march, detective sergeant. We continue it so that their deaths will not be in vain. Good day, sir."

She moved past him to exit the room, but then she stopped when he spoke out: "I understand your position, Miss Goldman, but these men who are after you—they are determined and very ruthless. I'll find out who they are, but it will take more time. I'm asking you to stay in protective custody until I can do that."

"I'm sorry," she said, facing him at the doorway, "but death awaits all of us, and I imagine that we don't really have a say in when it occurs."

He stood looking at her for a moment, and then walked over to the doorway. "Here," he said, "let me walk you out."

Stepping out into the hallway, he let the other men exchange brief greetings with Goldman, and then he led them all down the corridor towards the exit of the grand headquarters building, with Goldman walking by his side, a slight, petite figure next to his imposing presence.

Coming to the end of the hallway, he turned the corner to enter the large lobby when he almost bowled over a young female who was walking in the opposite direction.

"I beg your pardon, miss," he blurted out. "I didn't mean to—Nellie? I mean, Miss Bly?"

"Detective Sergeant Falconer," Nellie Bly said, straightening out her hat. "Fancy seeing you here. And Inspector Penwill, Officer Halloran, and Detective Waidler, as well—how nice to see you all again. But I don't believe I've met this gentleman."

"Ah, this is Inspector Houllier from the French Surete, Miss Bly," Penwill explained. "He is assisting us on an investigation."

"Oh, my…from France?" Bly said, shaking Houllier's hand. "How fascinating."

She then turned to look at Goldman standing next to Falconer. "Why, you're Emma Goldman, the so-called Red agitator," she said, wide-eyed.

"And you are Nellie Bly, the infamous circumnavigator of the globe," Goldman responded drily. "How are things as a celebrity reporter?"

"Oh, not much of a reporter these days," Bly replied with a smile. "I was trying to write some fiction recently, but it hasn't really worked out, so I'm looking at my options now."

"Well," Goldman said, "if you ever want to contribute some anarchist writings, let me know."

Bly chuckled. "Why, thank you, but what I'd really like is an interview with you. Could we arrange that, perhaps?"

"I am sorry," Goldman said, "but I don't trust reporters. Perhaps Detective Sergeant Falconer here could assist you with a juicy story, though? I take it you are acquainted with him?"

"Yes, we worked on cracking a case from last year, so you could say that we know each other somewhat."

"Well, from the looks of it, I think there is room to get to know each other a little better. Good day to you all."

Goldman and Timmermann then walked away and stepped out through the large front doorway of the building, and Falconer looked down at Bly. "So…what brings you to headquarters?" he asked.

"Unfortunately for me," she said, "I heard that Miss Goldman had some sort of an incident with a renegade carriage last night, and my sources tell me that it likely wasn't an accident. So, I had hoped to speak with her about it today, but as you can see, those hopes have been dashed."

"Yes, she is, as you can see, very eager to get out of here."

"So, is there any truth to that? That is was not an accident last night?"

"Well, I'm sorry, but there's an ongoing investigation—I just can't say anything at this point."

"Yes, I see. Well, gentlemen, so nice to see you all again after last year's rather thrilling adventure. Detective sergeant, I do hope you will keep me posted as to any developments in Miss Goldman's case that you can share."

"Yes, I'll keep that in mind, Miss Bly."

"So nice to see you today," she said, extending her hand. He took it and they shook hands, but they did not let go and only stared at each other for a moment until Penwill finally broke the silence: "Um, well then, chaps, I suggest we get a move on now—shall we?"

"Right," Falconer said, finally releasing his hand from Bly's. "Good afternoon, Miss Bly."

"Good afternoon to you, gentlemen," she said, and then she walked away and exited the front doors, as Goldman had just moments earlier.

"*Mon Dieu,*" Houllier said. "I have met the incredible Nellie Bly. I am stunned."

"Well, old boy," Penwill said, "that's New York for you."

"And much prettier in person, I must say," Houllier said. "*Tres belle filles.*"

"Yes, well, I suppose we should be getting on," Falconer said.

"Yes," Penwill said. "And actually, Inspector Houllier and I must take our leave of you—we have a slight lead on the Meunier case."

"Oh?" Falconer said. "And what's that?"

"Well, we've had alerts out to all the local arms and explosives manufacturers to be on the lookout for Meunier in case he tries to purloin some dynamite, and one of them has just been in touch with us—seems that a small crate of dynamite sticks has just gone missing down on the docks."

"Well, that's not good."

"No, it isn't. So, we're going to go check it out. We'll let you know what we find out."

"Great. And why don't you take Jimmy here just so you have a police department representative with you?"

"That would be splendid."

"Jimmy, mind if you tag along?" Falconer asked.

"Not at all, sir," Halloran said. "Happy to."

"Great," Penwill said. "Well, then, we'll see you all a little later. Cheerio."

"See you later," Falconer said, and Penwill, Houllier, and Halloran disappeared out the doors leading to the street.

"So, where are we headed, boss?" Waidler asked.

"We'll wait for Winter and Kramer, and then go pay a little visit to this Black Swan joint. Let's go back upstairs."

The two men then headed up the stairs to the Detective Bureau in the bustling headquarters building of the New York City Police Department.

55

Penwill, Houllier, and Halloran followed the shipping manager, a man named Bowles, into his office down at the New Jersey Southern Freight Station on Rector Street along the Hudson River. Outside the small office, in a cavernous space filled with desks, filing cabinets, and noisy telephones, dozens of shipping clerks energetically attended to their duties of accounting for tons and tons of freight that came in daily on the great ships moored tightly to the crowded docks three stories below. There, where the blended stench of dead fish and sea salt rose onto the docks like a thick blanket of putrid fog, the shrill sound of whistles mixed with the noisy workings of dozens of steam-powered cranes slowly yanking wooden pallets full of dry goods out from the deep bowels of the ships and down to the waiting arms of beefy dockworkers.

Bowles, an employee of one of the firms that shared the space, gestured for the policemen to take a seat, and then he himself sat down behind his desk that overlooked the crowded and noisy quays below. "Well, gentlemen," he said, "I appreciate you coming down here today."

"Certainly, Mister Bowles," Penwill said. "I'm sure we can all appreciate how serious a missing crate of dynamite is."

"Very serious, sir," Bowles said. "And I can assure you, we are doing everything in our power to track it down, but I'm afraid it may very well have been stolen—which is a first for us."

"We understand," Penwill said. "Now then, you are shipping manager here in Manhattan for the American Forcite Powder Company out of New Jersey, correct?"

"Yes," Bowles replied. "The plant and works are out in Landing, and we get shipments everyday down on these docks and distribute our products nationwide from here."

"So, this crate that went missing," Penwill said. "How many sticks would be in it?"

"Well, it's fortunately not a large item. One of those particular smaller crates carries approximately eight cylinders, I'd say."

"Still a lot of explosive power, though, correct?"

"Oh, yes. One of those cylinders could completely wipe out this office and those above and below us. The sticks are generally meant for removing rock and minerals, you see."

"Yes, of course. So, you were saying outside that one of your security guards saw a suspicious character nearby last night?"

"Yes, that would be Graves, one of our overnight guards. I asked him to be here so that you could meet with him."

"That's good, thank you."

"Here, let me go see if he's waiting outside," Bowles said, and he got up and exited the office.

"How the devil does one suddenly lose a crate of dynamite?" Penwill said, looking at Houllier and Halloran.

"Yes, it is most alarming," Houllier said. "One would think that security is very tight for these things."

"Especially after this company had an accidental explosion out at their plant back in April."

"An accident? This is true?"

"Oh, yes. A very large explosion out there—killed seven men, unfortunately."

"My…*c'est terrible.*"

Bowles then walked back into the office trailed by a young man in a brown suit. "This is Mister Graves, our security man," he said, taking a seat along with Graves.

"Ah, yes, Mister Graves," Penwill said. "Thank you for meeting with us."

"Certainly, sir," Graves said.

"So, you apparently saw a suspicious character near your storehouse last night?"

"Yes, I did, sir. I only caught a glimpse of him walking away up Rector Street, but I did see him, and I thought it odd."

"Odd, why?"

"Well, we don't see many people down here at that hour, and he seemed rushed as he walked away."

"Could you describe him?"

"I'm sorry, but he was too far away, so I didn't see his face. But generally, I'd say he was of medium height—maybe five feet eight or so—and he was dressed in dark clothing and wore a dark crusher hat. And then there was his limp."

"Limp? What sort of limp?"

"Well, I noticed that when he walked away, he had this sort of limp, as if he was injured, or was perhaps lame, in some manner."

"I see."

"*Monsieur* Graves," Houllier said, "did you notice anything misshapen about his form? His back, perhaps?"

"Misshapen, sir?" Graves said. "No, no, I can't say that I noticed anything. But of course, he was carrying a canvas bag on his back, so that might have hidden something from me."

"A canvas bag?" Penwill said. "Perhaps to carry away your missing crate."

"Yes, makes sense to me," Bowles said.

"Mister Bowles," Penwill said, "I assume you have very tight storage protocols for the dynamite."

"Oh, yes, absolutely. These sticks are kept in a locked storage house after retrieval from the boats, and they're further kept inside locked cages within the storage house. So, it's near impossible to get to them without a key."

"And who would have those keys, sir?"

"Well, I would, inspector, and then also my two assistants, Tom Underwood and Frank MacLeish. But we've already confirmed their whereabouts last night—they were both at home miles away from here. And I can absolutely vouch for the two of them—they've worked here for years and are very loyal, upstanding members of our company."

"Understood. And no sign of a break-in at all? Damage to doors or locks—that sort of thing?"

"No, indeed, inspector. That's what beats me about this—I can't figure out how this damned crate got taken out from under our noses."

"Well, I can assure you, sir, that we will take all of this under careful consideration and keep you posted as to the investigation. The New York City Police Department is making this one of its highest priorities, you understand?"

"Yes, I do, sir. Thank you."

"Well, then, we'll be off now. Again, we appreciate your time today, gentlemen."

"And thank you, inspectors," Bowles said, as they men all stood up.

"We'll see ourselves out," Penwill said. He then exited the office, followed by Houllier and Halloran. Outside, down on Rector Street, He stopped and turned to his companions. "A man with a limp," he said. "I think we know who that is."

"Yes," Houllier said, wiping his brow with a handkerchief. "Meunier somehow managed to get a hold of this crate, and now things are most urgent."

"Agreed," Penwill said. "We must confer with Falconer as soon as possible. Meunier is planning to act soon, and we must spare no efforts in stopping this man. Come, gentlemen—back to Mulberry Street."

56

"Well, it's clear to me that Meunier is the suspect who took the crate of dynamite sticks," Falconer said, sitting at his desk in the Detective Bureau on Mulberry Street. "The question is: where is he going next with it?"

"Agreed," Penwill said, sitting nearby with Houllier, Halloran, Waidler, and the two new additions to Falconer's team—Winter and Kramer. "We've got bulletins with his photo spread out across the city now in the various station houses. We've also alerted certain large venues that might be a target. But your city is very large, gentlemen—it's like looking for a needle in a haystack, as they say."

"Well, the only thing to do is to keep spreading the word," Falconer said, "although feeding it to the newspapers could create a panic. We can only hope that some vigilant officer walking the beat somewhere spots him soon."

"Yes, hopefully," Penwill said. "For now, though, since it's been a long day, would anyone care to join Inspector Houllier and me for a drink?"

"We'd like to, inspector," Falconer said, "but we're going to head up to that saloon that our carriage driver suspect apparently frequents—see if we can get any leads on this organization that he's a part of."

"Understood, say no more," Penwill said. "We'll see you in the morn', then?"

"Yes, have a good evening, gentlemen," Falconer said. Then he looked over at Waidler, Halloran, Winter, and Kramer. "Boys, ready to go check out this joint up on Thirty-Sixth?"

The men all nodded and grabbed their jackets and hats.

"Good luck," Penwill said.

"Thanks," Falconer replied. "All right—off we go."

He then started walking out towards the hallway leading to the exit of police headquarters, trailed by the other men, on their way to the Tenderloin and the place known as "Satan's Circus."

57

Falconer, joined by his men, walked up to the front entrance of the Black Swan Saloon on 36th Street as the sun fell beyond the high bluffs of New Jersey across the Hudson River to the west. The streets were busy at this hour with pedestrians of all sorts—small-time bunco men looking for a good swindle; prostitutes noisily plying their wares to game-some men out on the town for a night; young, dirty orphans causing mischief and mayhem before being chased down the street by irate street cops—and Falconer had to dodge people on the sidewalk as he stepped up to the door.

Moving inside, he glanced around the surprisingly quiet barroom as his colleagues spread out along the perimeter. To the left, a tall, sullen bartender with thinning hair and thick forearms glared at them, and then went back to his business of cleaning mugs and wiping the bar clean. In the back, at several round tables, a bunch of men quietly sipped their frothy beers and played cards, some of them stopping momentarily to eye the detectives suspiciously before focusing back on their game.

Another bartender—this one younger and boyish, but with an arrogant, testy look about his face—walked into the barroom through a door leading to the back of the place and stopped briefly to size up Falconer. Then he walked up to the tall bartender and whispered something in his ear, and the taller man nodded subtly.

Falconer motioned for the men to stay back as he slowly started walking up to the bar. Stopping a couple of feet from the two bartenders, he held out his badge. "I'm Falconer with the Central Detective Bureau down on Mulberry," he said. "Got a minute?"

"What's doin'?" the taller man said.

"We had an incident last night down on Forsyth Street where a driver deliberately ran over some people with his carriage."

"That's too bad," the bartender said.

"Yeah," Falconer said. "Well, the suspect had a napkin from your place in his pocket, and he had written down the address where this incident took place down there. We're wondering if you've ever seen this guy here." He then held out a mug shot of the carriage driver taken earlier in the day.

"Nope," the bartender said, looking briefly at the photograph.

"What about you, kid?" Falconer asked the younger man, who stared back icily and then glanced quickly down at the mug shot. "No, never," the younger man said.

"I see," Falconer said. "What about this?" he asked, showing the men a drawing of the tattoo that was found on the suspect's upper chest.

"What is that?" the older man asked.

"It's a tattoo that this carriage driver has on his chest," Falconer explained calmly. "Ever seen it before? Those letters like that?"

"I don't typically check out guys' chests for tattoos," the taller man quipped.

"I take it that's a no?" Falconer asked, and the man shook his head briefly, stating, "Sorry, cop."

"What about you?" Falconer asked the younger man. "You ever seen something like this?"

"Can't say I have, sir," the young man said with a smile. "Probably just the initials of his old lady, I'd suspect."

"Well, then," Falconer said, "I'm sure you two won't mind if I make the same inquiries with your guests here?"

"Go right ahead," the older bartender said tersely.

"Thanks," Falconer said, and then he walked back to Waidler, Halloran, Kramer, and Winter lurking in the shadows by the walls.

"The barkeeps are playing dumb," Falconer said. "I don't trust a word they say, but I told them we'd like to ask these customers if they've ever seen our suspect or the tattoo we found on him. James and Jimmy, mind if you do that for me?"

"Sure thing, boss," Waidler said. "Come on, Jimmy."

The two men then ambled over to the tables as Falconer gathered with Kramer and Winter by the wall. "Look, gentlemen," he said to them, "I think you're going to have to pay this place another visit in the near future—send a message to these guys. Not tonight, but soon. They are, shall we say, not treating this seriously, so maybe we need to use a different method of persuasion. Understand?"

"Absolutely," Kramer said.

"Yup," Winter said. "We got it, boss."

"Good, then," Falconer said. "When Waidler and Halloran are done in a moment, we'll shove off. Something strange about this place. I can't tell what, but I sense it."

"Think they're involved with this mope we have on ice back at headquarters, sir?" Winter asked.

"I don't know," Falconer replied, "but we'll find out soon enough, I can tell you that."

Waidler and Halloran then walked back to where Falconer was talking to the two officers, and Waidler gave the predictable news: "They're not saying anything—playing dumb."

"Yeah, I figured," Falconer said. "Let's get the hell out of here."

He then led his men outside onto the street, and they all headed over to Broadway to catch a cable car down to the Mulberry Street headquarters.

58

The man sat at the worn desk overlooking the busy street below and fingered the stick of dynamite.

Wonderful. Eight cartridges. All so smooth and well manufactured. So much explosive power. How to utilize them, though? One, all-encompassing, grand event? Or perhaps several smaller ones? No matter. There is time enough.

He stood up in the dark apartment and peered more intently at the people walking below.

So many New Yorkers going every which way, oblivious to my plans. None of them have any idea. Capitalist lambs.

He smiled and went back to his seat, unfurling a map of Manhattan and its environs.

59

The grim-faced interloper sat in the back of Ritter's Lokal, a German beer joint down on 2d Street on the Lower East Side where many of the German radicals in town were known to mingle. He knew German himself—had learned it from his parents as a boy—and that is why he was recruited for this job by his superiors. The place was full of them—German workers and agitators bent on bringing down the American State and installing their own vision of an anarchistic utopia based on a network of worker cooperatives and mutual aid societies. They were all speaking German, too, and many of them were likely Jews, he surmised. They were dirty, vulgar, and drinking their beers with abandon in the grimy, smoke-filled bar.

He scanned the crowded barroom in search of his target, a young anarchist neophyte who had been tagging along with Red Emma Goldman of late: Ernst Ginsberger. Twenty-three years old, slim of build, light-brown hair, and with a fiery demeanor when pontificating to a crowd.

Ginsberger was supposed to be in the saloon this evening—the assassin's own compatriots had assured him of this intelligence based on their contacts within the anarchist sphere—and he had studied a photograph of the young rabble-rouser for some days now.

After several minutes of looking around to no avail, he heard a ruckus at the door and glanced over to see several young people energetically shouting rude imprecations as they barged inside. There, in the front entrance, with two young ladies hanging onto his arms, he saw him: Ginsberger—insolent, haughty, and probably intoxicated. An easy mark this night, the man thought.

He watched as Ginsberger and his companions slowly and haphazardly waded through the crowd and took over a small, round table in the center of the room. As they sat down, Ginsberger raised his hand and shouted to the waitress over near the bar. Soon, the quiet spy saw her bring over a round of beers for the group, and he settled into watching the young radical holding court at the table.

He sat there watching unobtrusively and cleverly, waiting for the right moment, the perfect opportunity, when—hopefully—his target would run to the washroom alone, or would step outside into the warm evening air out in front of the noisy tavern. But it would take time—if the opportunity came at all.

He sat there patiently for the next forty minutes, quietly drinking his own beer and fingering the switchblade and small revolver in his pocket, and occasionally feeling the false beard set upon his face with a layer of spirit gum.

Everything is fine.

Then, at precisely 10:45 PM, he saw the young man, Ginsberger, finally stand up and whisper something into the ear of the young woman sitting next to him, and then walk slowly back towards the washroom in the back hallway of the place.

Getting up out of his chair, the man flipped a dime onto the table, straightened out his jacket, and moved quietly, like a ghost, through the crowd towards the back, as well. Dodging several people in the hallway, he came to the door to the washroom and opened it. Walking inside, he immediately saw his quarry in the back, standing unsteadily over the trough, with no other men nearby.

Good. No one else about in here.

He stepped into a stall and closed the door. Extracting the knife, he calmly opened the door again, walked back out, and moved over behind Ginsberger, who was still attempting to relieve himself over the trough in the corner. Stepping just behind and to the left of him, the assailant reached up, cupped his hand over the young anarchist's mouth, and shoved the knife deeply into the side of his neck.

Ginsberger struggled where he stood and attempted to shriek out, but the killer's strong grip on his mouth refused to yield. Muscling the gravely wounded man backwards, the quiet assassin dragged him into a stall, turned him forcefully around and down over the toilet, and pierced the man's back several times—first, near the spine, and then, several times into the lungs and kidneys. He then let the dying man fall gently to the floor on his back and, to make sure of things, slashed the trachea in one, final motion.

Stepping back out of the stall, he quickly secreted the knife in his pocket, exited the washroom, and turned left towards the back exit of the establishment. Stepping outside, he quietly descended the small, wooden staircase to the alleyway and disappeared into the crowds that filled the nighttime streets of the Lower East Side.

60

Falconer awoke to a loud banging on his apartment door over on Manhattan's West Side. Sitting up in bed, he scratched his face and let out a deep exhalation.

Exhausted.

He heard the banging again, and then Waidler's voice: "Sorry, but we need to see you, boss."

He got up out of bed, threw his trousers on, and yelled out from his bedroom: "Coming!"

Walking out to the main room of the apartment, he stood next to the locked door. "Is that you, James?" he asked.

"Yeah, sorry," Waidler replied from the other side of the door. "We've got a body...an anarchist down at a bar on 2d Street."

Falconer quickly unlocked the door and opened it to reveal Waidler standing in the hallway with Halloran. "An anarchist?" he said to them. "Who?"

"Guy by the name of Ginsberger," Waidler said, walking into the apartment, followed by Halloran. "Ernst Ginsberger. A young radical just off the boat, but apparently a friend of Goldman's."

"Damn it," Falconer said. "Ginsberger...I don't know him. Is he prominent in the movement?"

"People say not so much. But he was clearly trying to be—he was hanging out with Goldman and Aronstam and had already made some crazy speeches to groups down there. I guess he fancied himself a big anarchist leader someday."

"And how did he meet his end?"

"Multiple stab wounds. Found on the floor of the toilet at Ritter's Saloon, but nobody saw it happen."

Falconer walked away a few feet, slowly rubbing his forehead with his fingers.

"Well, that's not good," he finally said. "Here, let me get dressed quickly and we'll head down to Oak Street."

61

Falconer paced in front of the desk of Detective Michael O'Brien down at Oak Street as Waidler and Halloran sat nearby. O'Brien sat patiently behind the desk after having just briefed the men on Ernst Ginsberger's grisly murder that occurred at Ritter's Lokal the night before.

"So," Falconer said, "we have just very vague descriptions of this bearded young male who followed Ginsberger into the washroom, correct?"

"That's about it, unfortunately," O'Brien answered. "No one got a very good look at him, and he disappeared down the alley out back."

"Do we know if Ginsberger was having any girl problems? Any affairs with married women perhaps?"

"Nope. He seemed to be unattached, with several lady friends, but nothing indicating that there was some sort of a lovers' triangle going on."

"Well, then, chances are it wasn't a personal matter," Falconer said, looking at all three men. "Agreed?"

The men nodded.

"Then why was he targeted?" Falconer asked, walking over to a window. "He's not considered a great gun in the anarchist world—just a young neophyte trying to attach himself to the movement, a bigmouth trying to get seen. So why kill him, of all people?"

"Maybe his big mouth got a little too big?" O'Brien suggested. "He offended somebody with his wild anarchist talk at some meeting?"

"Could be," Falconer said, walking back into the center of the room. "But that sounds kind of thin. I don't see this sort of killing being about some inflammatory comment made at a beerhall gathering. You said that Ginsberger was getting acquainted with Goldman?"

"Yes. Everyone we've managed to speak to has said the same thing: he was sort of becoming a favorite student of hers, it seems."

"Well then, gentlemen, I think we have a political assassination on our hands. It was a firm statement made by the same group that's been going after Goldman—take your anarchist views out of this city, or else."

"Really?" O'Brien asked. "As we've acknowledged here, this Ginsberger kid was pretty much a nobody—a hanger-on."

"But he was clearly in Goldman's circle," Falconer pointed out, "and the anarchists in town were getting to know him. They just picked a target in that circle and sent their message—a message meant to instill fear in all of them."

"So where do we go from here, boss?" Waidler asked. "We obviously don't have much on this guy who did it."

"No, we don't," Falconer said. "We'll just have to keep running down any leads we can get. Meanwhile, I'm going to go pay the professor a visit. I'll see you gentlemen back at the bureau."

"Got it," Waidler said.

"Detective," Falconer said to O'Brien, "thanks for your time today and please keep us posted as to anything that you might come up with."

"Will do, detective sergeant," O'Brien said. "And good luck on your end."

62

Levine sat at his desk at the Columbia College School of Law and studied the drawing of the tattoo that Falconer had just placed before him. Falconer watched him intently, waiting for any response, but the professor said nothing. Instead, he just kept peering down at the drawing and even gently moved a fingertip over the initials, as if copying the delicate movements of the police artist who had rendered it.

"Hm," he finally said, still looking down at the drawing. "Fascinating. 'PF.'" He then looked up at Falconer. "And you saw the same initials on the knuckles of the assailant up in Cohoes?"

"Yes," Falconer answered. "Right on his middle two knuckles—I saw them as he held tightly onto a branch coming out of the cliff. It was unmistakable, but I didn't think anything of it at the time."

"Yes, I see. Two men with the same cryptic initials tattooed on their bodies. Two men who have both tried to take Miss Goldman's life recently. I agree with you then: these initials signify some bond, some joint purpose or motivation. The tattoos are a symbol of a unified mission."

"But what do the letters mean? That's the problem here. We just have no idea."

Levine got up out of his chair and walked over to his extensive collection of books that sat packed within a long, fixed wall of shelves in his office.

"Let me see here," he said vaguely as he moved his hand slowly across a line of volumes. "Ah, yes—here."

He removed one book and brought it back to his desk. Sitting down, he held it up to Falconer. "Heckethorn's 'The Secret Societies of All Ages and Countries,'" he said. "Most helpful."

"Secret societies?" Falconer asked quizzically.

"Yes. This is a compendium of secret societies and orders that have existed across the globe throughout the ages. It was written almost twenty years ago, so it's still very topical."

"You think it might be helpful in identifying our suspects and their group?"

"Yes, perhaps," Levine replied, rifling through the pages of the book. "From what I have heard about your mysterious adversaries, they do not appear to belong to a sect of any of the well-known secret societies that we know of."

"Like?"

"Like, for instance, the Illuminati, who originated in Bavaria in the latter part of the eighteenth century. Or, of course, the Freemasons, who are still very much active across the globe."

"I've heard of the Freemasons, but not this Illuminati group. Who are they?"

"They existed largely in Bavaria during the time of our own country's founding, but they were banned by edict after only ten years or so after the Bavarian government and the Catholic Church, in particular, grew suspicious of the group's motives."

"What sort of suspicions?"

"Essentially that the Illuminati were behind the French Revolution and were attempting to sow further revolution across Europe and install a radical, anti-clerical, anti-monarchical society."

"I see. And the Freemasons? You don't see any connection to them here?"

"It's hard to say, of course, but I see this mysterious group you're dealing with as being something new, something that has merged aspects of various secret societies into one, new organization."

"What would you think their main purpose is?"

"Again, it's very hard to say at this point, given that we know almost nothing about them. But considering that they have likely tried to murder Miss Goldman and probably did murder this anarchist acolyte, Ginsberger, I would think that they are animated by a deep antipathy for communistic and socialistic societies and for those pushing anti-capitalist views in general. And…"

"And what?" Falconer asked, leaning forward.

"And…well, they likely possess a corresponding hatred of ethnicities and cultures that are not, shall we say, like their own."

"Racism," Falconer said, leaning back in his chair.

"Yes, and probably religious bigotry, too."

"How so?"

"Goldman is Jewish, as was Ginsberger. And as you know, there is a strong anti-Semitic strain that permeates this country, even today. As a Jewish man, I still encounter it daily. And there was something that you told me about your interrogation of the carriage driver who tried to run over Goldman that convinces me of this further."

"And what's that?"

"You said that at some point, the suspect told you that he and his unknown compatriots would protect so-called real Americans, and you wouldn't be able to stop them."

"That's correct."

"Real Americans. What does that mean to you?"

"I'd say that the suspect and his pals don't like certain other citizens," Falconer replied, sitting back in his chair.

"True. And, in fact, these men do not even consider other citizens to be actual Americans. You agree?"

"I do. And let me guess: these other Americans who don't really belong here are…Jews, Negroes, Chinese, Muslims—that sort of thing?"

"Yes, I'm afraid, and it would seem that this secret society that is bent on protecting the country from the hordes of immigrants coming here every day will now revert even to murder to get their message across."

"It seems possible, professor, but how to break into this secret society? They seem very adept at maintaining their secrecy. We're having a tough time finding any leads, and that carriage driver won't break."

"Well, you must simply keep on pursuing any angle that you can, and I'll try to find any clues by studying my various books on these secret orders. I already feel like I know which one has probably been an important influence on the group's methods and beliefs."

"Oh? Which one is that?"

"The Assassins."

"Assassins?"

"Yes, the Order of Assassins was a part of a Shiite Muslim sect called the Nizari Ismaili that operated in the mountainous areas of northern Syria and Persia in the Eleventh and Twelfth centuries. It was formed by a man named Hassan-i Sabbah, a missionary who became known to Crusaders at the time as the Old Man of the Mountain. His sect ruled these mountainous areas with an iron fist, but they did not have a standing army, so they had to rely on a select band of specially trained killers called *fida'i* to enforce their rule. The *fida'i* were skilled warriors who conducted espionage and assassinated particular enemies whenever it was deemed necessary, and they instilled absolute fear wherever they went."

"Hm. Sounds like a novel."

"Yes, but it was all very real. The Assassins were disciples of Hassan who ingested hashish as part of their ritual, and in fact, that is where the name 'Assassin' comes from. Our own word, *assassin*, is derived from the Latin term *assassinus*, which in turn was a corruption of the Arabic words *al-Hashishiyyun* and *hashashun*, or 'hashish-eater.'"

"Fascinating," Falconer said. "I never knew that."

"Well, these assassins were very good at what they did," Levine continued. "And perhaps it was the hashish-induced fervor that allowed them to accomplish their misdeeds under difficult circumstances, because they were generally on suicide missions and didn't survive the assassinations themselves."

"Well, that's too bad for them. And how did they typically eliminate their targets?"

"Interesting that you should ask that. They were, in fact, very well known for using a dagger to accomplish their goals. No other instrument or methods were utilized—just the dagger."

"And you think that perhaps the group we're dealing with has been inspired by this ancient order of assassins?"

"It's hard to tell, but Ginsberger was killed by a dagger of some sort, and the group certainly has similarities to the *fida'i*."

"Well, I'd appreciate it if you keep looking into this, professor, and please let me know if you find any clues worth investigating."

"I surely will. Oh, and before you leave, if I may change the subject, I have more information that might potentially be helpful to you and the inspectors concerning our French bombing suspect, Meunier."

"Really? Please, go on."

"You said previously that Inspectors Houllier and Penwill had investigated whether current vice-presidential candidate, Whitelaw Reid, had had anything to do with the trial and execution of Ravachol when Reid was serving as ambassador over in France earlier this year."

"Yes, that's correct."

"And that they had found nothing in his service in France that would indicate he had any influence on the proceedings against Ravachol."

"That's right. It was a dead end."

"Well, that may be the case, but I have been looking further back into Reid's history, and you are aware that he was editor and owner of the New York Tribune prior to serving as ambassador?"

"Right, and still is the owner."

"True. He has been the owner of that powerful newspaper since 1872, and thus, he is a very important man with a very influential voice in the country."

"I'd agree with that. So, what does this have to do with Meunier?"

"Well, you know of the anarchists who were hanged for the Haymarket bombing in Chicago?"

"Sure. Goldman said it was the guiding force for her and her gang of anarchists."

"That's right. It is the seminal incident that has influenced so many anarchists around the world—the martyrdom of five men in Chicago, which has inspired so many others to take up the bloody work of bombing and killing in the name of anarchism."

"Like Berkman."

"Yes, like Berkman. And Ravachol."

"Ravachol? He was inspired by the Haymarket bombers?"

"Well, he included no express statement saying as much in the scant writings that he left for posterity, but nonetheless, it is well understood at this point that all of these French dynamiters look to the Haymarket five for inspiration and direction. In fact, people who knew Ravachol have said that he would mention the five men when talking about the need to attack the establishment and sow destruction throughout society."

"You mentioned five, professor, but there were only four men hanged as a result of the Haymarket bombing."

"Ah, yes," Levine said, smiling, "that is true, but you forget about Louis Lingg, the fifth suspect."

"Lingg?" Falconer asked.

"Yes. Lingg was a young and charismatic German-born anarchist who was swept up in the prosecution of the Haymarket suspects. He insisted that he had no part in the bombing, but nonetheless, he was convicted and sentenced to die like the others."

"So, what happened to him?"

"He cheated the hangman in the end. Another inmate smuggled in a blasting cap for him, and Lingg set it off in his mouth in an act of suicide and defiance on the evening before the scheduled hanging. Unfortunately for him, the resulting explosion was not immediately fatal, and he lingered in agony for six hours until finally succumbing to his wounds."

"Well, that's a nasty way to die."

"Yes, indeed, but importantly, Reid supported the executions."

"So, we have a powerful owner and editor of a major newspaper who was on record at the time for not having any sympathy for the five accused Haymarket bombers headed to the gallows. And now that very influential newspaper owner is a candidate for vice-president in the national election happening in two months."

"Yes, and we also have a violent acolyte of Ravachol probably loose in our city now, and he almost certainly has taken notice that that newspaper owner who publicly called for the hanging of the Haymarket defendants is currently running for vice-president."

"Taking out Reid would be a great victory for anarchist bombers everywhere around the world, wouldn't it, professor?"

"Yes, a wonderful victory. Especially since Reid and his running mate, President Harrison, are both known to be ardent foes of anarchism. And our French dynamiter, Meunier, might actually have the perfect opportunity coming up here in the city shortly."

"How's that?"

"I read in the papers recently that the Union League Club is hosting Reid for a large campaign dinner and rally at their clubhouse on Rogers Ave. in Brooklyn on the seventeenth," Levine explained. "A large crowd is expected, too. Hundreds, if not thousands, will be parading and cheering in the streets."

"That does seem like a perfect opportunity to cause lots of destruction and casualties, and to assassinate a very important man who wanted the Haymarket men hanged."

"Yes. A most inviting opportunity for a dangerous anarchist, if I may say so myself."

"Well, thank you for this valuable insight, professor," Falconer said, standing up. "I will meet with Penwill and Houllier about this, and keep you posted as to developments."

"I appreciate that," Levine said, also standing up. "These are trying times, and we must be vigilant."

"Agreed," Falconer said, placing his bowler on his head. "We'll keep in touch?"

"Yes—as always."

Falconer then turned and headed out through the door into the hallway, on his way back to the Mulberry Street police headquarters.

63

"That is a very good theory, I must say," Penwill said to Falconer as they sat in the Detective Bureau with Houllier, Halloran, Waidler, Winter, and Kramer. "Very compelling."

"I agree," Houllier said. "This man, Meunier, bombed a café in Paris as revenge for Ravachol's execution, and it is clear that he is not finished exacting retribution from Ravachol's enemies."

"Apparently, this gathering for Reid out in Brooklyn on the seventeenth is going to be big," Falconer said. "You think that's his ultimate target?"

"It seems like a very attractive one," Penwill replied. "If I were the bomb thrower, I'd be looking to it—mass casualties, a crowd to slip away in, chaos and pandemonium, et cetera, et cetera."

"Right," Falconer said. "And because Reid was a well-known supporter of executing the Haymarket suspects, this fits in very well with the revenge motive. We need to alert Reid and his people. Anyone know where he is at this time?"

"I can find out," Waidler said, getting up out of his chair. "Just give me a minute."

"Sure thing," Falconer said. "Thanks."

Waidler then walked out of the office and Falconer turned back to the others. "Well, if Meunier is here," he said, "he's certainly been keeping a low profile. No reports of anyone seeing him from the various precincts, inspector?"

"Nothing, I'm afraid," Penwill replied. "I suppose Meunier lost track of Boucher and just turned his attention towards Reid, given the campaign season. Of course, this is all conjecture—we don't know what he's up to, unfortunately."

"True," Falconer said. "These anarchist types are just puzzling to me. They complain about the government and society and yet they don't really present any viable alternative—they just want to tear everything down with no plan or organization. Just blow everything up and let the rest of us clean up the mess."

"Yes," Houllier said. "They are despicable excuses for human beings. *Ce sont des animaux.* They are animals—nothing more."

"But crafty animals nonetheless," Penwill interjected. "We mustn't underestimate their reserve for cunning and trickery. These men are often-times from the low classes, and yet their actions can betray a certain level of refined guile and ingenuity that could make the most high-born and educated master criminal envious."

"No argument with you there, inspector," Falconer said.

Waidler walked back into the office and sat on the edge of one of the desks. "I just got word down the hall," he said. "Reid is about to leave on a trip out to some campaign rallies in Ohio. He leaves on a train tonight."

"That makes things tough," Falconer said. "We need to alert him and his staff. Any idea what train he's on?"

"Looks like the campaign has its own train leaving from the Jersey City station at six tonight," Waidler replied.

"That gives us a few hours," Falconer said. "But I'm thinking we need to do more than just alert Reid and send him on his way."

"Really?" Penwill said. "What did you have in mind?"

"The threat is getting serious, and I don't think we can sit back and do nothing at this point. How would you feel, inspectors, about joining the vice-presidential candidate for the ride out to Ohio?"

Penwill and Houllier looked at each other, appearing surprised.

"I don't have a problem with it," Penwill said, looking back at Falconer, "but you really think our presence is necessary?"

"I'm sure Reid has security men, but you two know Meunier much better than they do—if they've ever heard of him at all. And at this point, I could see Meunier trying just about anything to make a statement. So, I think it's a precaution we should take."

"Well, I'm not sure how we manage to get included with his party on the trip," Penwill said.

"You leave that to me. Inspector Houllier, have you ever thought about visiting the American Midwest?"

"I have," Houllier answered, "and now would be as good a time as any."

"*Tres bien*, sir," Falconer said. "Let me make some calls."

"Oh, and boss," Waidler said, handing a small, yellow envelope to Falconer, "I also saw this telegram for you out in front."

Falconer took the envelope and scanned the message inside. "What the hell?" he said.

"What is it?" Penwill asked.

"Here—take a look," Falconer said, handing the telegram to him.

Penwill looked down at the message and read it out loud: "'Detective Sergeant Falconer, I know that you are trying to crack the case involving Miss Goldman's assailants. Please know that this organization is more dangerous than even you think, and that it rises to the highest levels of society. I cannot reveal myself at this time, but I can suggest to you that you and your men should start with the men at the saloon. They are a part of it. Sincerely, a friend.'"

Penwill handed the message back to Falconer, who took it and placed it in his breast pocket.

"I'm not sure what to make of it," Falconer said, appearing lost in thought. "This person knows all about the attacks on Miss Goldman, and about our investigation—and even about our visit to the Black Swan place. It's a little shocking, to be honest."

"But this man is obviously an ally," Houllier said. "In fact, he even makes that clear to you by calling himself a friend."

"I agree," Falconer said. "So...who could it be? Some sort of spy or informant who has infiltrated the group?"

"It would appear so," Penwill said. "And if that is the case, then this is an incredible stroke of good luck. You have a man on the inside who has taken you into his confidence. I say that you must take him at his word and heed what he says."

"Does anyone disagree with Inspector Penwill?" Falconer said, looking around at the men, none of whom said anything.

"Well," Falconer continued, "seeing that no one is speaking up, I'll say that I agree with the inspector here—we don't know who this person is, but he knows about us, and he appears to want us to succeed in finding out who these assassins are and bringing them to justice."

"So, what now?" Penwill inquired.

"We need to get you and Inspector Houllier on that train headed to Ohio," Falconer answered, "and then..."

He turned to Winter and Kramer, who had been sitting silently against a wall for the entire conversation.

"Yes?" Penwill asked.

"And then," Falconer continued, "I think we'll have Officers Winter and Kramer here pay the Black Swan another visit."

"Well, jolly good show," Penwill said excitedly. "We're starting to make some progress. Now, lads, let us all find these bastards and then retire for a good cup of tea."

"Sounds good to me," Falconer said. "Gentlemen, let's go alert Byrnes and Steers and then start to ruffle some feathers."

64

Falconer walked up to the front entrance of the Black Swan Saloon late in the evening trailed by Waidler, Halloran, Kramer, and Winter. He looked in a window and then turned to face the men. "All right," he said. "The men we spoke to the first time we dropped by are in there now, and there are a few others loitering at tables, but it looks pretty quiet. I'll stand guard out here with Waidler and Halloran. Winter, you and Kramer go inside and ask these men again about the photo of the carriage driver who almost killed Goldman, and about that tattoo we've seen."

He reached into his jacket and pulled out the mug shot of the carriage driver and the drawing of the tattoo. "Here's the photo and the drawing," he said. "Now listen— they're going to rebuff you and play dumb again, and that's when you start leaning on them a bit...let 'em know that the gloves are off now. All right?"

"Sure thing, detective sergeant," Winter said, "but, uh, what sort of 'leaning on' are you thinking?"

"Any kind that you consider appropriate to get the message across, officer," Falconer answered. "Understand?"

"I think I do," Winter replied.

"Just know that you are authorized at the highest levels of the department to conduct yourself in any manner you deem necessary," Falconer said. "These men are killers—or at least they're involved in a conspiracy to commit killings. So, as far as I am concerned, certain extraordinary steps might have to be taken to ensure 'officer safety' in the course of your investigations. Are we clear?"

"Got it," Winter said.

"Very clear," Kramer answered.

"If things get a little too hot for you, then Waidler, Halloran, and I will come in as backup," Falconer said. "Just know that."

"Thanks," Winter said, "but I think we'll be fine."

He grinned at Kramer, who smiled back at him, and then they opened the door and entered the bar.

65

Winter stepped into the saloon and then stopped, glancing over at the bartender, who glared back at him. Nodding to Kramer, he then walked over to the bar and stood before the sullen man, who was cleaning a glass. "How ya' doin', bud?" he said to him, doffing his bowler. "Quiet night, huh?"

Kramer stepped up to the bar a few steps away and turned around, staring at three men who sat leering back at him from over at a table

"It's okay," the bartender said to Winter.

"Can I get a whisky?" Winter asked.

"Sure," the bartender said. "What brand?"

"Got any Roxbury Rye?"

"Coming right up," the man said tersely. He then turned around and grabbed a bottle from the many that sat like shiny sentinels in front of a large mirror affixed to the wall behind the bar. Turning back, he poured a shot of the whisky and handed it to Winter, who dropped a quarter on the bar.

"Thanks," Winter said. "Say, can you give my partner here a bottle of Bucks Beer, too?"

"Sure," the barkeep answered.

As the man fetched the bottle for Kramer, Winter turned and examined his surroundings. Three grim-faced men sat huddled together at a table on the other side of the room, but apart from them, no other people were present. Winter watched them momentarily, but then his observations were interrupted by a voice coming from his left. Turning in that direction, he saw the younger bartender who had appeared the last time they had visited the place walking into the barroom from the back drying his hands on a dish towel. Winter locked eyes with him and felt immediately that the kid was itching for a fight, such was the antagonistic look upon his young face.

Turning back to the taller and clearly older bartender, Winter pulled out the mug shot of the carriage driver suspect and placed it on the bar. "Say," he said, "you ever seen this guy around here before?"

The bartender looked down at the photo briefly and then peered directly at Winter. "I told you guys before that I ain't never seen him," he said tartly. "Didn't you hear me the first time?"

"Well, what about this here tattoo?" Winter asked, ignoring the man's disagreeable affect as he shoved the drawing in front of his face. "You ever seen that tattoo before, pardner?"

"Nah," the man replied with a sneer, "I never seen it before. Just like I said to your pals the last time. Got it?"

"Well, I heard you," Winter said, gulping down the shot of whisky, "but the thing is, I think you are lying to me, my friend. Is that what you're doing here? You lying to an officer of the law?"

The bartender stood up straight and glared back at Winter for a moment, then spoke in a haughty, condescending tone: "You can take what I said any damn way you want, cop, and then you can take your ass out of here along with your little date over there. You might be cops, but I know plenty of other higher-up cops who could have your job in a second if I complained to them. So, why don't you do yourself a favor, huh? Go take your little detective act elsewhere and don't ever show your face in here again, see?"

Winter smiled as if impressed with the bartender's airs of importance, then he took the empty shot glass in his hand and tossed it up in the air a couple of times. "Well, you're a pretty tough guy," he said to the man. "Hey,

Kramer—did you hear this guy? He said we'd better get outa' here or he'll get his pals over at headquarters to give us our walking papers. Can you imagine that?"

He then turned back to face the man, who remained standing with his arms folded in front of him. Looking past the man, Winter motioned to the large, ornate mirror that backed the bar. "Say, that sure is one swell mirror you got back there," he said. "I'd say that cost a pretty penny. Is that true?"

The bartender remained still as a statue, however, and refused to answer.

"It'd be a shame if something were to happen to it," Winter said. And then he suddenly reared back and threw the shot glass directly at the mirror, just inches from the bartender's head, shattering it into hundreds of pieces.

The bartender ducked instinctively, and then—seeing what Winter had done—reached down behind the bar and raised a large wooden club up over his head with the clear intent to brain the offending officer. Winter, however, reached over the bar, grabbed the man's arm quickly with two powerful hands before the man could bring the heavy club down, and yanked him violently over the bar. Throwing him down to the floor on his back, Winter then smashed the man in the mouth with a meaty fist, and the man's face exploded in blood. Winter then pulled the dazed victim up and flung his face into the bar, resulting in the man falling to the floor in a heap.

Turning to his right, he saw the younger man running down alongside the bar towards him, but Kramer intercepted the interloper mid-stride by smashing his bottle of beer squarely against his forehead, and the young man fell back behind the bar with a groan. Kramer then hopped over the bar and began kicking the hoodlum in the ribs as he lay cowering in pain.

Winter heard a sound to his right and saw the three men at the table throw their chairs back and begin to approach him menacingly. "Oh, you three, too?!" he yelled to them with a grin. "I shoulda' figured as much. You guys look like pieces of shite who *would* be with this crew."

The three men spread out and continued to slowly approach him, and he saw that they now had extracted knives from their pockets. Resisting the desire to pull out his revolver, he reached down instead and grabbed the large, wooden club that the taller bartender had been brandishing just moments before. "That's it, boys," he said to the three men. "Come a little closer now."

The three men looked at each other and then turned and suddenly rushed him. He swung the club mightily at the closest one, striking the man solidly against the side of his head, and the man fell heavily to the floor. The other two got to within a foot of him, swinging out wildly with their knives, when he saw Kramer suddenly burst forth from the side of the room and take down one of them by the legs.

As Winter jousted with the last malefactor, he saw out of the corner of his eye Kramer rolling over on the floor and manhandling his own attacker into a twisted bundle of arms and legs. Kramer then quickly rolled back on top of his unsuspecting prey and wrenched his arm upwards and behind his back, and the man screamed out in pain. The screaming ended, however, when Kramer struck the man hard in the face with a swift kick that left the assailant lying senseless on the floor.

The third attacker swung his knife again at Winter's face, and Winter managed to parry the blow with the wooden club. But then the man started getting closer to him, and Winter could feel the air from the knife's thrusts blowing gently onto his face, and he decided then that extreme measures had to be taken to avert injury. Swinging the club one last time at the thug's face to gain some distance, he then reached down and pulled out his loaded .38 caliber Colt Lightning revolver. "Well, lookie here," he said to the man with a smile. "Forgot I had this."

The man stepped backwards slowly with a pained look on his face. "Now, where you goin'?" Winter asked him, and then he leveled the gun at the man's legs and shot him once in the knee, and the man toppled over in pain.

Just then, Falconer, Waidler, and Halloran burst into the bar, weapons drawn. "You men all right?!" Falconer yelled. "Heard a shot."

"Yeah, just me," Winter said sheepishly as he pointed to the whimpering suspect on the floor clutching his knee as gun smoke wafted through the room. "This one got too close for comfort with his knife—had to bring him down, sir."

Falconer looked around at the all the wounded men lying on the floor. "Who's the main guy?" he asked.

"Over there under the table," Winter said, pointing his finger at the inert form of the tall bartender lying on the floor.

"Right," Falconer said, walking over to the stricken man. "Jimmy, will you grab me that mug of beer on the table there?"

Halloran picked up a half-filled mug of beer on a table and handed it to Falconer, who immediately started pouring the beer on the dazed bartender's face. "Wake up," he said to the man.

As the bartender came to his senses, Falconer knelt next to him. "You remember me?" he said to the man, who blinked several times and winced as he regained consciousness.

"I know who you people are," Falconer continued. "You can't hide anymore in your little secret society. We're onto you and we're going to bring your whole outfit down. When you clean yourself up, go tell your damned bosses that. Understand?"

"You…you can't come in here and do this and get away with it," the man said haltingly through bleeding teeth and lips. "You're dead, cop, and your men, too. Just like the filth you're protecting. We're putting an end to it."

Then the man started laughing, and Falconer got to his feet. "Boys," he said, looking at his men, "I think this place looks a little too clean and put together—let's leave a little message for the owners."

He then lifted a chair up over his head and threw it behind the bar, smashing many bottles to the floor. Waidler, Halloran, Winter, and Kramer started to follow suit, throwing over tables, breaking glasses, and crashing chairs onto the hard floor. After several seconds of this, Falconer then lifted his hand to signal the men to stop. "All right, that's enough," he said. "They'll get the point."

"Hey, boss," Waidler said, "you might want to take a look at this."

Falconer walked over to where Waidler was standing and saw him looking down at an overturned table. "What is it?" he asked.

"Looks like a little slot or drawer attached to the underside of the table," Waidler answered. "Could be a place to quietly place a message or delivery of some sort."

Falconer knelt and examined the small wooden slot about four inches wide and six inches long that was attached by screws to the underside of the table. Reaching inside with his fingers, he felt a paper of some sort and extracted it. It was a small, white envelope containing a folded sheet of paper. Removing the paper, he looked down and examined the words written on it:

Cadere

Directives:

1. Eliminate EG.
2. Continue surveillance.
3. Prominent Jew – Jewtown.

SO ORDERED

Falconer turned to the men standing near to him. "Well, I'll be damned," he said. "These are instructions."

"Instructions?" Waidler asked. "What sort of instructions?"

"Instructions to kill," Falconer said, taking a few steps as he scanned the paper again. "Here—take a look and pass it around."

Waidler took the paper from Falconer and read the words printed on it, then passed it to Halloran, who, after reading for several seconds, handed it in turn to Winter and Kramer.

"What do we do with this?" Waidler asked finally. "It seems clear that this is our mysterious group, but who is it? And what does 'Cadere' mean?"

"I don't know," Falconer answered. "Sounds foreign—perhaps Spanish—but we can find out. Whatever it means, it appears to be the name of our illustrious gang of assassins."

"And there's no address given," Waidler said, "so we don't know where it came from."

"No, they wouldn't be so sloppy. But notice that they did mention continuing to target 'EG.'"

"Emma Goldman."

"Right. They didn't try to disguise that much."

"Well, do we take it with us?"

"Yes, James. Someone left it in there, so now it's officially abandoned property and we can take it. And they'll realize shortly that we now have in our possession one of their orders to kill someone, and that'll rattle them a bit."

"All right," Waidler said, placing the envelope and note into his jacket pocket. "Sounds good."

"And I'm going to have Professor Levine meet us at headquarters if he can," Falconer said. "He's quite good with foreign languages. For now, let's get the hell out of here, gentlemen. These thugs have some cleaning up to do."

He then turned and headed for the door, and the other men followed, leaving the broken and trashed barroom behind them.

66

Penwill sat in vice-presidential candidate Whitelaw Reid's special car as the campaign train rumbled through the night somewhere in central New York State. Across from him, Houllier dozed peacefully in his own seat while Reid and a few of his staffers quietly conferred across the aisle in their own plush, cushioned seats covered by red velvet. A few security men, meanwhile, stood like lifeless, sculpted idols at each end of the car—watching, waiting, and scanning the windows for any suspicious activity.

Penwill looked outside again and saw only the black night and the occasional dark silhouette of a grove of trees or a farmhouse rushing by. He wondered if this was all futile—if he and Houllier were simply being led astray, out into the American heartland, for a meaningless campaign trip while Meunier was actually getting ready to attack a different target back in the city. The theory made sense, at least—that Meunier would want to send a message of revenge by assassinating one of America's most prominent newspapermen who had enthusiastically and loudly called for Ravachol's execution, especially a newspaperman who was currently running to be vice president of the United States.

But would the slippery Frenchman with the hunchback come all the way out here, onto the long, flat prairies, so far away from the teeming city where he could better hide and disappear into the crowds, in order to accomplish his deadly mission? Penwill thought not and mused with some agitation that the dark-eyed bomb thrower was at this very minute getting ready to toss his sticks of dynamite into a bustling café in Greenwich Village, just as he had done in Paris already.

The train car jostled slightly as it went over a bump and he saw Houllier wake and look around momentarily, then lay his head back against the window and fall into slumber again.

He then glanced at Reid to his left and saw the man staring intently at some papers being shown to him by an aide: a speech to be made in Cincinnati, likely. Reid did not appear perturbed in the least about the possibility of a French assassin being on his trail, and Penwill remembered how the candidate had seemed slightly confused and irritated to learn that two foreign service detectives were being placed on his train to protect him against a bomb threat.

He looked down at his watch—11:00 PM—and then gazed out the window again. He thought of Meunier, the radical devotee of Ravachol, and of Falconer and his men, who were now probably tramping about through the dark, New York City streets in search of the other mysterious assassins who were targeting the very radicals whom Meunier represented.

Such a strange world, he thought. Killers and fanatics, both the hunters and the hunted. He looked out the window again and saw only the darkness, and he reached into his jacket and placed his hand on one of his British Bulldog revolvers sitting in its holster, as if doing so would somehow help make the world seem safe and ordered again. And then he waited.

Saturday, September 10, 1892

67

Falconer glanced up from his desk in the Detective Bureau and saw Waidler leading Levine in from the hallway. "Ah," he said, getting up out of his chair and approaching the two men, "glad you could make it, professor, and sorry to intrude on your weekend."

"Not a problem at all," Levine said, nodding to the other men gathered in the office—Winter, Kramer, and Halloran.

"Here, please have a seat," Falconer said, moving a chair near to Levine. "I have something I want you to see."

"Really?" Levine said, sitting down in the chair. "I'm very intrigued."

"Well, the other night we had a little altercation at that bar up on Thirty-Sixth, and we discovered a little mail slot attached to the underside of a table in the barroom."

"Hm. A mail slot under a table? That's odd."

"Yes, it is, but what was really interesting and concerning was what we found inside the slot: an envelope containing instructions for somebody."

"I see. And what sort of instructions?"

"Here, see for yourself."

Falconer then handed the envelope with the note inside to Levine, who carefully extracted the note and read for several seconds. Levine then placed the note back into the envelope and looked up at the men. "Well, this is a fascinating development," he said.

"I agree," Falconer said, taking the envelope back.

"These are clear instructions to commit murder and conduct surveillance on anarchist groups within the city."

"And it's clear that one of the persons targeted is Goldman. EG."

"Yes, I saw that immediately, too. She is obviously still a priority."

"And this mention of targeting some 'prominent Jew.' Any doubts about this group's motivating force?"

"None. It is obvious that his group is stridently anti-Semitic and—equally likely—stridently 'anti-foreigner,' I'd say."

"I think you're exactly right, professor," Falconer said, walking a few steps inside the circle of men. "It's not too difficult to see, I'm afraid. But what's confusing is this prominent reference to 'Cadere,' at the top of the page. Any idea what that might mean? Sorry, but we're not really the greatest with foreign languages."

"Yes, in fact, I do know what it means, gentlemen. It's Latin, and it means quite simply, 'fall'—or perhaps more accurately, 'to fall.'"

"'To fall?'" Falconer said. "What the devil does that mean?"

"Well, secret societies and groups often use symbolic language to identify themselves. Thus, instead of identifying itself with more literal terms, a group will use a name that is more symbolic, mysterious, and, frankly, eye-catching—like the Illuminati I told you about recently."

"Yes, I get what you're saying, professor. It makes sense, but 'to fall?' That's kind of a strange name for a band of assassins, don't you think?"

"It could mean any number of things. To fall into sin, or the fall of society. We just don't know, though, and perhaps that is the whole point—that only those admitted into the group can know and the rest of us are, as they say, kept in the dark."

"I think you're right, but we're in agreement that 'Cadere' or 'to fall' appears to be the group's name?"

"Yes, that appears to be the case by how prominent it appears at the top of the page. You are facing a group operating in the shadows that calls itself, 'Cadere.' Truly fascinating."

"And, as usual, the question for us now is where do we go from here? We don't know where this 'High Council' meets or where it sends its directives from—or who's even on it. We have a name now, but we're still in the dark, as you said."

"But what you do have is an informant or spy working with you. You obviously don't know who this person is, but you do know that he is on the inside, or at least close to the inside of the group. And, hopefully, he will be in touch with you again very soon."

"That's true. We do have that."

He then looked over at Waidler and Halloran. "Meanwhile, do we still have men on Goldman?" he asked.

"We do," Waidler answered. "Shadowing her day and night."

"Well, I'm sure she's pleased about that," Falconer said with a smile. "And let's also keep eyes on the saloon—see if anyone of note shows up."

"Will do, boss," Waidler said.

"Professor, thank you again for dropping by and giving us your input on this," Falconer said, shaking Levin's hand.

"Glad to," Levine said. "Anytime, and please keep me posted as to developments."

"We will do that. All right, then, men—let's head out."

"Oh, by the way," Levine said, "any word from Inspector Penwill?"

"No, not yet, but they're leaving Ohio tonight. I assume that it's been an uneventful journey so far, and it'll probably be a quiet ride back."

"Excellent," Levine said, smiling. "Very good to hear."

68

H oullier sat inside the rumbling train and finished reading a story in the New York Daily Tribune about how all the grand government buildings in Paris were undergoing a major cleaning and restoration before the opening of Parliament. He then placed the newspaper down and looked at Penwill sitting opposite him, reading his own newspaper. They had been riding along in Ambassador Reid's campaign car for some time after having stopped in Cedarville, just outside of Dayton, to spend a day with Reid's mother.

Then, after having stopped momentarily at a station in Steubenville along the Ohio-West Virginia border, the train had gained steam again and was headed towards the long railroad bridge that traversed the great Ohio River. It was late at night and most of the passengers on the train were sleeping comfortably in their seats. Houllier, however, was pensive, wondering where on earth his nemesis, Meunier, was lurking. They had checked the train for suspicious activity thoroughly at each stop, to the point where Reid's campaign staff expressed frustration at all the delays incurred from so many precautionary measures. Now, they were headed over the river and briefly into West Virginia, and then onward to Pittsburgh and Philadelphia, before the final leg into Manhattan.

Houllier looked around and scanned the car. Virtually nothing was happening around him and the car seemed relatively quiet and peaceful as the eastern Ohio countryside whizzed by in the darkness outside. Some security men chatted and laughed together quietly at their posts at the ends of the car and Reid was safely ensconced in his sleeping compartment in the next car forward. Houllier decided to get up out of his seat and stretch his legs and use the lavatory. "I am just going to the washroom, my friend," he said to Penwill.

"Oh?" Penwill said, looking over his newspaper. "Jolly good."

Houllier then walked down the aisle past the various sleeping staff members and a few journalists, and then crossed over outside into the next car to reach the washroom. He went inside the small compartment, relieved himself, and then, while washing, scanned his face in the small mirror attached to the wall.

Tired looking, he mused *I am really not good with traveling by trains at all hours of the night.*

Stepping back into the corridor, he nodded at Reid's security man standing near the sleeping compartments, and then turned to cross back over into the main campaign car at the back of the train. As he stepped into the rear car and out of the rushing wind, however, he thought he heard something and stopped.

Qu'est-ce que c'est? Am I imagining things?

He stood still, waiting for another sound, to make sure that perhaps it was just something striking against the fast-moving train—a tree branch or a small rock, for instance.

Hearing nothing, he took a step to move down the aisle but then was stopped by the sound again.

Yes, indeed. A knock or thud. Where, though? Above me?

He looked up at the ceiling of the car and tried to pinpoint the location of the dull thudding sound. And then he heard it again, faintly.

Thud...thud...

Oui...above me...up on the roof...there is someone walking up there...

He immediately reached for his French Chamalot-Delvigne model 1873 11-millimeter revolver in his jacket and raced down to where Penwill sat reading his paper still. "Charlie," he said in a hushed voice. "Quickly—a man is up on the roof now. I will tell the men at the front and then climb up—you go to the back."

"Good god," Penwill said as he rose quickly out of his seat and brandished one of his revolvers. "How the devil did someone get up there?"

Houllier turned and ran back to the front of the car where the two security men appeared anxious about the ruckus. "Gentlemen," Houllier said to them quickly, "we believe there is a man on the roof. You stay here and cover the inside and we will go up."

"Got it," one of the men said.

"And please alert your man in the sleeping car," Houllier instructed.

"Will do," the man replied.

Houllier then stepped out into the wind and noise between the cars and looked around the corner of the rear car, spotting a ladder affixed to its side panel. Looking quickly back the other way, he could see in the distance the land slowly descending until it met the approaching riverbed and the great railroad bridge that spanned the river, and he knew then that they were about to cross the Ohio into West Virginia.

Reaching up, he grabbed the ladder firmly and pulled himself up as the ground rushed by just a few feet away from him. Ascending the ladder quickly, he peered down the length of the roof of the car and spotted a dark figure halfway down, slowly walking towards the rear.

Meunier.

Houllier struggled up to his feet and leveled his revolver at the figure. "MEUNIER!" he shouted over the noise of the train and wind. "T'ARRETE, BATARD!"

In the darkness, he saw the figure turn slightly, and then crouch down quickly near to the edge of the roof of the car.

Mon Dieu, what the hell is he doing?

He walked slowly towards the crouching figure, but as he got to within twenty feet of him, he saw the man pull something out of his jacket. Houllier's heart raced as he realized in the dim light what it was: a stick of dynamite. "ARRETER, FILS DE PUTE!" he yelled at the man. "STOP!"

The man, however, ignored his commands and instead, pulled out what appeared to be a box of matches and carefully lit the fuse. Houllier aimed his revolver and pulled the trigger twice, but the man laid down flat just before the shots rang out and simultaneously smashed one of the windows just inches below him and threw the stick into the car. Houllier let off another round but missed striking the man by inches as the man rolled back to the center of the roof and got to his feet quickly.

Just then, Houllier saw a glowing object fly back out of the window and drop quickly into the darkness towards the river.

The dynamite.

He immediately fell to his stomach and held tightly onto the roof as best he could, waiting for the explosion, which came seconds later. The enormous sound and force shook the train roughly and he feared that it would be shaken off its tracks and fall into the river, but he was relieved to see that it remained moving steadily on its way towards the other shore. He looked up then to find his mysterious adversary slowly creeping towards the back of the car. Penwill suddenly appeared at the top of the other ladder that ascended at the rear of the car, and Houllier saw that his friend was aiming his own revolver at the attacker.

Standing up, he slowly moved towards the trapped man to arrest him, but suddenly the man stepped to the side of the roof, looked back at him and Penwill briefly, and jumped into the river. Houllier ran to where the man had leaped and crouched down carefully, scanning the dark river below, but he could see no one on the surface—just a bubbling little circle where the bomber had plunged into the river's depths just seconds before.

Penwill crawled up to him and looked down to the river, too. "Well," Penwill yelled over the noise of the train and rushing wind, "looks like we missed him again! Not sure if he can survive the fall, but we can alert the locals and start a search. At least I got the dynamite out of the car!"

"Ah, it was you!" Houllier shouted excitedly. "I thought for certain that we would all be blown up, and then I saw the little stick fly out into the night like a bird! Good thinking, *mon ami*. You have saved us from certain catastrophe!"

"Yes, well, I only wish we had caught the bugger. Let's get off this roof and see to the ambassador!"

"Yes! Let us go down!"

The two men then slowly crawled back to the ladder and descended to the landing as the powerful train surged across the long, dark bridge towards the West Virginia shore in the distance.

69

Falconer stood with his men and Penwill and Houllier in Byrnes' second floor office at the Mulberry Street headquarters. Byrnes sat in his chair, quietly smoking a cigar after having just heard a summary of the attack on Reid's campaign train on its way back from Ohio. He placed the cigar in a crystal ashtray on the desk and looked up at Falconer and the inspectors. "So," he said, "no word on the manhunt out near the river?"

"Nothing yet, I'm afraid, sir," Penwill said. "They've got many men and dogs searching both sides of the river, but no trace of Meunier."

"And you're sure it is Meunier, as opposed to some other lunatic agitator?"

"Inspector Houllier got the best look at the man, sir," Penwill said, looking over at Houllier, "and he feels certain that it was, indeed, Meunier."

"Inspector?" Byrnes said, looking at Houllier.

"Yes, superintendent," Houllier said, "I saw his face very briefly and it appeared to be Meunier. Plus, the way he walked was strongly indicative of a man with Meunier's physical deformities."

"I see. And does anyone appear to know of this in the press? I haven't seen anything."

"No, sir," Falconer answered. "The ambassador agreed with us that we should keep this all very quiet for now, and thus, the authorities conducting the search out there are just telling the press that they're looking for an escaped inmate from the local jail."

"Good," Byrnes said, picking up his cigar again. "The last thing we need is a public panic that a French dynamiter is on the loose."

"Yes, sir," Falconer said.

"So, what's next?" Byrnes asked. "Do you think this Meunier character will try to come back to New York, or will he just flee the country?"

"We believe that—given his failure the other night—he won't give up," Penwill replied. "The ambassador is clearly his target of revenge, and these French anarchist bombers do not scare easily and are very persistent, I'm afraid."

"Understood," Byrnes said, taking a drag of his cigar. "And what of the ambassador? Is he suspending his campaigning, I hope?"

"Unfortunately, no," Falconer said. "He's a very stubborn man and told us that he will not be intimidated by violent anarchist bomb throwers. In fact, he's getting ready for a large campaign gathering in Brooklyn this weekend."

"Brooklyn?" Byrnes said, sitting up straighter in his chair. "This weekend? After he nearly got blown up on his train?"

"Yes," Penwill said. "As Detective Sergeant Falconer said, Reid takes a hard line on anarchist agitators and he is determined not to be cowed by them. He is planning on attending a dinner and rally with Republican groups out at the Union League Club on Bedford Ave."

"And how many supporters are expected at this rally?" Byrnes inquired.

Falconer looked at Penwill, who slowly turned to Byrnes and spoke: "Well, sir, they are expecting above a thousand persons in the streets."

"Good god," Byrnes exclaimed. "More than a thousand people in one place? It's a perfect target for a blood-thirsty bomber such as Meunier."

"We know," Falconer said. "We've tried to dissuade Reid, but he won't budge—he says it's giving in to the barbarians."

"Well, then, we're just going to have to take exceptional efforts to watch over this rally, gentlemen," Byrnes said. "If Meunier is here again, I'm certain that he'll try to blow up a bomb in that crowd. So, do what you need to do, Falconer. If you need more men, get them with my approval. Stop at nothing to prevent an incident. Do you understand?"

"Absolutely, sir," Falconer said.

"Good," Byrnes said. "And Inspectors Penwill and Houllier, I congratulate you on your efforts on that train. Our country owes its thanks to you."

"Thank you, sir," Penwill said.

"*Merci beaucoup*, superintendent," Houllier said. "I appreciate your kind words."

"Thank you, gentlemen," Byrnes said. "And Falconer, keep me posted."

"Will do, sir," Falconer said. "Let's go, gentlemen."

He then turned and headed out into the hallway, followed by the two inspectors and Waidler, Halloran, Winter, and Kramer.

70

Falconer strolled into the Detective Bureau the morning after the debriefing with Byrnes and sat down at his desk. He had been busy over the past eighteen hours recruiting men to help watch over the upcoming weekend political rally in Brooklyn and was about to send out more requests when Waidler came into the room behind him and spoke: "Boss, I got something for you—think you'll be interested."

"Morning, James," Falconer said. "What do you have?"

"Looks like another message to you from that unknown informant with our band of assassins," Waidler said, handing a small, white envelope to him.

Falconer took the envelope and looked at the address typed on its front:

Det. R. Falconer

Detective Bureau

300 Mulberry St.

New York, NY

Opening the envelope, he then unfolded a piece of paper and read the type-written message:

Falconer:

I applaud your handling of the men down at the Black Swan. Now they know that the police are onto them. However, this means that they will increase their efforts and stop at nothing to achieve their malevolent goals. Thus, be ever vigilant—they are dangerous!

I would like to meet you in person, but we must be exceedingly discrete. Meet me alone at 1:00 pm Thursday at the park benches directly behind the Beethoven statute in Central Park. Do not say anything to me—just sit near to me and feign reading a newspaper so that I can speak. I will have further directions. I know what you look like. I will have on a yellow necktie with eyeglasses.

A friend

"Well, I'll be damned," Falconer said, looking up at Waidler and the others. "Our friend wants to meet me in Central Park tomorrow at one. He says he'll have more directions."

"So, what do we do?" Waidler asked.

"We meet him. But just me—he insisted that I be alone. However, I'll have you and Halloran keeping watch from a distance. All right?"

"Sure thing."

"Meanwhile, any idea where the two inspectors are this morning?"

"They said they had an appointment with Reid out at his mansion in Harrison. Something about trying to convince him to cancel his rally this weekend."

"Really? Well, they'll need a little luck with that."

Waidler grinned and then sat down at his desk to sort through his own telegrams and messages, and Falconer sat back in his chair, thinking of

Penwill and Houllier and their meeting with the vice-presidential candidate, Whitelaw Reid.

71

Penwill looked ahead at the imposing structure as the wagon bearing him and Houllier ambled up the driveway of Whitelaw Reid's impressive estate in Harrison, New York. As they got closer, he could see how truly immense it was: the grand, stone castle built in the style of the imposing castles that lined the Rhine in Germany.

"It is *tres magnifique*, my friend," Houllier said.

"Indeed, Prosper," Penwill said. "And it's practically brand new. The old place burned down several years ago, and so they've been building this castle since then. They just opened it up this year, actually."

"Well, clearly the ambassador is an important man. I didn't know newspaper men could become so wealthy."

"Well, I'm sure he's done well, but I think most of this was actually bought with his wife's money. She has a very wealthy father."

"Ah, yes, I see. The easiest way to become a millionaire: marry a woman who is already one."

Penwill chuckled as the driver pulled the wagon to a stop in front of the large front doors of the castle. "Well, here we are, Prosper," he said.

He climbed down from the wagon, followed by Houllier, and immediately saw a man approaching from the house. It was Leominster Finch, Reid's personal secretary.

"Ah, inspectors," Finch said enthusiastically. "So nice to see you again. I hope the train ride up was quieter than our return to New York?"

"Yes, very much so," Penwill answered. "No bombs this time, fortunately."

"Well, the ambassador is waiting for you," Finch said. "Just follow me, gentlemen."

He then led the two men into the front entry hallway, the walls and floor of which Penwill observed were made of a most exquisite pink marble. Above a large, ornate fireplace, he could see a very fine-crafted frieze that extended along the top of the marble walls. He stopped momentarily to gaze at the amazing detail, and Finch walked back to him. "Ah, yes," Finch said, looking up at the frieze. "Sculpted by the well-known firm, Salviati and Company, and imported from Italy."

"Most impressive, Mister Finch," Penwill said. "I'm sorry—shall we?"

"Yes, please," Finch said. "Ambassador Reid is just up the staircase here."

He then led the two inspectors up a shiny, marble staircase at the end of the hallway and down a hallway to a large, wooden door, which he opened. "Please, gentlemen," he said, "after you."

"Why, thank you, Finch," Penwill said, walking by him to enter the room.

"*Merci, Monsieur Finch*," Houllier said, following Penwill in.

The three men then entered a spacious, well-furnished office that over-looked a large, green lawn below. Standing over near two great windows that allowed plentiful sunlight into the room was Reid, who turned and spoke: "Ah, inspectors—so nice to see you again. I hope you had an uneventful journey?"

"Yes, we did, ambassador," Penwill replied. "Thank you for seeing us."

"It is my pleasure, gentlemen. Please, have a seat."

The three men then sat down in a group of ornately carved and well-lacquered chairs standing in the middle of the office, and Reid offered the men a drink.

"No, thank you, ambassador," Penwill said, "but we appreciate the offer, of course."

"Yes, of course," Reid said. "Now, how can I help you?"

"Well," Penwill said, "we understand how you feel about the upcoming rally this weekend, but nonetheless, we must impress upon you the extreme danger posed by this anarchist, Meunier, and we would urge you again to consider canceling the event."

Reid smiled wanly and sat motionless for a moment, as if gathering his thoughts, and then he spoke in a calm, almost reassuring tone: "Gentlemen, I know that this man is still out there, and he may likely be entertaining the idea of attacking me at the rally. I recognize the seriousness of the threat and I obviously don't wish to endanger any of my Republican supporters. Nevertheless, and after careful thought, I have concluded that we must go on with the campaign and not let these anarchist troublemakers interfere with our work."

He raised his hands up in front of him and gestured excitedly as he continued: "Can you imagine if we give in to these people? What message will be sent? It will be that any crazed bomb thrower who hates America can, with the slightest threat, completely muzzle us and send us hiding in our bunkers. We cannot give in to that, gentlemen. We cannot let the barbarians and criminals win. We must stand up and face them and destroy them with our words and with our might. It is the only way, I am afraid."

Penwill looked down at the floor briefly and then looked back up and smiled slightly at Reid. "I understand your position, ambassador," he said, "and, in fact, I salute you for being committed to it. But still, I have grave worries about the security of this event. We will have many men mingling in the crowd and working the perimeter, but it is impossible to cover every square inch."

"Yes, I know," Reid said, "but I am confident that my security men, in conjunction with you and your friends with the New York and Brooklyn police departments, will be able to thwart any attempted attack. The security will be extremely tight and any attacker like Meunier will find it extremely difficult to accomplish his goals."

"Yes, well, I suppose you're right, sir," Penwill said. "We thank you for your time and we will see you at the rally."

"Yes, thank you, gentlemen," Reid said, standing up to shake hands with the two men.

"Thank you, ambassador," Houllier said. "We can see our way out."

"Oh, nonsense," Reid said. "Finch here can lead you back to the front and your cab that is waiting. Good day, gentlemen."

"Good day, sir," Penwill said, and then Finch led the two inspectors quietly back out into the hallway and downstairs to their waiting wagon, where they would begin their journey back to Manhattan twenty miles away.

Thursday, September 15, 1892

72

Falconer strolled down the tree-lined Mall in Central Park while quietly smoking a cigarillo amidst hundreds of other pedestrians enjoying the picturesque surroundings. The temperature had dropped to a comfortable sixty-five degrees in the past day and the mild weather had clearly drawn out many people who wanted to enjoy the burgeoning fall weather in the grand, lush park lying in the middle of Manhattan.

As he walked, he took note of the variety of citizens dotting the pleasant scene: two women wearing their finest afternoon dresses with ornate, flowered hats leaning off their brows as they walked chummily together and quietly chuckled over something known only to them; a man holding the reins as he slowly walked alongside a team of two miniature ponies drawing a small wagon carrying an obviously well-heeled mother with her young, scowling son; a swarthy, young father dressed in a three-piece suit gently holding the hand of his toddler dressed smartly in a little blue sailor suit; the quiet man in a black bowler sitting alone on the benches lining the Mall to the left, drowsily reading his newspaper with lit pipe billowing soft puffs of tobacco smoke into the air around him; and the strapping, mustachioed beat cop walking jauntily down the way while swinging his billy club by its attached leather strap and whistling an upbeat, marching tune.

There were hundreds of them, all either strolling down the wide expanse of the Mall or sitting beside it, taking in the fresh air away from the busy city streets and getting a brief break from the harsh, breakneck pace of the growing metropolis that surrounded them.

Falconer walked on, taking in the sights and sounds of the busy meeting place and all the happy people wandering through it, until, moving closer to the shores of the great lake ahead of him, he spied to his right the tall, commanding face of the great composer, Ludwig van Beethoven, set upon a tall base of exquisite, gray marble. Walking closer to it, he looked up and studied the bust of the great musical genius for a moment: thick, wavy hair growing out of the tall forehead; two, deep-set eyes set fixedly on something seemingly obstructing his way; the small, contentious frown expressing an unbreakable will and imperious swagger. Shrugging, Falconer then pulled a copy of the morning's newspaper out of his jacket pocket and looked beyond the statue, over to the benches where several people sat minding their business amidst the great murmuring crowd moving slowly down the Mall.

He walked closer and looked for a man in a yellow tie with eyeglasses and saw him sitting alone at the end of the bench to the far right, away from the other people. The man held a newspaper in his hands down near his lap and appeared to be deeply engrossed in a story. Falconer walked up and took a seat about two feet away from him and unfolded his own newspaper, bringing it up closer to his face to shield himself from the gazes of strangers.

"Thank you for coming," the man finally said after a few seconds. "We must be very short with this and discrete, as I said."

"Understood," Falconer said quietly. "Who are you? A member of Cadere?"

The man chuckled briefly. "Oh, so you know the name?" he asked. "I didn't think you'd be that far along. But yes—I was a member of it, until things got too out of control and wrong. Then I started rebelling."

"Are you still in their good graces?"

"So far, I think, but one never knows with these people. They are very tight with security and could expose me at any time."

"So why are you doing this?"

"Because it started out as something noble and grand, and then it descended into something ugly and…well, un—American, in my opinion. I could no longer be a party to such despicable behavior."

"Who controls it?"

"Well, there are many who have a say in its direction, and many of them are some of our nation's most enterprising and successful power-brokers in business, finance, and politics. But there is one who is really controlling things at this point. He has made his imprint felt and they have allowed him to pervert the society's original aims."

"Do you have a name?"

"I do, but first, we need to arrange for you and your men to come get evidence of the group's misdeeds and its organization—documentary evidence that will help you bring down the whole place, as it deserves. I have taken a small apartment in the Tenderloin—55 West 37th Street, Apartment 402. Meet me there just before dusk tomorrow—say, seven o'clock. I will give you everything I have, and everything you need to bring them down. You have that address?"

"Yes."

"Good. And again, be discrete. Make sure no one follows you. They have men everywhere."

"Everywhere? Like where specifically?"

"In the halls of government. In the corporations…even in your police department."

"You haven't said what their overriding purpose is. What is it that they want exactly?"

"To control how the country works, thinks, and looks. To get the country back to the way they believe it should be—the way they believe it was meant to be."

"And what the hell does that mean?"

"I think you know what that means, detective sergeant. I think you're aware by now what their animating motive is."

"Purity of blood," Falconer said after a pause. "A permanent, white, Christian, controlling class. Am I correct?"

"You are," the man said, seemingly surprised. "You are a very perceptive man."

"But I'm just one man."

"Yes, but one man can destroy an entire wooden bridge by simply removing one, key supporting strut—one essential element to the bridge's structural integrity. Pull that one strut out, and…the whole bridge collapses. You don't need an army to do that."

"Well, that's encouraging."

"I must go, and we've been here much too long already."

"Wait. I need that name."

"Of course. Walter Bliss."

"What?" Falconer said incredulously. "*The* Walter Bliss? The millionaire?"

"The same," the man said calmly. "All roads lead to him, but it will be difficult to show that."

"So where do we begin?"

"By meeting me as we've arranged. Now I really must go. Until tomorrow evening."

The man then moved to stand up, but Falconer stayed seated as he spoke again: "I never got your name."

"A friend," the man said quietly before striding off and disappearing into the crowd walking down the Mall.

73

Houllier walked over to the dresser in his room at the Occidental Hotel and grabbed a necktie out of the top drawer. Standing before the mirror that was attached to the wall behind the dresser, he fixed the tie snugly around his collar and straightened it for effect.

Tres bien.

He then checked his watch: 6:30 PM. Right on time for dinner with Penwill down the block at a small café.

Circling back to the small bed that was set against the wall across the room, he sat down and looked at the pile of papers and envelopes that he had just left there. One manila envelope caught his eye—a large yellow one stuffed with photographs—and he finally picked it up and reached inside. Pulling out several photographs, he selected one and held it up in front of his face: Ravachol.

The unrepentant bomb thrower was shown standing in prison garb alongside two swarthy policemen dressed smartly in military uniforms and wearing large bicorn hats emblazoned with fancy cockades on their front. Houllier studied the prisoner's face. It appeared calm and relaxed— almost serene—and betrayed no sign of fear or dread of his approaching execution.

How, he wondered, could a man be so composed, so self-confident and poised as he faced certain death by guillotine? What was going through his mind as he spent those last few days lingering in his cell and waiting for the great blade to drop and send him to eternity?

He placed the photograph down and looked at another one in his hand: a police mugshot of Ravachol taken after he had had been arrested following a violent scuffle with several officers at a restaurant on the Rue Magenta. The arrestee's normally combed hair was in disarray, and his chiseled good looks were now marred by bruises and cuts arising from the arresting officers' blows and kicks. And yet, the stark defiance and unyielding rectitude in his own personal beliefs were still readily apparent in his faintly detectable smile and smug expression, and Houllier found himself admiring for a moment the determination and commitment of the doomed prisoner in the face of a lost cause and impending death.

This is why they follow him, he thought. *This is why he is not truly dead. He lives on and is celebrated for his defiance of authority and his absolute commitment to his cause. You knew that this would happen upon your death at the hands of the executioner, didn't you? You knew the Meuniers and the Francois and all the other frightful anarchists would follow in your footsteps and continue with your work. You are not dead, after all. And perhaps you are even stronger now.*

He placed the photographs back in the manila envelope and stood up. Grabbing his jacket, he slipped out of the room, locked the door behind him, and headed to the stairway leading down to the lobby of the hotel.

74

Falconer walked up to the front steps of 55 West 37th Street with Halloran, Waidler, Winter, and Kramer right behind him. It was a five-story walk-up, and, at this hour—7:00 PM—the street was relatively quiet as the sunlight slowly faded away and the more welcomed, cooler evening air seeped in between the buildings and along the sidewalks, lending some much-needed relief to the city's overheated denizens.

"Well, this is it," he said to the men. "Let's head up—Apartment 402."

He then led the men up the stairs and into the old apartment building, the floors of which creaked and groaned as they slowly moved up the stairwell to the fourth floor. Reaching the top, he signaled for the men to stop, and peered down the hallway, which was silent and devoid of life.

"Draw your weapons," he instructed. "You never know who might be watching or waiting."

As the men did as they were told, he unholstered his large .45 caliber revolver and started walking down the hallway, constantly scanning his surroundings for the slightest movement. Reaching Number 402, he turned to face the others. "I'll knock," he said. "Just be prepared for anything."

Rapping lightly on the battered and scarred door, he waited to hear some sign of life, but there was just silence. He knocked again, louder this time, and waited for several seconds, but there was no response or sound from behind the door. He then tried the doorknob and found that it was unlocked. Turning back to the men, he nodded briefly and then turned the doorknob slightly and gently pushed the door open. He looked inside and saw an unkempt, barren apartment that was still partially lit by the fading sunlight creeping in through two large windows directly opposite him. Sitting in a chair in front of the windows, and facing away from the door, was a figure, silent and unmoving.

Falconer moved closer and spoke: "It's us. Are you all right?" But the figure remained still as a statue and said nothing in return. Falconer looked back at the men, and then said quietly, "Something's wrong. Cover me."

Waidler motioned for the others to spread out into the room and positioned himself in the doorway in case anyone tried to enter from the hallway. Falconer then slowly approached the sitting figure until he came around to face him: it was the man, the "friend" who had met him in the park, and he was motionless with his eyes staring straight ahead at the windows.

"James," Falconer said quietly, motioning for Waidler to approach. Waidler quickly walked up and looked closely at the man. "I think he's dead," Falconer said.

Waidler reached down and felt for a pulse on the man's neck. Turning to Falconer, he shook his head. "No pulse, boss, but...he's still warm."

A noise suddenly came from above them out on the stairwell—a quick, jarring sound of perhaps a door closing or a heavy object falling to the floor. Falconer looked up at the ceiling and then quickly over at the men. "Up on the roof!" he said. "Jimmy, you stay here with the body."

He then ran out into the hallway, joined by Waidler, Winter, and Kramer. Sprinting up the last two flights of stairs, they came to a heavy, metal door that clearly led out to the roof of the building. Falconer tried to push it open, but it wouldn't budge. "Here," he said to Waidler, "help me shove it open—he must have put something behind it."

The two of them then rammed their shoulders into the door, and it moved slightly, but still, it would not allow entry onto the roof. They tried a second time, and it moved ever so slightly again. "Something heavy behind it," Waidler said breathlessly.

"Here, boss," Winter said from behind them, "let me give the son of a bitch a try."

Falconer and Waidler moved to the side and let Winter move his bulky frame closer to the door. Sizing it up for a moment, the officer then stepped back slightly and rammed a large shoulder directly into the middle of the door, and it moved a foot.

"Good work, Winter!" Falconer said, moving to squeeze through the opening. "Let's go!"

He then disappeared through the opening and the other men quickly followed.

75

Falconer ran a few steps out on the roof of the building and then stopped, scanning his surroundings. "See anything?" he asked the men.

"Nothing," Winter said.

"Nope," Kramer replied.

Falconer walked a few more steps with his revolver at the ready and looked out over the sea of buildings that stood like a great chain of mountains jutting into the sky.

"There!" Waidler yelled, pointing to a corner of the building. Falconer looked and saw a figure clad in black standing on the short, raised wall that surrounded the entire rooftop. The man quickly looked back at him, turned again and hopped off the building, and disappeared.

"What the hell?" Winter said. "Did he jump?"

"Just to the next building," Falconer replied. "Let's go!"

He then led the men in a run over to the corner and looked down. The man had landed across the short gap onto the next rooftop about twelve feet below and was now running away towards the far side of that rooftop.

"Let's go, boys!" Falconer yelled before holstering his gun and quickly jumping to the lower roof, followed by the others in quick succession.

He ran quickly and could hear his men just behind him as he saw the suspect pause at the far side of the roof and appear to look across at the next building. Clearly, the gap was much farther this time, and the man was hesitating. But then Falconer saw him walk backwards a few steps, run directly at the short wall in front of him, step up onto the wall in full stride and leap out across the expanse in between the buildings. The man then landed hard on the next roof and quickly got up.

Falconer kept running directly at the short wall ahead of him and determined to make the same leap. As he got closer, he saw that the gap was perhaps eight feet across and felt he could make it. Running at full speed, he stepped up onto the wall and pushed off hard, flying across the gap with the alleyway far below. He then landed with a thud and rolled over. Getting up quickly, he saw his men standing back at the wall of the second rooftop and then turned and looked at the mysterious figure who was running away. Turning quickly back to his men, he yelled to them: "Who's the best shot?!"

He saw the three men look at each other with a surprised look, and then Winter yelled back: "Kramer is!"

"Kramer!" Falconer yelled at the officer. "Can you get a shot off?!"

He then saw Kramer pull out his revolver and step up onto the small wall on the edge of the building. Crouching down, Falconer could see the suspect about to arrive at the far side of the rooftop that they were both occupying, and he looked to see if Kramer could get off a shot or two. The stoic officer stood up on the wall and had his revolver extended out at arm's length, and he was clearly trying to find a bead on the target. Then, just as the man was about to jump again to the next rooftop, Kramer fired off two rounds in quick succession, and the suspect fell to the ground, clutching his leg.

"You got him!" Falconer yelled. "Nice shot!"

He then started running over to apprehend the stricken man, who was already getting to his feet despite his apparent wound. They were now three stories up over the street, and Falconer could hear all the people and wagons and activity below on the busy thoroughfare. He ran hard now, and just as the man was about to try and somehow leap to the next closer rooftop, Falconer dove and grabbed him by his legs, and the man groaned loudly and fell again to the surface of the roof. Struggling to get up again, the man flung his fists as Falconer's head, and Falconer managed to parry the blows and get a hold of the man's jacket.

"Stop resisting!" Falconer yelled. "Or I'll shoot you!"

The man ignored the commands, however, and flailed with his legs, trying to kick Falconer off him. Falconer grabbed the legs to thwart the attack and then punched the man hard in his ribs. "I said stop resisting!" he yelled again, smashing a fist into the man's mouth. The man, dazed, tried to crawl away, but Falconer got up and, grabbing his jacket again, flung him hard against the low wall lining the edge of the roof over 37th Street. The man emitted a pained moan, and Falconer stood several feet away from him. "You're under arrest," he said to him, wiping a little blood off his own face. "Get on your stomach."

But as he slowly walked over to place handcuffs on him, the man got up to his knees and looked over the wall to the street below. He gazed back at Falconer briefly, and then reached up and flung himself up and over the wall with a surprising quickness. Falconer ran the last few steps and looked down towards the street. "Damn it all," he muttered.

The man had fallen towards the street but had landed in a large wagon full of large, burlap sacks filled with some sort of soft grain, for he was now slowly getting off the wagon and limping away down through the crowd of people who mingled and stared at him.

Falconer watched as the man quietly disappeared down the street, and as he rued his inability to properly take the suspect into custody, he glanced back to where they had struggled and noticed several items littering the surface of the roof. Walking over, he bent down and examined them: a small box of matches, a few coins, and a folded piece of paper. Unfolding the paper, he glanced at what was hand-written on the page:

Manhattan Council Meeting

153 Christopher St.

8:00 pm, Sun. Sept. 18

Folding the paper back up, he placed it in his jacket pocket along with the matchbox and coins and pondered what the note meant. Then he heard the voices of his men calling to him back on the other roof, and he turned and slowly walked back to speak with them.

76

Falconer stood with Waidler and Halloran below the reviewing stand near the entryway to the large Union League clubhouse on Rogers Avenue in Brooklyn. It was 8:00 PM on Saturday, the evening after the chase on the rooftops, and several thousands of enthusiastic Republican voters now stood cheering and shouting in the large plaza that stretched out in front of the detectives. A band was playing up on the stand while the crowd waited expectantly for the scheduled speakers, and fireworks were going off high above everyone. Meanwhile, the ornate clubhouse itself was lit up like a gigantic Christmas tree, with rows of gas jets and electric lights brightly lining the entrance, and other lights shining through the windows of the great building. This brightening effect was topped off by four electric arc lights that illuminated the whole plaza wherein the cheerful throng congregated.

The event's hosts had made sure, too, to decorate the building in a way that was fitting for a party in honor of the future vice president of the United States: American flags draped down from every window and hung over the arched entrance to the building, while other colorful banners fluttered brilliantly in the wind from the flagstaff that rose out of the building's cupola high above.

Falconer, who had just arrived after having attended the autopsy of their still-unnamed informant, turned to Waidler and spoke loudly into his ear, as the crowd was generating such a tremendous noise that it was difficult to hear one speak. "Are the officers in place around the plaza?"

"Yes," Waidler replied, equally loudly. "We have men all over, some in the crowd, some on the periphery. And, of course, Reid is surrounded by our men and his own."

"Good," Falconer said above the noise. "But with this crowd, there's no way we can cover everything. If Meunier tries to strike here, he has a chance to succeed. There are just too many damned people."

Waidler nodded as the crowd started singing along with the band's latest offering, and Halloran couldn't suppress a smile at all of the rejoicing happening around them.

"You ever seen a bigger crowd, Jimmy?" Falconer asked the young officer.

"No, sir. This is the biggest for me."

"Well, Reid and the other speakers should be coming out soon now. The sooner we get them out of here, the sooner we can go home."

Waidler nodded again and looked out across the jammed plaza.

"So where are Winter and Kramer?" Falconer asked. "They've got the rifle with them?"

"Correct, boss," Waidler said, pointing across the plaza at a darkened building that stood over the whole crowd. "They're up on that roof over there, ready to take a shot if we can get Meunier in sight."

"Well, good, but it'd be tough to get a safe shot off in this crowd. And what about Penwill and Houllier?"

"They're walking around the outside of the crowd, just trying to keep an eye out," Waidler replied. "They said they would report back here when Reid starts his speech."

"Good," Falconer said, gazing out at the mass of humanity that danced and screamed with ebullience in the cooling evening air.

Just then, the crowd got louder and appeared to start cheering in the direction of the reviewing stand. Falconer looked up and saw Reid walking out with a wide smile on his face, joined by Senator Joseph Hawley of Connecticut and the local U.S. Attorney, Jesse Johnson, among other dignitaries. Johnson moved to quiet the crowd, and, within moments, was able to make his introductory remarks. Then, Hawley approached the front of the reviewing stand and the crowd let out a great roar of approval. Motioning for the people to let him speak, he then began to expound on the blessings of the Republican Party and the benefits of keeping President Harrison and his new running mate, Ambassador Reid, in office.

After hearing Hawley's speech for about ten minutes, Falconer turned to Waidler and Halloran. "I'm going to go check on Winter and Kramer in the building across the way. Be alert and keep an eye out for Meunier—especially when Reid makes his speech."

"Got it," Waidler said, and then Falconer moved off across the street, through the tightly packed crowd. Making his way across the plaza, he kept looking out for the small, swarthy Frenchman with the slight limp who was potentially carrying sticks of dynamite to explode in the middle of one of the speeches. It was strange, he thought: the notion that everyone around him was smiling and laughing, unaware of the great danger that possibly lurked within the great folds of people that converged in the plaza, while he, charged with protecting them, was extraordinarily tense, agitated, and fearful that at any moment, a bomb might go off and kill many of them.

He fought his way through the people and finally came to the front of the building that rose three stories over the plaza. Showing his badge to the two officers standing guard, he moved inside, ascended a staircase to the top, exited out onto the roof, and walked over to where Winter and Kramer stood leaning against a four-foot wall that extended around the perimeter of the roof.

"Hey, Detective Sergeant," Winter said. "Big crowd, eh?"

"It certainly is," Falconer replied, looking down at the people. "How are things up here?"

"Oh, just fine, sir. But it might be a little hard picking out this little hunchback out of that crowd down there."

"Yes, I know. How you doing, Kramer?"

The quiet officer was leaning against the wall looking down the barrel of his Springfield 1871 rifle and scanning the crowd for his target. "Just fine, detective sergeant," he said. "But I agree—hard to get a clean shot off in this crowd."

"Understood," Falconer said. "Just do your best, and if something happens, use your best judgment."

"Will do."

"All right, I'm headed down to go find Inspectors Penwill and Houllier," Falconer said. "Carry on, gentlemen."

"Yes, sir," Winter said. "All good up here."

Falconer then went back to the stairwell and descended to the first floor. Exiting the building, he looked to his right and noticed a large body of marchers coming up the avenue.

The parade.

This would be the large evening parade of political supporters that was scheduled to walk by the clubhouse right before Reid made his speech. It would mean more people—and more potential victims.

Falconer moved to his right to go around the crowd that was now separating within the large avenue to let the marchers go by. He saw that, out in front, a platoon of mounted policemen was trotting up jauntily towards the clubhouse, and, behind them, walking together, were the parade's grand marshal and his chief of staff. And finally, behind these parade officials, were the many political groups and clubs that packed the avenue with shouts and song.

Falconer headed back across the plaza towards the reviewing stand, and, after several minutes of pushing and shoving, managed to arrive back to where Halloran and Waidler now stood with Houllier and Penwill. Penwill was speaking with a man in plain clothes, and when Falconer stepped forward, the Englishman turned and greeted him. "Good to see you, old boy. This is Mister Enright, head of security for the ambassador."

"How are you?" Falconer said loudly over the din of the immense crowd cheering behind them.

"Just fine, detective sergeant," Enright replied. "The ambassador is about to address the crowd, and we've got men all around."

"That's good," Falconer said. "So, whereabouts are they positioned?"

"Oh, all around the stage, and dispersed in the first several rows of people here," Enright said. "I'd say we've got good coverage."

"Excellent," Falconer said. Then he looked up and saw Reid slowly approaching the front of the stage after having just been introduced to the raucous crowd by Senator Hawley. Falconer looked back at the people, who must have numbered several thousand at this point, and then back to the stage. And then he looked farther back at the large clubhouse that rose ominously over all the people.

Strange, he thought. *But…could it be?…*

He turned back to Enright and shouted into his ear: "So did you say your men are all outside now?"

"Yes," Enright confirmed. "We've got them all out here converged on the stage for maximum coverage."

"So, no one inside the clubhouse right now?"

"No…no one. Is there an issue?"

Falconer turned to Penwill and Houllier and motioned quickly for Waidler and Halloran to step closer. "Quick," he said to them, "there's no one watching the inside of the clubhouse and I'm worried we've got a vulnerability. Let's go!"

He ran up the steps leading to the top of the reviewing stand and made for the entrance to the building, joined closely by the other men behind him. As they entered the large, well-decorated lobby, he pulled out his revolver and pointed to the stairs, yelling out to the men: "James, Jimmy—check out this floor! Inspectors—let's head up the stairs. Every room needs to be checked!"

He bounded up the stairs to the second floor with Penwill and Houllier close at his heels, and the three men began to clear all the rooms that overlooked the reviewing stand below. As Falconer entered each room, he would see various supporters gazing out the windows and cheering the ambassador's speech. He would then move on to the next room, leaving the surprised onlookers standing with mouths agape and confused looks.

After several moments, the three men met again out in the hallway having seen no sign of their French anarchist target. "One last floor," Falconer said, motioning to the stairs again. "Let's head up."

Reaching the top of the stairs, they fanned out to check all the rooms on the floor that overlooked the stage upon which Reid was at that moment exhorting the crowd of well-wishers to rise up for a Republic victory in November. Falconer ran to the door of the room closest to him, and, right before entering, quickly gazed down the hallway to see Houllier quietly entering another room, with handgun raised.

77

Houllier slowly pushed the door open and peered inside. It was darkened and appeared full of junk and pieces of furniture stacked high on top of each other—a clubhouse storeroom, likely. He entered a few feet with his revolver at the ready and looked out the open window across the room. He could see the tops of the buildings across the street and hear the great cheers of the crowd below interspersed with vague shouted words from a single male speaker: Ambassador Reid.

Stepping in a few steps, he looked to his right at a large mass of furniture piled together and decided to go check behind it. Moving lightly on his feet, he could feel the sweat dripping down from his brow and hear the faint sound of his labored breath as he tried to keep his eyes moving back and forth around the room, ready for any sudden movement.

Arriving at the corner of the mass of furniture, he quietly steeled himself, took a deep breath, and swung quickly around the corner with his gun pointed in front of him.

Nothing.

Walking slowly along the back of the furniture pile, he came to the other end and moved quickly around another corner, again seeing no one in front of him. He then stopped for a moment, listening for any sound of someone who might be hiding behind the junk and the desks, chairs, and tables that were thrown together around the room.

Hearing nothing, he kept walking alongside the front wall and came to the open window. Looking down, he saw Reid gesticulating as he spoke, and then the immense crowd that looked like a sea of little heads floating together as far as the eye could see. He then turned and moved towards another pile of furniture standing about three feet away from the window. Aligning himself at the edge of the closest corner of the pile, he again took a deep breath, got his revolver ready, and moved swiftly around the corner: nothing once more.

Taking a deep breath, he decided that the room was empty and moved to go back out into the hallway and find the others. Stepping forward, he suddenly felt a crash against his head and fell to the floor, stunned. He tried to regain his vision as he lay in pain but could only see little, shining stars dancing across the room like lit sparkles on Bastille Day in France.

Rubbing his head to ease the throbbing pain, he slowly looked back in the direction of the open window and saw a figure. It was a man with his back turned, and the man was doing something with his hands in front of his body, such that Houllier could not quite tell what. He tried to get up, but his body would not respond properly, as if someone else were controlling his hands, limbs, and torso, and as he lay struggling to move, he could hear the muffled sound of voices below. He tried to form coherent thoughts and make sense of where he was, and slowly, bit by bit, he began to remember that he was in a room, searching for the suspect, and there were people below, lots of them, unsuspecting and defenseless, and the vice-presidential candidate, Reid, was speaking before them.

He looked back at the dark figure and saw something shining behind him—a light? A lit match perhaps? But no, it was no light or match or lantern—it was sparkling wildly like those sparklers that people lit up and waved in the air at joyful celebrations. Houllier tried to avoid the unfortunate truth that was now forming in his brain: that the man held a bundle of dynamite sticks and had just lit them and was about to toss them lightly down onto the reviewing stand below. And then it all became clear to him.

Meunier.

He looked quickly around his body for his revolver that had dropped out of his hands when he was first struck, and he saw it a foot away, lying next to a chair. Looking back at the man, he saw that the anarchist was now slowly walking towards the window and would toss the deadly explosives in seconds. Turning back to the gun, he reached out as far as he could, but he was still several inches away from it. Gathering his limited strength, he then rolled his body over once and managed to get close enough to grasp it. Raising it in front of his eyes, he cocked the lever but then saw that the man—Meunier—was at that moment raising the bundle of dynamite and about to throw it out the window.

So Houllier decided to speak: "Theodule…."

It was the simplest thought that he could conjure up, the simplest utterance that he felt might stop Meunier for just a second, for a brief moment that would allow him time to aim the gun.

And Meunier did stop.

The anarchist looked back briefly, appearing surprised that Houllier was awake and speaking. And that was the moment when Houllier took aim and fired one shot at Meunier's dark torso. He missed his mark, however, but did hit his nemesis elsewhere, for Meunier winced and dropped the dynamite sticks, grabbing his forearm. Houllier raised himself up with all his will and strength and moved to grab the bomber by his legs. Meunier in response grabbed Houllier by the neck and started to pound at him with one fist, but Houllier managed to trip the would-be assassin and they both fell to the floor. Struggling to grab the suspect by the neck, Houllier shouted at him: "*C'est fini, Meunier! Arretez de resister!*"

"*Jamis vous batard!*" Meunier shouted back. "*Je vais tous vous tuer!*"

The two men struggled some more, and while doing so, Houllier noticed with a horrifying realization that the sticks of dynamite lying just a couple of feet away were still lit. Smashing a fist into Meunier's face, he then scrambled to his knees and struggled over to the sticks and doused the flame just as it moved to within an inch of the explosive cartridges.

Turning back to Meunier, he saw the man staring at him for an instant, and he felt the anarchist's rage and turmoil at having been thwarted so close to achieving his desired result. Meunier then turned away and rapidly made for the door, and Houllier sprang to his feet and followed him. Arriving out in the hallway, he saw Meunier running down to a room at the end of the hallway and disappearing within. Just then, he heard Falconer's voice behind him and looked back to see the detective running towards him from the other end of the hallway.

"What's happening?" Falconer asked hurriedly.

"Meunier!" Houllier shouted. "I just stopped him from throwing dynamite and he has gone into the last room!"

"Let's go!" Falconer yelled as he sprinted by Houllier, who followed close behind. The two men approached the door to the last room on their left, and Houllier looked at Falconer, who nodded. Falconer then turned the doorknob and swung the door open, leveling his revolver at the interior. Houllier looked and saw the room was empty, but a window was open. Running over to it, he looked down with Falconer and saw Meunier climbing the last few feet down a tree that rose high alongside the exterior wall of the building from the yard below. Falconer raised his gun, aimed, and fired a couple of shots, but the man escaped unharmed and ran off to a small, stone wall that lined the yard. Houllier then watched as the French bomber struggled up onto the wall and looked back at them.

"Ca ne s'arrete pas la, Meunier!" Houllier yelled out over the lawn. "Je t'aurai! Je t'aurai, Meunier!"

"*Je ne suis pas Meunier, mon ami!*" Meunier yelled back at the top of his lungs. "*Je suis Ravachol! Je vis! Je suis Ravachol!*"

Then, he dropped out of sight on the other side of the wall and disappeared.

Houllier sighed and dropped his head, anguished that he had failed to capture the renegade anarchist.

"What was it that you said to him?" Falconer asked.

"I said that this was not the end," Houllier replied quietly, "and that I would get him in the end."

"And what did he say back to you?"

"He said that he wasn't Meunier. He was Ravachol and that Ravachol lives."

"I see."

"I am sorry that I failed to get our man," Houllier said, shaking his head.

"It's all right. The important thing is you stopped him from achieving his mission of blowing up the ambassador and hundreds of other people down there. So, you did succeed. You succeeded very much, and you will get him in the end."

"Yes. Yes, we will."

"Come on. Let's go get the others."

The two men then walked out into the hallway and headed down the stairs as the rousing cheers of the crowd out in the plaza reached a crescendo and the noises of the celebration reached high up into the sky over Brooklyn.

78

"Well, gentlemen," Byrnes said as he stood behind his desk, "you did a fine job averting a catastrophe last night. Especially you, Inspector Houllier. It sounds like our suspect was only seconds away from successfully throwing some dynamite down on that reviewing stand when you stopped him in his tracks. The city and the country are indebted to you."

"*Merci*, Superintendent Byrnes," Houllier said. "I am only sorry that I let him get away."

"Do not worry, inspector," Byrnes said. "You clearly wounded him, so he will be slowed down now and easier to spot. I'm just wondering if you think he will continue to try and target the ambassador despite his wounds."

"If I may, superintendent?" Penwill said.

"Yes, by all means, inspector."

"Meunier is a radical and a fervent acolyte of Ravachol," Penwill said, "but I would wager that, having been wounded now by Inspector Houllier and knowing that we are close on his trail, he will not be inclined to further his deadly aims. Frankly, I believe that he will try to give us the slip and head back to Europe."

"Falconer?" Byrnes said.

"I tend to agree," Falconer said. "Meunier knows that he barely escaped with his life last night. I would think that he has finished making a statement here and will flee now."

"Understood," Byrnes said. "Well then, let's alert all of the wharves and points of departure in Manhattan—let everyone know that Meunier may be seeking to get on a ship."

"Will do, sir."

"And how is the ambassador reacting to the attempted bombing?"

"He and his aides are refusing to halt their campaigning. They said that they understand the dangers, but to stop going out and having rallies would be to send a message that any crazy anarchist can control our elections. They also fear that letting this news get out could strike fear in the voters and thus, suppress the vote in November. So, they were adamant that we keep this out of the papers, sir."

"Well, I can't say that I agree with Reid on that one, but I can't control a candidate's national campaign. Meanwhile, what is the latest on this other group that you've been investigating?"

"Well, we had the unnamed informant helping us, but unfortunately, he was found dead a couple of nights ago. We chased a suspect up on the roof, but he got away. We did, however, find something of interest in a note that apparently fell out of the suspect's pocket."

"Oh? What's that?"

"It's an address for a meeting happening tonight. Something about a 'Manhattan Council.'"

"Manhattan Council? Council for what?"

"We're thinking that it's a part of this secret order, sir. Clearly, our informant was silenced because he was giving up information on them, and this assassin that we lost up on the roof must be a part of the organization."

"So, a meeting tonight, you say…and I suppose you're wanting to do a little surveillance on them?"

"That's correct, sir. We'll sit back and see if we can find out who's showing up."

"And where is this alleged meeting place?" Byrnes asked.

"It's at 153 Christopher Street, sir," Waidler chimed in. "It's the location of the Saint Veronica Church, but it's in the process of being built—they just have the basement finished at this point."

"Really?" Byrnes said. "That's odd. Why meet in the basement of an unfinished church?"

"Apparently they're already holding masses in the basement," Falconer replied, "but I'd say that a building under construction wouldn't attract much attention because it's just a whole lot of stones, tools, and debris right now."

"I understand what you're saying," Byrnes said. "Well, do what you need to do and find out what this meeting is about and who's attending."

"Yes, sir," Falconer said. "Oh, and one other thing."

"Yes, Falconer?"

"When I met with that informant, he told me that the group was controlled by some very high-up people in business and government. But I only got one name from him—a man who the informant said was the controlling figure at this point—the overall boss."

"And who was it?" Byrnes inquired.

Falconer hesitated, looking at the other men for a moment, and then he turned back to Byrnes. "Walter Bliss," he said.

"Bliss?" Byrnes said, wide-eyed. "Walter Bliss, the railroad mogul?"

"Yes, sir. Our informant was very clear on Bliss' role at the top."

"Well, I must say that I'm rather surprised," Byrnes said walking a few steps away from his desk. "Bliss is certainly a character, a man-about-town, and he is never at a loss for making headlines in the papers. But the head of a cult of assassins? It seems almost absurd."

"Bliss has been known to make certain anti-immigrant comments in the papers. And that would fit with what the informant said was the group's stated purpose."

"Yes, I know that he's been one of the more vocal critics of allowing immigrants into the country in recent years. But murder? That's a new one for me."

"Unfortunately, we don't have much to go on except the informant's statement to me, which is now useless given his death. But I did want you to know who the informant fingered as the leader."

"Yes, yes, thank you, Falconer. And let's keep this in this room, understand?"

The men all nodded.

"If we were to make a public allegation without hard evidence," Byrnes said, "Bliss would make a big stink of it."

"Understood, sir," Falconer said.

"All right then, carry on, gentlemen. And be careful out there tonight—there's no telling what this band might pull if they're exposed."

"Right, sir. Thank you."

Falconer then turned and led the men out of the office and to the stairs leading down to the front entrance of the headquarters building. As they gathered at the bottom of the stairs, he turned to Waidler. "Did you go out to the church on Christopher earlier this morning?" he asked.

"Yeah," Waidler answered. "Didn't see anything but we went up to check out the door leading down to the basement. It's a big, wooden door with a metal lock that needs a key. Not sure how we'll get in tonight if it's locked up."

"Well, we can't break it down or shoot the lock. That would attract too much attention."

"Agreed."

"You said it's a lock that takes some sort of a key?"

"Correct."

"I think I might have someone who could help us out. Let's go pay a visit to the Fifth Avenue Hotel. Boys, we're going to take a little trip uptown right now. Inspectors, we'll see you here at 7:00 PM?"

"Jolly good," Penwill said. "We shall see you back here this evening."

"Excellent," Falconer said. "And thanks. All right, gentlemen, let's go."

He then stepped down the front stairs of the headquarters, followed closely by Waidler, Halloran, Winter, and Kramer, and bounded down the sidewalk, headed for the elevated train that would lead them uptown to the 5th Avenue Hotel.

79

The crowded streetcar pulled to a stop on its tracks in front of the opulent, six-story 5th Avenue Hotel at the intersection of 5th and 23d Street. Falconer and the other men hopped off the car and sauntered over to the front entrance of the enormous, brick and white marble building.

The sidewalks were busy at this late afternoon hour with pedestrians determined to get to the next destination in their packed Sunday schedules, and the streetcars and horse-drawn wagons and hansom cabs jostled for position out on the avenue as they navigated their way north and south on the wide thoroughfare.

Falconer looked up at the five-columned front entrance of the hotel and then briefly turned and surveyed the southwestern corner of the lush Madison Square across the avenue. "All right boys," he said, turning to them, "shall we go in?"

"Uh, detective sergeant?" Halloran said. "Can you tell us why we're here?"

"Sure. We might need to enter the basement of the church through a locked door tonight, and so, we'll need someone who can do that for us. And I'll bet he's inside the hotel right now."

"He? Who's he?"

"Come on inside with me," Falconer said, and he moved through the large front entrance into the hotel's bustling, marble-lined lobby. Stepping over to a wall amidst the many impeccably dressed hotel patrons and uniformed staff members scurrying about, he scanned the capacious room, looking out into the sea of top-hatted and tuxedoed men chatting amiably in groups and smoking cigars as their wives gave sweaty-browed porters directions for their luggage piled high onto wheeled carts. His men waited patiently as he looked, moving his eyes constantly from group to group, until finally he spoke out: "There, over near that group of swells standing next to the tall, potted plant: that's our man."

"Who, detective sergeant?" Halloran asked as he craned his neck to see.

"Who are you spotting, boss?" Waidler asked.

"The droopy-faced mug who's standing next to the men over there," Falconer answered. "See him?"

Waidler and Halloran looked over at a man with a bowler standing against a wall.

"That one," Falconer said. "Just watch—he's about to swipe a wallet now."

Falconer looked on with the other men as the lurking man slowly straightened up, moved towards the group of well-heeled men standing with their cigars and canes in hand, and suddenly bumped into one of them. Turning to face the subject he had run into—an older, gray-bearded man who had the look of a lifelong aristocrat with plenty of money in his bank accounts—the man in the bowler reached out with both hands to steady the old gentleman and appeared to apologize profusely to him. He then bowed deferentially and moved on through the crowd, heading towards the front entrance of the hotel through which Falconer and the men had just walked.

"Get ready," Falconer said. "He's headed our way. Did you see what he did over there, Jimmy?"

"Uh, I think so, sir," Halloran responded.

"That was a classic move by one of the best pickpockets on the east coast," Falconer said. "And here he comes now. Winter and Kramer, grab him quietly and usher him outside."

"Got it, boss," Winter said. "Come on, Kramer—you grab one arm and I'll get the other."

Kramer nodded and stepped forward discretely as the unknowing thief walked up near to them on his way out of the hotel. The two officers then reached out simultaneously and grabbed the man's arms firmly, and Winter spoke quietly into the man's ear with a smile: "Let's go, bub—we saw what you did over there. Quietly now."

The two officers then moved him outside, followed by Falconer, Waidler, and Halloran. Stepping over to the front wall of the hotel, away from the entrance, they quietly searched his pockets as he expressed surprise and bewilderment, and Winter finally fished out a long, black wallet, and handed it to Falconer. "So, what's that, pal?" Winter asked. "I'm betting it ain't yours. Am I right?"

The man, appearing to be in his mid-forties and wearing a thick mustache, demurred excitedly: "But I don't understand, gentlemen...I-I was just leaving the hotel after visiting a friend—that's all. I have no idea what this is about."

"What this is about, Poodles, is lifting that old dandy's wallet," Falconer said, holding up the purloined leather wallet. "And you're caught dead to rights."

"Um...'Poodles,' sir?" the man said incredulously. "Why, I'm not sure what you mean by that."

"Stop it, Poodles," Falconer said, handing the wallet to Halloran. "I know who you are and I was wised up recently about you probably hitting some marks in the hotel here this week— and look what happened."

The man only rested his head glumly back against the hotel's wall and said nothing.

"Poodles?" Halloran asked. "Is that this guy's name?"

"Gentlemen," Falconer said, "meet Terrence 'Poodles' Murphy, perhaps the most accomplished pickpocket on the east coast. So how are you, Poodles? I heard you had to do a stint in the pen back in Pennsylvania."

"Um…yes, sir, officer," Murphy answered quietly. "Three years…got out in eighty-seven."

"You were working back then with your partner, Pretty Jimmy Wilson, correct?" Falconer asked.

"Uh, yes, I was, actually. He got two-and-a-half years with me at Eastern Penitentiary. Not sure where he is now."

"I see."

"So…what are you gentlemen going to do with me? Throw me in the Tombs?"

"Not necessarily," Falconer answered. "Yes, it was wrong of you to lift that man's wallet, but we can get it back to him…in exchange for a little help on something."

"Um…help?" Murphy said. "What sort of help, sir?"

"Well, I know that your expertise includes picking locks. Is that correct?"

Murphy looked taken aback and looked at the other men momentarily, then turned back to Falconer. "Well…the truth is…I do have some experience in that…area," he replied slowly.

"Good, then. We're going to have to ask you to help us out this evening on a particular locked door, understand?"

"I can do that, sir. And this little incident here?"

"Don't worry about it," Falconer said, reaching out to Halloran with the wallet. "Jimmy? Can you bring this back to the old codger in there and then come back outside?"

"Certainly, sir," Halloran said, taking the wallet. "Be right back."

"There, you see?" Falconer said to Murphy. "No need to bring you down to the Tombs on this one. Just come downtown with us this evening for a little bit, and then we'll release you. You okay with that?"

"Absolutely, Detective Sergeant…uh…Detective Sergeant…what is your name, sir?"

"Falconer."

"Detective Sergeant Falconer," Murphy repeated. "I will be very happy to get you through that locked door, sir—with my thanks."

"Good. And here comes our boy, Jimmy, now. All right, gentlemen, let's go meet the inspectors and then head over to the church."

He then moved off, walking down the street, trailed by his four fellow police officers and their distinguished pickpocket-burglar in tow.

80

alconer stood behind a large supply wagon parked directly across from the partially built Saint Veronica's Church on Christopher Street. Halloran, Waidler, Poodles Murphy, and Levine stood by him while Winter, Houllier, and Penwill lurked behind a row of large barrels that stood on the corner fifty yards distant. Falconer looked at his watch and then turned to Levine. "Glad you could join us, professor," he said. "Thought you might be intrigued by all of this."

"Yes, indeed," Levine said. "Quite thrilling behind-the-scenes stuff."

"Well, it's just about eight," Falconer said, looking across the darkening street at the flattened construction site that would be a Catholic church eventually. "Anyone seen anyone out there yet?"

"No one, boss," Waidler said.

"Me neither," Halloran answered.

"Well, that's disappointing," Falconer said, taking off his bowler and wiping his sweaty forehead with his sleeve. "I was hoping that note we found up on the roof would lead us to a big meeting in this place."

"May I ask what sort of meeting you were expecting to take place, sir?" Murphy said.

"Not really sure about that, Murphy," Falconer answered, "but we were thinking it was going to be this sort of a meeting of a secret society type thing."

"Secret society?" Murphy said, his eyes widening. "That's interesting."

"Yeah, well, looks like maybe we were mistaken, unfortunately," Falconer said. "No one's coming around here tonight."

"Not so fast, boss," Waidler said, looking off to his right. "See over there?"

Falconer looked across the street and saw in the distance a woman dressed in a black dress followed by an older man, dressed in a suit and tie and wearing spectacles, slowly edging down the street towards the church grounds. They were creeping along the sidewalk very slowly and appeared to be trying to make their way down to the church as discretely and clandestinely as possible.

"Now who the hell are those two?" Falconer asked.

"Can't quite tell," said Waidler. "But if they're trying to be secretive, they aren't doing a very good job of it."

"If I wasn't crazy," Halloran said, peering closer at the two individuals slowly getting closer across the street, "I'd say those people look like—"

"Nellie Bly and Jacob Riis," Levine interrupted.

"What?" Falconer said, turning back and looking across the street at the two figures. "What the devil are they doing here?"

"I don't know, but I think it is them, sir," Waidler said.

"Damn it all to hell," Falconer said frustratingly. "Jimmy, can you go get their attention and get 'em over here?"

"Sure thing, sir," Halloran said, and then he crept out around the corner of the wagon and whistled shrilly once. Falconer watched as Bly and Riis stopped in their tracks and looked over at Halloran, who was now waving for them to join the men. The two interlopers then quickly jogged across the street and arrived at the wagon, breathlessly.

"Ah, there you are, gentlemen," Bly said with a smile. "We lost you on the way."

"Lost us?" Falconer said. "What the hell does that mean? Why are you here?"

"Why, to get the story, of course," Bly answered matter-of-factly.

"What story?" Falconer demanded.

"A story of some dark, secretive organization that might be responsible for some recent nefarious activities in this city—including murder."

"And how did you come by this information?"

"Why, from my sources, of course."

"What sources?"

"You know I cannot divulge that, detective sergeant—against the rules."

"If you're afraid I might give them a beating, you're right, Miss Bly."

"That was on my mind, actually," Bly said. "But rest assured, your secret is safe with Mister Riis and me—only we followed you here."

"That's just great," Falconer said. "So reassuring."

"Well, since we are here now," Bly said, "there's no sense in delaying your operation. What next?"

"What's next?" Falconer said exasperatedly. "What's next is you leave and forget this ever happened."

"I'm sorry, but we cannot do that," Bly said, crossing her arms.

"I can't believe this," Falconer said, turning to Riis. "Mister Riis, I'm a little surprised at you."

"I'm sorry, detective sergeant," Riis said, "but Miss Bly was insistent that she would be reconnoitering this scene tonight, and I just couldn't let her do it alone."

"Right," Falconer said. "I figured."

"Really, detective sergeant," Bly said. "We will not intrude on your activities tonight and will just hang back and observe."

"That's comforting," Falconer said dismissively.

"Boss, what we do now?" Waidler asked. "Cancel?"

Falconer hesitated a moment, then looked out across the street at the church construction site. "No," he finally said, "it looks like no meeting ever happened, but we should at least check out the church basement, just in case. Murphy, you ready?"

"Yes, sir," Murphy answered. "Just show me the way."

Falconer motioned for the other men to get ready to cross the street with him, and signaled to Bly, Riis, and Levine to follow up in the rear. As she situated herself behind the policemen, Bly exchanged brief pleasantries with Levine, and Falconer looked back with an exasperated glare. He then turned to Halloran. "Jimmy, please signal the inspectors to join us," he said.

"Got it," Halloran said, and he walked over several paces and waved his arms at the other men down the street.

"All right, everyone," Falconer said, "there's no telling who might be down in that basement, so be alert. James and Jimmy, draw your weapons."

Waidler and Halloran did as instructed while Falconer pulled out his own revolver and looked across the street again. "Let's go, folks," he said.

He then ran across the street, signaling to the inspectors and Kramer and Winter as he ran. Arriving at the church property, he looked down at a small set of stone steps and the large wooden door at the bottom. Houllier, Penwill, Kramer, and Winter arrived at a trot, and Penwill spoke up upon seeing Bly and Riis: "Well, by golly, it's Miss Bly and Mister Riis—fancy seeing you here. We've got quite a party now."

"Hello to you, inspector," Bly said.

"Yes, and I think you met Inspector Houllier already," Penwill said.

"Yes, *bon soir*, inspector," Bly said, smiling.

"*Bon soir, mademoiselle*," Houllier said, doffing his hat.

"And these two gentlemen are Officers Winter and Kramer, Miss Bly," Penwill said. "Gentlemen, this is Miss Nellie Bly the journalist, and this is Jacob Riis, also of the newspapers."

"Good evening, officers," Bly said.

"Well, I'll be," Winter said, peering excitedly at Bly. "Never thought this old beat cop would actually meet a famous person on the job. Look at that, Kramer—it's really Nellie Bly."

Kramer nodded slightly, and then Falconer interrupted their chat: "All right, people, let's get back to the task at hand. Murphy, you think you can figure out that lock?"

"I can certainly try, detective sergeant," Murphy said. "If I may?"

Falconer nodded and Murphy descended the several steps to the wooden door. Bending down, he peered through the keyhole that was set in a large, bronze escutcheon. He then reached into his pocket and pulled out two long, metal pin-like instruments. Placing one into the keyhole, he bent it slightly and then inserted the other metal pick into the hole, as well. Jiggling the picks for several seconds, he then caused the door lock to emit a clicking sound and quickly extracted the picks, placing them back into his pocket. "What is it you French say, Inspector Houllier?" he asked. "*Voila*?"

"Well done, Murphy," Falconer said, walking down the steps. He then pressed down on the door handle, pushed gently, and the door opened slightly. "Looks like your job is done and you can go. But a reminder: if you say anything of this to anyone, you can bet that we will find you, understand?"

"Absolutely," Murphy said, smiling. "Not a word, not a word."

"Good, and thanks," Falconer said. "Oh, and one other thing: you're done operating in the 5th Ave Hotel, got it?"

"Yes, sir," Murphy said, tipping his hat. "Message received. Good evening to you all."

He then walked up the steps and ran across the street, disappearing into the darkness.

"Well, I can see that he's not a regular employee with your police department," Bly said.

"One does what one has to do, Miss Bly," Falconer said. "All right, gentlemen, we're going in. Weapons at the ready. Winter, do you all have those gas lamps?"

"Got 'em, boss," Winter replied, holding out two, small gaslit lamps.

"Let's light 'em up," Falconer said. "I'll take one, and Jimmy, you hold one, too."

"Yes, sir," Halloran said, walking over to Winter and taking the lamps and lighting them. "Here you are, detective sergeant."

"Thanks," Falconer said, taking one of the lamps with his free hand. "Ready everyone? Good. Then let's go in, nice and easy." He then motioned for Waidler to open the door wider.

"Um, one thing, detective sergeant?" Bly said quickly.

"Yes, Miss Bly?" Falconer said.

"Isn't this a violation of the group's rights, if you don't have a search warrant?"

"It's not their church, Miss Bly," Falconer answered. "It's the Catholic Church's property, so this mysterious band of assassins can't complain if we go in and look around."

"Well, then, maybe the Catholic Diocese might have a problem with this," Bly said.

"Yeah, maybe," Falconer said, and then he turned and moved across the threshold of the doorway, disappearing into the darkness beyond.

81

alconer crept into the darkened basement hallway with his lamp in one hand and revolver in the other. He stopped momentarily to listen but heard nothing. He then turned and motioned for Halloran to walk along the opposite wall, with the others following. He kept walking down the hallway until he came to an opened doorway on his right. Sidling up next to it with Halloran and Waidler just behind him, he peered into a large room and saw what appeared to be a makeshift chapel with rows of benches and a raised alter on his left. He then motioned for Waidler and Halloran to enter the room and check it for any movement.

As the two policemen moved quickly but silently inside, Falconer looked down the hallway again. He could see a few more doorways in the dim light, and then the hallway ended where it intersected with another perpendicular hallway. He motioned for Penwill and Houllier to come up next to him, and they arrived almost instantly. "Why don't you two go check those other doorways with Kramer and Winter?" he whispered to them. "I'm going to help clear this chapel with Waidler and Halloran."

"Understood," Penwill whispered in reply, and then he signaled for the two officers to join him and Houllier, and the small band of men slowly walked down along the walls of the hallway, revolvers in hand.

Falconer turned to Levine, Bly, and Riis and held his index finger up to his mouth. "Stay here and be very quiet," he whispered. "We're just checking out the chapel here."

The three nodded in reply, and Falconer then moved rapidly into the large chapel. He could see that Waidler and Halloran were already on the other side, checking out the pews and various hidden corners and crevasses in the wall, and so he turned to the raised alter and moved over to look behind it. Seeing nothing, he looked back out onto the pews. It was just a drab, nondescript chapel in a basement of a church under construction—nothing more.

He then saw movement to his right and raised his revolver, but it was only Penwill leading the other men into the room. Penwill walked up onto the alter and spoke to him, slightly louder this time: "The basement is empty. There's no one here at all."

"Yes, that seems apparent," Falconer said, speaking in a normal voice this time. "If anyone met here tonight, they've already gone."

"Boss, no one in here," Waidler said, walking up to the alter with Halloran.

"Yes, that seems to be the case," Falconer said, putting his revolver back into its holster. "Jimmy, could you go bring the others in, please?"

"Yes, sir," Halloran replied, and then he walked out of the room momentarily and returned with Levine, Riis, and Bly.

"Well, everyone," Falconer said, "there's no secret meeting here tonight. I guess we were wrong about that note that our friend dropped up on the roof."

"But it was very clear," Penwill said. "8:00 PM tonight at this address. It just doesn't make sense."

"Yes, but we were out there for some time," Falconer pointed out. "And we saw no one enter this place."

"Indeed, we did not," Penwill said.

"Could it be," Houllier interjected, "that someone was alerted to the fact that the suspect's note was left on the roof, and therefore, the meeting was abruptly canceled?"

"That's always a possibility, I'm afraid," Falconer answered. "We just can't be sure, of course."

"Or perhaps," Levine said, stepping forward, "the meeting did take place tonight here at this address, but it did not occur in this basement."

Falconer looked at Levine, as did the others in the room, and then he spoke: "Not in this basement, professor? Then where could it have occurred?"

"It is just speculation at this point, of course," Levine said, "but perhaps it occurred just below us."

"Below us?" Falconer said quizzically. "But there's nothing below us but earth and brick and mortar foundation."

"Perhaps," Levine said, "but there is the slight possibility that this group meets in secret, as-yet-undiscovered chambers built below this building."

"But that is *fantastique*, professor," Houllier said. "How can you just say there might be secret chambers below?"

"Well, it has to do a bit with American history," Levine answered, slowly walking around the group. "American history and a little private sleuthing if you will. Plus, some plain conjecture, of course."

"Go on, professor," Falconer said.

"As some of you might know," Levine explained, "General George Washington took command of colonial forces here in New York City at the beginning of the Revolutionary War. He knew that the British would try to take the city sometime in 1776, and so when he set up his headquarters down on Broadway at the bottom of this island, he also took up residence in the Mortier House just south of where we stand right now—at the intersection of present day Varick and Charlton Streets."

"And how does Washington's temporary residence in New York relate to alleged hidden chambers beneath us?" Falconer asked.

"Well," Levine continued, "Washington knew that the British could potentially bombard his headquarters and residence from the river, or even invade the island very quickly, which would necessitate a quick and, shall we say, stealthy escape north."

"And so?" Penwill asked.

"So," Levine said, "there have long been rumors—unconfirmed, of course—that Washington had a series of underground chambers and tunnels built near to the Mortier House in early 1776 so that he and his wife and staff could have a rapid means of escape undetected from the invading British forces up on the streets. And we are presently standing just north of where the Mortier House used to be. We are standing directly along the expected escape route that Washington would have taken in an emergency."

"Well, this is rather fascinating, professor," Falconer said, stepping closer to him. "But if no one has ever found these secret chambers, how can we expect to find them?"

"Admittedly, that is a difficult question to answer," Levine replied. "But again, if it were true, it would present the perfect clandestine meeting place for our mysterious band of assassins. I would imagine that if the chambers did exist underneath this spot, the entrance would be somewhere out there, perhaps closer to the Hudson's shores. Or, then again, there could be an entrance that we have just not discovered inside of this church basement."

"Well, this is a whole lot of conjecture, professor," Falconer said, "but I suppose it's worth a try to find some sort of entrance in here. Let's all take a careful look around, especially at the floors, all right?"

"This is grand!" Bly said excitedly. "A secret entrance to a long-forgotten series of tunnels that George Washington himself built in the moment of crisis in our nation's founding. Imagine, Jacob!"

"Yes, Nellie," Riis said, "I am almost speechless. What a story this would make."

"Let's not worry about the story just yet, please," Falconer said. "Let's first see if this thing really exists. Come on—break up into two groups, each with a lantern."

He then moved off with the two inspectors, Bly, and Riis, while the others formed a group utilizing the light from the lantern that Halloran carried. Moving out into the hallway, he led his companions slowly towards another doorway leading into an anteroom off the main chamber. Walking in, he raised the lantern higher and looked about the room: there were a few desks against the walls, some cabinets fastened above them, and some boxes piled up in a corner. "Anyone see anything?" he asked, looking back at the others.

"Nothing," Riis said, peering around the darkened room.

"Same for me," Bly sighed. "Nothing."

"I'm afraid there isn't anything in this room," Penwill said.

"Yes, I think you're right," Falconer said. "Let's go into the next one."

They moved out into the hallway and walked a bit farther until they came to the next doorway. It led into a storage room of some sort, which was cramped and difficult to navigate, being stuffed with a large amount of church supplies and furniture. Falconer led the others in and searched the room for a few minutes, ultimately finding no trace of any trapdoor.

They did this is succession, moving on to two more rooms and thoroughly searching for any sign of an entrance to an underground tunnel, but found nothing. Falconer finally turned to the others and motioned for them to head back to the main chamber. "I think we've searched every room down here," he said, "and the others apparently haven't any success, either. Let's head back to the main room."

As he led them back down the hallway in the darkness, holding the lantern high, he called out to the other group: "James! We can't find anything, so we're headed back to the chapel!"

Waidler called back immediately from out in the darkness: "Got it, boss! Nothing over here, either!"

"Well, we tried, folks," Falconer said. "Maybe it's like the professor said: there could be some sort of entrance out there on the street, or along the docks."

"Yes, it was a longshot," Penwill said, "but worth the effort while we were here."

They came to the entrance to the chapel and walked in, meeting the others. "Well, professor, I'm not saying your theory is wrong just yet," Falconer said. "There could be some sort of passageway leading from the street or the river, as you said."

"Yes, I know this all sounds quite farfetched, ladies and gentlemen," Levine said, "but I'm not ready to disavow it yet."

"Well, we'll just have to keep looking," Falconer said. "Meantime, it's clear no meeting happened in here tonight. Let's head back to the street."

He started walking out with the others but then stopped when he noticed Bly over near the wall behind the small alter, gazing upon a collection of marble figurines of Jesus and other biblical characters that stood fixed against the ornate back wall. "Miss, Bly," he said, "are you coming?"

"Oh, yes, sorry," Bly said with a smile. "I was just admiring these little statuettes here. Such wonderful detail and craftsmanship. I wonder who sculpted them."

"Well, you'll have to come back and take some more time with them when the church is open," Falconer said.

"Yes," she replied, softly touching the side of the figurine of a young shepherd boy standing with his staff and a flock of sheep. "I'll make sure to do tha—"

Suddenly the figurine moved slightly, and a portion of the wall appeared to start moving backwards. Bly yelped and stepped back a couple of feet, appearing frightened at the sudden movement of the chapel wall.

"What the hell?" Falconer said, stepping forward and grabbing her by the arm.

The others slowly started moving into the room again, and Waidler, Halloran, Winter, and Kramer pulled out their revolvers. Penwill stepped forward and peered into the doorway that had opened in the wall, then turned to Levine. "Well, professor," he said with a grin, "I think Miss Bly has just stumbled upon George Washington's secret underground chambers."

82

Falconer gently moved Bly behind him, as if to protect her, and then he raised his lantern and peered into the opening in the chapel wall. The hidden doorway was about five feet high and two feet wide—certainly large enough for a grown man to walk through. He then turned to the others and spoke: "It looks like our evening isn't over quite yet. And professor, you might have just helped discover one the great historical finds of the century. Is everyone all right with going in? You don't have to if you don't want to."

He looked around at the others, who all nodded eagerly. "All right, then," he said, "gentlemen, keep your weapons handy, and Miss Bly, Mister Riis, and Professor Levine, you stay in the back—understand?"

"Yes, detective sergeant," Bly replied.

"Understood," Riis said.

"Yes, of course," Levine said.

"Okay, then, here goes," Falconer said. "Follow me—quietly."

He raised his lantern a little higher, held his revolver up near his shoulder, and then bent down slightly and walked through the doorway. As he moved slowly into the space, he saw that some stone steps started to descend just a few feet in front of him. He turned and pointed them out to the others, then started walking again. Arriving at the top of the stairs, he started walking down until he came to a wide, brick hallway that, to his surprise, was brightened with gaslights fixed to the walls every twenty feet or so. He gazed down the hallway and saw no one, and then walked back a few steps and whispered to the others: "As you can see, they've got working gaslights on down here, so be careful—we could encounter our suspects."

Turning forward again, he walked slowly down the hallway as Waidler, Halloran, Winter, Kramer, and the two inspectors spaced out along each wall with their revolvers at the ready. About forty feet down the passageway, he saw an opening leading into a much larger space. Pointing at this, he motioned for the men to stay along the walls and be ready for contact with any armed suspects.

He then walked up to the edge of the opening and looked inside the large, brick and stone room. It was clearly a meeting place of some sort and was lit by the same gaslights that adorned the passageway. At the far end of the room, there was a long, marble table with a large, decorative wooden chair behind it. As Falconer walked into the middle of the space and got closer to the table, he saw a series of painted inscriptions high up on the wall behind the chair. He tried to make out what it said but it appeared to be in Latin.

Turning, he signaled for Halloran and Waidler to go check out the exits at the far corners of the room. He then realized that there was a second level to the space, with some sort of balcony wrapping around it. "Winter and Kramer," he said quietly to the two officers, "go find a way up to that balcony and check it out." The two men nodded and quickly walked off.

Falconer then turned to Levine, who was standing behind with Riis, Bly, Houllier, and Penwill. "Professor," he said, "do you see that writing up there on the wall? Any chance you know any Latin?"

"I have some experience with it," Levine said, walking forward. "Let me see here..."

Falconer watched as Levine raised his index finger as if pointing to the words on a page of paper as he read. Then, after a few seconds, Levine turned back to him and the others.

"Amazing," he said.

"What?" Falconer asked.

"Do you see those two words in Latin up there?" Levine asked, pointing at the wall. "The two larger words that are above the picture of the large Christian cross?"

"Yes, I do," Falconer answered. "What does it mean?"

"Puritas Fortitudinem," Levine said. "Purity is strength."

"Purity is strength?" Bly asked. "What on earth do they mean by that?"

"It's their code, Miss Bly," Falconer answered. "By purifying the racial make-up of the citizenry, the country becomes stronger—becomes more unified and good."

"So, purify it by making it completely Caucasian, I suppose?" Bly said.

"Yes, and wholly Christian, too," Levine said. "Other religions, like my own Judaism, or Hindus, or Moslems, are regarded as the other…the enemy to be removed and destroyed."

"Good heavens," Riis said as he gazed up on the wall.

"Why, this is like the Klan that has caused so much trouble and bloodshed in the south," Bly said.

"Only they don't wear hoods," Falconer said. "Instead, they move about in the open, working their jobs and walking down the street just like you or I, posing as normal citizens, but then they meet in the night and concoct their plans to, as the professor said, destroy those whom they feel threaten their unique vision of the world."

"Except they do display this little code on their bodies, it appears," Levine said.

"What do you mean, professor?" Falconer asked. "Wait—Puritas Fortitudinem…P.F. It's the tattoos that we've seen on the group's members."

"Yes," Levine said. "Here is the answer to your mystery."

Falconer looked at Bly as she gazed up at the wall again for several seconds, and then turned back to the men. "This is incredibly frightening, gentlemen," she said. "So, they are committing murders, assassinations, kidnappings?"

"They are," Falconer said, stepping up onto the raised platform that served as a base for the marble table and chair. "And they have to be stopped."

"But how?" she asked. "If they roam about society with nothing but hidden tattoos, how can you expose them?"

"There is an old saying in the military, Miss Bly," Penwill said, stepping forward. "Cut off the head of the snake, and the body will die."

"So, the head," Bly said. "Find out who the leaders are, and remove them, then the organization fails?"

"Something like that," Penwill said. "If one can take away the controlling headquarters of a group, oftentimes, the group then becomes muddled and lost, and can be easily surrounded and eliminated."

"I like what you're saying, inspector," Falconer said. "The question is, how do we find out who runs the headquarters, so to speak?"

"Well, you yourself said our recently deceased informant had said that the railroad magnate, Walter Bliss, was at the top."

"Walter Bliss?" Bly said excitedly. "You can't be serious."

"Unfortunately, we are," Falconer said. "We had an informant on the inside who told me Bliss is one of the controlling parties, but this informant was just found dead. So, we don't have much to go on now."

"Walter Bliss at the head of a murderous society bent on eliminating all non-white, non-Christian people from the country," Bly said. "Jacob, this could be the story of the decade, if not the century."

"It is truly remarkable," Riis said. "And horrifying."

"Well, don't get your hopes up for a story at this point," Falconer said. "They first have to be brought to justice, and I'm counting on you both not to divulge any of this."

"Yes, of course," Bly said.

"Absolutely," Riis said. "This is too important."

Falconer saw Waidler and Halloran coming back into the room from a corner exit. "All clear, boss," Waidler said. "Only some locked doors and another long hallway that appears to be headed towards the docks."

"Got it," Falconer said. "Thanks, boys."

He then looked up and saw Winter and Kramer exploring the balcony. "Hey, Winter!" he yelled out. "Anything?"

"No, sir!" Winter yelled back. "Just an empty balcony up here."

"Well, if they had a meeting here at eight, it was a short one," Falconer said to the others gathering around him. "No one's here."

"What do you suggest we do now?" Penwill asked.

"I don't know," Falconer answered. "We've apparently found a head-quarters of some sort, but there's not really any evidence of their activities present."

"Uh...sir?" Halloran said from behind the marble table.

"What is it, Jimmy?" Falconer said.

"I'm seeing some drawers right back here," Halloran replied, "and you might want to see this."

"Drawers?" Falconer said, walking around the table, followed by the others.

"Right here, sir," Halloran said, pointing at a set of wooden drawers fastened to the back of the table. "And there's something inside this one."

Falconer looked down and saw inside an open drawer a large binder or book with the title, "Order of Cadere – Meeting Registrar," printed in fancy calligraphy on its cover. He reached down and picked it up and set it on the marble table.

"What the devil," Penwill said, stepping closer. "What is that?"

"It looks like some sort of record of the meetings that take place here," Falconer answered as he flipped through the pages. "I'm seeing dates and times and lists of last names of attendees."

"Really?" Penwill said. "Good god, this could be a treasure trove of information."

"I agree," Falconer said. "Let's see…let me just take a look at today's date."

He flipped through several more pages and then peered down at a page. "Yes, looks like we just missed it, folks," he said. "It says here in fresh ink that they met tonight and adjourned at approximately 8:15 PM."

"So, we did just miss them, confound it," Penwill said.

"At least I have a bunch of names in attendance," Falconer said. "Here, everyone, gather around a take a look."

The others moved closer to the table and looked at the page as Falconer held the book up.

"There must be thirty names there," Penwill said.

"And I, in fact, recognize some of them," Levine stated. "Some of them are very prominent men in our city."

"*Incroyable, messieurs et mademoiselle,*" Houllier said. "You have found the map to the very heart of this sinister organization."

"Yes, Inspector Houllier," Falconer said, "but I don't see a listing for Walter Bliss anywhere."

"But look there at the top of the list of today's attendees," Bly chimed in. "'G. Bliss.' You know who that is, don't you?"

"I'm not sure, honestly," Falconer said.

"Wait," Levine said, "'G. Bliss'…for George Bliss."

"Exactly, professor," Bly said, smiling. "Bliss' eldest son who allegedly works for him and is one of the elder Bliss' fiercest supporters."

"Right," Falconer said. "Now I remember him. I've seen him in the papers, always spouting about the latest assault on his father's golden image."

"Well, we, too, know all about Bliss and his sons across the pond, Falconer," Penwill said. "Indeed, they are regarded as the greatest hornswogglers and humbugs your good country has ever created. Always good for a laugh."

"But unfortunately, they're good for murders now, too, inspector," Falconer said. "We can't take this book with us—they'd realize that someone is onto them and then just disappear into the night. We have to leave it and figure out how to take advantage of this knowledge that we've gained."

"Well, we can focus on the son," Waidler said. "Maybe tail him."

"That's a good start," Falconer said. "Let's all head on out of here, shall we? We've done enough for one night."

He placed the book back in the drawer and closed it, then pointed the way back to the stairs leading up to the basement of the church. The group then started walking out of the large room and made it to the stairs, where they all ascended to the basement. As Bly and Falconer followed the others and approached the stairs, she touched him on his arm.

"Thank you for allowing us into this little investigation," she said. "I appreciate it very much."

"Well, you were already here, and I suppose we had to let you into the circle at that point," Falconer said.

"I want you to know that I won't be saying anything about this to anyone," she reassured him. "Not even to my mother."

"Well, I appreciate that, Miss Bly."

She stopped him at the bottom of the stairs and let the others move up to the street ahead of them.

"Just a brief word, detective sergeant," she said to him.

"Sure."

"I want you to know that this story is very big, and it could be a huge win for a journalist and a newspaper that publishes it first."

"Yes, I know that."

"But I want to keep it secret because I know that you want to keep it secret. That's important to me, detective sergeant."

"Well, thank you, Miss Bly."

"It's the least I can do. After all, you did jump off the Brooklyn Bridge last year and saved me from certain drowning."

"That's all right. No need to return any favor. I was—"

"I know you were just doing your duty. That's what impresses me about you, detective sergeant. Not many men would have done that—even if they felt a certain duty."

She then turned and started slowly walking up the stairs, but he spoke out and stopped her after a few steps: "It wasn't just because of my duty."

She turned and stood on the steps, staring at him momentarily, and he wasn't sure if he should say anything more.

"What was that?" she asked.

"I…I just said that I didn't jump off the bridge that night just because of my duty as a policeman."

"I see," she said, tugging absently at her hair. "Well…what exactly do you mean?"

He walked forward to the bottom step, and they appeared to be almost looking eye-to-eye because she was standing several steps up. He looked down at his shoes and wrestled with the words that were swimming in his brain, and he became acutely aware that she was staring at him.

"I…well…I…"

"Yes, detective sergeant?"

"The truth is, by that time," he said haltingly, "I think I had taken a liking to you, Miss Bly. I liked your liveliness, your drive, and your concern for the safety of the citizens in the city. When that man threw you off the bridge all tied up like that, I just couldn't let you go without trying to do something to save you. I just couldn't."

She stared at him for several seconds and he wasn't sure if he had offended or alarmed her, and he almost wished he hadn't said anything. "Well, maybe we should just head up with the others here," he said awkwardly as he moved to walk up the steps.

"No," she said, stopping him with a hand on his chest. "I actually appreciate you very much for telling me that. We have not seen much of each other since you last visited me in the hospital after that terrible ordeal in the river, and frankly, I've missed your presence."

"Well, thank you," he said, looking at her again. "I've wondered about you, too. I've wondered what you've been doing these past several months, and…how your mother is doing—that sort of thing."

"I've wondered about you, as well," she said, smiling, and he suddenly felt a weight lift off his shoulders, and he wanted then and there to walk off with her, back into the caverns and passageways, and talk into the night. But then he remembered that they had to leave, and that the men were waiting up on the street above, so he smiled back slightly and pointed at the top of the stairs.

"I…think we'd better catch up to the men," he said.

"Yes, yes, of course," she said. "How very rude of me to keep you here while they are waiting."

She turned and quickly bounded up the stairs, and he watched her from below, and he realized that he was smiling slightly again. He took a deep breath and chuckled to himself. "Oh, boy," he said, still smiling.

83

Falconer sat at his desk the morning after he and his companions had explored the tunnels beneath the Saint Veronica Church. Before him was the just-released coroner's report on the death of the mysterious informant who had met him in Central Park. He gazed down at the pages and looked for the coroner's ultimate conclusions concerning the cause of death. After skimming through several pages, he arrived at the final page, read through it, and then sat back in frustration. He looked down at the page again and read the final couple of paragraphs once more, just to be sure.

"Morning, boss."

He looked up and saw Waidler and Halloran entering the room with coffee mugs in hand. "Good morning, gentlemen," he said to them. "I'm just looking through the coroner's report on the death of our informant, and it's not good."

"Oh?" Waidler said. "Why not?"

"Well, it says here that they can't find any external cause of death," Falconer answered. "They only conclude that our guy died from apparent heart failure—basically, an undetected congenital problem that suddenly reared its head."

"But we know that that suspect up on the roof had something to do with it," Waidler said. "There's no doubt."

"Yes, I agree, James," Falconer said, "but apparently, they just couldn't find any sign of a struggle, no external cause of death, which is troubling. Except…"

"Yes?" Waidler said.

"Except there's this other doctor—Doctor Albright—who writes in a little footnote at the bottom of the page that he disagrees and believes there is some evidence of poisoning. I guess this was overruled by the coroner and the other docs, who weren't convinced."

"That's odd," Waidler said.

"Yes, it is," Falconer said, "and I think we need to go pay this Doctor Albright a visit and find out what he's talking about."

"Sounds good," Waidler said. "When should we go?"

"How about right now?" Falconer said. "Finish your coffee, boys— we're going to go ask this doc a few questions about poison."

84

Falconer walked up to the front desk of the city morgue in Bellevue Hospital, followed by Waidler and Halloran. A young woman sat behind the desk arranging papers and folders, and Falconer coughed slightly, getting her attention. "Yes, sir?" she asked.

"I'm Detective Sergeant Falconer from police headquarters," he said, showing his badge, "and these are two of my men. We're working on a case involving an unidentified decedent whose body was found at 55 West 37th Street on September 16. We've reviewed the coroner's report on this individual, and we'd just like to speak with one of the doctors if possible—a Doctor K. Albright?"

"Yes, certainly, sir," the receptionist said. "Doctor Albright is just in the back. If you'll give me a moment, please."

"Yes, thank you," Falconer replied.

The receptionist then exited through a door behind the desk and Falconer turned to the other men. "Well, that was easy enough," he said.

"Strange that this doc identified some evidence of a poisoning, but the others didn't see it," Waidler said.

"Yeah, well, you know docs," Falconer said. "They all think that they're right and there can't be an opposing view."

Waidler and Halloran chuckled momentarily, and then composed themselves quickly when another young woman—pretty with wavy brown hair pulled up into a bun and wearing eyeglasses—suddenly entered through the doorway behind the desk. "Yes?" she said, with no sign of a smile. "Can I help you gentlemen?"

"Um, yes, miss," Falconer replied. "We're detectives from police headquarters and one of your receptionists just went to get Doctor Albright for us. Could you please see if he's available?"

The young woman stared at Falconer for a moment, and then, with a curt, "Certainly," she turned and exited the room again.

Falconer turned to face Waidler and Halloran and smiled a little. "Well, that one wasn't too friendly for some reason."

The young woman with the eyeglasses then reappeared suddenly from behind the door and stood before the men again. "Yes?" she said. "How can I help you?"

"I don't understand, miss," Falconer said. "Again, we're looking for Doctor Albright."

"Yes, I know that," she said, smiling this time. "So, again—how can I help you?"

"I'm not following you, miss," Falconer said.

"Uh, boss," Waidler said, stepping forward, "I think you're speaking to the doctor right now."

"What?" Falconer said. "Oh, right. Sorry, doctor—I was just a confused for a moment there."

"Yes, I know, detective sergeant," the doctor said. "It happens quite often, actually. I can't tell why."

"Yes, well...we appreciate you meeting us today without an appointment," Falconer said. "We just had a few questions concerning your comments on the autopsy report of the decedent found at 55 West 37th Street on September 16."

"Yes, the young Caucasian male who has not yet been identified," she said.

"Correct," Falconer said.

"What would you like to know?" she asked.

"Well, the coroner concluded that this was simply a case of congenital heart failure," Falconer said. "No external cause."

"Yes, that's true," she said.

"But you disagreed. You reported that there was some evidence of poisoning."

"Correct, detective sergeant."

"Would you mind explaining what you meant? I will be frank—we are investigating this as a murder."

"Yes, I figured as much. Here—come into this side office with me so that we're alone."

She turned and led the three men into an anteroom with a large table and several chairs, and several bookshelves stocked full of thick medical treatises.

"This is better," she said, taking a seat along with the men. "So, why do you think it was a murder, if I may ask?"

"Because we found the decedent in his apartment right after he expired," Falconer replied. "And I chased a suspect from rooftop to rooftop just minutes after."

"I see," the doctor said. "Then I believe my suspicions were correct. With your circumstantial evidence, it's very evident to me that this man was poisoned just moments before you arrived at his apartment."

"But what is the evidence that you found? And why do these other doctors disagree?"

"Well, as to the other doctors, I cannot answer that. But sometimes these physicians can be very...well...set in their ways."

"And as to the evidence of poisoning?"

"It's not overwhelming, but it is there. In examining the man's body with my colleagues, and hearing of the scene of the crime, it became apparent to me that this man was killed quickly and probably without his awareness."

"Why do you say that?"

"Because there were no signs of convulsions, physical injuries, diarrhea, vomiting—that sort of thing. So, there clearly was no struggle, and if a poisoning did occur, it was not a long lasting one."

"What about arsenic? I know that it's a popular choice for would-be killers because one can't taste it, and it's difficult to detect in the body later."

"Yes, but arsenic takes time to work, and it results in those very symptoms that I just mentioned, retching and vomiting, falling into terrible convulsions. This victim appeared peacefully at rest in his chair, as you well know. So, it wasn't arsenic."

"Then what?"

"Well, after my colleagues had finished their work, I lingered a bit and looked over the body some more. I, in fact, bent down closely to the man's skin, and smelled it."

"You smelled his skin?" Falconer asked.

"Yes."

"Why would you do that?"

"Have you ever tasted a batch of bitter almonds, detective sergeant?" she asked.

"No," he replied. "Can't say that I have. I don't like almonds."

"Um, pardon me, miss," Halloran said from across the table. "I like almonds, and I've smelled those sort—the bitter ones. I hate them."

"Yes, well, some almonds do have that bitter smell, unlike the typical batch that smells and tastes rather sweet," she said.

"So, what of this?" Falconer inquired.

"There is something else that smells just like those bitter almonds, detective sergeant," the doctor answered. "Cyanide."

"Cyanide?" Falconer said. "I've heard of it—another very toxic poison, and very quick acting."

"True," she said. "It's not necessarily easy to detect in an autopsy, and it also results in tissue and organ breakdowns that are often seen in naturally occurring events, like heart attacks and heart or pulmonary failures."

"And I take it you detected this bitter almond smell on his skin?" Falconer asked.

"Yes, and on his urine sample that was taken from his pants. And I also would like to add that his skin had a rather pink, almost cherry-colored glow to it, which is another indication of potential cyanide poisoning."

"So, why didn't your colleagues detect all of this, doctor?" Falconer asked.

"We were wearing masks, detective sergeant, and the smell on the skin is not strong. As I said, I had to lean down closely to the body to detect it. The other doctors simply never thought to look. They were convinced that the medical evidence all pointed to sudden congenital heart failure, which of course is a common cause of death."

"So, the question is, how did our suspect on the roof give the poison to our victim?" Falconer asked. "Perhaps mixed it in a drink?"

"Doubtful," the doctor replied. "Inhaling cyanide in gaseous form is much more potent and lethal than ingesting it."

"But how would this victim not be aware of some cyanide gas? And how would the suspect manage to get him to inhale it?"

"Did any of you see any signs of cigarettes, cigars, pipes, that sort of thing?"

"I don't recall seeing anything," Falconer said.

"Me neither," Waidler said.

"There was a pipe, actually, sir," Halloran said, sitting up straighter in his chair.

"Really, Jimmy?" Falconer said.

"Yes, sir," Halloran said. "I saw it over in the corner of the room, lying under a small table. I didn't think anything of it at the time—sorry."

"That's okay," Falconer said. "Doctor, could this pipe be the source of a cyanide gas?"

"If your suspect convinced the victim to smoke a tobacco that was subtly flavored with almonds," she replied. "Does anyone know if almond-flavored tobacco exists?"

Falconer looked at Halloran and Waidler, and Waidler spoke: "Sure. I've seen it marketed."

"Well, then, there's your answer, detective sergeant," the doctor said. "This victim sat down with the suspect and likely smoked a pipe filled with tobacco that was laced with cyanide. It's not too far-fetched a scenario."

"No, it isn't," Falconer said. "In fact, it makes perfect sense. But one thing: if our victim was smoking tobacco with cyanide in it, how come our suspect wasn't affected?"

"I would imagine that he simply made sure to be well-distanced from the smoke when your victim lit up," the doctor opined. "Perhaps even standing by an open window. One would have to be quite close to it to suffer any ill effects."

"Well, thank you for your opinions, doctor," Falconer said. "Again, we appreciate you speaking with us today, and I can assure you that next time, I'll know who you are."

The doctor finally smiled again. "Are you saying that there's definitely going to be a next time, detective sergeant?"

"Well, unfortunately, we deal with dead bodies quite a lot, doctor," he replied. "I'm sure that if you continue working for the coroner, you'll be seeing us again. Thank you again—we'll show ourselves out now."

"Yes, certainly, detective sergeant," she said, standing up with the men. "Please keep me apprised of this situation if you don't mind. That man suffered a terrible death. A quick death, but terrible nonetheless."

"Agreed, doctor," Falconer said, doffing his bowler. "Have a good day."

He then walked out of the room and headed for the stairwell, joined by Waidler and Halloran.

85

"So, this Doctor Albright believes that your unidentified informant was poisoned by cyanide?" Byrnes asked from behind his desk.

"That's correct, sir," Falconer answered, as he stood with Penwill, Houllier, and Waidler. "She dissents from the other doctors' opinions, but she did provide these compelling reasons."

"Yes, yes, I can't argue with you there, Falconer," Byrnes said, scratching his chin. "And it makes sense, actually. This group that you've been investigating would want this informant eliminated, obviously, and poison appears to have done the trick. So, what are we doing now?"

"Well, Officers Halloran, Winter, and Kramer are tailing Bliss' son, hoping that it'll lead somewhere," Falconer said. "We think the son is high up in the group's hierarchy."

"Well, tread lightly, Falconer. Bliss is, as you know, a powerful man in this town, and his son is equally well-connected. I don't need any bad press coming to us by having one of your men rough up the son."

"Understood, sir. We're just trying to shadow him and see where he leads us."

"Yes, of course. And I agree that you don't have enough evidence at this point to charge anyone, even after discovering this mysterious lair under the church."

"Yes, not yet, but soon, we hope."

"Well, keep at it," Byrnes said, looking at the men, "but this stays in this office, understand."

"Yes, sir," Falconer replied. "Thank you."

"And by the way," Byrnes said, "any news about Meunier's trail, inspectors?"

"Well, perhaps it's good news for you, superintendent," Penwill said. "We aren't sure, but we have indications that perhaps he made his way back to England or France. The Special Branch is investigating this now."

"Understood, gentlemen. Then, I suppose that means we'll be losing the both of you shortly."

"Yes," Penwill said. "I believe that soon, Inspector Houllier and myself will have to head back to London or Paris. But in the meantime, we are happy to help Detective Sergeant Falconer here with this band of assassins that he's been tracking."

"Good, good," Byrnes said. "The city certainly appreciates your assistance in this matter."

"Certainly," Penwill said.

"But of course, superintendent," Houllier chimed in.

"All right then, men," Byrnes said. "Good luck."

"Thank you, sir," Falconer said.

He then pointed to the door and led the men out into the hallway.

86

Winter stood alone in the shadows on the corner of 5th Avenue and 36th Street and looked over at the front entrance to the swanky Millennium Club that stood like a great, marble symbol of American extravagance and wealth. He had been standing vigil over the exclusive gentlemen's club for the rich and powerful for a couple of hours as Halloran lingered on the other side of the avenue, away from the glare of the gaslights and the constant activity at the grand building's entrance.

Winter glanced over at the younger officer, and then looked farther back on the street to where Kramer was sitting atop a parked hansom cab, playing the part of a simple cab driver working the city streets at night. The three of them had been on the trail of George Bliss, 42-year-old heir to the Bliss fortune and favorite son of his vainglorious, provocateur father, and had tracked the younger man to the opulent Millennium Club, which was headed by the father and included some of the wealthiest people in town as members.

He turned back to look at the entrance of the club again, reached down, took out a flask, and took a quick drink of some whisky.

No harm. To hell with 'em.

He then stuffed the flask back in his pocket and suddenly stood still: the tuxedo-clad younger Bliss had finally appeared at the entrance to the clubhouse across the street and appeared to be instructing some men to bring up a carriage. Winter watched as the young financier spoke with a young paramour hanging onto his arm for several minutes, and then a fancy black carriage headed by a small team of elegant horses rode up and came to a stop curbside in front of the couple. Winter watched as the club's doormen helped the two up into the carriage and then sent it off down the avenue.

Stepping out slightly into the street, he waved at Halloran, and then did the same to Kramer back with the cab. Within seconds, Kramer had guided his horse up to the two officers, and they jumped in and sat back as the cab roared off away from the curb.

"You sure that's him?" Kramer yelled down from his seat above and behind the cab's small passenger compartment.

"As sure as I'm sitting here on my big Irish arse!" Winter yelled back. "He's with some lady-friend, too."

"Well, he's probably just going back to his joint," Kramer said.

"Nah, he's headed west," Winter said. "His place is over on the East Side. Let's just keep an eye on him."

Kramer guided his horse slowly behind the fancy carriage at a distance as it wound itself west to Broadway, then south into the heart of the noisy Tenderloin. Approaching the intersection of 31st Street, the carriage suddenly turned west again and ambled past numerous gin joints, bordellos, and dirty dance halls.

"Now, where the hell is this swell going?" Winter asked loudly. "Why would such a rich guy like him come over to this pigsty?"

"Somethin' must be up, my friend," Kramer said from above.

"I agree," Winter said. "When he stops, leave us off at a distance. All right?"

"Sure thing, pal," Kramer said.

"You think he's meeting someone over here?" Halloran asked Winter.

"Why else would this fancy dude be coming over to these parts, Jimmy?" Winter responded. "Let's just see who he meets."

Winter watched outside his window as the large carriage kept rolling west until it finally came to a stop next to the curb at a slightly quieter section of midtown.

"He's getting out," Halloran said.

"Yup," Winter said. "Jimmy, let's get out here and see where he goes. Keep at a distance, boy, you hear?"

"Got it," Halloran replied.

"All right, Kramer, you okay parking here for a bit?" Winter asked, looking up at the officer sitting high up on his driver's seat.

"Sure thing," Kramer answered. "But if I hear anything bad, I'm coming fast with my two guns."

"Sounds good to me, pardner," Winter said. "All right, Jimmy, you take the other side of the street and I'll go down on this side. It looks like he's moving down a bit towards Eighth. Remember—Falconer just wanted us to see what he's up to, not try to take the guy down."

"Understood," Halloran said.

The two men then split up and walked slowly down the street on opposite sides. Winter could see Bliss walking westward along the sidewalk by himself, and the carriage remained parked along the street. Coming alongside it, he pulled his hat down low over his brow and looked away, and then, when he was finally past it, he kept moving slowly behind his quarry, perhaps thirty yards distant. After several more seconds, he saw Bliss suddenly turn left and disappear into an alleyway. Slowing up, he looked over at Halloran, who was watching intently, and nodded subtly at the young officer. Halloran then quietly walked across the street and started walking with Winter.

"Did you see that, Jimmy?" Winter asked him. "He went down this alley here."

"I did see it, Mister Winter."

"Well, make sure your gun is handy, if need be. I'll go in on this closer side, and then you follow on the other side of the alley a few seconds later, okay?"

"Yes, got it."

"All right, here goes," Winter said, and then he walked several paces forward and turned left into the alley. Peering down the slim space between the two buildings that rose on either side of him, he saw no sign of Bliss, so he ventured a little farther into the alley. He looked back and could see Halloran doing the same: gliding slowly along the opposite wall, pistol ready in his hand.

Walking several more steps, Winter gazed forward into the dim light and saw two men standing together and talking in the distance near a large barrel.

Bliss and some other mope. Interesting...

He watched as they spoke for several seconds, and then he signaled for Halloran to quickly join him alongside the wall where he stood in the darkness. Halloran nodded and soon was standing right behind him, pressed up against the dirty, brick wall.

"Is that Bliss right there?" Halloran whispered.

"Sure is," Winter said quietly. "All dressed up in his finery that costs more than our salaries and meeting some pin-head in a back alley. Kind of odd, wouldn't you say?"

"Yes, I would agree. Should we grab them?"

"Nah. Falconer didn't want that, as I mentioned, so we'll just follow him afterwards."

"Bliss?" Halloran asked.

"Nope," Winter replied. "The other guy. We follow him back to wherever he goes and then eventually we take him down and get him to talk. Know what I mean?"

"Sounds good."

"Okay, then, let's back off and head back to where the cab is. When this little minion of Bliss comes out of the alley, we tail him. Okay?"

"Understood."

The two officers then quietly retraced their steps and moved out onto the sidewalk of 31st Street, where they would await the appearance of George Bliss' mysterious new contact.

87

The young lawyer, Meyer Weintraub, stopped for a moment in his speech to a large crowd of immigrant workers at an assembly hall on the Lower East Side and allowed their raucous applause to play out. He was almost finished with his remarks to the mainly German and Eastern European followers of the Autonomist branch of anarchism in New York City, and he was pleased that the crowd had been noisily receptive to his words.

He took a deep breath and then spoke again: "To conclude, my fellow Americans—yes, Americans, for that is what you are despite the ill treatment you face every day on these shores—I am just a young, undistinguished attorney with—like you perhaps—very little money in my pockets. But I will fight and keep fighting for your rights and your equality in this land, and I will not shrink from their intimidation or their threats to silence me! Let us go forward and make the world anew and fight the dark forces that would keep us under the boot and hidden away from the blessings of this country!"

The crowd roared again as he stepped away from the dais and received a quick handshake and congratulations from the master of ceremonies, and then he took his seat along with the other speakers at the back of the stage.

A half hour later, he was exiting the assembly hall to the well-wishes of the spectators, and, after speaking again momentarily outside with the meeting's organizers, he placed his hat atop his head and cheerfully walked down the street, pleased with his place in the movement and his status as a frontline warrior in the legal battles to ensure the rights and dignity of the immigrants struggling together in the packed tenements of Lower Manhattan.

That went well. Anya will be pleased when I tell her, and I will keep doing the work that the thousands of others cannot do for themselves. This country does have an inherent tendency towards kindness and goodwill, and we have hope….

88

F alconer stood alone under a gas lamp and smoked a cigarillo. He had been waiting for her to come out of the saloon for the past hour and thought this was a better course of action than to simply interrupt her again with her band of followers and friends inside the place. He heard the noise of some drunken revelers down the street and glanced in that direction, and then turned back to the entrance of the establishment. He saw the door open wide and Emma Goldman came out finally, surrounded by several companions. As they all spoke gaily to each other following their evening of drinking and storytelling, Falconer stepped off the curb and saw that she had seen him. He walked slowly across the street and could see that she was smiling now.

"Detective Sergeant Falconer," Goldman said, "I see that you are still tracking my whereabouts."

"Occasionally, Miss Goldman," he said. "And how are you these days?"

"I am fine, for the most part, thank you. But such is not the case for my Sasha, whom I just learned recently was subjected to a sham trial and was sentenced to twenty-two years in the penitentiary. Twenty-two years, Falconer!"

"Well, I'm sorry about that, but he did try to kill a man."

"But this is outrageous!" she said excitedly. "Twenty-two years in a hole in the ground, forgotten by civilization and beset by the brutes of the prison system. It is not right, and I will fight this sentence to the last extremity."

"I'm sure you will, and I imagine you might succeed in helping him."

"We can only hope," she said quietly. "So, why have come out this night?"

"I wanted to warn you. I know that you've not been targeted recently, but we have come across certain evidence recently…evidence concerning who was trying to assassinate you these past few months, and they are still out there."

"Evidence, you say? What sort of evidence? Who is it?"

"I can only say that it is a group that hides in the shadows and is led by some very powerful men," he replied. "We are not there yet with proof that will hold up in court, but we are trying. I just ask that you be very careful these days—they aren't finished."

"And what is their grievance? Why are they so hell-bent on killing me?"

"They are a group devoted to maintaining the purity of the population, and that means white Christians, and that also means that you—a Jewish immigrant who rails against the American system and government—are the enemy. You are everything that they despise—an intelligent woman who is of a different culture and religion, and who is a threat to their power. Do you understand?"

"Oh, I understand very well," she said calmly. "I understand all too well. It appears that your land of the free is actually not so free, after all. Do you agree?"

"I suppose I do," he said.

"Well, then, your warning is appreciated, and I shall take appropriate precautions, but I will not bow down to their threats."

"I know you won't. And I won't, either."

"I know that, too. We are not so dissimilar."

"Maybe," he said, grinning slightly. "I'll be in touch."

He then walked off across the street and headed for the elevated train.

89

The groggy janitor lugged his bucket and mop out to the pews in the Sharrai Zedeck synagogue on Henry Street. It was early in the morning—six o'clock—and he wanted to get the floors cleaned well before the rabbi and his assistant appeared for the day. He dropped the bucket to the floor and stood up straighter, intending on dipping the mop into it, but then he noticed something out of the corner of his eye in the growing sunlight that seeped into the temple's windows. He turned slightly and looked up over the rabbi's podium and started with a fright, dropping his mop.

"My god," he said. "Oh, my god."

He then ran out through the front doors and raced as a fast as he could to the Madison Street police station five blocks away.

90

Falconer hopped off the police wagon with Waidler in front of the synagogue at 38 Henry Street. A small crowd of mourners lingered together near the entrance, clearly overcome with grief. "Let's head in," he said to Waidler, and then the two men moved to the entrance and entered the building. Inside, Falconer spotted Detective Stan Crawford from the 7th Precinct on Madison Street amongst several other officers and lay persons. Crawford looked up and nodded at them, and then walked over.

"Hey, Robert," he said to Falconer. "Glad you could make it."

"How you doing, Stan?" Falconer said. "This is James Waidler, a detective with us at Mulberry."

Crawford shook Waidler's hand and then turned back to Falconer. "Well," he said, "we learned that the victim was a lawyer for some of the anarchist groups down here, and then we were told to call you guys down. Does this make any sense to you?"

"Yes, it does, I'm afraid," Falconer replied, looking up at a rope with a noose that hung from a beam angling down from the ceiling. "So, what do you have?"

"Well, the janitor was cleaning this morning when he looked up and saw victim hanging from that rope," Crawford said. "He beat it on down to our station and we came over immediately. We know who the victim is—his wallet was still in his pocket. His name is Meyer Weintraub, a twenty-five-year-old lawyer who represents these anarchist types in their fights with landlords, in their criminal court cases—that sort of thing. Apparently, he's been earning a name as a very vocal supporter of their causes—a real firebrand type."

"Any witnesses to what happened?" Falconer said.

"No," Crawford replied. "No one saw anything, or at least we haven't found anyone. We do know that he was at a rally last night at Wilzig's Assembly Hall on 4th Street. He finished his speech and then left alone, according to some witnesses. No one knows what happened to him next."

"And I take it he's a Jewish lawyer—correct?" Falconer asked.

"Well, yeah," Crawford answered with a puzzled look on his face. "But what does that have to do with it?"

"And he worked closely with people down here who were aligned with the anarchist movement?" Falconer asked, ignoring Crawford's inquiry.

"Yeah, definitely," Crawford said. "I'm hearing that he was basically rising in the ranks of those who are looked upon as leaders of their movement—a talented speaker, apparently."

"Right," Falconer said. "Well, we know who did this."

"You do?" Crawford said. "How? There aren't any witnesses and no evidence left at the scene."

"I know," Falconer said, "but it's clear who's responsible."

"Mind telling me how you're going to prosecute someone when you don't have any witnesses or identifying evidence?" Crawford asked, incredulously.

Falconer looked up at the rope again, and then turned back to Crawford. "I'm not going to bring these people in to be prosecuted," he said. "Thanks, Stan," and then he nodded at Waidler and the two men walked back outside to the street.

91

Bly hurriedly entered the sparkling lobby of the Bliss Building on 5th Avenue. A crowd of reporters was already assembled, as well as scores of admirers who struggled to get a glimpse of the famous railroad magnate, who, along with his wife, Agatha, and son, George, was expected to make a grand entrance at any minute from their upstairs apartment.

Bly had heard that Bliss was back in town after vacationing at his opulent mansion in North Carolina and would be making some sort of big announcement in the lobby of his famous building that had his surname etched into the concrete over the front entrance. Through her sources at her old newspaper, The World, she had learned that Bliss was likely going to announce a run for governor of New York State and make the long-expected transition from business mogul and constant presence in the newspapers' society pages to the government.

As she walked between the many persons vying for a good spot to see the event, she bumped into Fred Sullivan, her old cohort and fellow scribe at The World. "Nellie!" he exclaimed, eliciting the concerned glances of several onlookers nearby. "What are you doing here? I thought you'd be out at the farm and writing novels still."

"Oh, pshaw, Fred," she said dismissively. "You know I was never cut out for that novelist thing. And I'm not officially working for anyone, mind you, but I do have a lead on something."

"Really?" he said, eyebrows raised. "What, pray tell?"

"Sorry—can't," she answered apologetically. "It's top secret, as they say, but it could be big, Fred. Really big."

"Well, I'm all ears, girl," he said, "but I understand your position. Oh, look—here they come."

Bly craned her neck to get a look at the wealthy couple and son coming down the shiny, golden stairs of the fancy high-rise. "Here," Sullivan said, offering her a space in front of him. "It's a good vantage point."

She moved over a step to be in front of him and thanked him, and then gazed at the Bliss family walking down the steps towards a lectern set out in the lobby. The elder Bliss appeared as she remembered him from her reporter days: tall, a little rotund, a ruddy complexion, and with a thick mane of brown, graying hair sitting atop his head and a similarly colored, well-manicured goatee. He wore a dark suit with a fancy necktie and smiled approvingly at the throng that greeted his entrance enthusiastically as if he were a Roman conqueror.

His wife, Agatha, much younger than his 72 years, was slim and silent, a pretty woman dressed in a dark dress who said little and smiled wanly at the crowd. Then, behind her, the son from a different wife, George, in his early forties with slick-backed, dark hair and wearing an equally expensive suit and tie, smiled confidently at the crowd, seemingly convinced of his father's greatness and his own special place in the world.

The assembled people clapped and cooed until Walter Bliss, joined nearby by several security men, finally raised his hands to quiet them down. He then looked from side to side and spoke: "Ladies and gentlemen, this is a beautiful day here at my building, and it's so wonderful to be joined by all of you. We just got back from the lovely State of North Carolina, and it's beautiful down there, but it's not like New York. New York—the greatest city in the world."

The crowd cheered at his words and it took several moments before they quieted down to give the man a chance to speak again.

"But, my fellow citizens," he continued, "we're not here to talk about the weather outside. We're here to talk about a new beginning. A new beginning for this city and this state. We are seeing this once-great city crumble with crime and disease, brought here by people who came from God knows where. You know them—these people living twelve persons to a room, children everywhere, never washing, not even speaking English. Yes, you know the type."

The clapping and cheering grew louder again, until Bliss once more signaled for quiet.

"But we're here to put a stop to this nonsense," he said. "We're going to take this city and this state and bring them back to the way they used to be, when it was a bright, shining place for true Americans to work and raise their children in peace. Let me tell you, ladies and gentlemen—we're going to do it, that's right. So, as of today, I am announcing my candidacy for governor of the great State of New York, and we are going to win. We will win, and win big, ladies and gentlemen."

The people in the jammed lobby then erupted in a huge cheer, and Bly looked around and was impressed with the fervor that she saw, and she looked at Sullivan and smiled. Then Bliss again moved to silence his supporters and spoke in conclusion: "We thank you for coming out today—such a lovely crowd. Thank you for being here, my dear people, and God Bless America and our great state."

He then turned to lead the others up the golden staircase again, and the reporters started shouting out questions, and Bliss stopped suddenly and turned back to answer several of them. After a brief back and forth with the newspapermen, who wrote feverishly in their notebooks as the bombastic new candidate spoke forth, he turned once again to ascend the stairs, but then Bly pushed her way to the front of the pack and yelled out: "Mister Bliss, does the word 'Cadere' mean anything to you?"

Bliss stopped and turned, looking for the female voice that had uttered the strange question. Bly raised her hand and spoke out again as the other reporters looked at her in wonder: "Um, Nellie Bly, sir."

The crowd murmured with excitement upon learning who the young woman was: Nellie Bly, the great reporter/adventuress.

"Does the Latin word 'Cadere' mean anything to you or to your son here, sir?" she asked again.

Bliss glared down at Bly, and she could see below him the son also staring stone-faced at her. There was a moment of awkward silence in the room until Bliss finally smiled again. "Well, well," he said. "Do you see, ladies and gentlemen? We have none other than the famous reporter, Nellie Bly, here with us today. It's great to see you, Miss Bly, and sometimes I've wondered where you've gone—maybe you're just not so famous anymore, I don't know. But I'm not sure what you're talking about, so whatever it is, you should check your sources."

He then turned and walked up the stairs, followed by his wife, son, and retinue, and Bly just watched them go up before she was suddenly barraged with greetings and questions herself from the adoring people.

92

F alconer looked over at the shabby apartment building across the street in Hell's Kitchen as Winter and Kramer stood by. It was morning, and the rising sun revealed the grimy street lined with old and dilapidated buildings and sidewalks littered with rubbish and junk left by residents and shopkeepers the previous evening for the occasional ragpicker to come by and collect. As people walked briskly along the sidewalks, Falconer turned to the two officers and spoke: "So, you're sure this is the place where he stays?"

"Yes, sir, boss," Winter answered. "We followed him back here after he met Bliss, Junior, and he's been going in and out for a couple of days."

Falconer looked over at the decrepit building again. "Looks like a place a thug working for the Bliss family would call home," he said. "And you think he'll be coming out soon?"

"Yeah," Winter replied. "He's been coming out the past couple of mornings at nine o'clock or so. Then he goes down the street for a coffee."

"Well, then let's just wait and see if he's on time again today, gentlemen," Falconer said. "Winter, why don't you and Kramer head down the block a bit and wait near the corner there? I'll keep watch here with Halloran. If he comes out, converge on him and bring him down—we have our warrant now."

"Got it," Winter said, and then he traipsed off down the street with Kramer.

"Okay, Jimmy," Falconer said, "let's just see if our little minion appears on the street here in a minute."

"Yes, sir," Halloran said. "Do you really think Mister Bliss, the millionaire, is responsible for these assassinations going on?"

"It's looking like he is. Hard to believe, though. I've always viewed that guy as sort of a clown, one of those ringmasters in the circus—not as a real danger to the community. I guess we can always misjudge people."

"Yes, sir. And I hear he just announced a run for governor."

"What? Governor?"

"Yes, it's in the papers today. He just announced that he's running."

"Well, that's not good. A guy like that moving into a position of power in the government. What's next?"

"And I guess he has a big following, too. Being famous and all."

"Right. I figured. Wait a minute—look, Jimmy."

Falconer pointed across the street to where a young man was walking out of the old apartment building. "Is that him?"

"Yes, sir. That's him."

"Good. Let's start walking across the street but try to stay behind him."

"Got it."

Falconer waited a few seconds as the young man across the street pulled his cap down over his brow and started walking down the sidewalk towards Winter and Kramer. He then nodded at Halloran and started walking diagonally across the street, careful to avoid passing wagons and carriages. Signaling to Halloran to move across to the sidewalk and follow up directly behind the man, he quickened his pace and started gaining ground on the hoodlum. Just as he was about to hop onto the sidewalk, however, his quarry suddenly glanced over his shoulder and stopped—leering directly at Falconer. The man then bolted down the sidewalk, with Falconer close at his heels.

Falconer watched as the man—clearly fleet of foot—raced down the sidewalk between unsuspecting pedestrians, wandering dogs and cats, and well-stocked apple carts, and then approached the corner. Just as he was about to spring across the intersection, however, Winter and Kramer jumped out from behind a newsstand and moved to bring him down. The young malefactor, though, immediately shoved an older man straight into them and managed to evade their grasp.

Running after him, Falconer saw the man sprinting down the sidewalk unconcerned about the many people being tossed and thrown aside before quickly turning at the next corner. Falconer sped around the corner, too, and saw the suspect getting farther away, so he attempted to run faster despite the many people filling the sidewalk. The man kept running hard, jumping rabbit-like between people and leaping high over boxes and feed bags left for store owners, and, just when Falconer felt that it was futile—that his target was going to escape and delay the investigation further—he glanced ahead and saw the man look quickly back at him just as a young patrol officer, athletic-looking and solidly built like a boxer, stepped out of a grocery store, directly in the way of the fleeing sprite.

The man and the officer, who had time to brace for impact, met with a thud, and the suspect went down to the sidewalk, groaning. As the officer bent down to hold him fast, however, the man rolled away and somehow managed to leap up, raise his fists, and take a large swing at the young officer's head. Falconer slowed up and watched in wonder as the officer deftly parried the blow and landed several hard jabs to the face and hooks to the ribcage. Then, as the lunging criminal took one last swing with his fist, the officer ducked quickly, rose, and struck the man with a hard blow to the jaw, knocking him senseless to the ground.

Falconer ran up as the officer was placing handcuffs on the dazed man, and, when the arrest was completed, Falconer smiled at him. "You were pretty good with those fists, officer," he said, showing his badge. "Detective Sergeant Falconer for the Detective Bureau. You a prizefighter when off-duty?"

"No, sir," the officer said, grinning slightly as he stood up. "Just learned a few things on the street, is all."

"Well, I thank you for bringing our suspect down," Falconer said. "He could be an important break in a big case."

"No worries at all, detective sergeant. Just part of the job."

"What's your name, officer?"

"Schlager, sir."

"How long you been on the force?"

"Just a few years, sir. I thought about becoming a lawyer for a bit, actually, then figured that would be kind of boring, so I signed up to be a cop instead."

"That's an interesting choice, Officer Schlager. But I respect it. I once knew a detective who did the same thing, and he was an outstanding man for the force."

"Thank you, sir."

Just then, Winter, Kramer, and Halloran ran up and surrounded the stricken prisoner.

"This is Officer Schlager, gentlemen," Falconer said. "He just gave our suspect a little well-earned beating."

"Well, I'm all for that, boss, as long as the guy deserved it," Winter said.

"We'll take it from here, Schlager," Falconer said. "And again, thanks for your assistance here."

"No problem, sir," Schlager said. "It was just good timing, I guess."

"Perhaps," Falconer said, grinning. "Okay, boys, get this man out of here."

Halloran and Kramer lifted the suspect up by his arms and started walking him slowly back on the sidewalk. Falconer and Winter then nodded to Schlager and turned to follow, but Falconer suddenly stopped and looked back at the young officer. "Schlager," he said, "you ever had an interest in joining the Detective Bureau over at headquarters?"

"Ah…no, sir," Schlager said slowly. "Can't say that I ever thought I'd have that opportunity, to be honest."

"Well, you interested?"

"Sure, detective sergeant. That sounds very interesting."

"Good then. Where do you work out of?"

"West 47th Street."

"Got it. Just give me a little time and I'll clear it with your sergeant."

"Yes, sir. I appreciate that. Thanks very much."

"Don't mention it," Falconer said. "We could use another guy who can handle his fists like you."

He then turned and walked off to join his men and their newly arrested suspect.

93

Falconer and Waidler strolled into the interrogation room at The Tombs the day after the arrest of John Fitzgerald, known associate of George Bliss. Fitzgerald sat in a chair with locked chains on his ankles and handcuffs on his wrists, looking glum and perturbed. Falconer walked over to another chair a few feet from him and sat down, and Waidler did the same. Then Falconer lit a cigarillo and offered a cigarette to Fitzgerald. "Care for one?" he asked.

Fitzgerald looked at the two detectives warily, and then nodded slowly. Falconer pulled a cigarette out of a pack and lit it, then handed it to Fitzgerald, who took it with two hands and smoked copiously.

"Well, we know who you are," Falconer said, leaning back in his chair. "You're John Fitzgerald of 264 West 39th Street, a sometime barman and bricklayer who's been in and out of jail for the past ten years. You're also an associate of millionaire George Bliss and a member of Cadere, the secret society devoted to ridding the nation of non-whites and non-Christians. Isn't that correct, Fitzgerald?"

Fitzgerald looked at Falconer for a moment, then took a drag of his cigarette again and placed it down in an ashtray on a small table next to him. He then looked back at Falconer. "I don't know what you're saying about this Bliss character, or that...society or whatever that you mentioned."

"Cadere, or The Fall," Falconer said. "You meet beneath the church that's being built down on Christopher Street. We've been there, Fitzgerald."

"Still not sure what you're talking about," Fitzgerald said.

"Really?" Falconer asked. "Even though you've got that tattoo on your chest—the two initials, PF, for 'Puritas Fortitudinem?' Purity is strength?"

Fitzgerald squinted his already deep-set blue eyes and sat back in his chair, looking at his two interrogators.

"We know what you're about," Falconer said, "and we have you on conspiracy to commit murder. You're looking at the chair up in Sing Sing, and George Bliss doesn't give a damn about you now. So, if you want to help yourself, you'd best tell us what Bliss asked you to do the other night."

Fitzgerald looked at Falconer for a moment, and then reached out and grabbed the still-lit cigarette from the ash tray. Taking a drag, he smiled. "I'm sorry, gentlemen, but you got the wrong guy. I ran yesterday because I was just scared that this woman I was with recently went and lied to the cops about me—that's all. I'm no conspirator about anything, and I sure as hell ain't one to hobnob with millionaires. So, I got nothing to say to youse guys today."

"All right, Fitzgerald," Falconer said, getting up. "But we'll see you again—trust me."

He then stepped out of the room, and Waidler followed.

"No rough stuff today?" Waidler asked.

"I try not to go there if I can help it, James," Falconer answered. "Let's just let him cool his heels a bit and talk to him again, shall we?"

The two men then moved down the hallway headed for the exit to the great stone jailhouse.

94

Walter Bliss, joined by several bodyguards and newly hired campaign advisors, exited the grand front doorway of the Millennium Club with a horde of reporters held back on either side by police officers and security men. The reporters yelled out questions and pleaded for a response, but Bliss just nonchalantly waved them off with a smile and an open hand. But then one aggressive reporter's pointed question rose above the others and stopped the business tycoon in his tracks just steps away from his gilded carriage: "Mister Bliss, is it true that you're a member of a secret cabal that the police are investigating for murder and kidnapping?"

Bliss turned to face the reporters, smiled, and appeared speechless for a moment, but then he raised an index finger at them as if to reproach a child and spoke: "Now listen, I don't know where this inflammatory information is coming from, but clearly it's an attempt by my opponents to smear me and hurt my campaign. This is nothing but a hoax perpetrated by someone who doesn't want me to win, and it's going to fail, I can tell you that—it's going to fail. The Democrats have made a mess of this state. The cities are full of crime and unproductive immigrants, and the do-nothing Democrats' record on the economy is, frankly, not good. Their economy is terrible, as you know, and they are afraid of us, to be honest. They are afraid of us because we're in the race now and we're looking very good in the polls. Very good, indeed."

"Do you have anything to say to the police department given this allegation against you, Mister Bliss?" a reporter quickly shouted.

"I would say that the police department is largely full of Tammany types and Democrats who don't want me to win," Bliss said calmly, "and frankly, there will be changes when I do win, I can promise you that."

"What about your son, George?" a reported shouted above the resultant cacophony of voices. "What do have to say to the rumors that he's being investigated, too?"

"I'd say that you're a very terrible reporter, honestly," Bliss quickly snapped, glaring at the scribe, "and your paper is truly worthless. You need to find a new job. Now if you'll all excuse me, I have an important meeting to make."

He then stepped up into a carriage and it immediately pulled away from the curb, followed by a gaggle of reporters chasing it on foot before it disappeared around the next corner.

95

Falconer stepped off the streetcar on the Bowery and walked east on Hester Street deep into the heart of the Jewish district. It was early evening, and as the sun fell beyond the buildings to the west, a coolness finally began to settle over the densely populated tenements that filled this crowded quarter of the great city.

He had walked these busy streets before—many times, in fact, as a beat cop—and was familiar with the community, but he had never really taken notice of the people who lived, worked, and died here. He had investigated beatings, thefts, kidnappings, lost children, murders, and had always gone about his business quietly and efficiently—because that was his job. But he had never taken notice of the people—never *truly* taken notice of them. Never really looked at them. Seen them. Talked to them. *Heard* them.

They seemed so different to him, in dress and manner, and in the way they carried themselves so seriously and devoid of humor when he was in their presence. He did not judge them, though, as others did—the others who called them derisively, "Heebs," "Kikes," and "Sheenies." They were simply different from him, these hard-working immigrants who oftentimes spoke a foreign language and had—many of them—only recently arrived from Poland, Russia, Germany, and other far-off lands.

He saw them at work, through the windows of their dank and cluttered shops, often from eight in the morning until eight at night—sewing garments, fixing clocks and watches, laundering clothes, or baking bread: these stoic people who worked for hours and hours, and then returned to their eight-to-a-room tenements for the night, only to return to their grinding, noisy sweatshops in the morning for another long day. He saw them on the streets, peddling wares or selling fruits and vegetables, or working as dusty rag-pickers with their carts and barrels full of refuse. He saw them pray, too, when he entered their synagogues on cases, praying on their knees with Torah in hand, or standing with palms raised and opened, murmuring soft prayers, sometimes even weeping.

These immigrants were different than he was, he knew, but he did not understand why they were demonized and forsaken, or even worse—persecuted and ostracized and sometimes murdered simply for being who they were or for praying to their God.

He walked down Hester Street and looked around the sidewalks that were still very crowded, and he watched all the Jewish people. Women were leading children by the hand, men were gathering outside shops and rubbing their foreheads of sweat after the long day of work. Older men were sitting on stools with canes in hand, nodding silently as the cool evening breeze drifted down the corridor formed by the great tenement buildings stretching up into the sky.

Falconer felt out of place on this street, a lawman dressed in suit and tie, a son of an army officer and his New England-born bride, both themselves children of Irish immigrants. He did not live in the tenements or work in the sweatshops or pray in the synagogues. He did not know this world; he only came into it when his job demanded it. He himself felt like a foreigner, like he did not belong here and was being watched and stared at.

He came to the corner of Hester and Essex Street, leaned against a tall light post, and lit a cigarillo as the many people walked by and around him, heading home or out to eat perhaps. They were doing exactly what Christians were doing at this hour—nothing more and nothing less. Just being people.

They weren't dirty or foul smelling; they were regular people, people just making a living and raising kids.

He stood there, wondering why they were treated so differently, so harshly by a large portion of the population. Were they a threat somehow? Were they quietly undermining the fabric of American society, slowly bringing in their own beliefs, customs, and languages to the peril of others already entrenched across the sprawling continent?

It all sounded so absurd in his mind. Another faith allegedly poisoning the character of the American people. And now this group, this mysterious band of criminals known as The Fall, lurking in the shadows, and devising their malevolent plans to rid the streets of impure heathens and foreign invaders. This was a dangerous new game that they were playing, and nobody knew about it—nobody except his men in the Detective Bureau and perhaps a few others.

He felt alone on the street corner—alone with his knowledge of this new evil that he faced. Alone with the feeling that it was all too great for one man, or a small group of men, to bring down and destroy. Alone with the thought that somewhere at this very hour, at some location within the large, beating city with its thousands of drawing rooms, back alleys, and hidden, little crevasses, an assassin was slowly getting closer to an unsuspecting target whose only offense was looking different, or talking in a different language, or praying to a different God.

He turned and headed back towards the Bowery and to unknown events along the perilous, dark path that he was now treading.

96

The veteran plain-clothes sergeant waited underneath an awning of an old building as the rain pelted down onto the street before him. The sky had darkened as the afternoon moved towards evening, and then the hard rains had come in, giving relief to the thousands who had been enduring the last vestiges of the fall heat.

People ran swiftly through the rain as he stood looking out for the carriage that was scheduled to pull up in front of him at the appointed hour, and the rain made a steady humming sound punctuated by the occasional roar of distant thunder.

He thought of what he was about to do—how he was essentially betraying those with whom he served and betraying the city itself. But then he thought of his struggles, of how he could not pay for his family while others on the police force with less experience and less accomplishments were given promotions with higher pay over him, and how he was left to work more and more cases and fall more and more into debt in this accursed city of demons and pandering sycophants.

He had been approached recently by a mysterious representative of an unknown party offering a princely sum if he would only deliver certain information concerning an ongoing, secretive investigation. And he was also told that by his acts, he would be exhibiting great patriotism and would help to ferret out corruption and foreign-led machinations harmful to Americans.

He had thought about it for a bit, had thought about how he had never been given any accolades or commendations over the years despite all his work and efforts, and how he had a right to the finer things in life and to a more comfortable future like others.

And then, after pondering these issues, he had decided to agree to the exchange, and had spent some time at the Mulberry Street headquarters finding out what the unnamed party wanted to know. And now he was about to deliver the information on this rainy, windswept night in Lower Manhattan.

A carriage interrupted his thoughts by suddenly pulling up alongside the curb in front of him. The carriage driver waved, pointing down to the door of the carriage, and he immediately walked forward. Approaching the carriage door, he saw it swing open, and he slowly stepped up into the passenger compartment. Sitting down, he wiped the water off his sleeves, fingered his revolver, and stared at the slim man sitting opposite him. He was on the younger side—perhaps in his mid-thirties—and was balding and dark-eyed, with an expressionless face that was hard to read. The sergeant said nothing for a moment, and then, to combat the anxiety that was coursing through his nervous system, he issued a warning to the young stranger: "I don't know who you are, or who you work for, but just know that I'm pointing my revolver at your belly, and if there's any funny business, you go first."

The man smiled and raised his hands as if to reassure him. "I can promise you, sergeant, that there will be no funny business," he said with a slight smile, "and that, in fact, I am alone with my driver and we are not armed. Would you like to check that?"

"No, no need," the sergeant replied. "Just wanted you to be aware that I know how to use this and if we had any problems, I'll have no compunction about defending myself."

"Well then," the man said, "now that we have that out of the way, let me ask you: do you have the list of names for me?"

"I have a list, but it's not on paper," the sergeant said. "It's in my head. You understand—if something were to happen to me, you don't get any names."

"Ah, yes, understood," the man said, reaching in his pocket for a pen and notepad. "I see what you mean. So, can you please recite the names then, and I can write them down?"

"Nope," the sergeant said. "Money first."

The man paused and sat back in his seat. "All right," he said, appearing surprised, "that's perfectly fine. Here you are."

He took out a thick envelope and handed it to the sergeant, who opened it quickly and started counting the many bills that were contained in it. After twenty seconds or so, the sergeant put the bills back in the envelope and secreted it inside a pocket in his jacket. "Thanks," he said to the man. "Are you ready?"

"Certainly," the man said.

"Okay then," the sergeant said, "the investigation is headed by a detective sergeant in the Detective Bureau by the name of Falconer. He has some men with him—Winter, Waidler, Kramer, and Halloran. And they also happen to be working alongside a couple of cops from across the pond, actually—a French guy named Houllier and an Inspector Penwill from Scotland Yard. Not sure why, but they're a part of it, too, from what I've heard. That's all I got."

"Thank you," the man said. "Are these correct spellings, as far as you can tell?" He handed his notepad to the sergeant.

"Yeah, that looks about right, I think," the sergeant said, handing the notepad back.

"Well, wonderful," the man said. "Sergeant, you've done a fine thing here this evening, helping to expose corruption and illegality within your police force."

"How so, corrupt?" the sergeant asked.

"That, sir, would take a very long time to explain," the man said, "but unfortunately, I am late for a meeting, and so I must take my leave of you. We thank you again for your service in this matter."

"Understood," the sergeant said slowly. He moved to exit the carriage, but then turned back right before stepping out. "Hey, nothing bad is going to happen to those guys, right?"

"Of course," the man said, smiling. "Just being held accountable in the manner deemed appropriate by city authorities."

"Well, good," the sergeant said. "Thanks."

He then turned and stepped onto the sidewalk and watched as the dark carriage pulled away and disappeared down the rain-soaked street.

97

Falconer walked up to the nondescript brick apartment house on 4th Street near the Bowery. He had arranged with Emma Goldman to meet at her apartment for the purpose of asking her a few questions about the recently murdered lawyer, Meyer Weintraub, and she had given him the address to the building. He stepped up to the front door and knocked, and within thirty seconds, a middle-aged woman dressed in evening attire appeared. "Well, hello, young man," she said, smiling. "How can we help you?"

"Well, ah...I have an appointment to see Miss Goldman here," he replied slowly. "Does she live here?"

The woman's smile quickly faded, and she sighed. "Yes, she does," she said, "but she's not here right now."

Falconer looked beyond the woman and saw several scantily clad young women lolling about on chairs and couches in the front drawing room. It occurred to him then that he was standing before the head madame of a bordello, and he wondered how in hell Goldman had come to rent a room in such a place.

"So...she does live here?" he asked the woman.

"Indeed, she does, sir," the woman replied casually. "I imagine you are wondering why she would take up residence with us—am I correct?"

"Well, now that you ask, I am a little confused. I think you would agree that she's not really the type to…"

"To provide our particular services?"

"Correct, ma'am. No offense intended."

"None taken, Mister…"

"Falconer. Detective Sergeant with the Central Office Detective Bureau," he said, taking off his bowler.

"Well," she said, folding her arms in front of her. "A policeman—are we in trouble now?"

"No, ma'am. Not at all. I'm merely seeking to speak with Miss Goldman about a different investigation."

"I see. Well, the truth is, Emma was looking for a room to rent, and we had one, so she joined us, and she soon learned to her surprise what we do here. But it's all worked out in the end—she is a very talented seamstress and has been very helpful in sewing our dresses lately, and we, of course, help her with food and that sort of thing. She's a lovely young woman and doesn't deserve the mistreatment that she gets in the press."

"I think you're right there, ma'am. So, she isn't at home?"

"No, I'm sorry to say. In fact, I haven't seen her since yesterday. She didn't come home last night."

"That's odd. I communicated with her just recently and we agreed to meet here at this hour. She hasn't sent any messages to you?"

"No, none," she said, starting to appear concerned. "Is she in any danger, detective sergeant?"

"I'm not sure, frankly," he said. "But I'll look into it, I can promise you that."

"Well, thank you," the woman said. "I really don't know what's going on, or why she hasn't been in touch since yesterday. It's not like her."

"Yes, I understand," he said, placing his hat back on his head. "Well, good afternoon to you. I'll keep you posted."

"Yes, yes, thank you, detective sergeant," she said. "Thank you, very much."

He then turned and stepped down to the sidewalk and rubbed his forehead. *Now, where the hell are you, Goldman?* he thought. *What game are you playing now?*

He walked rapidly down the street, headed towards a cable car to make it quickly over to the Mulberry Street headquarters and his men.

98

Levine opened the envelope and read the telegram as he sat in his office at the Columbia College of Law:

Fri., Sept. 30

Can you meet me at 8:00 PM tonight at the corner of West and Horatio near the river? New developments in the case involving Goldman, etc.

Falconer

Interesting, he thought. *Must be something big. But why meet in some industrial area down near the river?*

He placed the telegram back in its envelope and resolved to meet the detective sergeant as requested. Whatever Falconer's reasons for meeting in such an odd location, he was sure that there was good reason for it and Falconer would explain.

99

Falconer walked into the Detective Bureau offices three days after his visit to Emma Goldman's flat on 4th Street. Feeling frustrated and anxious, as if great walls were suddenly starting to close in all around him, he sat down at his desk with a thud and stared at some papers lying before him. Then he heard the voice of James Waidler from a few feet away. "Anything wrong, boss? Did you find anything out about Miss Goldman?"

Falconer looked up at the young detective and saw Halloran sitting nearby, too, staring at him with a look of concern on his face.

"No," he finally said to them. "Nothing on her, unfortunately. She's not up visiting her family in Rochester, and she's not out on the road giving lectures. It's like she's just vanished into thin air, I'm afraid. And now I think we have another problem."

"What's that?" Waidler asked.

"I've just been contacted by the professor's colleagues up at the law college. He didn't show up for his classes yesterday and no one's heard from him since Friday. They wanted to know if I had seen him at all."

"Hasn't been seen since last week?" Waidler said. "That's strange."

"Indeed, it is, James. I fear something has happened to him."

"Like what, sir?" Halloran asked from over at his desk.

"I don't know, but it's not like the professor to just disappear on his students like that. The school has already had some officers go over to his apartment, with no luck. So, I'm starting to worry that someone is behind this."

"You mean a kidnapping?" Halloran asked, standing up.

"Yes, or worse, so let's all head on over to his office and see if we can find anything that might give us a clue about what happened. It's a long shot, but you never know."

"But why would someone kidnap the professor?" Halloran asked. "He's not a part of the anarchists, and I don't think he's wealthy or anything."

"There could be other reasons, Jimmy," Falconer said.

"Like what?" Waidler asked.

"Well, the professor isn't officially a part of our investigation into Cadere," Falconer answered, "but he's aware of it, and he was down there with us underneath the church that night."

"So...you think this is tied to Cadere?" Waidler asked.

"I do," Falconer said. "First, Goldman, and now the professor. It can't be a coincidence. I think they're starting to move on us now, and so we all need to be very vigilant and ready for anything."

"But how would they know the professor is aware of things?" Halloran asked.

Falconer looked around the room at the other detectives at work and then turned back to Halloran. "I'm sorry to say," he said, "but I think there might be an informant in our midst here at headquarters. It's the only way they would've learned about the professor, so we need to keep quiet for now. We only keep things to ourselves or to Steers or Byrnes—understood?"

"Got it," Waidler said.

"Yes, sir," Halloran answered.

"Good," Falconer said. "Now let's head up to the professor's office. But first, Jimmy, go grab Winter and Kramer. James, you get a message to the inspectors over at the Occidental Hotel and tell them to be on their guard about all of this, and to meet us here tonight at six, all right?"

"Will do," Waidler said, and then he grabbed his jacket and walked off out into the hallway.

"So, how are we going to deal with all of this?" Halloran asked. "I mean, Cadere starting to go after people we know."

"We're going to meet them head-on," Falconer answered as he grabbed his bowler. "We're going to bring them down—all of them—with no mercy. Let's go."

He then rushed off with Halloran at his heels.

100

Falconer and his men followed Levine's secretary, Miss Brittle, into the office that was lined with shelves stuffed with thick, legal treatises and other dusty books and papers. He turned to her and doffed his bowler. "Thank you, Miss Brittle. We'll just look around and see if there are any clues as to his whereabouts."

"Yes, thank you, gentlemen," she said weakly. "I don't know what could have happened to him. We're all just beside ourselves with worry. You understand."

"Yes, we do, ma'am. And I can assure you that we are going to do everything we can to find him—I promise."

"Yes, I know you will. Thank you, detective sergeant."

She then turned and exited the office, and Falconer looked at the men standing around him. "Well, let's get to it," he said. "We're looking for anything—anything at all—that might shed light on his disappearance: a note, an address…anything to give us a start. All right?"

The men nodded and then started to search all around the office for any clue that might give them hope for the professor's safe recovery. Winter and Kramer started to remove books delicately from the bookshelves, scanning their interiors for any note or memorandum that might have been left in haste; Halloran and Waidler began to open and search the various drawers in Levine's old, wooden desk; while Falconer searched the pockets of the several jackets that hung limply from a coat rack standing in the corner of the room.

They explored the office for a half an hour, desperate to find a lead, until Falconer finally called a halt to their efforts. "Well, I hate to say it, boys," he said, "but it looks like there's nothing here. Let's go tell Miss Brittle that we're going to head out."

He started walking out into the hallway, followed by Waidler, Kramer, and Winter, but then Halloran suddenly called out from near the desk: "Sir—here's something."

"What's that, Jimmy?" Falconer asked, walking back into the office.

"There's a little note down here on the floor," Halloran answered, crouching down and clutching a small piece of paper. "He must have tried to toss it into the trash bin but missed."

"Let me see," Falconer said.

Halloran handed the piece of paper to him and he read the message written on it silently to himself.

"What's it say, boss?" Waidler inquired.

"It's a message asking him to meet last Friday night down on the west side near Horatio and West concerning a break in Goldman's disappearance," Falconer said slowly.

"Who's it from?" Waidler asked.

"It's from…me," Falconer said, looking up at the men.

"You?" Waidler said.

"Yes, but I obviously didn't write it," Falconer said, folding the paper and placing it in his jacket pocket. "Gentlemen, we have someone playing tricks on us at the present moment, and I think we all know who's behind it."

"Cadere," Halloran said quietly.

"Yes," Falconer said. "This has moved into a new phase, and we need to move with it. I fear that these thugs might have murdered both the professor and Miss Goldman, and I'm sorry to say that. We need to be on guard at all times because clearly, they are targeting us now. And we have to hit back and hit them hard. There's no time left for strategizing."

"Well, I for one welcome any of these mopes to come try something with me, boss," Winter said. "Time to put some of 'em in the hospital."

"Or six feet under," Kramer chimed in. "I agree—the gloves are off."

"We're all on the same page then," Falconer said. "Good. Let's go get the inspectors and meet with Byrnes and Steers about this. And, for now on, no one travels alone—understand? We always travel in pairs at least and have your weapons at the ready. One of these sons of bitches approaches you, you put a hole in him. Got it?"

The men nodded in unison.

"All right," Falconer said. "Follow me."

He strode out of the office, headed back to Mulberry Street headquarters.

101

"So, you see, sir," Falconer said to Byrnes as they stood in Byrnes' office surrounded by Falconer's men and Chief Inspector Steers, "this is urgent now and has risen to a much more dangerous level. We need to act fast and with more men."

"Yes," Byrnes said, walking slowly behind his desk and appearing more pensive than usual. "I understand that Professor Levine is your friend and that Miss Goldman depended on you for her safety for a while. It is all very concerning, but…"

Falconer waited for Byrnes to continue, but the venerable head of the police department hesitated, looking down at the floor.

"But what, sir?" Falconer asked.

Byrnes looked over at Steers, who shrugged and appeared resigned to some unspoken unpleasantness.

"But," Byrnes began, "unfortunately, the word has come down from the police commissioners that this investigation must halt. They gave no reason why, Falconer, but they were adamant: your men must stand down and end all official investigations into the Bliss family and this alleged crime ring that you speak of. We will hand over the information about the professor and Miss Goldman to Missing Persons, but as of now, I'm sorry to say that you and your men are off this case."

"What?" Falconer said, stepping forward. "Are you serious, sir? We can't get off the case—we are the case. We know what's been going on and we are in the best position to take them down."

"I'm sorry, Falconer," Byrnes said, "but the Police Commission is, as you know, higher up than I am—I cannot go against their commands. I fought this hard, but it was clear that they wouldn't budge. They want you all off the case—for whatever reason, perhaps political considerations, I don't know—but I am ordering you to stand down and cease your investigations in your official capacity as a detective sergeant in the Detective Bureau. I don't know why they made this decision."

"I do, sir," Falconer said, grimly.

"Why then?" Byrnes asked.

"Because Cadere—The Fall—got to some members of the Commission, or perhaps to all of them. My informant warned me that they have people placed in the highest positions of business and government, and this is obviously their work. They made this happen, sir."

"That's a pretty inflammatory statement to make," Steers said from the side of Byrnes' desk.

"I'm sorry, Chief Inspector, but it has to be true," Falconer said. "There's no other explanation."

"Well, I'm sorry, but I have to agree with Chief Inspector Steers here," Byrnes said. "We don't have any evidence of this group infiltrating the Police Commission. They might have made this decision based solely on, as I said, political considerations. This investigation is a powder keg for the city. You're saying that some of our most notable men might be responsible for kidnappings and murders. But, in any event, I must repeat my orders: do not under any circumstances continue with this investigation in your official capacity as a detective sergeant in the Detective Bureau during official work hours. Do you understand?"

Falconer paused, his gaze meeting Byrnes', and then he spoke: "Yes, I do understand, sir. No more investigations in this case in my official capacity as a detective sergeant."

"Very good then, and I'm sorry, Falconer," Byrnes said. "We will get this information on the disappearances to the Missing Persons Unit, and that will be all."

"Right," Falconer said. "Understood, sir."

He then turned and motioned for his men to follow him outside the office, but as he got to the door, he heard Byrnes speak again: "Oh, Falconer?"

"Yes, sir?" Falconer said, looking back.

"Be careful out there," Byrnes said gravely. "You understand me?"

"I do, sir," Falconer said. "Thank you."

He then turned and walked out into the hallway, joined by his men.

"Um, mind telling us what just went on in there, sir?" Winter asked. "What the hell was the superintendent saying about being careful out there after he just pulled us off the case?"

"It was his way of telling us to keep going," Waidler answered with a grin. "Only we have to do it when we're officially off-duty. Correct, boss?"

"Correct, James," Falconer said. "Byrnes can't buck the Commission officially, but he was giving us his blessing to keep investigating when we're officially off-duty. So, we keep going, men. This isn't over for us."

"But, uh, just one question, boss," Winter said. "What if looking into something must have to take place during the day, when we're all on-duty?"

"Well, then, I'll officially give you time off during those hours," Falconer said. "Understand, Winter?"

"A hundred percent," Winter said as the others chuckled. "Sounds good to me."

"All right then," Falconer said. "We are officially off-duty now that it's getting late, so let's go get the inspectors."

He turned and started walking down the hallway towards the stairs, followed by the others.

102

"We're here to see Inspectors Houllier and Penwill," Falconer said, holding out his badge to the front desk clerk at the Occidental Hotel on Broome Street. "We're on police business."

"Oh, yes, I see," the clerk said, appearing a little surprised. "But they left late last night, and we haven't seen them return, I'm afraid."

"Last night?" Falconer asked incredulously. "Did they say where they were going?"

"I'm sorry," the man replied, "but the clerk on duty at the time just mentioned in passing today that they went out at around 10 P.M. and haven't come back. Is there something wrong?"

Falconer grimaced. "Maybe," he said. "Can you please let us into their rooms? They might be in danger."

"Um…yes, certainly, officer," the clerk answered, turning to get a key from the wall behind the desk. "If you'll all follow me."

He then exited from behind the desk and led Falconer and the other men towards the stairwell leading upstairs to Houllier and Penwill's rooms.

103

"Nothing," Falconer said angrily as he stepped out into the cool evening air outside the Occidental with Waidler, Halloran, Kramer, and Winter. "Not a damn thing to give us a clue as to where the inspectors went last night."

"I hate to say it, boss," Waidler said, "but maybe they got a fake message from you, just like the professor did."

"Yes, I think you might be right, unfortunately," Falconer said grimly. "I think we all know what's going on here. These bastards with The Fall are trying to make all of us disappear, and now I think they got to the inspectors by duping them."

"Well, that means we're next," Winter said.

"You're right," Falconer said. "So, we all need to be extremely careful, as I've mentioned. Let's go down to Mulberry and formulate a plan. Come on."

He walked off with his hand inside his jacket, gripping his loaded .45 revolver, and the others followed.

104

Falconer walked into the Detective Bureau with Schlager in tow and clapped a couple of times to get the other men's attention. "Listen up," he said. "This here is Officer Matthew Schlager from the West 47th Street station house. You might remember him."

"Oh, yeah," Winter said, sitting up straighter in his chair. "This here guy was the one who collared our little friend over in Hell's Kitchen. How ya' doin', buddy?"

"Not bad, thanks," Schlager said, nodding.

"He's officially joining our bureau," Falconer announced, "so make sure you make him feel at home. We can use an extra officer. Have a seat, Schlager."

The young officer pulled up a chair as Falconer put one foot up on another chair and addressed the men. "So, here we are, gentlemen," he said. "I've briefed Mister Schlager here on everything, and now we're in a very dangerous predicament, and we can't even investigate it officially. The way I see it is, this group has now resorted to kidnapping and possibly even murder to keep their little scheme a secret, and we need to put an end to it. The question is, how?"

The other men looked at each other, as if waiting for someone else to offer up a solution, and then Waidler finally spoke: "Boss, I'd say we have to draw them out and catch them in the act, and then do whatever's necessary to lead us to the top."

"Yes, I agree," Falconer said, "but we've already gotten a couple of them in custody, and they didn't seem inclined to break ranks. They've given us nothing."

"Kramer and I would be happy to have a go at one of 'em, sir," Winter said. "We'll see how hard they really are."

"It may come to that, Winter—thanks," Falconer said. "But my first concern is to find out where the inspectors and the professor and Miss Goldman are right now—if they're even alive."

"Sir?" Halloran said from his seat.

"Yeah, Jimmy?" Falconer said.

"Maybe we could lay in wait with a next target and catch them trying to pull another kidnapping," the young officer suggested.

"What do you mean by a next target?" Falconer asked.

"Well," Halloran continued, "it seems to me that everyone who has been kidnapped recently is either a known anarchist type, like Miss Goldman, or a person who knows about The Fall's secret hideout under the church."

"What—you mean us?" Falconer asked.

"No, sir," Halloran said. "I was thinking actually of Mister Riis and Miss Bly. They were down there that night, too, as you recall."

Falconer's heart felt like it leaped up into his throat, causing him to almost fall over.

Nellie. Damn it.

"God, I forgot," Falconer said removing his foot from off the chair. "You're right, Jimmy—they will be after them, if they haven't already. Quick—James, you, Winter, and Kramer get ahold of Riis' address and get over there now. I'll head up to Miss Bly's place with Jimmy and Schlager here. Meet back here in a couple of hours. Let's go!"

He grabbed his bowler off a coat rack and ran out of the bureau, and the other men scrambled to follow, as other uninformed officers on duty stepped out of their way and looked on with confusion.

105

ellie Bly placed the evening copy of The World next to her on a table and yawned. The house was quiet now and her mother had almost certainly turned in for the night upstairs. She looked across the drawing room at the window that looked out over 35th Street and wondered if she was missing out on something in life—on a great, groundbreaking story perhaps, or maybe a fancy soiree that was happening uptown, or perhaps even some raucous political gathering that was occurring at that hour as Election Day approached.

She wondered, too, if she had made the right decision to leave the newspaper business a year earlier to make the quick transition to being a celebrated novelist. None of it had panned out, and now here she was, unemployed, unmarried, and living with her mother in a great, big city that seemed to swirl around her with life and activity.

And then, she thought of Robert. The man who had saved her life from a crazed murderer just eleven months earlier when she was thrown off the bridge to certain death a hundred feet below. Robert had jumped in, too—to save her—and he had succeeded. Robert, the mysterious, impenetrable detective who—she couldn't deny it—was devastatingly handsome and…inalterably decent.

He had surprised her by hinting at his true feelings for her back on the night when they had gone underground and found the secret lair of the murderous group she was trying to expose. He had made it clear to her—and she, to him—but then, the constant churning of life had taken over. The investigations into corrupt millionaires and the stress of finding new sources and leads, and then more murders. It had taken over, and she wondered if they might never regain that moment there in the stairwell leading back to the street, when he had smiled at her for once—the first time she had ever seen him really smile, and she had melted inside and wanted him to reach out and touch her. Robert…that quiet, hard, strong, and solitary man. That good man…

A brief, dull sound suddenly interrupted her thoughts. She turned to look back towards the kitchen where the sound had come from. A thud of some sort. Perhaps Maggie dropping a broom. She would still be back there, cleaning up before turning down the lights and retiring for the night.

"Maggie?" she called out. "Maggie, are you all right?"

She heard no response, so she stood up and walked slowly towards the small hallway leading to the back kitchen. "Maggie?" she said again, this time slightly louder. "Are you there?"

She went through the hallway and peeked into the kitchen and saw no sign of the young housemaid. "What the devil?" she said to herself.

She then looked over at the corner where the door to the backyard and alleyway was and saw that it was slightly ajar.

Hm. Must be out back doing something or other.

She walked over to the door and looked out but saw no sign of her. "Maggie?" she called out into the blackness. "Do you need help, dear?"

Starting to feel anxious, she contemplated just shutting the door and looking upstairs, but then she thought of the possibility that Maggie had fallen perhaps and was hurt outside, so she slowly descended the wooden steps to the ground and tried to see in the deathly silent darkness. "Maggie?" she said again. "Are you out here?"

She walked a few steps out into the yard, towards the fence that separated the property from the alley and listened for any sound. But she heard nothing—only a light wind and some distant sounds of people down the street.

And then she felt it. A faint, warm air on the back of her neck, lightly brushing against her skin. Like the wind, but also full of certain smells—food, and alcohol, and tobacco. Air that felt like a breath...

106

Falconer raced up the front steps of Bly's stone walk-up on 35th Street, joined by Halloran and Schlager. He knocked quickly on the door as he looked over at the window to his left, which still showed some lights on inside the home. Hearing no response, he knocked again, louder this time, and shouted: "Hello! Open up! It's Detective Sergeant Falconer of the police! We need to speak to you! Open up!"

He waited for another minute and then was just about to knock again when he suddenly heard the lock being undone. The door then opened slowly, revealing Bly's mother standing in her nightgown with a look of confusion on her face. "Detective Falconer?" she said shakily. "What's wrong? Why are you here so late?"

"I'm sorry to wake you, Miss Cochran," he said, "but we have reason to believe that your daughter is in danger. Is she here?"

"Why, yes, somewhere, as I don't believe she went out. Please, come in."

The three men stepped inside and removed their hats, while Bly's mother called out: "Nellie? Where are you, dear? Detective Falconer is here on some important business."

There was no sound from anywhere inside the house, so the woman called out again: "Nellie? Are you there? Maggie, please come quickly now!"

She turned to face Falconer. "I don't know what the problem is," she said. "They were both here when I went to bed, but they're not answering. I don't understand."

"May we please take a brief look around, Miss Cochran?" Falconer asked.

"Why, yes, of course. I don't know where they could have gone. This is worrisome."

"Well, just give us a minute, ma'am. Let's go, gentlemen."

The three then moved off and went searching around the home, on all three floors, until—after several fruitless minutes—they met again down in the drawing room.

"Did either of you check the backyard area?" Falconer asked them.

"Not me, sir," Halloran answered.

"No, sir," Schlager said.

"Well, let's go out back through the kitchen and do that," Falconer said. "You never know."

He led the men through the short hallway into the kitchen, and immediately noticed the door to the backyard that was open. "Look," he said. "The door."

"I got it," Schlager said, and he quickly moved over and went through the door and down the stairs into the backyard. Halloran, meanwhile, began to check the kitchen for any sign of a struggle. Rummaging through the pantry, he stopped suddenly and looked over at Falconer. "Shhh—sir, did you hear that?" he asked.

"What?" Falconer said.

"I just heard something. Like, a moaning sound or something, coming from over here." He walked over towards a closet set back in the corner of the pantry, and Falconer joined him. Standing still, they both listened for any sound, and then, after a few seconds, Falconer heard it: a moaning, faint but perceptible, coming from behind the door to the closet. He unholstered his gun and motioned for Halloran to do the same, and then grabbed the doorknob and flung the door open. Lying at the bottom of the closet was Maggie, Bly's housemaid, tied up with rope and gagged with a cloth.

Falconer quickly knelt and untied the gag, and the housemaid emitted a loud breath, followed by a torrent of excited exclamations: "Oh, my God, sirs, they tied me up! I didn't see them and suddenly they grabbed me! It was horrible! I thought I was going to die! Please help me!"

"It's okay, miss," Falconer said soothingly as he untied the ropes. "Just a second here and we'll have you loose and safe. It's going to be all right."

He threw the last of the ropes to the side and helped her to her feet, and then led her to a chair in the kitchen. "Now, sit down and take it easy," he said. "We're the police and you're safe now. Can you tell us exactly what happened?"

"Yes, thank you," the young woman replied breathlessly. "I was just cleaning up at the end of the evening and was about to start turning off the lights when someone grabbed me from behind here in the kitchen and held my mouth tightly so that I couldn't even scream. I struggled but it was of no use, and they threw me down near the pantry and tied the cloth over my mouth very tightly and then the ropes, and then they threw me down in the closet."

"Did you ever see them?" Falconer asked.

"No, not at all," she answered. "I'm sorry—I just couldn't get a look. It happened so fast."

"And I suppose you never heard or saw anything relating to Miss Bly?" Falconer asked.

"No, sir," she replied dejectedly. "I saw her lounging in the drawing room earlier, but never again after that."

"I understand," Falconer said. "It's all right. We're going to try and find out what happened to her."

"This might help, sir," Schlager said, walking back into the kitchen from outside. He held a long hairpin in his hand. "I found this just down the stairs in the grass, and it's got blood on it, I'm afraid."

Falconer took the hairpin from him and examined it. On the end of it was a wet smear of fresh blood. "Do you recognize this, miss?" he asked, turning to Maggie.

"Why, yes," she answered quickly. "That's Miss Bly's hairpin. I saw her playing with it as she read the evening paper in the drawing room earlier."

"And looks like she might be injured, by the signs of it, sir," Schlager said quietly.

"Well, maybe," Falconer said. "Unless the blood belongs to one of our assailants. Let's go speak to the neighbors—maybe they saw something."

"Right," Schlager said.

"Yes, sir," Halloran stated.

"Miss," Falconer said, kneeling in front of Maggie, "Officer Halloran here will stay with you and Miss Cochran while we go get you some help, all right?"

Maggie nodded slowly. "And what of Miss Bly?" she asked. "What's happened to her?"

"That's what we're going to find out," Falconer said. "I can assure you of that. It'll be okay."

"Yes, yes, I sure hope so," she said.

"You just rest here for a bit, and we'll be back, all right?" Falconer said, and she nodded again with a slight smile.

"Okay, Jimmy, just wait here for a bit, and we'll be right back," Falconer said.

"Got it, sir," Halloran said.

Falconer then walked out to the front of the home with Schlager, headed to the front doors of the homes that stood adjacent to Nellie Bly's residence.

107

Falconer sat with his men in the Detective Bureau after a long, fruitless day searching for any sign of their missing friends and Emma Goldman. He worried that the press would soon be inquiring about the missing anarchist leader, given that she had not been seen or heard from in days. He interrupted his ruminations, though, to inquire into Jacob Riis, who had also been present when they found The Fall's secret meeting chamber underneath the streets of Manhattan.

"So, Riis is safe?" he asked, looking at Waidler, Winter, and Kramer.

"He is," Waidler answered. "We got to his home in time, alerted him, and now we've got him and his family holed up in a safe house out in Jersey."

"Great, thank you," Falconer said. "At least that's one target they can't get to."

"So, what's next?" Waidler asked. "We've got no clues."

"I know," Falconer admitted. "And each day that passes will make it harder to find them. I think you men need a rest—we've been going all night and all day. Head on home and we'll meet again in the morning. Are you all situated in pairs?"

"Yes," Waidler answered. "Jimmy comes home with me, Kramer stays with Winter, and we thought Schlager here could stay with you, boss."

"Well, I'd like to be able to agree to that, Mister Schlager, but unfortunately, I can't," Falconer said. "I have a few things to do overnight."

"But, boss, you said yourself that we need to travel in pairs all the time," Waidler said. "It's dangerous for you to be alone with all this going on."

"I know it's not optimal, but it just has to be that way for tonight," Falconer said. "Don't worry—I'll stick with the crowds. It'll be all right."

"All right, then," Waidler said. "Schlager can also join us at my place."

"Thanks," Falconer said. "Then I'll see you all tomorrow morning. Get some rest—we're going to need it."

The men then grabbed their jackets and hats and slowly shuffled out of the room, leaving Falconer and a few other late-night detectives working silently at their desks as the hands on the clock affixed to the wall over Falconer's desk slowly moved towards seven o'clock at night.

108

Falconer approached the swanky Millennium Club on 5th Avenue at 8.00 PM and was stopped at the front entrance by a large doorman, who asked if he was a member.

"No," Falconer said, showing his badge. "Police."

"Oh, I see," the doorman said, looking down at the badge. "So, is this something that I can help you with?"

"No, it isn't," Falconer said.

"Well, I think I'm going to need some sort of an idea of why you're here, sir," the doorman said.

"What you need to know," Falconer said, stepping closer to the man, "is that you're getting damned close to getting hauled in for obstructing an officer. Now step aside or I'll have you in The Tombs in the next twenty minutes."

"Hey, it's okay," the doorman stuttered. "No offense meant here, officer—just trying to do my job."

"I get it," Falconer said, "but as I said, I'm on police business from police headquarters and I need to enter this building—got it? And it's Detective Sergeant."

"Right, understood, detective sergeant," the man said, moving aside. "Sorry to trouble you."

Falconer brushed past him, walked up the front steps, and moved into the lobby of the grand building. He was immediately greeted by the sight of lush, elegant, wood-paneled walls stretching high up to a vaulted ceiling, with two, sweeping, marble staircases leading up to a ballroom. He could see some smartly dressed people loitering at the top of the staircases and heard a speaker inside the ballroom bellowing to a crowd that was laughing and applauding intermittently.

Moving deliberately up one of the staircases, he arrived at the top and saw some of the tuxedo-clad men look over and stare at him. He disregarded their befuddled looks and moved over to one of the entrances leading into the large, glistening ballroom that was filled with hundreds of well-heeled diners. Stepping inside, he decided to walk over to a long bar to his left that was filled with various guests eagerly seeking to refill their glasses.

As he stopped at the bar and leaned back against it, he looked over at the raised table at the end of the room where a dozen or so distinguished-looking men were sitting and he saw that the speaker was Walter Bliss, dressed in evening finery and standing at a small lectern positioned on top of the table directly at its middle. Bliss was in the middle of a campaign speech, Falconer surmised, and the crowd of affluent supporters sitting at the many round tables covered with expensive silverware and aged bottles of wine seemed completely enraptured by his presentation, smiling and clapping whenever the millionaire made a particularly biting remark or caustic observation. Falconer pulled out a cigarillo and lit it, listening intently to the railroad mogul's words.

"We've decided to answer the call to public service," Bliss said, "because the state right now is in terrible shape, and we've got to get back to where we used to be, when we weren't overrun by these hordes of immigrants who can't even speak a word of English and bring in their filth, their crime, and their little children who run around like rats in the streets. Did you ever see them? These kids? They're not in school, people—they literally just run around, stealing, pickpocketing, causing mischief, and they just ruin the city for normal people. It's a disgrace and we are going to put an end to it."

The people cheered again, and Bliss had to pause, smiling back at his fervent supporters. Then, as the applause quieted down, he continued. "But, of course," he said, "there are those who don't want our great country to get back to where it was."

Falconer heard the crowd groan audibly.

"Oh, yes," Bliss said. "They want to tear down this great country and cause general mayhem. They are not real Americans—they're Reds and traitors, in fact—and they want to harm us with their schemes and criminal enterprises. Like the police—did you hear this one? They've got a bunch of so-called detectives down at headquarters who actually tried to accuse me falsely of being a part of some mysterious cult. Can you believe that, ladies and gentlemen?"

The crowd started to boo and hiss, and Falconer could feel their anger rising.

"That's right," Bliss continued, raising his voice even more. "These dirty cops are trying to upend my campaign already—it's very clear. They are trying to defeat us with their false claims and made-up stories, but they won't succeed. They won't succeed at all because of good people like you— good Americans who love our flag and love our great heritage."

The people erupted with applause, and Falconer looked around the room and realized that Bliss was much more than a just a celebrity million-aire who appeared regularly in the society pages of the newspapers. He was also a skilled manipulator and a self-righteous con man. Falconer had come across such men in the past—men who knew how to play on people's hopes and dreams and fears, and who would exploit these vulnerabilities to enrich themselves. Those men were troublesome, but this man who stood up on the dais was much more: he was dangerous.

He stamped out his cigarillo in a crystal ashtray lying on the bar and started walking towards the exit. Moving past several tables, he then saw several men coming into the ballroom from the hallway, one of whom was Bliss' son, George. Dressed impeccably in an expensive tuxedo and sporting his neatly combed, dark hair, the younger Bliss walked up to Falconer and smiled. "You're Falconer, right?" he asked. "Yeah, it's you. I'm wondering why you're here, Falconer, after your bogus investigation got thrown in the dustbin. Are you here to apologize to my father maybe? Make up for your past ineptitude and ask for forgiveness?"

Falconer stared at Bliss for several seconds and then slowly walked up to him, stopping just inches from the shorter man's face. "Now why would you know something like that, Bliss?" Falconer asked. "The halting of an investigation. That's not something that's known or out in the papers, so I'm wondering if you've been in touch with someone in my department. Maybe even a police commissioner perhaps? Is that what happened?"

Bliss just smiled. "Nice try, Falconer, but it is well known at this point," he said. "Sorry, but you're fast becoming the biggest joke in town—a fool of a detective who just isn't good enough to play with the big boys. So good luck dealing with drunks and tramps on your beat—we need cops to patrol the dirty streets of the Lower East Side, too."

Falconer grinned. "I'm going to enjoy bringing you down, Bliss, as well as your two-bit con man father. Until then."

He tipped his hat, shoved Bliss aside with his shoulder, and headed towards the staircase.

"Hey, Falconer!" Bliss said from behind him. Falconer turned and looked back.

"You might want to be careful out there," Bliss said, smiling slightly. "You offended a lot of people with how you treated my father recently, and they might be a little angry."

Falconer stood for a moment and then turned and walked down the staircase towards the street.

109

O n the journey uptown to his apartment building, Falconer thought of what the younger Bliss had said to him back at the campaign dinner about being careful. George Bliss was, like his father had been earlier in his career, a pampered rich boy who took enjoyment in mocking others and feeling superior. But he was always careful to not go over the line. He had uttered his words to Falconer ostensibly as a helpful warning, but it was really a veiled threat—a promise of things to come.

Falconer didn't need to be warned, though. He knew they would be coming soon, as they had come for Goldman, Penwill, Houllier, and Levine. They had sent a clear message: "We will eliminate anyone in our way and will stop at nothing." And so, as he stood on the sparsely populated cable car traveling uptown to his apartment during the late hour, he remained ready—ready for the assassins who were lurking out in the night, bent on removing all impediments to their corrupt, darkened vision.

The cable car finally came to his stop, and he hopped off, ready at any minute to draw his .45 revolver from his shoulder holster or his other handgun secreted in his pocket. He looked around the intersection as the car rambled off towards the north and saw a few people walking on the shadowy sidewalks, and others gazing out their open windows high over the street. He started walking towards his building about a hundred yards up the block on his right, and passed several locked-up stores and cafes, and the dark alleyways that separated the buildings on the block.

Scanning the scene with his eyes that darted to the left and right, and also to his rear occasionally, he saw no one of note, and so he kept walking with the expectation now that it would not be this night—there would be no confrontation with The Fall and he would arrive at his apartment door and get a respite from the deadly cat-and-mouse game that this had become.

As he got closer to his building's entrance, he saw a couple of lamp-lighters up ahead, standing below one of the street's gas lamps, an elongated pole in one of the men's hands and a ladder held over the shoulder of the other. As he walked by them, they looked at him briefly, with caps pulled down low over their brows, and they nodded, and he nodded back and kept walking.

And then, the thought came to him.

It's after 9:00 PM and those lamps are never lit this late in the evening.

He turned quickly, removing his revolver from his side, and saw the men dropping their pole and ladder and extracting something from their pockets. He was quick with his gun, but they were just as quick, and, as he shot off a round at one of them, he dove to his right to shield himself behind an old cart that was parked on the street. He heard the report of their guns as he flew through the air and landed with a painful thud behind the cart, and he instantly got up on his knees and peered around the cart, searching for them. One was running away, holding his upper arm with his other hand, obviously wounded. The other was crouched down and sprinting towards an alleyway next to the closest building.

Falconer took aim at the dark figure right before he disappeared into the alley's entrance and pulled the trigger. The man stumbled to the sidewalk and Falconer knew that he had hit him. The stricken suspect nonetheless got up onto his hands and knees and, groaning in pain, crawled away. Falconer stood up and, with gun at the ready, trotted after him. Approaching the alley's entrance very carefully, he peered around the corner of the building and saw the man, still crawling in pain and unarmed, inching his way deeper into the dark tunnel between the two adjacent buildings.

Falconer was upon him in seconds and slammed the man to the ground with a well-placed foot between his shoulder blades.

"Agh!" the man yelled out.

"Turn over," Falconer said, but the man just wheezed and ignored the command.

"I said, turn over!" Falconer said louder, kicking the man in his side.

"Ow, goddamn it!" the man yelled out, rolling over onto his back. "You son of a bitch!"

He was around thirty years old, with large, dark eyes and black hair, and, in Falconer's mind, appeared to have the crazed look of a lunatic.

"You're with Cadere, aren't you, pal?" Falconer asked, his gun pointed at the man's head.

"To hell with you, Falconer," the man answered, smiling.

"Well, you know my name, so you've answered my question, frankly," Falconer said. "So, where do you have my friends hidden?"

"Um...in Nellie Bly's closet," the man replied, smiling again.

"So, you're a comedian, are you?" Falconer said. "I see. That's fine."

BLAM!

The bullet tore into the man's knee and he screamed out in agony as Falconer pointed his gun at the other knee.

"I asked you a question," Falconer said. "What have you all done with my friends, Miss Bly, Penwill, Houllier, Levine, and Emma Goldman? I need an answer."

The man gritted his teeth and then spat at Falconer. "Never, you pathetic cop," he sputtered. "You're done, Falconer. Someone else will visit you very soon—trust me."

"I get it," Falconer said. "You want to protect someone. I'm sorry to hear that."

BLAM!

The man screamed out again in pain as he reached down for his other leg, now bleeding from a new gunshot wound. His cries reverberated throughout the cavernous alley, and people began to peer out of their windows, so Falconer grabbed him by his collar and dragged him several feet behind a row of large barrels.

"All right, one last time, my friend," he said to him. "Where are my friends? Are they alive? Maybe this one will convince you."

He pointed the gun directly at the man's groin and spoke again: "You might be willing to give up the use of your legs. How about this?"

The man looked down in terror and then back up at Falconer and finally held up his hands. "Wait! Wait! All right! All right! I'll talk..."

Falconer lowered his revolver and took out a cigarillo. Lighting it, he looked down at the man again. "Tell me where my friends are, if they're even alive," he said. "This is your one chance."

"I'm not sure where they are right now, but they are alive," the man said, groaning as he spoke. "They don't tell me these details, but I do know they'll be bringing them to the headquarters on Friday at 9:00 PM to decide what to do with them."

"The headquarters," Falconer said. "You mean beneath the church on Christopher Street?"

"Yeah," the man said. "9:00 PM this Friday—they'll be deciding what to do with them then. I swear, that's all I know."

"All right," Falconer said. "You'll be taken into custody tonight and given medical attention. But if you've somehow given me a load of lies, it'll be the end of you, understand? We'll make you disappear from The Tombs."

The man nodded. "I swear, it's the truth," he said. "But don't tell them I told you—they'll kill me. They don't mess around."

"I can tell, pal," Falconer said. "I'll be right back with help."

He turned and strode back towards the street, leaving the stricken assassin lying in the darkness and lingering gun smoke of the bleak alley.

Wednesday, October 5, 1892

110

Falconer sat at a round table in Brackley's Tavern joined by Waidler, Halloran, Winter, Kramer, and Schlager. He had instructed them to meet there instead of at the Detective Bureau to avoid any further leaks from the unknown mole who was certain to be operating still inside the Mulberry Street police headquarters. He had just finished telling his story of the previous night's events near his apartment building and wanted to formulate a plan of attack against The Fall.

"Well, nice work, boss," Winter said with a smile. "That little rat knew what was good for him."

"But can we trust what he says?" Waidler asked. "He might have just been telling you a lie to stop the pressure on him."

"You're right there," Falconer replied. "But the way I see it, we have no choice—we have to approach this as if he gave us the truth. We can't just ignore it."

"Agreed," Waidler said.

"So, here's what I propose," Falconer stated, making sure that there were no patrons listening nearby. "Tomorrow night, I enter the basement of the church and take the path down into their headquarters. You all wait outside for any stragglers after I flush them out. We'll have you positioned across the street behind any cover you can find, and you will have authority to use deadly force, if necessary. It's clear that any member is now a conspirator to murder and kidnapping, at the least, and they aren't playing around. So, don't hesitate to bring them down, understand?"

"But you can't go down in there alone," Waidler interjected. "There's likely to be dozens of them—if this meeting is really taking place. You won't have a chance against those numbers."

"It's all right," Falconer reassured him. "I won't directly confront all of them—I'll just roust them a bit so that they feel the need to get out of there, and then I'll join you up on the street. We can hopefully get lots of them rounded up and free up our friends."

"I gotta' say I agree with Detective Waidler here, boss," Winter said. "At least take Kramer and me down with you, just to give you some backup."

"I appreciate that, Winter," Falconer said, "but it'll be all right—trust me. Just be ready with your rifles up top."

"Well, you got it, boss," Winter said resignedly.

"Falconer and his boys," a voice said from behind Falconer. He turned around and saw Brackley, the jocular longtime owner of the tavern, walking towards the table while drying his hands with a dishrag. He was around fifty, with a tanned complexion and a thick mop of wavy, brown and gray hair, and was built like an aging yet still formidable middleweight prize-fighter from Limerick. Although known to oftentimes engage in hilarity and barroom antics with his workers and patrons, he could also be irascible at times, and occasionally took it upon himself to physically remove drunken reprobates from his establishment.

"Ryan," Falconer said. "How's things?"

"Oh, not too bad," Brackley answered, resting his hands on the top of Falconer's chair.

"These are my men from the bureau," Falconer said. "Waidler, Halloran, Winter, Kramer, and Schlager. Gentlemen, this is Ryan Brackley, owner of this place."

The men all nodded at the barman, who grinned back. "So, what brings all you gents in here this evening?"

"Oh, just recapping the events of the day, I suppose," Falconer said. "Good beer, by the way."

"Thanks," Brackley said. "Only the best for you boys. I always appreciate it when there's a few cops nearby."

"You've had problems in your place in the past?" Winter asked.

"Oh, on occasion," Brackley replied. "You know how it is. These gangs and the no-good drifters...they come in here and try to get wise with me every now and then."

"But Ryan here usually can deal with them on his own, believe me," Falconer said.

"Yeah, but I'm getting old now, Falconer," Brackley said, smiling. "I'll leave it to these young guys here for now on." He pointed at Halloran and Schlager. "All right, back to work—thanks for coming in and I'll see you around."

"Yes, we'll see you," Falconer said, and the tavern owner turned and walked back towards the bar.

"All right," Falconer said, "are we all set for tomorrow night?"

The men nodded.

"Let's meet at the bureau tomorrow night at 8:00," he said. "We'll get squared away and then head over for the operation. And, needless to say, no one else hears about this."

The men all nodded again and indicated their approval.

"I have somewhere to go right now," Falconer then said, "but I'll be back at the bureau in about an hour. I'll see you all later."

He then grabbed his hat and headed out to the street with the intention of making his way over to the wharves on the West Side.

111

The 9th Avenue elevated train came to halt at the 14th Street station and Falconer hopped off and joined the multitude of other passengers moving down the staircase to the street. Arriving at the bottom, he turned and walked west a couple of blocks on 14th until his destination appeared on his left right before the street terminated at the bustling dock of the Hoboken ferry: the Empire Hardware Company.

Moving inside the large building, he dodged various customers as he worked his way to the front desk. Behind it, he could see the cavernous store full of employees addressing customers' requests down the many aisles separated by large shelves containing sundry items or machinery parts, or up on the second-floor landing that went around the entire perimeter of the establishment.

Stopping for a moment to observe the hectic goings-on inside the vast building supply center on the West Side's crammed docks, he likened it to an anthill that swirled with the activity of thousands of frenetic worker ants, each completing a designated task amidst the overarching chaos of the whole.

Scanning the front desk area, he was unable to spot the object of his search: friend and manager of the store, Ralph Hartwig, a man he had met a few years earlier when he was called upon to help stem the tide of graft and extortion that was quickly enveloping the wharves courtesy of several power-seeking gangs.

He walked up to the counter and hailed a wiry clerk with a full, gray beard and a seemingly immovable grin. "Afternoon," Falconer said. "I'm looking for Ralph. Is he around?"

"Yeah, sure," the man said, still smiling. "But maybe you want someone who actually knows what they're talking about?" The man chuckled at his little jibe, and Falconer smiled, too.

"No, it's okay," he said. "Ralph will do just fine—mind grabbing him for me?"

"No problem, pardner," the man said, "Be right back."

The man walked off and disappeared behind a doorway on the side of the store, and Falconer leaned against the counter, admiring all the men at work around him. *These are the men who are truly responsible for the growth of cities like this,* he thought. *It's not the millionaires and the boards of directors—it's these men who come into the stores and gather the necessary tools and supplies and equipment, and then struggle inch by inch, bead of sweat by bead of sweat, to turn the plans into reality and lift those amazing buildings and immense ships up to fruition. It's these men who actually get it done—the builders and creators. The men who give us this modern world but get none of the credit.*

A burly bear of a man suddenly walked through the side door into the front counter area followed by the gray-bearded clerk.

"Falconer," the man said, smiling. "What brings you here, my friend?"

"Hiya', Ralph," Falconer said, grinning. "I was just in the neighborhood and I remembered that I had a little request for something and thought you might be able to help me."

"Well, I'll see what I can do," Hartwig said. "But first, did you get any problems from my guy here, Jeff?"

Falconer looked over at the clerk, who was still grinning wide, and then turned back to Hartwig. "Nah," he said. "He was very helpful, and very complimentary of you, Ralph."

"Oh, I'm sure," Hartwig said, smiling. "He's a barrel of kindness. Ain't that true, Jeff?"

"Who, me?" the clerk said. "Only the highest of compliments from me, Ralph. Don't you know it."

"Falconer, meet Jeff Navarre," Hartwig said. "He's been here a few years after we found him on the doorstep one rainy night. I'm still not sure what he does here, but I'm told we gotta' keep him. So here he is. Jeff, this is Detective Sergeant Falconer from police headquarters."

"Pleased to make your acquaintance, detective sergeant," Navarre said, saluting Falconer.

"Same here, Mister Navarre," Falconer said.

"So, how do you two gentlemen know each other?" Navarre asked.

"Well, a couple of years ago," Hartwig explained, "we had some of those Whyo creeps cracking skulls down here if people weren't playing their game, and they dropped by one day and threatened to sink some of us in the river if we didn't cough up some cash every month. Well, we got word over to the local precinct and Falconer here came down with some of his boys and ended the problem. So, ever since, he's been on my list of special customers, if you know what I mean."

"Well, that works for me," Navarre said, smiling even larger.

"So, what do you need, Falconer?" Hartwig asked. "We'll try to set you up."

"Well, it's a little strange, Ralph," Falconer answered, reaching into his pocket and handing him a slip of paper, "but I assure you, it's important and needed. What do you think?"

Hartwig looked at the paper for a few seconds and, by the look on his face, appeared slightly taken aback. "I see what you're saying," he said, "but I think I can take care of this. I have a guy down the block who owes me a favor, and he can come up with this, no problem. Can you give me 'til tomorrow, say…two o'clock?"

"That works for me," Falconer said. "I appreciate this, Ralph."

"My pleasure, Falconer," Hartwig said, handing the paper to Navarre. "Jeff, take this down to Morgan's on Bank and West, and ask for Tom. Tell him I need it by tomorrow at two o'clock, and it's important. We can settle up later on. Got it?"

"Sure thing, boss," Navarre said. "We'll get you what you need, detective sergeant."

"Thanks, gentlemen," Falconer said. "I know it's a big request and I appreciate your discretion in the matter.

"We understand," Hartwig said. "We'll see you tomorrow."

"Great," Falconer said. "'Til then, gentlemen."

He then turned and started walking back towards the door.

"Hey, Falconer!" Hartwig shouted.

Falconer stopped and looked back. "Yeah, Ralph?" he said.

"Be careful…know what I mean?" Hartwig said.

Falconer tipped his hat and smiled, and then turned and exited the store to the street.

Friday, October 7, 1892

112

Falconer sat at a table in Benedetti's Café on Mulberry Street, quietly sipping his coffee. He looked down and checked his watch: 8:05 PM. He would sit for a little while longer, alone with his thoughts, and then would head over to meet Waidler and the rest of the men on Christopher Street, near the unfinished church that was currently the focus of his mind.

He pondered the haphazardness of it all. What if the information that the wounded suspect had provided to him was all fabricated? What if no one would be down there beneath the church this evening, and his friends, Penwill and Levine, Houllier and Miss Goldman, and Nellie Bly were simply gone—dead somewhere, never to be seen or heard from again, perhaps floating out in the river?

He felt for his revolver at his side, and then for the smaller one fastened to his belt on his back. He had brought extra rounds, and had two knives and a blackjack, as well, but he felt that it might not be enough down in those caverns. He had made his plan, had thought it through for several days, and believed that it could work, but perhaps he was just heading into a disaster instead, and very soon he, too, would be dead—tossed into the river by some low-level soldiers from The Fall.

It was too hard, he thought—too hard to try and bring down a powerful, secretive organization with no help from the police department or the city authorities. He had his men, but that was all. They were just six in total—six men arrayed against a well-funded and well-organized, vicious group of perhaps hundreds, led by some of the most powerful figures in the country, and bent on molding the country to its corrupt vision. How could he succeed? How could he save the others, if, in fact, they were even alive now?

He took another sip of his coffee and glanced around the small café that contained only a handful of patrons at this hour. He placed the cup back down on the table and felt angry—overwhelmingly angry, bitter, desperate, and lost.

"How are you, Falconer?" a female voice asked from his left. He looked over and saw Madame Benedetti, the proprietress of the establishment, walking slowly over to him from behind the counter.

"Madame Benedetti," he said, forcing a smile, "I'm very well. And you?"

"Oh, you know how it is," she said. "Getting by. But to be honest, you don't look so good tonight. Something troubling you, Falconer?"

"Oh, I'm all right," he said, looking at his cup on the table. "I guess I just have a job to do, but I don't think I can do it."

"You mean police work, eh?"

"Yes, ma'am."

"Don't you have any help? You got the big police force—lots of detectives and officers to help."

"No, unfortunately. I'm not getting help on this one—just me and five other men. That's it."

"Why is that?"

"Because people can't make the tough decisions," he answered cryptically. "They want to hide unpleasant things and act like they don't exist. And some people even like the bad things and want them to continue. So, they use their power to do that."

"Ah, politicians, hm?"

"Something like that," he said, laughing.

"Well, you got those five men."

"Yes."

"Five good men, I can tell. There's a lot that five good, decent men can do in this world. And with you, that makes six."

"Maybe."

"You see, Falconer, they can't take a stand for the innocent people," she said, pointing an index finger for effect. "They are too soft or too concerned with retaining their power and prestige. They are too weak and afraid. They cannot make the difficult decisions that are necessary, and they need you to do it for them. You understand? They need you."

He sat back and thought about what she had just said and wasn't sure how to respond.

"They need you to step forward and do what is necessary," she continued. "You. The city—the people out there on the streets and in the tenements—they need you, too. That's why you joined the police and became a detective. But I think you already know that."

"Yes," he said slowly. "Yes, perhaps. Thank you, Madame Benedetti."

"You be careful, Falconer," she said, slowly turning back towards the counter. "But I know that you are ready for this job, whatever it is."

She then walked off and he sat quietly for a moment, contemplating what lay ahead and what he intended to do on this night. He reached into his pocket for some change and placed it on the table before him, and then stood up and walked out the door.

PART III

113

The men up ahead were standing close together on the dimly lit sidewalk as Falconer approached them on Christopher Street. It was approximately ten minutes to nine and he could see that Waidler, Halloran, Winter, Kramer, and Schlager were ready at the appointed place and hour. He strolled up and waved and Waidler signaled for the others to gather.

"Gentlemen," Falconer said, "how are things?"

"All stable, boss," Waidler replied. "Very quiet and no signs of anyone going in."

"Well," Falconer said, "clearly, if there is a meeting tonight, they'll be entering from some other location."

"Right," Waidler said. "We've gone around the perimeter of the church a few more times and couldn't find anything. Sorry."

"It's all right," Falconer said. "We'll find it eventually, and, in fact, I'll bet it's somewhere down near the wharves. You men ready?"

The men nodded, and Winter held up a hammer and screwdriver he had procured at headquarters. "Took care of the door lock over there, as you asked, boss," he said. "It's open."

"Thanks, Winter," Falconer said. "And your weapons are ready?"

"Yeah," Waidler said, walking into the middle of the group. "We'll have Schlager and Kramer here with the rifles, standing just down inside these two stairwells for cover." He pointed to a couple of stone stairwells that led down from the sidewalk to the basements of two adjoining buildings, then directed Falconer's attention to a large pile of heavy burlap bags that stood like a small pyramid off the curb ten feet away. "Winter and I will be at either end of that pile of sacks with the shotguns," he continued. "And finally, Jimmy here will be down at the corner with his revolvers."

"Good," Falconer said. "As I've mentioned, I don't know how things will turn out tonight, but you just need to be ready in case they come out from their hideout and appear up here on the street. You are to arrest any of them who show their face, but if they raise their weapons in any way, shoot them. Understand?"

The men all nodded in unison, and then Waidler spoke again: "I really think you should reconsider your plan to go down there alone, boss. It's too unsafe."

"I know what you're saying, James," Falconer replied, "but we can't risk being found out too soon if a few of us go down together. I'll be careful, as I've said, and I'll only try to roust them. But your point is well taken." He then turned and looked across the street at the unfinished church. "Well, it's about time, I suppose," he said. "I'm going to head over now. Good luck to you all and stay alert."

He then stepped off the curb and walked across the street, scanning the area for any potentially hostile malingerers. Approaching the stairwell leading to the church's basement, he looked back once at Waidler and the others, tipped his hat, and then turned and descended the steps.

114

Falconer reached the bottom of the stairs and walked over to the large door leading to the church's basement. Removing his revolver from his shoulder holster, he gently pushed the door open and peered inside. Seeing no one, he descended the inner stairs and arrived at the basement floor, where he lit a match.

Moving quickly down the hallway, he entered the chapel and moved over behind the alter. Scanning the various figurines that stood there, he saw the small figurine of the shepherd boy with the sheep and gently pulled on it. The secret door opened, and hearing nothing within, he moved through it and down to the wide, brick-ceilinged corridor that was, as on his initial visit, lit with torches fastened to its walls.

Walking carefully down the side of the corridor, he held his revolver at the ready in front of him, and, after about ten seconds, he began to see the vague shape of the familiar, open doorway leading to the large meeting room. He stopped momentarily and squinted, attempting to focus on what was inside. Stepping forward several more feet, he suddenly heard a voice coming from the interior, and he realized that it was that of a man sitting in a chair at the far end: "Come in, Detective Sergeant Falconer…we've been expecting you."

Falconer stepped forward another few steps and saw that the man was not alone: there were a couple of other men standing slightly behind him, silent and stone-faced.

"It's all right," the man in the chair said. "Do come in—please."

Falconer walked closer to the open doorway, and as he did, he saw that there were many more people inside the room, in fact: a couple of long rows of men on either side—perhaps 80 of them in all—standing silently at attention and looking at him.

"Yes, it's perfectly all right, detective sergeant," the man in the chair said. "I see you heard about our meeting. Please come inside."

Falconer stood for a few seconds and then stepped slowly into the room, keeping his revolver pointed in front of him, until he reached the middle. He then stood and looked directly at the man sitting in the chair. He was perhaps fifty years of age, with dark hair speckled with gray swept back above his forehead, revealing a high hairline bisected by a prominent widow's peak. He was dressed in a dark suit with a black shirt and burgundy tie, and wore several, shiny rings on his fingers.

"Well then, welcome to our abode, as it were," he said with a smile. "I didn't expect to ever see you down here like this, but at this point, it's clear that you're very good at what you do. So here we are."

"Yes," Falconer said calmly. "Here we are."

"Oh, you needn't keep that gun pointed at us," the man said. "We're no threat to you."

"Thanks," Falconer said, "but I'd like to keep it handy, all the same, if you don't mind."

"Well, I'm sorry to say this," the man said, "but I do mind, actually. And I think you already know that we can't allow you to have a loaded gun pointed at people in here, so you'll need to hand it over—with your other weapons, too, of course." He nodded at the line of men to his right, and the entire front row immediately pulled handguns out of their jackets and pointed them directly at Falconer.

"You know that you can't win this fight," the man said. "Please do the prudent thing and hand over your weapons. It's the only choice now. Then we can have a safe conversation."

Falconer hesitated, looking over at all the raised revolvers pointed directly at his chest, and then, realizing that he had no moves, he finally lowered his gun, dropping it to the floor. The man in the chair signaled with a wave of his hand and several of the men standing near to Falconer walked up to him quickly and patted him down for any more weapons, extracting his second revolver and the knives and blackjack. They then left him standing in the middle of the room and returned to their places in the rows.

"There," the man said. "That's better, right? No reason for sudden unfortunate incidents down here. None of us wants that."

"So, what now?" Falconer asked.

"Well, I was going to ask you the same question. Do you mind letting us know why you've come down here to see us tonight?"

"It has something to do with several friends of mine who've been kidnapped, or perhaps killed, by your organization."

"Oh, yes, right. Your friends. Well, they aren't dead, you'll be happy to know. But we might have to go that route, I'm afraid. They are too dangerous to our movement, it seems. They are here tonight, actually, and they were going to hear of our decision concerning their fate."

He turned to the man standing behind his right shoulder and whispered something to him, and the man left the room out the back door. The man in the chair then turned back to face Falconer. "I'm sorry for getting in the way of things for you," he said, "but we simply could no longer bear these intrusions that you and your friends were committing. You were just getting too close, and something had to be done, and so, we acted. Do you understand?"

"I understand that you've broken the law of the State of New York, and perhaps some federal statutes, as well."

"Maybe," the man said, standing up and coming around to the front of the table, where he leaned back and folded his arms in front of his chest. "But it's getting to the point where we are the law, in fact. Does that make sense?"

"Not really."

The back door suddenly opened, and Falconer saw several men leading in the bound and gagged forms of Penwill, Houllier, Goldman, Levine, and Bly, who all stepped gingerly into the room and appeared tired and anxious.

"Ah, here we are," the man at the table exclaimed. "Your friends, in the flesh. As you can see, they are still very much alive despite their compromised state."

"Well, I suppose I should give you thanks for that," Falconer said drily.

The man grinned. "Yes," he said, "I know that it's not the best show of hospitality on our part, but as I mentioned, you and your friends have become enemies of our movement and our cause, and this simply cannot be tolerated."

"And what cause is that?"

"What cause? Why, the recapturing of the American character and the American way of life. It is the single most important initiative going on in our country right now. The war to take back America."

"A war, huh? And who are the warring parties? I haven't heard of Congress declaring war on anybody."

"We don't need Congress," the man said, stepping away from the table and walking a few steps towards Falconer. "We are a patriotic group of men taken from all walks of life in America, from all industries and all levels of society, all devoted to the central principle that Anglo-Christian culture, that great bastion of human progress and human productivity, and led by the male head of the household—the man, who knows what is best for his family and his country—must be preserved and fostered in the face of increasing attacks from without. We must save our great country from the foreign hordes that currently threaten it, Falconer. They are at the gates and the walls are crumbling."

"Foreign hordes?" Falconer said. "I take it, you mean Jews, Chinese, Middle-Easterners, and other non-whites in general, right?"

"Well, that is a bit simple, but yes."

"The negroes, too, I suppose?"

"Indeed. They are becoming increasingly troublesome and impertinent for such a low and uncivilized race."

"And how are you proposing to stop these hordes? Are you going to murder all of them?"

"No, of course not," the man said, smiling. "That would be too difficult logistically, and we are not mass murderers. We occasionally have to remove certain key figures, that's true, but in general, we are contemplating a system of purification whereby these degenerate and unproductive drains on our society are told to leave—or else. It is time to simply let them know that they are not welcome here. They don't look like us, dress like us, talk like us, or act like us, and a good Christian society cannot live long with such festering wounds riddling its body. We must remove those who already here, and then lock the gate. It is the only way to save our people."

"I see," Falconer said, "and my friends here are some of those festering wounds." He looked over at Penwill, Houllier, Goldman, Levine, and Bly, who stood in a line in the corner of the room, unable to speak or move.

"Well, certainly your professor, who, despite his intellectual gifts, is yet another troublesome Jew with questionable views," the man said, looking over at the prisoners. "And Miss Goldman is the same—a filthy, vulgar Jewess with a big mouth who wants to topple society and create anarchy and lawlessness. We can't have that, Falconer—you know that. And as for the inspectors and the famous Miss Bly, well, they are condemned merely for attempting to reveal us. They cannot be allowed to undermine this great, glorious movement taking over the country. So, they must go, too."

"So, what about me?" Falconer asked. "I suppose I'm in for it, too, given that I've led the investigation into your group."

"You actually present a more difficult question, Falconer. You are a very formidable policeman—a man of action and fortitude, and character. You are actually someone we would be very interested in working with. If you joined us, you could become an important man—someone who could lead the charge and be heralded by future generations as one of the great knights of the crusade to save the white, Christian race. Do you understand?"

"Not really," Falconer replied nonchalantly. "I never saw myself as some savior type."

"Well, you are someone we would value very much, if only you would see things our way and be open to our cause."

"I don't think I can do that. I'm a policeman, as you know, and I generally don't care for people who murder and kidnap."

The man chuckled. "There you go again," he said. "Characterizing us as common thugs and killers, as opposed to dedicated soldiers and protectors of the American way of life."

"I'm not sure what you're referring to. As far as I remember, the Declaration of Independence says that all men are created equal, not just white men."

"Ah," the man said. "Quoting Jefferson. Very good…very good, indeed. But he and the other great men of that age—Washington, Madison, Adams—they did not believe that the negro was actually equal to a well-educated, cultured, Christian white man. That notion was absurd to them. You must know that."

"No, I don't know that. All I know is that my father fought with the Union in the war to free the slaves and allow them an equal place at the table. He and his fellow soldiers fought, and some died, for that cause. And they won, Mister...I'm sorry, I didn't get your name."

"Just call me Ames," the man said.

"Very well, Mister Ames," Falconer said. "As I was saying, the Union won, and the Confederates lost. Your cause—it lost."

"Not so fast. That was a war of oppression—not a noble war. The North had too many men and too much materiel—the South's cause did not have a chance in the end because of simple arithmetic. But it still lives on and still has momentum. Go down to the South sometime and see what life is like there. I don't think you'll like it." He smiled slightly, as if satisfied with his latest barb.

"No, thanks," Falconer said. "I've got enough cheap, low-down white supremacists to deal with up here."

"You're really very humorous," Ames said, "for a condemned man facing his death."

"Well, like they say, you've gotta' make the best of things, right?"

"Yes, indeed," Ames said, taking a seat in his chair again. "But, alas, it seems that our attempts to sway you to our side have failed. And that is most unfortunate, because now I must inform you that our only other recourse is to move you out of the way. It is the decree of this council therefore that you and your friends will be sentenced to death. Your bodies will be taken out into the middle of the river and dropped beneath the waves, to disappear forever. And that is a pity for you, I must say. But you have forced the issue."

"I see," Falconer said. "And I understand. Sorry to decline your invitation, but a man has to be true to himself."

"This above all," Ames said. "To thine own self be true, and then it must follow, as the night the day, thou canst not then be false to any man."

"Very nice. Your own?"

"Shakespeare. Polonius to his son, Laertes, Act One, Scene Three of Hamlet."

"Very impressive. May I have one last request?"

"Certainly. What is it?"

"A last smoke?" Falconer said, gesturing to his jacket pocket. "Your men generously left my cigarillos and matches."

"I don't see why not," Ames said. "We are gentlemen, after all."

"Thanks," Falconer said, and then he reached slowly into his pocket and extracted a cigarillo and a box of matches. Lighting a match, he carefully lit the cigarillo and placed the box back in the pocket. "You know," he said, taking a deep drag of the cigarillo, "I've been doing some thinking these last few minutes, and although you've made this decree about our fate and all, I just don't think I can let you do that, Mister Ames."

"Oh, really?" Ames said, smiling and looking around at his men, some of whom were also smiling or chuckling. "And what do you propose to do about it, I wonder?"

"Well, I think actually I'm going need to end your cause and your operation right here and now, frankly. You're just a public menace."

"I see. But you're out of options, Falconer."

"Well…not quite," Falconer said, slowly taking his hat off and bringing it down in front of him as if he were holding a bowl. "You see, your men searched me and all, but they didn't quite cover everything." He then took his cigarillo and gently lit the three, broken sticks of dynamite that he had secreted in his bowler prior to arriving at the church. The fuses lit and immediately started burning down towards the explosive cartridges, which he had cut earlier in the evening to allow for their being placed inside the hat. He then looked up at Ames.

Thanks, Ralph…I owe you for this one…

"What the devil are you up to?" Ames said, standing up out of his chair.

"I'm purifying this place," Falconer said as he quickly threw the three burning sticks to his left, right, and front, respectively. He then started sprinting towards his friends in the corner of the room as the mob of men tried to escape the bombs. He knew that they only had a few seconds before the sticks detonated, and so he ran hard directly at Bly and Goldman, and, just as he got to within a few feet of them, he yelled out to the others: "Inspectors! Professor! Get down!" And then he leaped forward with all his might, reaching out for the two women, as the room erupted in a bright, roaring flash.

115

Falconer was on the floor of the alcove to the great underground meeting hall and was trying to make sense of his surroundings. Lying on his stomach, he raised his head slightly with his ears ringing and saw smoke, fire, and rubble all around him, as well as some bodies back closer to the middle of the room. He looked around closer to where he lay and saw Goldman, Houllier, and Penwill starting to move on the floor, apparently not injured—at least not seriously.

He wondered where Bly and Levine were and then remembered what had happened: he had tackled both Bly and Goldman at the same time and had covered them as they all hit the floor, but then the concussion of the dynamite explosions had blown him off them several feet away. He now looked for Bly desperately through the thick smoke hanging throughout the room but could not spot her. Then he saw a dark figure moving away to his left, towards the doorway leading out the back of the meeting room, and he realized that it was Ames, and he had two others with him. He got to his knees and looked again and realized that Ames was armed with a revolver and was shepherding both Bly and Levine out the doorway.

Getting to his feet, he walked quickly over to Goldman, who was sitting up slowly, and helped remove her gag. "Are you all right?" he said loudly over the din of fire and destruction happening all around them.

"Yes, I think so!" she yelled back, rearranging her spectacles that had miraculously stayed on her face through the explosions.

"Stay with Penwill and Houllier," he said into her ear. "They'll take you up to the street."

"Yes, all right!" she shouted back at him, and then he turned and hopped over to where Penwill was helping Houllier to his feet and removing his gag. "Sorry about that, gentlemen," he said loudly. "It was the only way to get out of this."

"Oh, don't worry, old boy," Penwill exclaimed, grabbing his arm. "Glad to see you're all right, too!"

"Listen—Ames has taken the professor and Miss Bly out the back," Falconer said. "I'm going to follow them. You help Miss Goldman up to the street—my men are up there."

"Right," Penwill said. "We've got it!"

Falconer then moved quickly to the doorway and exited the alcove. The corridor he entered was, like the others, walled with bricks and lit by a series of torches fixed to the walls, but a thick blanket of smoke now hung over everything, and he struggled to see what was happening ahead. He thought he could see figures moving and heard shouting. Moving quickly along one of the walls, he could tell that the corridor was longer than the others he had been in, and he walked rapidly along the wall for what appeared to be well over thirty yards.

Coming to an intersection with another corridor, the smoke started clearing and he could hear more of the shouting to his left, down the bisecting corridor. Turning and making his way down its length, he followed the noises of the voices and eventually came to a dark staircase that led up towards the street. Stopping to make sure that no one remained on the stairs, he could smell the unforgettable scent of the sea and quickly bounded up the steps. Coming to a doorway at the top that was ajar, he carefully looked out and saw that he was down along the wharves, with the large, wooden docks right above his head and the Hudson River slowly lapping the shore just feet away.

"So, this is where they entered," he said to himself. "Very clever."

Looking around, he heard the voices again above him on the docks and near the street—tense and strained voices of men trying to make their escape. He focused, though, on his paramount concern: finding Bly. Stepping out of the doorway, he jogged approximately thirty yards in the darkness up the wet embankment that slowly rose to street level and crept up along the side of the old, wooden dock. At the top of the rise, he could see large buildings across the street—warehouses, workshops, and adjoining coal yards devoted to servicing the steady stream of shipping that came in through the crowded docks twelve months a year. Close by, running headlong every which way through the streets, he saw about thirty or so men desperately trying to escape apprehension. And yet, he still could not spy Ames, Levine, or Bly.

Stepping up onto the dock, he walked quickly back towards the street and arrived at the sidewalk just as most of the men were disappearing down alleyways or darkened side streets. Then, out of the corner of his eye, he spotted three figures walking briskly towards a large warehouse to his right that stood alongside the docks. He squinted in the dim moonlight that was augmented slightly by the glare of gas lamps fixed to the street and could see that it was Ames forcing Levine and Bly to run into the building at gunpoint.

Realizing that he himself was presently unarmed, Falconer nonetheless took off at a gallop down the sidewalk, running after the armed kidnapper and his two friends who were at that moment disappearing into the large, brick building that loomed over the quiet docks and immense ships standing like great jagged-peaked mountains in the dark night.

116

Waidler peered across Christopher Street at the unfinished church and saw nothing. He and the others had heard the great booming sound moments earlier, and he wondered what had happened. Then they had begun to see smoke rising over the church and he feared that Falconer had run into something bad down below and needed help. But then he remembered Falconer's admonition to stay back and be prepared to apprehend anyone coming out of the underground tunnels, and so he had told the men to stay put and have their rifles ready. But nothing had happened in the past few minutes, and he questioned the wisdom of staying in their positions any longer.

Suddenly, he heard voices coming from down Washington Street, which intersected with Christopher on their left. The voices were getting louder, and he knew that they were somehow related to the events of the past several minutes, so he yelled out to the other men: "You hear that? We've got company!"

"Sure do, detective!" Winter yelled back. "Get ready, boys!"

Waidler peered over at the corner of Washington and Christopher and immediately saw approximately twenty men spill out into the street, carrying revolvers. He raised his shotgun and yelled out to them: "Police! Drop your weapons!"

The suspects ignored his commands, though, and instead, turned and quickly started shooting at him and the others. He flinched when a round slammed into the bags that were shielding him, and then he raised the shotgun and pulled the trigger.

BOOM!

He felt the shotgun dig into his shoulder upon firing and heard a chorus of other gunshots going off to his right and across the street. Quickly reloading, he looked and saw the men darting in various directions to avoid being hit and noticed one of them stop and turn to fire in the direction of Winter and Kramer, who was stationed in a stairwell behind and to the right of their position. The man let off several shots from his revolver, and Waidler heard Winter yell, "Damn—those were close!" Raising his shotgun again, he aimed at the man's torso and pulled the trigger. The man immediately flew off his feet and landed on the street, unmoving.

"You got the little bastard, detective!" Winter yelled before firing his own shotgun several more times across the street. Waidler then heard some shots coming from some upper windows of the three-story building just to the right of the church property, and he could see a couple of rifle barrels visible in the open windows.

"They've got two men up in those windows there to the right!" he yelled out. "Kramer and Schlager, can you see them?!"

"I've got one, far left window, second floor!" Kramer yelled back.

"Can you see where the other guy is?!" Waidler shouted.

The riflemen up in the windows let off some more shots, which landed close to where Winter and Waidler were hiding behind the big pile of bags.

"I think the other one is in the far-right window, second floor!" Waidler yelled.

"Yeah, I got him, detective!" Schlager shouted.

Waidler then waited a few seconds before the men in the windows appeared again, about to shoot. But then he heard Schlager and Kramer's rifles ring out in unison and the men in the windows fell back and were silent.

"Nice shot, boys!" Winter shouted over the sound of various gunshots coming from across the street. "Almost as good as me!"

The suspects had now taken cover in various positions across the street, and were firing steadily at Waidler and the others, and so Waidler instructed Kramer and Schlager to run down the street away from the church, cross over, and approach the suspects along the sidewalk. "Grab Halloran while you're at it!" he yelled over the erupting gunfire. "Try to surprise them from the side!"

"Got it!" Kramer shouted, and then Waidler saw him nod at Schlager and the two of them hopped up onto the sidewalk from their stairwells and ran down the street. Waidler then looked over at Winter at the other side of the pile of heavy bags. "Get ready, Winter!" he yelled at him. "When those guys come down the sidewalk over there, we rush them—understood?!"

"Sure thing!" Winter said in between firing his shotgun.

As the gunfire continued, Waidler looked over to his right and saw the three figures of Kramer, Schlager, and Halloran creeping down along the buildings across the street, weapons at the ready. Loading his shotgun again, he made sure that his revolver was ready for use and then watched as his three comrades started running quickly at the suspects from the side, firing repeatedly. He turned to Winter and yelled out: "That's it! Let's go!"

He then started running across the street at the gunmen who were focused on dealing with Kramer, Schlager, and Halloran on the sidewalk, and started firing at the unsuspecting men, hitting several of them. He saw that Winter, too, was firing rapidly, first with his shotgun and then with his revolver, and men began to drop one by one in succession near their hiding places.

As the five policemen converged on the rest of the suspects, Waidler saw weapons being thrown out into the street and heard men yelling out that they wanted to surrender. He ordered his colleagues to hold their fire and instructed the surviving gunmen to come out with their hands held high, and they obeyed.

Schlager, Kramer, and Halloran quickly surrounded the prisoners, who numbered approximately twelve, and Waidler ordered them to lie flat on the street with their arms outstretched. Approaching them carefully, he spoke out: "You men are under arrest for suspicion of kidnapping and murder. If any of you try to escape, you'll be shot immediately. You will remain where you are until police wagons appear, at which time you will do as you are told. Again, anyone moves, and my men will shoot you with no warning."

He then turned to Halloran. "Go contact headquarters, Jimmy," he said, "and get some wagons down here as wells as ambulances. Some of these men are still alive."

"Yes, sir, detective," Halloran said, and he quickly ran off towards the local precinct.

Turning back to Winter, Kramer, and Schlager, Waidler instructed them to keep watch over the suspects so that he could head over to the wharves in search of Falconer.

"Sure thing, boss," Winter said, looking at the men lying prone in the street. "These dopes won't be trying anything—right, gentlemen? I heard all you fellers go by some high falutin' Latin words that mean something like, 'strength through purity.' Is that so? Well, I got a big Latin word for you now, boys—I looked it up: 'Perdere.' You know what that means, gentlemen? It means, 'jailbird.' Now how do ya' like that?"

Waidler smiled and shook his head as Kramer and Schlager chuckled, and then he turned and quickly ran off towards the wharves just a couple of blocks away.

117

Penwill grabbed Goldman by the wrist and led her over to Houllier, who was dusting off his trousers and coughing intermittently.

"Here, Miss Goldman," Penwill said to her loudly amidst the burning walls and crumbling ceiling, "you go with Inspector Houllier here—he'll take you back up to the street and safety."

"Yes, thank you," she said. "I appreciate that."

"You take her up, Prosper," Penwill said to Houllier. "I'm just going to see if Falconer is back there."

"Are you sure?" Houllier asked.

"Yes, no worries, old boy. I'll be up right quick."

"Very well, Charlie. But be careful, *mon ami.*"

"Will do," Penwill said, and then he moved over towards the doorway leading to the back corridors. Stepping carefully through it, he inched along one of the walls in the smoky cavern until suddenly he felt his foot his something. Bending down, he realized that it was large revolver. Picking it up, he looked closer and saw that it was, in fact, Falconer's gun. "Well, I'll be," he said to himself. "What luck."

After checking to see that it was still loaded, he stood up and started walking down through the hazy corridor, keeping the gun pointed in front of him. Hearing nothing, he was about to turn back when he heard a banging noise coming from his right. Stepping in that direction, he saw that a wooden door was ajar, and the banging was continuing from somewhere inside.

Moving over to the door, he gently pushed it open and peered inside with Falconer's revolver at the ready. He saw that it was a small room with various desks and filing cabinets spread throughout, but no one was present. Then he heard the banging again and quickly discovered that it was coming from another room set off from the initial one that he was presently standing in.

Walking quietly over to another door that was ajar to his left, he pushed it open gently and saw a slightly built man with eyeglasses rummaging through several drawers of some tall filing cabinets standing against a far wall. The man was taking out many folders and piles of papers and was dropping them into a large, leather bag at his feet, and he appeared to be doing it with great agitation and urgency.

Penwill opened the door fully and pointed the gun at the man. "Hello there, chum," he said to him." The man turned and stood back a step with a look of fright on his face. "What are you up to, I wonder?" Penwill continued. "Are you trying to hide something perhaps?"

The man hesitated, and then spoke up haltingly: "I…um…I was just making sure that the fires didn't touch the items inside these cabinets— that's all."

"I see," Penwill said, walking into the room. "And what might those items be?"

"These?" the man said. "Well, actually, I don't rightly know, sir."

"Oh, really?" Penwill said, smiling. "Well, then, why don't you step away from the bag and cabinets so that I can take them off your hands?"

"Well, I really don't think that would be necessary," the man said. "We should be getting out of here—it could all come down any second."

"Yes, indeed, it could," Penwill said. "Then let me put it this way, my friend: step away from the bag or I'll shoot you dead with this gun. Do you understand?"

"Um…yes…yes, sir, I do," the man replied, stepping to his right slightly.

"Good then," Penwill said. "You're going to get on the floor on your stomach with your arms outstretched, and then I'm going to pack up this handy bag for you, all right?"

The man nodded.

"And then we're going to go up to the street to see my friends on the police force," Penwill said. "Because you are now under arrest, and you're my prisoner. So, get down on the floor now. Come on—hop to it, chum."

The man quickly did as he was told, and Penwill moved over to the cabinets and started throwing as many folders and documents into the leather bag as he could. After five minutes of rapid stuffing, he ordered the man to stand up, and they both exited the room and headed out to find a stairway up to the street.

118

Falconer burst through the open doorway to the warehouse and quickly took cover behind a large crate to his left.

Damn. Need a gun.

Looking around, he saw a large wrench lying on a countertop, and he quickly crawled over to it and grabbed it. He then froze in a crouching position and listened for any sounds. Within seconds, he heard footsteps at the far end of the floor. Standing up, he started moving from hiding place to hiding place on the floor, slowly working his way towards the sound. As he got close to the far wall, he heard footsteps ascending a staircase and moved in the direction of the sound. Arriving at the corner of the warehouse, he saw a standard U-shaped staircase that went back and forth up to the top of the building and heard the footsteps several flights up.

Running up to it, he was just about to start ascending the steps when he suddenly heard more footsteps approaching from behind him. He turned quickly with the wrench held high and saw to his relief that it was Waidler, who jogged up to him breathlessly and crouched down next to him. "Hey, boss," Waidler said. "I figured you might be over here and saw you entering the building, so I followed. You all right?"

"Yes, just fine," Falconer said. "But I could use a gun—you have an extra one?"

"Sure thing," Waidler said, reaching to his side and extracting a small revolver. "Here you go."

"Thanks," Falconer said, grabbing the gun. "I think the leader of the group has the professor and Miss Bly up those stairs, so we need to head up."

"Sounds good," Waidler said. "Hey, did something blow up down there?"

Falconer grinned. "I'll explain later," he said. "Let's go."

They both ran over to the stairwell and started moving rapidly up the steps, holding their revolvers in front of them. At each landing, they beheld another large, open floor containing mountains and mountains of supplies, cargo, and crating, and Falconer wondered if his quarry had taken Bly and Levine and hidden out somewhere behind one of the myriad heaps of shipping equipment. After reaching the top floor, they moved separately to find cover to the left and the right, and Falconer crouched behind a pile of crates so that he could survey his surroundings.

Hearing and seeing nothing, he motioned for Waidler to follow and they both crept down towards the other side of the floor that overlooked the docks. When they arrived, Falconer looked out a window and saw that an outdoor terrace extended away from the wall such that he could look directly down on several tall ships from, essentially, a balcony. Moving over to a doorway to the terrace, he stepped out with Waidler right behind and walked over to the edge of the building. "Well, James, they didn't come up here obviously," he said.

"Still hiding somewhere on one of the floors," Waidler suggested.

"Yes, I guess he managed to give us a slip on the way up," Falconer said, looking down at the docks, ships, and several cranes that he felt he could almost reach out and touch. "Let's head down again and see—"

"What is it?" Waidler asked.

"What the devil?" Falconer said, gazing down in between two massive ships that rested in their berths like enormous, sleeping whales.

"You see something?" Waidler asked, scanning the docks below.

"Down there between those two ships," Falconer said, pointing. "That bastard sure did give us the slip—he's on that launch right there trying to escape."

He looked down and pointed at a smaller passenger launch—perhaps 35 feet long or so and partially roofed—slowly moving away from the shore in between the two larger, three-masted barques that were tied up to their respective quays. The launch, however, had no sails and yet was still moving steadily towards open water.

"Yes, I see him holding the professor and Miss Bly at gunpoint, boss," Waidler said. "But how the hell does it manage to go like that?"

"It's a new electric boat they've been developing," Falconer replied, removing his bowler and jacket. "I've read about it."

"Really," Waidler said. "Incredible. Hey—what are you doing?"

Falconer made sure his gun was safely secured in his shoulder holster, looked out at a nearby crane that extended up about fifteen away from them, and then walked back towards the doorway.

"Boss," Waidler said, "you can't jump out there—it's too far."

"We've got no time," Falconer said, touching the outside of the building's wall to steady himself.

"Boss, no," Waidler again pleaded, walking up to Falconer. "It's too dangerous—let's run back down."

"I need you to go down and get the others and meet me along the docks," Falconer said, looking at him. "It'll be all right."

"But, boss—"

"James," Falconer said, grabbing Waidler's arm, "you'd make a great detective sergeant right about now—you know that?"

He then sped off towards the edge of the warehouse, running as hard as he could in the limited space. Right when he reached the edge, he leaped off, reaching out for the rope that hung limply from the nearby crane stretching into the night sky. As the arc of his leap started downwards towards the wharves far below, he felt his two hands meet the rope, and he held fast, feeling the momentary burn from its braided fibers.

Swinging wildly for a moment, he slowly managed to get the rope moving back and forth in a way that would enable him to jump to some rigging that fell from a high spar of the closest sailing vessel. Satisfied with his momentum, he came up close to the rigging on a final swing and let go of the rope, grabbing onto the sturdy brace that gently arced down to the ship's deck. Climbing hand over hand down the solid rope, he arrived at the deck of the great vessel and quickly ran to its gunwale overlooking the little slip through which the motorized launch had been moving.

The smaller boat was now almost out from in between the two large ships and was close to entering open waters. Falconer thus started running swiftly down the ship's long deck, jumping over ropes and barrels as they came across his path. As he did so, he kept looking to his left off the side of the ship, and he could see that he was getting closer to the smaller boat due to its relatively slow speed. Nearing the end of the deck, he glanced off the side and saw the boat just below, within jumping distance, so he ran up to the cathead that extended off the bow about four feet, hopped onto it, and leaped off its end, crashing onto the launch with a thud.

Rolling into the smaller boat's gunwale, he sat up and saw Bly and Levine struggling against their bindings and unable to speak due to their gags, and then he looked at the back and saw Ames reaching for his own revolver. Falconer, too, grabbed for his gun and let off a shot just as he felt a round graze his upper arm.

Rolling over to his left, he tried to find cover behind one of the numerous benches that were fixed to the deck, and searched for Ames, who had left the tiller and was somewhere near the stern, likely crawling on his hands and knees. Falconer crept in that direction along a middle aisle that separated the benches and watched for any bit of movement. Then a bullet smashed into a bench right near his head as he heard the loud report of Ames' gun sing out across the water again.

Peering over a bench, he saw Ames' head and shoulders briefly bob into view to his left, about fifteen feet away, before disappearing again. Falconer realized that the launch was still moving aimlessly through the waters, essentially rudderless, and that they were in danger of crashing directly into one of the docks or large ships that were moored in the vicinity. But he could not rush to the tiller to take control of the boat without being shot by his adversary, and so he determined to find Ames and neutralize him somehow, either by shooting him or beating him senseless.

Another shot whizzed by his head suddenly, sounding like a bee flying next to his ear in an instant, and so he crouched down lower to avoid being hit. Crawling to his left, he looked down and looked underneath the benches for a moment and saw Ames trying to hide behind a coiled rope near the side of the launch. He then crept another ten feet until he was directly to Ames' left. Raising his gun, he let off a couple of rounds which struck the gunwale inches from Ames' body. Then, just as he was about to fire off another round, he felt a terrific crash and fell violently down to the deck. Regaining his balance, he looked up and saw that the craft had sideswiped another large vessel and was now careening straight at a large sloop moored to a dock.

He looked over to where Ames had been and saw that the man was crawling desperately over to his gun, which had been jarred loose at the collision and had skidded down the deck. Falconer immediately stood up, ran between two benches, and dove for Ames. The two men met with a thud and fell together against the gunwale, and Falconer's gun dropped to the deck, too. Ames tried to get up, but Falconer grabbed him by his collar and punched him in the face, sending him back in a heap. Shaking his head momentarily, Ames turned and yanked a knife out of his jacket pocket, waving it threateningly at Falconer. The two men then both got up and squared off, trying to figure out the other's next move.

Ames made a couple of feints with his knife and then finally stepped forward and tried to slash Falconer across the neck, but Falconer managed to grab his opponent's arm and swing him violently against a bench, and the knife flew down the deck towards Levine and Bly, who were both still sitting in the corner of the bow trying to break free from the ropes that were tied around their wrists.

Falconer walked over to the stunned figure of Ames and picked him up by his jacket collar with two hands, and then smashed his fist into the man's jaw, sending him reeling to the deck with a groan. Turning him over, Falconer punched him two more times in the face until the bloodied man appeared senseless and finished. He then quickly ran over to Bly and Levine, and—with Ames' knife—cut their gags and ropes and tossed them into the water.

"Thank god!" Bly said excitedly with a great exhalation. "You found us!"

"Yes, it took some doing," Falconer said, "but we managed it. Are you both all right?"

"Yes, yes, I think so," Bly said. "Just need to take a few breaths."

"Yes, indeed, detective sergeant," Levine said. "Thank you so much for coming to find us."

"My pleasure, professor," Falconer said, "but I think we'd better get control of this boat—we're headed straight for that dock there." He nodded his head in the direction of a large wooden pier that loomed larger and larger as the launch slowly moved directly towards it.

"Here, allow me," Levine said, standing up. "I'll grab the tiller."

"Thanks," Falconer said. "Appreciate that."

He watched as Levine moved quickly down the boat until he reached the stern and grabbed the tiller to direct the boat away from the approaching dock. Falconer then turned back to Bly, who was wiping her brow with her sleeve.

"Well," he said, grinning, "I guess I've saved your life two times now."

"Yes," Bly said, smiling, "it appears that way, doesn't it? I think I'm going to have to start paying you to be my personal bodyguard."

"Or maybe you could just stop trying to crack all these criminal cases of mine," he said. "Maybe do some feature writing on some less dangerous topics perhaps?"

"Oh, but then I wouldn't get to see you anymore, detective sergeant," she said. "That would be unfortunate."

"Yes, I suppose so," he said, moving closer to her. "But then again, we could perhaps see each other under... other circumstances."

"And what might those be?" she asked.

"Oh...daylight instead of the middle of the night would be a good start," he said, moving closer still. "And perhaps a stroll in Central Park instead of in the back alleys of the Bowery. That would be a little more pleasant, don't you think?"

"Well, yes, I suppose it would be, detective sergeant," she replied slowly.

"Please...call me Robert," he said.

"Robert," she said, as if trying the word out for the first time in her life. "Robert...I like that. And please call me Nellie."

"Nellie," he said, his face now just inches from hers.

"Robert!" she yelled out suddenly, moving forward and shoving him violently aside. He looked up as he hit the boat's deck and saw that Ames was standing right above him and was beginning a downward thrust with his knife, but Bly had now taken his place as the intended target. He reached up vainly to stop the approaching blow but realized that he was too far away and could do nothing to protect her.

BLAM!

Ames staggered mid-thrust and the knife fell to the deck. He reached down towards his abdomen and Falconer realized that he had been shot in the back with the bullet exiting his front. Ames then stepped unsteadily towards his right, breathing heavily, and finally fell onto his back, unmoving. Falconer looked back and saw Levine standing just fifteen feet away, holding Ames' revolver that was now smoking from its barrel.

"Oh, dear," Levine said, looking at Ames. "Oh, dear."

Falconer quickly turned to Bly, who held a hand to her face as she stared down at the stricken man. "Now why did you go and do a thing like that?" he asked her, grabbing her hands. "You could've been killed."

"Well, maybe it was time I saved your life, Robert," she said calmly. "Did you ever think of that?"

Ames muttered something where he lay, and Falconer, Bly, and Levine moved over to him quickly and knelt. "What's that, Ames?" Falconer asked. "What are you trying to say?"

The wounded man turned his face to look at Falconer and, after a few labored breaths, spoke again in a weak, pained voice: "Ante ruinam ortum est."

His face then fell limply to the side and he appeared to stop breathing.

"What the hell?" Falconer said. "Did you hear that? Sounded like more Latin."

"Yes, it was," Levine said.

"Any idea what it meant, professor?" Falconer asked.

"Yes, I believe I do," Levine answered. "As far as I could make out, he said, 'Before the rise comes the fall.' That's it."

"I see," Falconer said, looking down at Ames. "Well, he won't be around when that happens."

They all stood up and Falconer looked at Levine, who still appeared shaken. "Here, professor," he said to him, taking the gun from him. "It's all right—you had to do it, and you saved our lives. Now, I think we need you back at the tiller before we crash into the dock."

Levine looked ahead and then back to Falconer. "Oh, yes," he said. "I've got it." He then ambled back to the tiller and began to guide the launch towards the nearest dock.

Falconer smiled at Bly, and then looked towards the shore and saw Waidler and the other men standing up on the wharf waving at them. "Look, Nellie," he said, pointing. "We've got some friends waiting for us."

She looked across the water at the men who were getting closer and closer, and then turned back to Falconer and smiled, too.

119

"Well," Falconer said to his men back in the Detective Bureau just an hour after they had reunited on the docks at the end of Christopher Street, "Miss Bly and the professor are filling out their statements and we've got the last of our suspects locked up downstairs. I suppose we should start filling out our own reports."

"Looks like a good night, boss," Winter said. "Got all those thugs rounded up, didn't have any serious injuries, and got our friends back safe and sound."

"Yes, Winter," Falconer said, "but unless one of those prisoners talks—which they don't seem inclined to do—we didn't get any closer to Bliss or to any of the other unknown leaders. We just don't have the proof, unfortunately."

"Not so fast," a familiar voice said from the doorway.

"Inspector!" Falconer said, looking at Penwill as he walked into the room with Houllier. "And Inspector Houllier—glad to see you both made it out okay."

"We did," Penwill said, grinning. "Thanks for shaking things up back there, old chum. And, in fact, we made some headway in the investigation, I'm pleased to say. But first, I think this is yours, Falconer." He handed

Falconer the large revolver that he had stumbled upon down in the smoky caverns beneath the Saint Veronica Church.

"My revolver," Falconer said. "Thank you, inspector—I thought it was lost forever."

"It actually did some good down there, Falconer," Penwill said. "I used it to confront a member of the group who happened to be trying to destroy loads of documents and records in a little side room after the explosions. I decided to confiscate said records and here they are for your perusal, my friend." He threw the large bag he had taken down in the caverns onto a desk in front of Falconer.

"Documents, you say?" Falconer said, opening the bag and taking out a large stack of papers.

"That's correct," Penwill said. "We had a brief look at some of them already, and they provide a lot: minutes, orders, names, addresses, reports… it's a treasure trove of damning evidence against Bliss, his son, and a bunch of other well-heeled toffs in town who were behind all this."

"Inspectors, I feel like it's Christmas Day," Falconer said, looking up at them with a wide grin.

"And that's not all," Penwill said, sitting down. "This little bookkeeper whom I arrested while in the act of trying to destroy the documents didn't want to say anything about his bosses, apparently worried about retribution. That is, he was quiet until we discussed the distinct possibility of him being sent to a nice little cell in your Sing Sing Prison for the few decades. Then, he started to sing like a lovely canary bird. He'll make quite a good witness, my friend."

"Well, inspectors," Falconer said, smiling, "you've earned your pay for the week. Let's all get settled in and write up those reports so that we can bring this to Byrnes in the very near future."

120

Superintendent Thomas Byrnes peered down at the array of documents covering his large, oak desk just seconds after Falconer had completed a half-hour recitation of the evidence inculpating the leaders of the The Fall in a broad conspiracy to kidnap and murder various perceived enemies of their criminal plot. Surrounding the superintendent were his own top lieutenants—Chief Inspector Henry Steers, Inspector Clubber Williams, and Detective Sergeant Charles McNaught—as well as Falconer's men—Waidler, Halloran, Winter, Kramer, Schlager, and the two visiting inspectors, Penwill and Houllier.

Byrnes lit a cigar and looked down again at the papers, taking a deep drag and letting out a large, billowy cloud of smoke. "Well," he said finally, "this is all very interesting."

"We think it's solid, sir," Falconer said. "Certainly, it's enough to get a warrant for all of these men—including Bliss."

"Ah, yes, Bliss," Byrnes said, nodding. "That will cause quite a stir—the famous millionaire currently running for governor, now caught up in a web of political intrigue and murder."

"We know that this is sensitive, sir," Falconer said, "and that it could cause a huge uproar, but the evidence is overwhelming."

"Yes, I can tell," Byrnes said.

"I think you know that there will be various people or entities allied with this group that will do all that they can to undermine this case," Falconer said. "Powerful forces—even on the Police Commission. They will try to destroy this department and even have our jobs, sir."

Byrnes looked down at the papers some more and took another drag of the cigar. He then looked up at Falconer. "Falconer, why did you become a cop?" he asked.

"I'm sorry, sir?"

"A police officer. Why did you become one?"

"Why…I suppose to help those in need and to keep the world a little safer, sir."

"Exactly. So did I, many years ago, and I'll be damned if I let some mysterious supporters of a reckless band of cut-throats keep me from doing my job. You go get your warrants, Falconer, and I'll handle the rest."

"Yes, sir," Falconer said.

"And it just so happens that Bliss is having a large campaign dinner for his wealthiest supporters over at his club on Fifth tonight," Byrnes said. "Might be a good time to pay him a visit."

"Yes, understood, sir," Falconer said, and then he turned and waved for his men to follow him out into the hallway and down to the Detective Bureau offices.

121

F alconer approached the grand entrance to the Millennium Club followed by his men and ten other uniformed police officers. When two large doormen moved to bar their entry, he stopped and held out the signed arrest warrants for Walter Bliss and his son, George. "We have warrants for the arrest of Walter and George Bliss," he informed them. "We're coming in and taking them into custody."

"Ah…yes, sir," one of the doormen said slowly, as if searching for words. "But…there's actually a big dinner going on in there right now, so…"

"Stop your chatter, bub," Winter said. "Step aside—we don't make appointments."

Falconer and the men then pushed the doormen aside and strode inside the fancy palace. Moving quickly down the central hallway, Falconer could hear the loud voice of Walter Bliss addressing the crowd from within the banquet hall. As he approached the main doorway to the large room, a hulking bodyguard joined by two others stepped in front of him and demanded that he halt. Falconer stopped and looked up at the man, who appeared to be over seven feet tall. "We're from the police department's Central Detective Bureau," he said. "We've got signed warrants for Walter and George Bliss, so you'll need to step aside."

He moved to go around the enormous man, but the giant's great hand grabbed his shoulder and shoved him backwards. "You don't just come in here and take Walter Bliss away, cop," the man said. "It doesn't work like that."

Falconer sighed and then looked behind him. "Kramer and Schlager?" he said, beckoning the officers.

The two plainclothes officers walked forward and stood before the imposing man. "You need to move aside," Kramer said quietly. "It's for the best."

"Oh, really, shorty?" the man said, smiling. "Are you and your fellow Tom Thumb here going to make me?"

"Tom Thumb," Kramer said, chuckling. "That's a good one. Really, it is—very, very funny."

The man started laughing, too, and he looked back at his cohorts, who were also starting to chuckle.

Kramer then suddenly grabbed the giant's forearm, pulled him forward, and twisted the arm up behind his back, causing the stunned man to yelp in pain. Schlager, meanwhile stepped forward and unleashed a sharp punch to the man's kidneys, sending him reeling to the floor.

The other two bodyguards moved forward but were stopped when confronted by Winter and Halloran's raised billy clubs. "I wouldn't, fellers," Winter said, "unless you want your noses rearranged."

Falconer looked beyond the bodyguards and saw the figure of George Bliss, dressed in a tuxedo, striding rapidly towards them from inside the banquet hall. "What the hell do you men think you're doing here?" he demanded. "Turn around and get your asses out of here or I'll—"

SMACK!

Falconer's fist rammed into Bliss' nose with a loud thud and the young man fell to the floor, moaning in pain and holding his face, which was now bleeding profusely.

"My nose!" he yelped. "You broke my nose!"

444

"Put him in cuffs," Falconer instructed one of the uniformed officers. "Let's go."

He then entered the banquet hall and walked with the other men alongside a wall on the way towards the front circular table where the millionaire, Walter Bliss, stood addressing the large crowd. As they got closer, Falconer could hear murmurs from the audience and Bliss finally halted in mid-sentence to look over at the men approaching the table.

"What the hell is this?" Bliss said. "You can't come in here."

Falconer nodded at Winter, who stepped forward and held out the arrest warrant. "Pardon me, ladies and gentlemen," he announced loudly, "but I got here a warrant for Walter Bliss' arrest for conspiracy to commit kidnapping and murder."

A loud, collective groan came from the crowd, and Winter held up his hand as if to calm the guests. "I know, I know," he said, "but we'll be quick about it and get this suspect out of here in just a few minutes, and then you can all get back to your fancy dinner."

Falconer then signaled for him to join him, and they both moved over to where Bliss stood as voices in the crowd started angrily objecting to the intrusion.

"Walter Bliss," Falconer said, "you are under arrest for conspiracy to commit kidnapping and murder. Turn around, sir."

"I know who you are—you're that joke of a detective who couldn't solve a crime if his life depended on it," Bliss sneered. "Falconer...yeah, Falconer...you can't just come in here and ruin our event. I'll destroy your career for this. You'll be nothing by tomorrow."

"I'll repeat myself, sir," Falconer said. "Please turn around so we can take you into custody." He motioned for Waidler and Halloran to step forward and the two men walked up and grabbed Bliss by the arms, attempting to turn him around, but Bliss shrugged them off violently. "DO YOU KNOW WHO I AM?!" he shouted in Falconer's face with a threatening stare, but Falconer grabbed the angry man by his lapels and threw him face-first down onto the table, sending silverware and plates flying everywhere.

"Do you know who I am?" Falconer said through gritted teeth closely into Bliss' ear.

He then stood up and looked at his men as Halloran and Waidler placed handcuffs on Bliss' wrists. "Let's get out of here," he said. He turned and started walking out of the great hall, followed by the others, while the dinner guests began to cry and wail, shout and protest at the sight of their beloved candidate being hauled out in handcuffs.

122

G oldman stopped momentarily in the middle of a speech she was giving to a gathering of workers and anarchists at an old assembly hall on the Lower East Side just a few days after Falconer and his men had rescued her from her ordeal with her kidnappers. She stepped to her left on the stage and picked up a glass of water on a table, took a drink, and then turned back to the hundreds of dark forms sitting before her in the smoky auditorium.

"So, you see, my friends," she said, "our work is not done—not nearly. We are faced with the oppressive and brutal tactics of a police state, allied with the great capitalist criminals sitting in their beautiful mansions on Millionaires Row, determined to stifle the speech and very lives of the workers like you who built this country!"

The crowd roared with approval.

"And if they think they can erase us," she continued, "if they think they can keep us under the boot of modern-day slavery, then they have another thing coming! The state is filled with immoral men determined to further the ends of their evil machinations, men who want you to remain under the yoke of oppression and greed, men who want you to work yourselves to the bone and then just disappear without any struggle or sound. Yes, my friends, the United States is now ruled by men who care not a whit about your lives or your sufferings! Men who...who..."

She stopped mid-sentence and looked out towards the back of the hall as the people murmured slightly. She was about to conclude her long speech but then thought that she saw something near the back wall, out where the people had entered two hours earlier.

"I…I'm sorry, ladies and gentlemen," she said slowly, still straining to see in the muted light. "As I was saying…"

She peered again and saw it—or rather, saw him—leaning back against the wall with the familiar cigarillo and bowler worn down low on his brow. It must be him, she thought—taller than the other figures back there, silent and puffing slowly on the cigarillo, arms folded in front of him. She recognized the figure, even in the darkness of the hall—the man with whom she had struggled for survival, the man who had saved her time and time again during that terrible period after Sasha had been imprisoned. He was out there in the hall, watching from the back, quietly and unobtrusively. It had to be him…she just knew it.

And then she looked back at the people, who were looking at each other and shuffling in their seats, unsure of what was happening. Gathering her thoughts, she took a deep breath and continued: "As I was saying, ladies and gentlemen, we live in an oppressive time when men in powerful places are doing everything that they can to keep you bound and gagged within the dank factories and the stifling sweatshops that prop up their vast corporations. They do not care one bit about you or your families because you are different than they are. You are what I call 'the other'—the people who have darker skin, who speak differently, who perhaps worship a different god. But sometimes there are other men…"

She looked across the tired and withered faces, grimy from a long day of work, and settled her eyes again on the tall figure leaning against the back wall.

"Sometimes there are men and women in this world who will stand up to the corruption and the lies and the injustices," she continued. "Brave men and women who will put their own lives in danger to soothe the persecuted and lift the downhearted—who will try to correct a broken world. We must look to these men and women, these lonely sentinels who stand with the downtrodden, who go out into the night to confront the danger and bring the powerful brutes to justice, and we must keep fighting for the better world that we know is possible."

The crowd erupted with cheers and applause, and as the people looked up at her with approval and admiration, she watched as the tall figure in the back slowly stood up away from the wall, moved to the main doorway, and quietly exited the hall.

123

Charles Francis, a young cub reporter for the New York Tribune, stood outside the courthouse with Jacob Riis and watched as the throng of other reporters and onlookers pushed and struggled to get a glimpse of the people exiting the building after Walter and George Bliss' arraignments were held. The story had hit the newspapers like a lightning bolt, and every crime reporter was desperately pacing the sidewalks in the hopes of gleaning new information from the very secretive police department and district attorney's office.

"Look there," Riis said, pointing at the stairs of the courthouse. "It's Falconer and his men coming out. Now those are the people you'd really want to speak to."

Francis watched as Falconer and his men stepped down to the street and moved through an opening in the crowd created by several large police officers wielding billy clubs. The men then started walking towards him and Riis on the sidewalk, and Riis turned to him and said, "Let me try and introduce you, Francis."

Falconer walked up with his men and smiled at Riis. "Mister Riis," he said, "how are you today?"

"Very well, Detective Sergeant Falconer," Riis answered, shaking his hand. "Thanks for asking. This is a new reporter for our paper, Charles

Francis. Francis, this is Detective Sergeant Falconer with the Detective Bureau and some of his men."

"How do you do, Mister Francis?" Falconer said. "This is Detective Waidler, along with Officers Halloran, Schlager, Kramer, and Winter."

"Pleased to meet you gentlemen," Francis said, doffing his hat.

"So," Riis said, "how did it go in there?"

"Oh, not too bad," Falconer answered. "But…."

"But what?" Riis asked.

"Oh, there was just something about how the D.A. and judge acted that I found a little troubling."

"How so, may I ask?"

"Well, I can't put my finger on it, but something seemed fishy in there, Mister Riis. This secret order has a lot of men in high places, and no one knows about it. And I'm worried, frankly, that they've managed to spread into the courts and D.A. offices, which would not be good, obviously."

"Well, that would be troubling, indeed," Riis said, "but surely it can't be so widespread as to prevent these agencies from doing their jobs."

"Maybe, but I wonder," Falconer said.

"You sound very pessimistic," Riis said.

"I'm just a policeman, Mister Riis," Falconer said. "I don't have a lot of power, really. I can only arrest someone and put them in jail for a few days. Yes, I can use lethal force, if necessary, but I must be justified in that—I can't just go out and shoot someone without cause. But the district attorney—he is the one who has true power and is really the last bastion against chaos and violence in the streets. He can bully the bully, as it were. If he has the evidence, he can potentially remove a man from ordered society for the rest of his life—or even send him to the electric chair. That is true power, Mister Riis. And if someone with that kind of power becomes corrupt—if the prosecutor himself becomes one of the bad guys and won't stand up and do the right thing, then we are all lost."

"I see what you mean," Riis said. "That is worrisome, indeed."

"Yes, it is," Falconer said, "but we will hope for the best. Have a nice day, gentlemen."

"And, uh, what is next for you and your men?" Riis asked.

"Oh, the cases keep hitting our desks," Falconer said, smiling. "We don't get a break."

"Yes, understood," Riis said, also grinning.

"Take care of yourself, Mister Riis," Falconer said, and then he turned and motioned for the other men to follow. Francis watched as they walked off, six policemen in plainclothes headed back to their bureau. "Very impressive group of officers," he said to Riis.

"Yes, Francis," Riis stated. "And do you know what they call them, actually?"

"I'm sorry?" Francis said absentmindedly as he watched Falconer and the men walking away.

"Byrnes' detectives in the Detective Bureau," Riis said. "Do you know what the newspapers call them?"

"No, I don't, actually," Francis said.

"The Immortals," Riis said, smiling slightly. "They call them The Immortals."

Riis took a deep breath and straightened his hat on his head. "Well, have a good afternoon, Francis," he said. "I shall see you back at the office later."

"Yes, sir," Francis replied. "Thank you."

He watched Riis step off the curb and walk across the street, and then he turned his attention back to Falconer and his men as they receded into the crowd again, disappearing from view.

124

Levine sat down at his desk and stared at his typewriter. It had been over a week since he had narrowly escaped death at the hands of the murderous secret order, and he wanted to set down on paper his thoughts and experiences over the past few months. He pondered what had happened, and how Falconer and his men had managed to track down the group and accumulate enough evidence to prosecute many of its members.

Looking down at his desk, he noticed what appeared to be a sealed telegram with his name on it. Miss Brittle must have left it there when he was out. He picked it up, opened it, and saw that it was a message from Falconer. Sitting back in his chair, he read its contents:

Professor:

Thank you again for doing what you did out on the boat that night. Although I'm sure it was difficult, you did save our lives, and for that, I am eternally grateful to you.

"A faithful friend is a strong defense: and he that hath found such a one hath found a treasure."

—Ecclesiasticus 6:14

Falconer

He placed the telegram back on his desk and smiled. Then he looked at the typewriter again and began to write.

125

Falconer sat at his desk in the Detective Bureau several days after the arraignments of Walter and George Bliss and their closest co-conspirators. He fumbled through some letters and telegrams and then picked up a new file: the disappearance of a young girl who lived down on Hester Street. He read the first few paragraphs of the initial pages when he suddenly realized that someone was standing next to him. Looking up, he saw two women gazing down at him, stone-faced. The closest one was a little shorter with brown hair cut above her shoulders and wearing round, wire spectacles. The other, standing just behind and to the side of the first one, had bright, blue eyes and longer hair that was pulled up underneath her hat. Falconer waited a few seconds for one of them to speak, but they remained silent, and so he finally spoke to break the awkward silence: "Um…can I help you ladies?"

"Maybe," the shorter woman said. "Or more likely, it is we who can help you, Detective Sergeant Falconer."

"Really?" Falconer said, standing up. "And how might you do that?"

"Well," the shorter woman said, "we are both aware, as is most of the city, of how you have cracked a secretive organization that resorts to kidnapping and murder to accomplish its nefarious goals. But maybe you aren't aware that this group is much larger than you think, and that it continues to operate with impunity."

"Well, I wasn't aware, exactly," Falconer said, "but I figured as much."

"Yes, well, we have certain information about its ongoing activities," the woman said, "and we are willing to collaborate with you as co-investigators in this effort to bring them all to justice."

"Collaborate?" Falconer said. "As co-investigators?"

"Yes," the woman said. "Here, allow me."

She pulled out a business card and handed it to him, and he read the contents out loud: "'Aguilar & Johnston...Private Investigators...No Case Too Small Or Large.' You ladies are...private investigators?"

"Yes," the woman said, "is there something wrong with that?"

"Well, no, miss," he replied. "I just didn't...expect this, frankly."

"Well, y'all know why we have to go private, don't y'all?" the taller woman suddenly interjected in a loud voice tinged with a decidedly southern drawl. "It's because y'all won't let women like us join your police force. You git that?"

"Uh...yes...I understand," Falconer said slowly. "I...I didn't mean to insinuate anything..."

"Well, y'all know why we're here," the taller woman stated flatly. "You gonna' git on board this train or no?"

"Wait, Miss Johnston," the shorter woman interrupted. "There's no reason to get excited here. I'm sure this is all very sudden for the detective sergeant. What do you think, sir? If we have valid information pointing to additional suspects—as we do—would you be interested in working with us to bring these men to justice?"

"Well, I suppose I would, uh, Miss Aguilar, is it?" Falconer said. "Anything to help solve the case."

He paused as Aguilar smiled and nodded approvingly, and then Johnston broke the silence: "Well, what are we all waitin' for? Git your jacket, Falconer, and let's get goin' here. There's no time to waste on this, people!"

He grabbed his jacket off the chair and headed for the hallway, trailing the two ladies who were already leaving him behind as they quickly headed out to the bustling streets of Manhattan.

Epilogue:
London Victoria Station
8:00 p.m. April 4, 1894

126

Penwill walked up to Houllier at the end of the loading platform at the crowded Victoria Station. They had been lingering in the area for an hour, searching for Theodule Meunier, who was reputed to be back in England after a two-year jaunt to North America and was supposedly going to be boarding a train at any minute according to intelligence sources. Penwill nodded at his friend and scanned the busy train station.

"Well, hopefully, we'll get our man tonight, Prosper," he said to Houllier. "It's been a long chase."

"Yes, my friend," Houllier said. "Much too long."

"Look," Penwill said, nodding to his right, "here comes the Old Man himself."

Penwill watched as William Melville, the sturdily built head of Scotland Yard's Special Branch, walked up to them and smiled. "Hello, boys," he said. "Anything yet?"

"Nothing, sir," Penwill replied, "but we still have time."

"Indeed, Penwill," Melville said. "This crafty fox may yet show. Well, keep your eyes peeled, gentlemen."

"Yes, sir," Penwill said, and Melville wandered off.

"It is funny," Houllier said. "For two years we have all followed this man around the world. We have gone our separate ways after the adventure in America, and now we are back again to ensnare this bomb thrower and bring him to justice. I am most proud to have worked with you, Charles."

"And I, you, Prosper," Penwill said. "Most proud indeed, whatever may happen—"

He stopped and stared down the platform, grabbing Houllier's forearm.

"What is it?" Houllier asked.

"There, just halfway down the platform, approaching us in the black coat and gray hat. Do you see him? That noticeable limp?"

"Yes...yes, I do, Charles. The right height, and the limp, and look how he tries to shield his face, but you can tell it is our man."

"Right. Let's head towards him. He's about to enter the car. And look over there—it appears Melville is on to him, too."

"Yes, let us go," Houllier said urgently.

The two men then started walking down the crowded platform, dodging passengers and weaving through the human traffic, until they came to within ten feet of their quarry. Penwill looked over at Melville, who nodded discretely, and then nodded at Houllier. The car's doors were opening, and the people were jostling to get onboard, so the two inspectors swiftly moved over behind the unsuspecting anarchist bomber and grabbed his arms. Meunier looked at Penwill and started to struggle as passengers gasped with fear. Meunier managed to wrest one arm free, but then Melville moved in and grabbed it again and, with the other two inspectors helping, shoved the suspect to the platform. Penwill and Houllier then carefully placed handcuffs on the stunned prisoner.

"Well, then, Mister Meunier," Melville said, standing over him, "my understanding is that you do understand the King's English, so let me tell you that you are, at long last, under arrest for Attempted Murder and Conspiracy to Commit Murder. You will be handed over to your countrymen and finally meet the justice that has been awaiting you, old man."

"No!" Meunier yelled out with a thick French accent. "To fall into your hands, Melville! You, the only man I feared, and whose description was engraved on my mind!"

"Well, thank you, my good man," Melville said, "but it isn't I whom you should have feared—it's these two men holding you who chased you to the ends of the earth and back and who tracked you here tonight. They are your true tormentors, Meunier."

Meunier looked up at Penwill and Houllier and appeared to be searching for words, but he could only gape in confusion and stunned silence.

"Let's go, Meunier," Penwill said, lifting him up. "Time to go visit Scotland Yard. We'll take him back, sir. Thanks for the assistance tonight."

"Very good, Penwill," Melville said. "And thank you again Inspector Houllier—it looks like your long chase is finally over."

"Yes, sir," Houllier said. "Thank you, very much."

Penwill then nudged Meunier, and, with Houllier's help, began to escort him off the platform to a waiting paddy wagon.

"Well, Charles," Houllier remarked, "I am glad that we got our man finally because I am very hungry at this minute."

"Oh, really, Prosper?" Penwill said. "Well, that's just grand because after we let our friend here off at Scotland Yard, I know of a wonderful place on Piccadilly Circus. Just outstanding food. Shall we?"

"*Mais oui*, my friend," Houllier said, smiling. "At last—a meal with the one and only Inspector Charlie Penwill of Scotland Yard in the infamous Piccadilly Circus…what could be better?"

The two men then trudged off through the train station, leaving the sounds of trains and whistles, people and horses, behind them in the London night.